A Sudden Wild Magic

A Sudden Wild Magic

DIANA WYNNE JONES

An AvoNova Book

William Morrow and Company, Inc.
New York

A SUDDEN WILD MAGIC is an original publication of Avon Books. This work has never before appeared in book form. This work is a novel. Any similarity to actual persons or events is purely coincidental.

AVON BOOKS
A division of
The Hearst Corporation
1350 Avenue of the Americas
New York, New York 10019

Copyright © 1992 by Diana Wynne Jones
Published by arrangement with the author
Library of Congress Catalog Card Number: 92-10860
ISBN: 0-688-11882-8

Library of Congress Cataloging in Publication Data:

Jones, Diana Wynne.
    A sudden wild magic / Diana Wynne Jones.
        p.   cm.
    ISBN 0-688-11882-8 : $22.00
    I. Title.
PR6060.0497S84   1992   92-10860
823'.914—dc20   CIP

First Morrow/AvoNova Printing: October 1992

AVONOVA TRADEMARK REG. U.S. PAT. OFF. AND IN OTHER COUNTRIES, MARCA REGISTRADA, HECHO EN U.S.A.

Printed in the U.S.A.

ARC   10   9   8   7   6   5   4   3   2   1

J
cop 1

I

Earth

1

The magical activities of Britain have always been highly organized. Anyone who doubts this should consider the Spanish Armada and the winds that so conveniently dissipated it—and perhaps further consider why even the most skeptical of historians accepts this convenient hurricane so calmly, as a perfectly natural occurrence. Or the doubter might also consider why Hitler, or Napoleon before him, never got around to invading Britain, and why we accept these facts, too, so easily.

A moment's unclouded thought should persuade anyone that these things are too good to be true. But of course, no one's thought *is* unclouded, for the very good reason that the organization has, for centuries, devoted itself to clouding it and making sure that most people perceive its activities as messy, futile, and mainly concerned with old ladies astride broomsticks. In fact, the organization is so ruthlessly secret that even the majority of those engaged in the various forms of witchcraft are unaware that their activities are being directed by a ruling council—which we shall call the Ring—carefully and secretly selected from the ranks of practitioners all over the country.

This council has had to work increasingly hard this

century. Its activities have, more and more, been forced to encompass the whole world. Most of its members agreed that this was a natural result of improved communications. The only person who disagreed was the one man of the Inner Ring.

2

His name was Mark Lister, and his actual title is a secret. He made his living with computers. It always pleased him that he should work at something so unrelated to witchcraft, and make good money at it too, without more than occasionally invoking his powers as magician. He dressed the part of a businessman, in expensive charcoal gray suits, kept his pale face meticulously clean-shaven and his pale hair most conservatively cut, and, since he was of average height and neither fat nor thin, he looked almost unremarkable. This pleased him too. He made just one concession to his secret activities: he always wore a wide-brimmed hat as a covert allusion to the Magician in the tarot pack. It did not worry him that, apart from the hat, most people found him both humorless and colorless. What did worry him was certain current trends in the world.

Thinking about these trends, Mark Lister started to feed certain data to computers in his office. It was idly done at first, in a spare moment, just to make him feel he was doing something to control something that had long gone beyond anyone's control. The answers he got back added up to something that so startled him that he set about designing a special program of inquiry. When this was done, he stayed in his office all night to run it.

His absence took careful planning. His wife, Paulie, was no mean witch herself, and Mark was not at this stage prepared to trust anyone, let alone Paulie. Halfway through the morning he phoned her with his excuse: an unexpected conference in Birmingham. This gave him time to set up a simulacrum of himself and send it to dine with another colorless simulacrum in Birmingham, in case Paulie—or an unknown—decided to check; and he had the rest of the day to recoup the considerable energy it took to do that. In the evening, as soon as his partners and staff had left, he set to work. First he had to bespell the office so that no cleaner or security man would be tempted to enter while he was there, and to make it seem as if the place were empty. He had to block telephones and fax machines so they would not distract him during the more delicate magic to come. All simple enough stuff, but if what he feared was true, he could not afford to put a finger wrong. By the time the office was silent and looked to any possible observer like the usual empty space lighted by greenish striplights, he was already shaking and sweating. He had to compose himself magically, before he started on the complex of tiny sendings to prevent anyone—*anyone*—from noticing the sort of data he would be receiving. Since his program was going to access a number of very secret files, further sendings were necessary to make what he filched invisible. He was not going to trust to technology alone in this.

"And all for nothing if it turns out to be my overactive imagination," he murmured. But he did not think it would, and he cast at his gentlest, strongest, and most careful.

When it was done, he walked about waiting for the excess ambience of power to die away. He did not want that to influence the computers. Even then, after he had at last tapped in the instruction to run the program, he found he was walking about still, in terror of accidentally influencing the running of it. It was absurd. He had worked with power ten years now. He knew how to control it. But he was still scared. He stopped and grasped a tubular steel chair with both hands—not precisely cold iron, he thought ruefully, but it should serve to negate anything wild he was putting out—and stood leaning on it whenever he was not needing to monitor the program.

Results gathered. Mark took his hands from the chair, intending to take printouts before asking for forecasts, and felt the tubular steel crunch and seem to crumble under his fingers. He looked down at it rather irritably. And stepped away in dismay. The steel portions were reverting to some kind of red iron-bearing sandstone speckled with crusty black granules. The plastic of the seat was curling into feathers of something yellowish and dry, which had a strong chemical reek.

Rather grimly, he dusted redness off his hands. The chair was surely only a symbol of his state of mind—he hoped—but it looked as if his worst fears were being confirmed, even before he had asked the final question.

He asked it. He took his printouts. He erased everything and went by careful, gentle stages back up his tracks, making sure that no trace of him, magical or technological, remained in any of the places he had tapped for data, or in the office either. Around dawn he picked up his briefcase and turned to the once tubular steel chair, ready to deal with that now. It stood in the middle of the space as an impossible curved framework of red earth, although the black nodules were now a pale sickly green. Mark frowned at them. Then, as an experiment, he spread a gently imperious hand toward the nearest green blob. It obeyed him by bursting. Twisting and writhing, it enlarged and threw out two round green leaves as it grew upon a white thread of stem.

"Hm," he said. "I seem to feel more hopeful than I think. All the same, you have to go." He gestured again, making it a stiff push from the elbow, and succeeded in teleporting the entire strange mess from the office building into the nearest skip, where he felt it crumble away. After this he was very weary. He rubbed his face and longed for coffee. "On the station," he decided. He also longed for his car. But that had to be left out in the parking lot in Surrey for verisimilitude. A man traveling by train was much harder to trace, too.

In the station buffet, over a large polystyrene mug of coffee, he allowed himself to wonder whether he had chosen the right member of the Inner Ring to take his discovery to. A lot hung on his deciding right. His first impulse had been to convene the entire Ring, but he still rejected that idea. The nine of the Outer Ring were all adepts and none of them was stupid, but there were those among them who came from walks of life that gave them rather too much in the way of downright common sense. These few were likely to pooh-pooh every one of his notions. He could hear Koppa Taylor or Sid Graffy now: "You can make computers prove anything! You only have to feed them the facts you want." True. And he had. Then he knew so little about any of them, beyond the most obvious things. Take Koppa, whom he knew best of all the nine. All that amounted to was knowing she had been born in California fifty years ago. He knew much the same sort of things about the other eight, and that was all. Secrecy was important. Personal details were supposed not to count when they communed together as the Ring. Disguises apparently dropped away at the higher levels where they were At One. Mark gave a small sarcastic grunt. If they were up against what he *thought* they were, then disguise and shielding at every level was entirely to be expected. He could not trust one of the nine not to be a spy.

That left the inner three. Damn it, he simply did not want to take his briefcase full of trouble to the old woman. He and she thought along such different lines. But he tried to leave his personal feelings out of it and consider them each dispassionately. Young Maureen? He smiled. Personal feelings were very much there. Every time he thought of her, he remembered the exact, scented, animal smell of her and the long-legged shape of her sharing that bed with him in Somerset. That had been some night! It had almost made up for Zillah. But he still felt Maureen was too—flimsy? flighty? There was no exact word for what he knew of her. It just meant he was not, after all, going to consult Maureen first. He needed a steady mind, and a keen one. Amanda? She had a mind, all right—too bloody right she had! He found himself wincing at the mere thought of her curiously luminous dark eyes. Oddly enough, at forty she was still considerably better-looking than Maureen and could pass for almost the same age. Mark was scared to death of her (in his secret soul where he hoped nobody knew), and he knew she would either reject his fears out of hand or pat him kindly on the head and take charge. So . . .

"The old woman then," he muttered, and with resignation, got up and bought a ticket to Hereford.

3

It was a muddled old farmhouse with a verandah on the front of it that somehow melted into a porch with a green door. A garden spread from it in successive waves of overgrowth—grass first, then longer grass containing leaves of long dead daffodils, then bushes, then higher bushes, several waves of those, including laurels—and finally a row of trees that generally flowered in spring, but were liable to be untidily in bloom most of the year. The house was quite hidden from the road. On the other hand, if you knew where to position yourself in the garden, you could have an excellent view of the road without anyone knowing you were there.

The old woman knew exactly where. She had been sitting there all morning, at various tasks, with Jimbo scratching diligently beside her and the cats stalking hither and yon in her orbit. Around her, the muddled house seemed to have spread into the grass, manifesting as flowerpots, tipped-over mugs of coffee, cane chairs, a basket or so, a colander, a kettle, a few cushions. All the day's work, the old woman thought, shunting a row of peas with her broad thumb along their pod and into the colander.

A car engine caught her ears. "Ah," she said. "At last!" And she raised her head to watch the local taxi

decant a passenger at her decrepit gate. Her squabby
eyebrows rose at the sight of the pale young man in
the sober gray suit who climbed out and turned to pay
the driver. "It's *him!*" she remarked to Jimbo. "And here
was I expecting someone about that poor girl! Must have
got my wires crossed. *Do* people like me get their wires
crossed, Jimbo? Well, there's a first time for everything,
they say. And whatever he wants, it's trouble. The poor
boy looks all in."

She watched him wait for the taxi to drive away and
turn to the gate, carrying that absurd hat he affected. She
watched him have the usual problems people had with
her gate. She grinned when it finally fell down flat in the
mud and he had to pick it up and prop it on the bushes.
But the look on his face sobered her as he came on up the
path, still carrying that hat and an expensive briefcase
with it. She quietly replaced the gate behind him and
waited for him to get to the place where visitors usually
found they could see her.

"Hallo, Mark," she said. "Important, is it?"

"Yes," he said. "Very." He stood and surveyed her,
a fat and freckled old woman wearing a red dress and
pink ankle socks, squashily embedded in a floral plastic
garden chair and busy shelling peas or something. Her
hair had been dyed a faded orange and fussily curled.
Her cheeks hung around her lax mouth, white where
they were not freckled, and her garden was strewn with
objects and aswarm with cats. As usual. He had forgotten all those cats. The place reeked of cat. His foot
pushed aside a saucer of cat food lurking in the grass,
and he was unable to avoid fanning at the smell with his
hat. And on top of all this, her name was Gladys. It was
hard to believe she was any good. "Expecting me, were
you?"

Gladys looked up. Until you saw her eyes, Mark
emended. Her eyes knew most things. "Expecting *some-*

one," she said. "I've been waiting out here all morning. It's been trying to rain. Nuisance." As if to prove this, a few warm drops fell from the overcast sky, splashing his hat and pinging on the colander. Gladys looked skyward and frowned. The drops instantly ceased. "A real nuisance," she said, and possibly grinned briefly. "What's the matter, Mark? You look like death. Take a seat before you fall down."

Her fat hand, with a peapod in it, gestured to the nearest cane chair. Mark walked over to it and settled himself, creaking, with his hat over his knees. Instantly he was in a ring of cats. They appeared silently from clumps of grass, from under bushes and from behind flowerpots, and sat gravely surveying him, a circle of round green and yellow eyes. Her ritual. He sighed.

"What can I get you?" she asked. "Have you had any breakfast?"

"Not really," he said. "There was no buffet car on—"

"They always forget it," she said, "on trains out this way. Jemima, you and Tibs."

Two of the cats disdainfully got up and walked toward the house.

"I've a lot to explain," Mark said.

"So I see from the size of that briefcase," she said. "Eat first. Get some coffee inside you at least."

There was, without any apparent disturbance, a wooden tray now lying beside him on the grass. On it was a rack of toast flanked by a glass dish of butter and a jar of marmalade. A bone-handled knife was laid carefully across a glass plate on top of a paper napkin with a pattern of puppy dogs on it. Beside that was a glass of orange juice, and milk in a jug that matched the plate. A mug with the words THE BOSS on it and a blue steaming coffeepot materialized as Mark looked. He felt considerable irritation.

"He'll need a strainer," Gladys said. As the strainer duly appeared, propped in a little glass bowl, she added, "They can't remember if you take sugar or not."

"I do, I'm afraid," Mark said, and tried to suppress his irritation. He had tried, any number of times, to persuade her that magic was not just something you used as a home help, and that she had skills too important to be squandered in this way. Most of the time Gladys pretended not to hear. When she did listen, she laughed and said she had plenty more where that came from, and besides, it never did anyone any harm to keep in practice. She looked at him challengingly now, knowing just what he was thinking, and he did his best to seem impassive. A glass bowl full of sugar cubes came to stand by the milk jug.

"Eat," she said. "You need the energy."

Mark laid aside his hat and wedged the tray across his knees in its place. Breakfast, however it arrived, was thoroughly welcome. As he buttered his toast, he saw the two cats return and, quietly and disdainfully, station themselves among the others. Gladys continued shelling peas until he was on his second cup of coffee. Then she looked up again, a sharp, full look.

"Go ahead," she said.

"Would it surprise you," asked Mark, "if I said Chernobyl was no accident?"

"I feel bad about that," Gladys said. "You know I do— we all do. *Damned* if I can see how none of us noticed that radioactive stuff until it was too late to do more than push it off to where there were fewest people to harm." She paused, with her hands on her fat thighs. "You're not saying that just to make me feel better, are you? Who'd *do* a thing like that?"

"The same people who distracted you with the bombing of Libya," he said. "Who'd cause World War Two, or the Cold War, AIDS, drugs, or—come to that—the greenhouse effect? Who isn't interested in our having a space program?"

"People," said Gladys. "This is people. You don't have to tell me the world's a crazy place. If it isn't stupidity, it's greed with most people."

"Yes, but *which* people?" he asked her. "Suppose I were to tell you the same people were responsible for all these things I just mentioned *and* a great deal more I haven't?"

She was silent. For a second or so he feared she was rejecting every word, and he sighed. She was too old. Her face was blank. Her mind was set. He should have quelled his fear and gone to Amanda instead. Then he saw that Gladys's expressionless face was turned toward something in the grass. Her lips moved. "Jimbo," she said faintly, "I'd have to ask three questions, wouldn't I?"

She was talking to that animal of hers. Some people claimed it was a monkey. Others declared it to be a small dog. Mark himself had never been sure which it was. All he knew was that it was brown and skinny. When it appeared, it scratched rather a lot—as it was doing now. He suspected this was a device to stop people looking at it too closely.

"I'd have to ask," said Gladys, "Who? and Why? and What proof has he? Wouldn't I, Jimbo? And why is he coming here with a tale like this when the Berlin Wall's down at last, and just as Russia and so forth start being more friendly?"

So her mind *was* working, after her own fashion. "That's all part of my proof," Mark explained quietly. "Ask yourself—or Jimbo—who might want all technologically advanced nations at peace with one another at the moment when the world's climate is changing."

"Sounds like a well-wisher," she said.

"Not if you consider that they started the global warming at the precise moment when we were all distracted by Chernobyl," Mark told her. "It's quite a pattern of theirs—they lull us, or they distract us until it's too late—and it quite remarkably often seems to be aimed directly at *us*, at magic users in this country. I've got pages of proof in my briefcase to—"

"Printout things!" said Gladys. "You know I can't make head or tail of those. Tell it plain."

Mark creaked about in his cane chair, wondering how to explain. "Well," he said at length, "let's begin with global warming. Do you know how much of this country will be left if the polar icecaps melt entirely?"

"I saw a map on the box," Gladys assented. "Not much." In the grass, the skinny animal appeared to paw one of her freckled bare legs. "I know, I know, Jimbo," she said. "He's on to something. I know that. It's the Who and the Why that worries me. *Who's* going to want the world at peace while they heat us up until we're all tropical and flooded?"

"The same people who wanted a war fifty years ago," Mark said.

"How do you make that out?" she said. "War *and* peace. That puzzles me. It doesn't make sense!"

"It does," he said, "if you consider all the inventions and discoveries that came out of the war. I'm not just talking about rocketry and nuclear power—I'm talking about the seven new forms of protection the Ring discovered during the Battle of Britain. I'm talking about the ways we're going to have to think of now to hold the water back, not to speak of all the new cooling techniques we'll need when the world gets hotter."

There was another long silence, during which a few more raindrops pinged on the colander and the breakfast tray. "Someone using us to learn things," Gladys said. "That's not nice. What proof have you?"

Mark reached his pale hand out to his briefcase. "For one thing, I called up records of all the plans, blueprints, and prototypes that have disappeared over the last twenty years. There's a hell of a lot. The significant thing is that two-thirds of them vanished so completely that they've never been traced."

"Oh, industry," Gladys said dismissively. "What about *us*?"

"Exactly," said Mark. "We don't keep records. For the important things, we use word of mouth."

They looked at each other across the littered grass. The bushes tossed as if a shiver had run through them.

Gladys levered herself from her plastic chair. "Up, Jimbo," she said fretfully. "Time I was getting lunch. This is all too much for me."

It sounded as if she had given the whole thing up. Mark followed her anxiously as she lumbered into the house, dutifully carrying the tray with him. It was dark and redolent indoors, of herbs, pine, cats, and bread. Plants—some of them tree-size—grew everywhere in pots, as if the garden had moved in there in the same way that the house had spread onto the grass. Mark fought his way under a jungle of tree-tall plants, which reminded him of the things you might expect to find growing in a bayou, and found her busy in the elderly little kitchen beyond.

"You didn't need to bring that tray," she said without turning around. "The cats would have seen to it. I've only chicken pies today. Will that do, with peas?" Before he could suggest he had only just had breakfast, she went on, "It has to be one of the Outer Ring, doesn't it? No one else knows enough."

"Yes," he said, sliding the tray onto a surface already full of flowerpots. Some toppled. He was forced to enhance the space in order to make room for the tray. She's got me squandering power now, he thought. "Can I help?"

"No, go in the other room and sit," Gladys said. "I need to be on my own when I'm thinking."

Mark went obediently, highly relieved that she was prepared to think about it, and sat on a hard sofa amongst the jungle, staring out beyond the lozenge-shaped glass panes of the verandah door. She had let the rain come down now. It was pouring outside, steady white lines of rain, and the room was nearly dark. The cats were arriving indoors around him. The cane chairs were now on the verandah, along with most of the other things. Mark sat listening to the rilling hiss of the rain, and it had nearly sent him to sleep by the time Gladys called him to lunch.

"You still haven't told me who," she grumbled. "Has he, Jimbo? If someone's using us for guinea pigs, I've a right to know, Mark."

Mark picked at a large, squashy commercial chicken pie and some remarkable bulletlike peas, sighed, and went with her, for security, to another level of the continuum, where he gave her his theory. He saw her eyes widen in the gloom of the kitchen.

"There's never been any sort of proof of *that*," she said. "Eat up. I don't want to hurry you, but I've got to get to the hospital. There's someone needing me there."

He was fairly sure he had lost her now, but he did his best to eat the pie. Anxiety caused it to form a hard lump, with corners, in his stomach. He watched Gladys encase herself in a transparent plastic mac and sort through a floppy purse for money.

"You can come too if you like," she told him. "I'm still thinking—and I'd like you to see this girl anyway. Coming?"

He nodded and followed her out into the soaking garden, where he was not particularly surprised to see the taxi that had brought him here once again drawn up outside the tumbledown gate. He climbed into it after her and sat curled up around the square pie in his stomach, wondering whether to feel hopeful or simply wretched.

4

It was clear that Gladys knew her way around the
hospital. She waddled swiftly ahead, encased in her
ectoplasmic mac, down an interminable corridor and
into an elevator. Mark thought, following her, that only
the raindrops on the surface of the plastic showed that
she was not in fact being manifested by some medium
or other. He was not surprised when none of the people
they passed seemed to notice her. He was putting out
the same kind of *Don't see*, but with an effort. Hospitals
always bothered him acutely. They were so full of pain,
and of pain's obverse, cheerful insensitivity—or was cru-
elty the word?

Gladys turned to him in the elevator. She looked intent
and busy, almost cheerful. "They brought this girl in
around five in the morning," she said. "The poor thing
was hurt bad, and she put out a call. Only one call.
Then she stopped and drew everything in—as if she'd
made a mistake. Anyway, she needed everything she'd
got just to stay alive with. Luckily I managed to hitch
on when she called. I've been monitoring her ever since,
and there's something *very* peculiar there. As a matter of
fact, when you turned up, I was *sure* it was going to be
someone come about her. You gave me quite a surprise.
I'm not often wrong that way."

Mark only nodded. The elevator shaft was like a section through the varied pain of the hospital. The lift carried him past the blinding worry of a parent, the grinding of a broken bone, the eating acid of an internal growth, fever dreams, and for a short—mercifully short—instant, the vivid agony of a knife slicing anesthetized flesh. He had to fight to shield himself.

It was still as bad when he left the elevator and followed Gladys down further corridors where they passed beds. This hospital was on some kind of open plan. Every few yards or so, a corner with windows held a cluster of beds. There were wrung faces on pillows. Women here and there sat up and, in the concentrated egotism of mortal sickness, greedily ate chocolates or stared while visitors harangued them. When they came to the place Gladys was looking for, that was a corner too. You could have taken it for a corner where equipment was dumped, had there not been a bed there. And here was relief. It was such blessed silence from the insistent pains of the hospital that Mark did not understand at once.

Gladys nodded at him. "Feel that? Did you ever know such shielding?"

Only then did Mark associate the silence with the bed around which most of the equipment centered. Silly of me! He marveled that the occupant of the bed seemed so young and small. Anyone who could block out that amount of pain while being so sick as this girl must be a powerful adept indeed. He thought he knew everyone throughout the world who had this kind of strength. But the thin, scraped face among the equipment was not the face of anyone he knew.

"Now, who are you, my darling?" Gladys wondered aloud. Her fat, freckled hands fastened on the girl's free arm, tenderly, gently. Her breathing grew heavy as she concentrated. "She's come from a long way away," she said. "Bad, bad. That car that ran into her crushed her in all down the other side, poor dear, and they haven't given her enough painkiller, the fools. There. There, Auntie Gladys has put in a few blocks for you, my love, so you can spend your strength on getting well." She turned over her shoulder to mouth at Mark, "What do you make of the color of her?"

Mark considered. The scraped, half-raw little face had the mauvish tinge of someone badly in shock. Carefully avoiding the abrasions, he put his hand to the sharp, unconscious corner of the girl's jaw. Mordant blue-gray pulsed from the contact, sickening and strong enough to make his stomach heave. He removed his hand. "She's been poisoned. It's no kind of poison I know."

"Me neither," said Gladys. "Worse and worse. Those fool doctors haven't even noticed. Give me your hand and we'll see what we can do."

She snatched his hand as she spoke. For a while they both concentrated in silence, drawing off the blue-gray sickening waves and feeding them to whichever of the various sumps would accept them, drawing again, casting the venom, drawing—until no more would be accepted.

"It was a massive dose, whatever it was," Mark said, "and it's antipathetic to most of the usual sumps."

"They did their best," Gladys said defensively. "So did we. Let's see if it's helped at all." She tapped gently at the girl's skinny arm. "Wake up, my darling. Auntie Gladys is here. Gladys is here to help. Wake up and tell Gladys what needs to be done for you, my love."

The girl's eyes had been half-open all along. Now, slowly, they were seeing. A weak but practiced consciousness played over first Gladys, then Mark.

"Friends, dear," Gladys said.

They could tell that the girl knew that. Her mouth made a mumble. It sounded like "Thank goodness!" But Mark, moving automatically to another plane of being, interpreted it there and exchanged a look with Gladys. The girl had tried to say "Thank the Goddess!"

"And may She bless you too," he said. "Where are you from?"

The girl's mouth mumbled again. Gladys, tenderly holding the girl's wrist in one hand and grasping Mark's hand with the other, was forced to join Mark, and both had to move to a more distant plane before the sounds made sense. The girl manifested there as a little flame, flickering and guttering, but somehow fresh and sweet.

"The Ladies of Leathe," the flame fluttered at them. "I wasn't careful enough and my Lady Marceny found out—found out, my love, my love—it wasn't done for the Brotherhood—it was wicked, wicked—and I tried to get away and warn you, my love—but I think she poisoned me—and they have traps out—I didn't know and I was caught—and my love has no idea—I must warn—"

"Where were these nasty traps, my love?" Gladys asked. "Tell Gladys and she'll take them apart."

"Through every band of the Wheel," flickered the flame. "Between the two of them."

"But *where*?" Gladys insisted gently. "Where did you come from, my love?"

"Neighbors," whispered the flame. It was down to a weak *phut-phut* now. "Next-door universe—the Brotherhood studies yours—but it was wicked—" The guttering light flared desperately. "I must warn him—"

And went out. On the pillow the eyes were still half-open but evidently saw nothing now. A green light that had been scribbling on a screen drew a straight green line.

"We'd best get out," Gladys said briskly. "They'll be along to see her any second."

They passed the nurse hurrying that way as they went. Both of them made very sure they were not noticed either by her or by anyone else they encountered, until they came to the parking lot, where the taxi driver was patiently reading a newspaper spread over his steering wheel. "Back home?" he asked Gladys. "That was a quickie."

"It takes all sorts," said Gladys. "And I can't wave a magic wand over all of them." The driver laughed.

Mark fell asleep on the way back, into dreams of drugs uneasily seeping and knives lancing, and did not wake until Gladys was heaving herself out of the taxi at her tumbledown gate.

"Well, how about that?" she puffed, somewhat triumphantly, as they walked up the muddy path. "The only way I slipped up was not seeing you and that poor girl were part of the same thing!"

Mark nodded. It had been proved to him over and over again that there was no such thing as coincidence in magic, but he still felt a kind of incredulous excitement, weary as he was. "You believe me now?"

"As soon as I set hands on her, I knew she wasn't out of *this* world. Didn't you feel the strangeness? It wasn't just the strange poison either."

Again Mark nodded. It was easier than confessing that touching the girl had told him nothing beyond the fact that she was poisoned.

Gladys shot a look at him as she unlocked her green door. "You're going to lie down and sleep while I look into this. Where do I tell Paulie you are?"

"Birmingham," he said. "The conference took longer than I expected. But she has to be able to get in touch with me there. I gave her a phone number. I'd better—"

"I'll do it," said Gladys. "It'll be a bad day when I can't tangle a few phone lines. She'll get a hotel receptionist who'll promise to give you the message. You get upstairs. There's a bed for you in the room on the right."

He stumbled his way gratefully up the shallow, creaking stairs, knowing there was some other anxiety in his mind, but almost too tired to place it. Traitors, he thought. Spies and traps. That was it. But he had warned Gladys. He could surely trust her to handle it. He found the room. He removed his jacket and shoes and fell on the bed, which proved to be as shallow and creaking as the stairs. He slept.

He slept, and the dreams of chemicals and lancets returned. But after a while, other things flitted behind those dreams, like birds going secretly from bough to bough inside the foliage of a tree. Behind the machines of the hospital, he had more than one glimpse of a blue fortress with five sides and odd-shaped towers, and occasionally there was rolling countryside with a subtly Mediterranean look. Eventually, as if the leaves dropped one by one from the tree and left the birds in full view, the hospital images fell away to show a deep tawny tone. He was somewhere very high up where everything was this curious color. There he accompanied several other people on what seemed to be an inspection of their borders and the defenses on those borders. He was relieved to find the defenses of Britain standing like a wall of amber. They were unbroken, and yet he had a feeling something was seeping under them. But as he tried to turn his attention to the defenses of Europe and the distant gamboge of America behind him, he found that the inspection party was moving on, outward and upward, on a voyage none of them had ever thought to make before. They seemed to be driven on by strong anger. He followed, in his dream, puzzled, and found that they came to the borders of the universe.

The dream image of this outer boundary beggared description, since there were many boundaries, all weaving and writhing and partially interwoven like thick, honey-colored rainbows. Some even seemed to occupy the same space as others. The dream was forced to simplify. At first it looked like a bucket of water into which concentrated tawny dye had been stirred. But when none of the watchers could make sense of this either, the dream simplified again, and they walked the edges of fields that were also seashores, stretching from them in all directions, upward, downward, slanting and standing on end, piled up into the sky, and piled likewise into the transparent amber depths below. Mark marveled in his dream. He had not known there were so many.

Most fields ended as simple seashore, though some had low walls with gates in them, and some hedges or lines of trees. But the party walked along its own shore until they came to one that was different, because it was defended. In the dream, it was represented as a tangle of barbed wire all around the amber field. Though it looked dark and unnatural enough, there were moments when it took on the look of a giant hedge of brambles. Beyond it, a stretch of sand had notices stuck into it at intervals: BEWARE MINEFIELD. Even in the dream, Mark was aware he was seeing an absurd diagram of a threat he would otherwise not be able to visualize at all. He, together with the rest of the party, surveyed the defenses glumly. There was no way into that field. Then his eyes fell on a large pipe, leading under the barbed wire from the field where he stood. In the distance, beyond the mined sand, he could just see the pipe disgorging a gush of substance from his own field into that other, defended place. There was no doubt that this place was the one he had been looking for.

Meanwhile, someone else in the party was pointing out that the defended field seemed to have a satellite. It hung in the distance far out over the center of the field. It looked like a writhing amber lens.

"Laputa," this person said.

"A James Blish city," said someone else.

Mark brought dream-binoculars out and took a closer look at the distant undulating lens thing.

This was where the blue pentagonal tower was, he discovered, although now he could see that the structure was in fact more like a walled city with a flat base, built of some kind of blue stone. As he swept his glasses across it, he saw that it was old and that there were people in it, looking back at him through binoculars not unlike his own . . .

5

M ark awoke to find Gladys standing panting at his bedside with a supper of fish and chips. This surprised him rather more than her announcement that Maureen and Amanda were waiting for him downstairs. He struggled up and leaned against the creaking head-board, beset with anxiety. "What time is it? How long have they been here?"

"A bit after midnight. They both got here around eight," she told him.

At least three cats were asleep on the bed. Another was curled up in his jacket. He stared at them with undiminished anxiety as he took the tray and thanked Gladys.

"It's all right," she said. "I wish you weren't such a worrier, but I suppose it's in your nature. Nobody knows where they really are."

Probably true, he thought. Every member of the Ring had carefully planned emergency arrangements, which they renewed and reorganized every week—like his own conference—so that no one in their families would know where they were. Neither Amanda nor Maureen could conceivably be a traitor. And yet, and yet . . . While he ate the withered and lukewarm fish and chips, his mind played with the idea of the traitor being one of their immediate families. Plotting the pattern of their absences would not help the traitor overmuch—it would merely become obvious that these happened during certain kinds of crises and at particular phases of the moon— unless one or the other of them had dropped a careless word at home. Careless words were very easy to drop to one's nearest and dearest. Mark himself was always most carefully circumspect in what he said to Paulie, but she was not entirely ignorant. She attended all the less secret ceremonies with him. She knew the office he held. He hated to think how angry she would be if she discovered how much of his duties he concealed from her. The other three must surely feel the same—at least, not Gladys: as far as anyone knew, she was a widow. But Maureen ran a troupe of professional dancers who were almost like a family to her, and she also had a succession of boyfriends, very few of whom had anything to do with witchcraft. The present boyfriend was a rough diamond—or, to be more honest, an unpleasant lout— who ran a music shop, and the kind of fellow who could well be in someone's pay. And Amanda? In addition to an obliging husband most people never saw, she had teenage children and, someone had told Mark, a sister living with her. It was surely too much to expect that Amanda had not dropped a word to her sister . . .

All the cats' eyes were on him, accusingly. He left the rest of the chips and padded off to the bathroom, where, to his exasperation, the toilet seat would not stay up. Another of Gladys's jokes, like her front gate. And quite probably, he admitted ruefully, wedging the thing with the toilet brush, the whole of his anxiety was some kind of displacement. Frankly, he was scared stiff of Amanda. It was the Aspect of the Mother in her that scared him most—though why it should, when he had no recollection of his own mother, he had no idea.

Amanda was leaning across the kitchen table when he came in, with a sheaf of Mark's printouts in her hand, talking trenchantly to Maureen. Upon her, Gladys's dim electric light seemed to play like the white shaft of a spotlight. It lit Amanda's hair blue-black, and the handsome lines of her face clear white. Her eyes glowed in it, compellingly.

"So this is what we've got," she said, and her voice was as clear and compelling as her eyes. "Another universe, one of many next door to this one, and in it a world probably much like ours, where they seem to have found some way of manipulating *our* world to *their* advantage. Their pattern seems to be to orchestrate a crisis—like a world war or an epidemic; AIDS, I suppose, is a good example—and then study what we do about it. If we solve the problem, they import our findings into their world."

Maureen, by contrast, was all reds and browns in the light—copper hair, tawny freckles, yellow eyes—and a brown jumpsuit clothing her long body, which was never wholly still. She writhed from a lotus position while Amanda was speaking and turned her kitchen chair backward, to sit astride it with her freckled forearms on its rickety back. "Don't forget their little habit of keeping *us* busy while they set up their experiments," she said. "That's the thing that really gets up my nose!"

"I was coming to that," Amanda replied. "There's no question that the pirate universe knows something about the way the Ring is organized. Either they tested us out during World War Two or we gave ourselves away keeping Hitler out. And since then they've flung things like Chernobyl at us from time to time to see if we were still on our toes, and finding we were—"

"Just about," Maureen commented, hitching her knees under her chin. "That one was a real closie."

"I know, but we did deal with it," said Amanda, "and I've no doubt that gave them the conditions for their latest experiment. Now they've handed us global warming, with the superpowers at least at an understanding, so that they can deal with it, while the Ring here in Britain is going to have its hands full with the country half underwater. That way, they can study how the Ring holds back the water, and make sure we haven't much left over to interfere with the technological approach. My guess is they want both magic and science out of this one." She turned across her shoulder to look at Mark in the doorway. "I hope you agree with my summary."

She said it with a strong and kindly smile, including him in the conversation because she had plainly known all along he was leaning in the doorway. He wished she would not treat him so kindly. It seemed to have something to do with the fact that she was both a professor of theology and a feminist, and it never failed to make him feel inadequate. "Perfectly," he said. "I couldn't have put it anywhere near as well."

Maureen turned as he spoke and half smiled too, looking up at him under her eyelids, full of the secret knowledge of that bed they had shared in Somerset. "We took a look at this other universe while you were asleep," she said, and her voice was full of the secret as well. It did not seem to perturb her that Amanda's brilliant eyes met Gladys's knowing ones across her, in perfect understanding of that secret.

It embarrassed Mark. "I was with you," he said curtly, coming to sit at the end of the table. "It seems rather well defended."

"I'll say!" said Maureen. "Mile-thick stoppers strewn with traps the whole way round. I saw it like a cell wall with hormone triggers against invading microorganisms."

"It was more like the ramparts of a prehistoric hill-fort to me," Amanda observed, "with sharpened stakes and pitfalls all over it. There was a culvert under the walls to take in what they learnt from us."

"Funny the way everyone sees things differently," Maureen said. "It's something I never quite get over at this level. Gladys said it was like the barbed wire on the Normandy beaches to her. Isn't that right?" she asked Gladys.

Mark turned to Gladys, startled that he and she had seen so much the same. "Or a very thorny wood," she said, dumping on the table a fat teapot clothed in a striped cozy. "Anyone but Mark take sugar? Good. Well let's get on and decide what we're going to do about these blessed pirates."

There was a short silence. Maureen's long hands, faintly mauve under the freckles, fidgeted around a mug with a picture of Garfield on it. "I'm too mad to think properly," she confessed. "I just want them stopped."

"One *possible* way is to stop their culvert. I expect we can find it," Amanda pointed out. "Stuff is bleeding off to them quite fast, and we ought to be able to trace where it goes."

"Out of the question," said Mark. "As soon as they realize we've stopped it, it'll be war. And they'll fight us with our own weapons, not to speak of their own, which we don't know about. I'm willing to bet they'll know as soon as we find the outlet. They have to be good to have had us under observation all this time without our knowing they had."

"Then I'll throw out another thought," Amanda said imperturbably. She seldom lost an argument, and never admitted it if she did. "How about putting up defenses even bigger than theirs?"

"Heavy job" was Maureen's comment. "Worldwide— it *might* work."

"They see those and it means war again," Mark pointed out.

"Well, anything we do and they notice is going to mean war," Amanda said in her most brisk and reasonable way. "Do you want to look into the possibility of rendering our universe invisible to theirs?"

"Which, if they find us doing, they'll just pirate too," Maureen observed. "I'm sure it would suit them very well to be invisible to us. Not wanting to be critical, Amanda, but they might even be hoping we'll think of that." She turned and stretched her legs the opposite way.

"And," added Mark, "none of these suggestions help with the greenhouse effect."

"We seem to be stuck with that, even if the pirates did start it," Amanda said. "I'd assumed—and since I'm simply throwing out ideas, I'm perfectly open to criticism, Maureen, though I wish you and Mark could contrive to be *constructive* for a change!—I'd assumed we'd get the pirates off our backs and then turn our attention to readjusting the climate." Her hands clenched around her cup fractionally. She was irritated.

Aware that she despised him, Mark found himself protesting, "I wasn't being destructive, Amanda! I just wondered if there wasn't a way to deal with both things at once. For instance, if we were simply to do nothing?"

Amanda's shapely black eyebrows came to a sharp point, exactly in the middle. An astounded crease grew between them, above her elegant nose. "Do *nothing*? At *all*?"

Maureen took this up eagerly. "Mark has got a point, Amanda. You must see that. If *we* did nothing and made sure none of the Rings all over the world did nothing, and just let the climate get hotter and the seas higher, then the pirates would have to stop the greenhouse effect themselves, don't you see? It's not in their *interests* to let everyone here die!" She was climbing about all over her chair in her vehemence, beating her mug on the table—and yet Mark was uneasily aware that it was all because the idea was his in the first place. Maureen was taking sides like a child in a school playground. There was even a faint jeering tone to her voice.

Amanda responded to the jeer. "Oh, perfect, Maureen! So we call their bluff. The only result, as far as I can see, would be that our world dies and the pirates simply start exploiting another one."

"I didn't mean—" Maureen and Mark began together.

"Oh, for heaven's sake!" Gladys interrupted. "We're not in business to do nothing, are we, Jimbo? It's obvious what we've got to do! We have to go *into* that universe and stop those pirates at their fun and games, for once and for all!"

In the ensuing silence, the creature called Jimbo appeared to climb into Gladys's lap. She hugged it and stared at them, a mulish and stony old woman.

"It's the only thing that makes sense," she said. "It's the only thing we ought to be discussing."

After another long silence, Amanda said, "I agree. How do we get there? Whom do we send? And what would a raiding party do when it gets there?"

Maureen, subdued and still for once, added, "Yes, and how do we keep what we do secret from these people? They must have the best intelligence in the world."

The discussion that followed this was, to begin with, slow and heavy and very, very serious. All four of them were overwhelmed with the nature of what they were discussing. This was war, against an enemy who knew all their weapons, and it made every other war look small and local and feeble by comparison. They knew their campaign had to be careful. It had to be good. And it had to succeed. It was clear to all four that, if they bungled, the pirates would finish them.

"Come on, come on!" Gladys said at length. "You've got to remember this is really no different from the way we went against Napoleon or Hitler. It's just bigger and in a new place, that's all. We need a smoke screen first. We're going to need to make it look as if we're powering up against this greenhouse thing. That's what we'll have to tell everyone else we're doing. It'll be too late when they find we're using the power another way."

"In that case we'll have to tell the Outer Ring," Amanda stated.

"Yes, we'll be breaking the rules, not telling them," Maureen agreed. "And—"

The Jimbo creature stirred in Gladys's arms. "Oh, don't give me that!" she said. "You young ones! You're all for breaking the rules when it doesn't matter, and when it *does* matter, you don't seem to know how to do without your precious rules! One of the things Mark spent all last night proving is that there has to be an informer pretty high up among us. So we have to break the rules. None of this is to go beyond this house and the wards I've put around it. Is that clear?"

"I second that," said Mark.

"You always were rather paranoid, Mark," Amanda said, but she gave in. So, after a little squirming and some clamor, did Maureen.

The discussion proceeded much more efficiently after that. They forgot how momentous it was to wage war on another world and simply discussed how to do it. Breaking into that world was the first major problem. The defenses they had all in their different ways perceived seemed truly formidable. This had them at a stand for a while, until Maureen pointed out that the satellite they had all noticed was far more lightly warded than any other part.

"Could we get in through Blish City somehow?" she asked. "It seems to be part of the pirating setup too."

"Somehow, somehow," Mark said. "There must be a reason they don't ward it so well. Can anyone think why?"

"Well, it can't be there just to make an easy way in," Gladys observed. "I sensed a lot of people there."

"So did I," agreed Amanda. "How is this for a working theory? Their defenses in the main world make it quite difficult for them to observe our world as closely as they want, so they have to build Laputa as a sort of observation platform. I saw Laputa myself as a sort of floating island—which is why I called it that, after *Gulliver*—but I suspect it's more on the lines of a pocket universe."

"I think you may be right," Mark said soberly. "And if you're right, then they won't need wards on the place, because that's where the main strength of their witchcraft will be."

"All gathered to spy on us and exploit us," Maureen murmured. "I think you're right too, Amanda."

"So an attack on Laputa ought to devastate them," said Amanda. "Of course, we'll need to research it more thoroughly, but let's plan on those lines provisionally. Now, how are we going to get a strike force to the place? Transition between universes is bound to cause all sorts of problems."

6

The discussion continued all that night and went on at intervals over the next month. Paulie Lister grew exasperated.

"Conferences, conferences!" she exploded to her lover. "Tony, I'm *sure* Mark's got a new woman, and I bet you it's that Maureen Tenehan! He only comes home to sleep!"

"Why do you let that bother you?" said Tony.

Maureen's dancers grumbled too. Maureen, it seemed, had strained a shoulder and was forced to make frequent visits to the only osteopath she trusted, who, it appeared, lived in Ludlow. But as her absences went on, little Flan Burke began to prove such a good deputy that most of the troupe foresaw that Maureen would lose her place to Flan and end up simply teaching the younger dancers. Maureen's boyfriend took the view that Maureen was doing it to spite him.

Somewhat the same opinion was held by Professor Amanda Fenstone's teenage children. They grumbled to their aunt that Mum's career seemed to mean more to her than they did. Why else was she always away giving lectures?

Only Gladys was spared human grumbling, and she often came back from another place to find herself in an accusing ring of cats long past their feeding time. For she took to sitting, hour after hour, on the Normandy beach forest borders of the pirate world, watching through notional spyglasses for any activity in Laputa-Blish (as it came to be called). Her skin grew flabbier and more blotched. Her feet were often numb, despite tartan socks and furry slippers, and she was tired. The other three worried about her. But Gladys was firm. This was the part of the task that she had set herself. As she said, she was the only one among them who was canny enough to watch without letting Laputa-Blish suspect it was being watched.

And her work bore fruit. One of the first things she was able to report was that there was always at least one observer in Laputa-Blish watching Earth. Often there were many more. They seemed to sit regular watches, and whenever the time came around for a group to be watching Earth, she became fairly sure that at least one was always focused upon the activities of the Ring.

"Let's give them something to watch then," Maureen said. "I'll start having everyone power up on the ecology from now on, something cruel."

"They'll be expecting us to," Gladys agreed, and went back to watching. As she moved away in her mind, she chuckled. Maureen was into ecology anyway. On the rare occasions Gladys had visited Maureen, she had found the flat full of tasteful green packages labeled *ozone friendly* and *ecologically sound*. The toilet roll had had *recycled toilet paper* printed on every sheet. *Could* one recycle toilet paper? she wondered, grinning as she drifted away, and if so, *how?*

During this stint of watching, she saw Laputa-Blish put out tenuous threads and translate them down to an earthly plane. Before she could trace them, they were gone. But she was ready for them next time they happened. She made one of her rare linkages with Jimbo and let him take her down, right down to his disquieting native ether. There she lurked, watching like a fox in a hole, and found that, as she suspected, the threads connected with the pirate world itself. She was lucky. It was a big joining that went both ways in all the planes of matter, and it lasted until her strength was almost gone.

"I think people were going back and forth, or supplies, or both maybe," she told Amanda, who came to put a rug around her shoulders and a mug of tea into her shaking hands.

"That stands to reason," Amanda said, going back to her careful checking of Mark's printouts. "It would be hard to make a pocket universe an entirely closed ecology. And I suppose the crew has to go on leave sometimes. Now, if only we could find out what sort of supplies they need regularly, we'd be home and dry. We could send our team in disguised as provisions."

"I'll see what I can get you on that," said Gladys. Lord! Amanda made a lousy cup of tea! Too intellectual, that was her trouble. Mind above tea. "You really think we're going to have to send people across?"

"Can you see any other way to get close enough to blast them *and* cope with all the surprises they're going to heave at us?" Amanda asked. "The Trojan horse idea still seems the best bet to me."

"You're probably right," Gladys agreed mournfully. Probably because she was so recently out of linkage with Jimbo, she found her mind full of earthy sadness, playing over all the brightest and best and most beautiful of the young folk associated with the Ring—feisty little Flan Burke, that lovely boy Tam, the nice-looking blond fellow who was Paulie Lister's lover, bossy Roz Collasso, and many, many more. Any of these could be chosen as storm troopers bound for Laputa-Blish. Such a waste. Such a shame. But no point mentioning that to Amanda.

"I'll have a look at the supplies they're getting," she promised. Disguise the kids as corned beef? Unless the citizens of Laputa-Blish turned out to be vegetarians. That would cause problems.

She was out of luck the next few watches, however. Laputa-Blish neither received nor sent anything concrete. All it did was move.

"*Move?*" Mark asked, startled.

"Bless you, they all move, these universes!" Gladys said. "Ours wriggles about, and theirs wanders up and over and around ours, and all the others do it too. Every time I go, there's a difference. Cup of tea, Mark, please."

Mark, who had spent his stint looking after Gladys in laboriously exploring ways and means of transferring matter between universes—the pirates had proved it *could* be done, otherwise he would have despaired—sprang to the kettle, and then stopped. "What about Laputa-Blish? Does that move?"

"Yes. It sort of jostles in a circle around theirs. The first time I went back to look for it, I thought it had gone," Gladys confessed. "But it was just around the back of them after all. I was in quite a panic till I realized."

"I'll need its course plotted," he said. "If it's moving about, our capsule could miss it and simply disintegrate in the void between. That void's giving me nightmares anyway. All sorts of things could happen to our team there. I *must* have a chart of how Laputa-Blish moves."

"You'll get it. When do I get my tea?"

"Now—at once," he said, diving to the stove through the jungle trees. They kept the kettle perpetually simmering these days. "Amanda left you some soup in a thermos. Want some?"

"Not if it's like her tea," said Gladys.

"It's not. She said her sister made it." Mark brought her the soup with her tea, and she did not refuse it. As he got back to work, she said sharply, "Did you feed my cats?"

"They make damn sure I do," he said. She chuckled. When he next looked, she was off again, or perhaps asleep, with Jimbo a dark, leggy, motionless heap on her lap. He got down to work again, grateful for the heavy warding Gladys kept around her house. Someone kept trying to contact him. He was fairly sure it was Paulie. It was sharp and possessive and had a female feel to it. Whoever it was had some difficulty penetrating Gladys's wards as more than a little nagging whisper. At any other time he would have answered at once, just on the off chance it was Zillah—even though Zillah was never possessive and had anyway made it plain that everything between them was finished—but not now. Transfer was fiendishly difficult. He kept wondering why, when the pirates could do something of this order, they needed to steal from Earth at all.

Gladys burst out laughing.

Mark jumped around to find her leaning back in her chair cackling, and Jimbo capering around her legs. "Are you all right?" he said cautiously.

"Oh, dear me, yes!" she said, wiping a tear of laughter away with her blotchy knuckles. "Oh Lord! You'll never believe this, Mark! I've found out what those big linkages are. I was fairly sure they were transferring people, and they *are*. They're women, Mark—girls for the troops! They just sent the lot of them back."

"Are you sure?" he said. Her earthy cackle unnerved him. He felt prudish dismay.

"Of course I'm sure! Every soul in Laputa-Blish at this moment is a man. Think I don't know the difference?"

"Then we've got our strike force," he said, divided between distaste and relief.

"That's right, dear," Gladys said. "Trojan women. Girls for the troops. Jael smote Sisera sleeping, and a few Jezebels for luck. I almost wish I could be going myself!"

Further careful observation confirmed that the resident population of Laputa-Blish was indeed all male. Amanda and Maureen gleefully set about choosing a group of the gifted, committed, and good-looking from which the strike force could be selected.

"It serves them right," Amanda said, briskly ticking names on her list, "for confining the use of magic to the male sex."

"Oh, but they don't," said Gladys, and her eyes met Mark's. "That poor girl in the hospital was a proficient, wasn't she?"

"We'd better get in touch with her," he said uneasily.

"All in good time. When she's ready to talk." Gladys stroked her animal. "Jimbo says she's still in shock yet. He thinks the pirates don't really understand about rebirth the way we do."

II

Arth

1

The High Head of All Horns and King's Vicar on Arth performed the final motions that transferred his visitors from Arth to their homes in the Fiveir of Leathe. Instead of doing it with his mind, which was the usual practice, he drew the symbols of the weave in the air with his hands and took vicious satisfaction in the way they burned green across his sanctum. Ozone crackled from wall to wall. Those ladies were in for a rough ride. Having done this, he sank into a seat, slung his heavy mitre onto its stand, and loosened his uniform with savage relief.

Nag, nag, nag! He could see them now, all the pretty faces gathered about his conference table, all the expensive and no doubt fashionable clothes, each one assaulting his nose with her own particular thick perfume—not to speak of assaulting his psyche with their dozen individual soft accusations. All claiming he had *hurt* them, for the Goddess's sake! Didn't they think he could see into their souls at least as well as they could see into his? Hurt, indeed! He knew them all to be as hard as nails, each one softly and inexorably set on having her own way. Well, they commanded in Leathe maybe, but not here in the separate small universe of Arth.

When he learned that this year's high-tide transfers would be bringing the entire Inner Convent of Leathe to see him, he rightly interpreted it as another attempt by Lady Marceny to get his soul under her domination. Report had it that she, and her mother before her, had possessed his predecessor in soul and mind too. The High Head had no doubt that the report was true. Marceny was the hardest and most inexorable of all the women of Leathe. She possessed most of the power in Leathe, but she was not satisfied with that, nor with having made a vicious puppet out of that son of hers. Not she. She wanted Arth as well.

The High Head had taken precautions, swiftly. Not only did he evoke the strongest possible wards for his own soul, but he made sure that every soul under his command was equally well protected. Arth's citadel had hummed with the application of powers—he could feel the wards pulsing away into the etheric spokes of the Wheel at this moment, withdrawing now the need for them was over. Unfortunately, the nature of the tides between universes meant that the ladies would have to stay overnight. The High Head made sure that they only came into contact with the strongest minds Arth could muster. Only those with a truly armored integrity were allowed to wait on them. This went for personnel from Maintenance Horn to clerks, cooks, and those who waited at table—everyone. He had even had to debar his friend and deputy, the Horn Head of Healing, from any dealings with the ladies and give his duties of attendance to junior mages. Poor Edward had deep uncertainties where females were concerned.

"You have surrounded us with woman-haters, Magus dear," was almost the first thing Lady Marceny said, opening her blue eyes wide and injured in his face. "Why?"

It was the first salvo of the hostilities. He bowed, smiling. "Oh, I don't think so, my lady. Just an average cross section of the men. You're simply sensing the pride we here in Arth take in keeping to our Oath."

"Really? You have made such *changes* since dear Peter's time, Magus," she replied, all honey and perfume and wide, wide eyes.

Thereafter it was assault and battery. Assault of the soul and battery of the mind, the High Head thought, running his hands through his hair. His hair was thinning and caught in strands between his fingers. He rather feared it grew thinner every time he had any dealings with Lady Marceny. There was something peculiarly avid and hungry in her that seemed to draw and suck the life out of you. Though the conditions of Arth tended to prolong a man's life far beyond the usual, he was sure Lady Marceny would have him old well before even home time. He sighed.

The first complaint on the ladies' agenda was that there had been so few results from otherworld. The High Head was naturally ready with figures. He pointed out that a steady stream of innovations was now flowing between otherworld and the Pentarchy, things both technological and magical. Particularly magical, he stressed. Since his predecessor, Magus Peter (under prompting from Lady Marceny's mother), had so cunningly reseeded the otherworld with the principles of magery, it had responded with a burst of fertility.

The ladies did not deny this. But the Lady Istoly, who was spokeswoman for home affairs, said reproachfully that the dear Magus seemed a little out of touch with the needs of the real world. "While you live peacefully here on Arth, the Pentarchy is in ever greater trouble," she told him. "I won't bore you with accounts of the other continents, but you do know—do you?—that at home the Sea of Trenjen has now joined up with Corriarden Bay in the north, making us into an island continent. Unless we can find some way to stop the oceans rising, the Pentarchy as we know it may vanish over the next century or so."

To which Lady Katny added, in dire, deep tones, "*Leathe* is beginning to erode." And Lady Moury spread papers on the table, saying, "I have here an outline of your plan to perform parallel mageworks on the otherworld, to cause waters to rise there by affecting its climate, and thereby elicit a solution to our own flooding. What became of this plan, Magus? Surely we should be getting some results by now?"

In vain did the High Head point out that this was a very large magework indeed; that although the work had been most satisfactorily performed, it took time for something that size to take effect; that they were even now getting preliminary results—

How *much* time? the ladies wanted to know.

"At least a decade," the High Head said firmly. "A fact which you will find stated in the plan, Lady Moury."

"But Magus dear," Lady Marceny said, all wide blue eyes again, "from our point of view, a decade is what you have now had. Aren't you getting any real results at *all*?"

He had defended himself by explaining such results as there were in detail. True, there was as yet no relevant mageworking, but on the technological front, moves were being charted. He went on to remind them that, just as time passed at different rates on Arth and in the Pentarchy, so it passed at another rate again in otherworld. "And," he said, "of course, you ladies all know that the relationship between our time and that of otherworld is notoriously capricious—possibly even chaotic. Sometimes five of their minutes pass to five of my months and nearly three of your years. Sometimes they seem to have had decades in half an Arth day. So for all we know, not enough time has passed yet in otherworld for those in charge of mageworks to have come up with any answers."

"I would have thought that all those observers you employ ought to have established *some* kind of ratio between our time and theirs by now," Lady Marceny retaliated. "Are you sure these men are quite competent?"

He bit back his anger and assured her they were. Only the fact that they both served the same Goddess kept him civil. The ladies were under no such restraint. They left him in no doubt that they wanted results and they wanted them *now*.

And it went on like this. They wanted him to do this, or that. He tried to make it plain that although his function was to serve the Pentarchy, this did not make him their servant (thank the Goddess!), and that he was only answerable to the king. But they were used to having menservants and blandly ignored the king. And Lady Marceny set continual traps for him. Over and over again she wondered aloud whether Observer Horn was quite efficient. Was it worth trying another system? Was *any* system that had to straddle two universes likely to be foolproof?

Each time he restrained his anger and assured her that Arth's method had stood the test of centuries now. If he opened himself to rage, he knew she would have him. He felt her all the time nudging at his wards, greedily waiting for him to lose control. So he did not lose his temper, much as he felt like screaming—and he could cheerfully have flung her several universes off, or even down to hellband, when, during the best dinner that Arth could provide, she went back to the subject of observers yet *again*.

"I only ask," she said, leaning sweetly toward him across the table, "because I've been trying a new method of observation for quite a while now, and I seem to have met with a hitch. This makes me sure that you must have your troubles too. In my case, it's maddening. Just as I was sure there was something firm to observe, the connection seems to have been lost. I must confess that I came to Arth hoping I could reestablish it, but I'm still getting nothing."

The High Head knew she had her own observatories, but it was unlike her to be so frank about it. Why, I believe she really is in earnest! he thought. "This happens," he said. "I confess to hitches in my time too."

"I hoped," she said, "that you might be able to advise me of some method that did not have so many problems."

"Willingly, my lady," he said. "Suppose you tell me something about your new method and how the hitch develops, and I will see what Arth can provide that might help you."

But of course, she would not tell him. She talked for the next half hour without saying one thing to the purpose, and he realized that this was just another attempt to get him off his guard.

Really, he thought, stretching in his chair, he *had* let her bother him badly, if he found himself reliving the ladies' visit like this! Arth discipline enjoined you to banish this kind of obsessive stuff with a short meditation followed by a short specific weave. But he was simply not in the mood. The most he could do was to utter his devout thanks to the workings of the Cosmic Wheel, which had placed him in Arth rather than left him on the estate of Lady Istoly, where he had been born. If you were born a man in Leathe, you joined the Company of Arth and hoped passionately that you would eventually be received into the Brotherhood. Otherwise your life was miserable. And he had been lucky, one of the fortunate tenth who passed all the tests, and luckier still to rise to High Head of the citadel.

Which reminds me, he thought. I have responsibilities. Better get on with the work those harridans interrupted.

He swung around and gestured at his wall. It responded by becoming a rank of mirrors, most of them apparently reflecting blue-clothed mages peacefully at work, though about a third had this reflection covered by a pulsing sigil. The High Head smiled as he collected these pulsing ones into the main reflector before his desk and gestured at them to elucidate themselves. This was a very useful adaptation of an idea from otherworld. Research Horn was still working to discover what otherworlders actually used it for.

The sigils spread to rows of print, most of them routine reports. Defense Horn was still having problems with those otherworld rockets. Housekeeping Horn was inundated, because a year's supply of goods had come over on the last of the tide. They requested help from either the cadets or the servicemen to unload capsules and stow provender. It would have to be the cadets who did that, because the newest recruits had been over for two days now and presumably knew their way around— enough to haul goods anyway. The servicemen had only come over in the carrier that brought the Ladies of Leathe, and thanks to those ladies, he had not even seen them yet. They should be about through with the rest of their induction by now. But here was Healing Horn—for which read Edward—wanting to see him about those same servicemen. Not yet, Edward, for Observer Horn was reporting some considerable etheric troubling centered on that spot in otherworld which they had learned to connect with the most useful mageworkings. And Maintenance had another leak in the atmosphere.

Maintenance Horn came first. That was a cardinal rule. The High Head indicated that they had his attention.

"It's due to the tides, sir," said the Duty Mage, briskly materializing in the mirror. "Tides always cause trouble, and this one's bigger than usual, and there seem to be eddies. We've thrown up some patching wards, and they'll hold till tonight, but I'm afraid it's going to take a full-scale magework to get it properly sealed."

"Get Augury and Calculus to give you their best times for the ritual then," the High head ordered. "I'll have fifty mages stand by."

Back to routine, he thought comfortably as the image of the Duty Mage dissolved. He called up Ritual Horn and gave them his instructions. Then he summoned to his reflector the otherworld site Observer Horn was so excited about. There was very little going on now. Hellband! It was high time something happened there. The Ladies of Leathe were not the only ones who were getting impatient. But the corner of his eye was catching the winged sigil flashing repeatedly in its mirror—Edward's sigil—which meant that his friend wanted him urgently. He let Edward know he was free.

"Coming now," said the mirror.

There was a delay while Edward traversed the corridors and ramps. As a healer, Edward claimed not to be very adept at projecting to a mirror. Oh, he could do it right enough, he always said when challenged, but walking was good exercise, and besides, having walked to where a person was made him feel as if he was truly meeting him. The other ways, he said, smacked of illusion.

Equally typically, when Edward actually arrived, he slid apologetically among the door-veils, ducking his head under the lintel. He always did duck, despite the High Head having several times stood him in the doorway and proved to him it was plenty high enough. And he advanced equally apologetically to put two steaming mugs on the worktop.

"I thought you could do with some coffee," he said, "after Leathe first thing in the morning."

"Rather than brandy?" said the High Head.

"Not straight after breakfast," Edward said, "though I did consider beer—Oh, blast you, Lawrence! Why do I never see your jokes?"

"You usually do in the end," said the High Head. "So what did you want to see me about? To make sure I hadn't become a Leathe puppet overnight?"

Edward laughed. The High Head was gratified to see that the possibility had never occurred to him. "Great gods, no! No, it's about this year's servicemen—I imagine you haven't had a chance to see them yet. I'm afraid you're in for a shock when you do."

"You mean the numbers are down? I saw that from the list. What happened? My guess is that the Ladies of Leathe quietly slung two-thirds of them off so that the Inner Convent—whom the Goddess bless!—could have plenty of space in the transfer carriage."

Edward shook his head. "No, it's not that. I talked to some of them, and they all say that this is all of them there ever were. I'm afraid it's worse than that, Lawrence. It looks as if every single district that owes us service, in every single Fiveir, has sent the absolute legal minimum, and on top of that, almost every lad is wrong in some way. I'd say the Corriarden district turned out their youth prisons for us. There's a lad from one of the north Trenjen places who can barely write his name— though he seems to have the rudiments of magecraft, so he's within the letter of the law, just. And as for the rest, I've seldom seen a set of sorrier physical specimens. About the only normal one is the son of the Pentarch of Frinjen, and he's only come because he had to—he'd be too old for next year's batch—and he's sulking like an infant over it. The rest are frankly demon fodder."

"What?" said the High Head. "Even from the Orthe? What have they sent?"

"A spavined centaur," said Edward, "and a gualdian with two left feet."

The two of them looked at each other. The Other Peoples of the Orthe were under the king's direct rule. Normally they took pride in sending the best of their youngsters for the year's service on Arth, and it was not unusual for them to send several members of all five Peoples. If they, too, had dispatched only the very least they were obliged to send, then things were bad indeed.

"I'm not saying the king's been got at by Leathe," Edward said anxiously. "Though he *could* have been."

"I doubt it." The High Head got irritably to his feet and strode from wall to window to wall. "The king may be as scared of Leathe as the rest of us, but he can hold his own or he wouldn't be king. I suppose we can be grateful to His Majesty for not coming here and giving us a piece of his mind like the Ladies of Leathe. Instead, he's simply made it plain that the entire Pentarchy has lost confidence in Arth. Edward, it's not my fault. I've worked like a demon to pull us out of the mess Magus Peter left us with. I've got everything running smoothly again—now this! What am I supposed to do?"

"Try to get some results on the latest experiment before the flooding at home gets much worse," Edward said. "And drink that coffee since I troubled to bring it." As the High Head stared at the mug as if it were an object from otherworld, he added, "I've got the assorted jailbirds, morons, and cripples lined up in the exercise hall. Want to come and give them your induction talk?"

"Give me five minutes," said the High Head. He picked up the mug and drank absentmindedly. "I know I've been telling you all along that I've got a bad feeling about this flooding project, and I suppose this may be why. But I have a horrible sense that there's worse to come. Do you?"

Edward shrugged. "Foreknowledge is not a thing I get much. Except about death, of course. I do feel a certain amount of death coming, I'm sorry to say. But," he added, sidling his apologetic length toward the doorway, "that's not unusual for a community the size of Arth. I'll have a Duty Mage put those servicemen through some exercises while they wait. It's always possible half of them will die of that."

2

B ad feeling or not, the High Head got swiftly to work to push his project onward. Using the correct imagery, he bent his mind to the necessary spoke of the Great Wheel. There, he deftly and expertly hooked up the threads of thought belonging to his otherworld agents and led the whole bundle to the specially crafted spindles on his worktop. The spindles spared him trouble by translating to matter again and giving him the result in his main reflector.

There were a good many agents out there. They were necessary, not only for information, but to balance the continuous stream of ideas that had lately been flowing from otherworld to Arth and the Pentarchy. The High Head, being in a hurry, took most of them into his mirror in clusters, each twist of thread representing a center of intelligent activity in that world. Most reported, as they had been doing all this past month, that the effects of Arth's project had been noticed. Otherworld seemed aware that its climate might be getting hotter and its seas rising. But not much yet was being done about it. Otherworld ran about wringing its hands and talked of planting appropriate vegetation or banning certain technology it believed harmful.

"For the Goddess's sake!" the High Head exclaimed. "What in hellband's use is *that*?" And he sent messages along the threads. *Get them moving. Tell them the effect is going to double in their next decade.*

Then he teased out the threads from the Islands. The magecraft of this site was usually among the strongest. Arth had run various tests recently and proved it currently to be in excellent working order. This was why Observer Horn regularly focused there. The High Head had great hopes of results here soon. First he focused again on the spot where observers had reported activity, but fine-tune it as he might, he found he could receive precisely nothing. Interesting. Every place in otherworld normally put out a certain amount of meaningless activity. The spokes of the Wheel were full of it, and junior mages had to learn to tune it out. But this area was not even putting out that. Most interesting. They must be using wards at least of the strength Arth had used against Leathe. Sadly, every single one of his Island agents was outside this area of silence, but this did not unduly perturb the High Head. This was the Islands pattern. When big mageworkings were afoot, they always closed down. Something was really happening at last!

In strong excitement, he flicked his two most important agents aside from the cluster. The first was serving as lover to a female known to be at or near the center of any magework performed. His image materialized in the reflector much as the High Head had seen him last on Arth—though this probably had little to do with the way the agent looked now, and was almost certainly simply the man's image of himself. Strange transmogrifications befell those who made the transition and became one with otherworld. This agent was—in his own mind at least—somewhat unshaven, bored, and a little drunk.

"Gods of the Wheel!" this agent said. "All I needed was *you*! What do you want?"

The High Head indicated he needed anything that might cast light on the area of silence slightly to westward of his agent. *Was* magework afoot?

"Do you indeed?" said his agent. "Then you're as wise as I am. It's obvious something's up. Bloody Maureen's pretending to have something wrong with her shoulder so that she can keep going off to that hag's place in Herefordshire, but that's all I know. You'd think someone who talks as much as that girl does would give *something* away, but not she! She's also collecting money. Cash is pouring in from all over the country—I'd no idea witches were good for so much. But she says it's for her new Green World Campaign—products made in conditions that don't hurt the ecology—you know the sort of thing. They're supposed to be buying a derelict factory somewhere up in the Midlands. Then they make green soap. The gods know if that's true or not. I've not been allowed near the factory—or the money, worse luck!"

He was, the High Head indicated, to investigate the factory.

"All right, all right! I know I should, and I've been trying. The bitch keeps putting me off. If I get you stuff on the factory, can I get shot of Maureen and come home? I really hate this world!"

The High Head of Arth forbore to indicate, even by so much as a flicker in the most distant spoke of the Wheel, that this agent was not coming home, ever. When a man underwent the ritual to make him one with otherworld, a change happened that seemed to be irreversible—but one could not let an agent know this, naturally. Instead, the High Head reminded his agent that he was serving as observer in the field as the result of misdemeanors as yet unexpiated and—because agents must be humored—inquired what exactly was so hateful in his position.

"I have to work in this music shop. I *hate* their music!" was the reply. "Let me tell you—"

The High Head cut into the stream of complaints he knew was about to follow by promising that, once the agent had firm information on the Maureen-female's purposes, the waves of the correct spokes would adjust themselves so that all would be well. He was careful not to promise that the agent could then come home, although he was well aware that he left the agent with that impression. Such prevarications were a regrettable necessity. He cut the agent off, still grumbling, and turned to the second one, the one set to monitor the most important male mageworker.

He had far less hope of anything concrete from this one. The inescapable fact that the Brotherhood of Arth was an all-male company made it impossible to place this agent as a lover. This male mageworker was decidedly heterosexual. So the agent had been attached to the mageworker's female partner instead, which was easy to do, because on Arth the agent had been blond, smooth, and handsome. As the image formed on the reflector was as handsome as ever, the assumption was that, whatever this agent had become, it still counted as good-looking in otherworld terms.

"I'm awfully afraid I can't give you very much to go on yet, sir, more's the pity," this second agent said. He was always very polite. He was one of those who hoped to ingratiate himself in order to get forgiven and recalled to Arth. Poor misguided Brother. "The woman I watch complains her husband is always away and too tired to talk when he comes home. She thinks he's got a new lover."

The High Head requested his agent to play on the female's fears to make her find out where the male really went.

"Oh, I did, sir," the agent said eagerly. "It doesn't take much doing, actually—she wants to know as much as we do. Last time he went, she took rather a risk, to my mind, and tried tracing him by witchcraft. But all it told her was that he seemed to go to that old woman's house in

Herefordshire, and she didn't believe that for a moment. It looks as if he's being too clever for us, sir."

This house in Herefordshire, mentioned by both agents, unquestionably was the site where Observer Horn had pinpointed the recent activity, and, the High Head mused, the elderly female equally unquestionably was the center of it all. He had many times attempted to tag her, but she gave him no hold, no excuse to plant an agent, nothing. She was wily. She slipped away from contact. She was powerful. There had been one occasion, when he was a good deal younger and less experienced, when he had made a rash attempt to broach her consciousness. She had risen up in anger, through every band and spoke of the Wheel, majestic and horrible, and threatened to kill him if he tried that again. Since then he had treated her with great caution. So if they chose *her* house for their activity, what they were doing was very important.

He was recalled from these thoughts by the agent saying piteously, "Sir? Sir, I would welcome it very much if I could be removed from this assignment. I'm not at all happy in it."

The High Head asked considerately wherein his unhappiness lay.

"It's not just that I have the feeling Mark Lister suspects me, sir. I think I can handle him. But I really hate that woman. His wife, sir. I really do!"

What was wrong with her? the High Head inquired.

"She's hard and mean—and stupid with it, sir. I think she's probably the most selfish creature I've ever known. I'll take any assignment you care to give me, sir, if only I needn't put up with her anymore. She makes me ill, sir!"

The High Head suggested that this seemed to describe all females. But since the agent was truly distressed, to the extent that his smooth face in the reflector was distorting in surges, the High Head made haste to assure him that he would be replaced as soon as another agent could be activated.

"Oh, *thank* you, sir!" said the agent. "You don't know how much this means to me!"

Know your men and keep them happy, the High Head thought, in considerable distaste at himself, as he cut the connection. That agent would now obtain him real information, quickly and in quantity. But since it did not do to play too many games with an agent's feelings, the man would have to be replaced—just as he was likely to be most use. Pity. The High Head sighed as he detached all the threads of thought from the spindles and left the agents to themselves again. He stayed in the Wheel himself, however, for he still had his contact to make with the third important female. She was almost as hard to tag as the old one. He had discovered she had a life-partner, but, to his chagrin, the two seemed perfectly faithful to each another. All attempts to plant a lover had been wasted. He had no success in tagging her mind, either. It was not so much that she resisted his efforts as that she seemed totally unaware of them. He just slid off the surface of her mind.

But in the course of his attempts to tag her, he discovered that she had young. This was excellent. None of the young knew very much, but they served to inform him when the female was moving, and if there seemed to be any unusual excitement brewing. They had been most useful in charting the response to Arth's last big test. The female had indeed been distracted by the small act of war Arth had organized, but when the noxious fumes had started drifting in from the continent—where the response of mageworkers had been surprisingly patchy— the young had told him that their dam had suddenly become alert and raced off to cooperate with the old female. The old one was known to them as "Auntie Gladys." They seemed to like her. They were disposed to like the High Head too. They thought of him as "Earth Angel," and they treated him with trust.

Then their usefulness had ended abruptly. The High Head had moved in on them as usual one day on a routine check. And found himself confronted with a sudden wild magic, passionate and strong. It was partly taught— enough to be conscious of itself—but hardly tamed, and it flung fluctuations all over the Wheel with a force that a full-blooded gualdian could hardly have equaled.

"How *dare* you!" it blazed at him. "Get out of these children's souls this instant!"

The High Head had been forced to retreat before the power of its anger, vainly protesting that he had always treated these young with kindness, that they liked him, knew him well, named him—

"I don't care *what* you think they think, or even what *they* think!" the wild magic stormed at him, and around him, and through him. "These are my sister's children, and I'm not having you nosing around inside them! It's unclean! And you're not doing it *ever* again!"

True to its word, the wild one had turned and thrown a rock-hard protection around those young. It was like granite. Powered by anger, that shielding formed an impenetrable twist right through every band of the Wheel. Nothing the High Head knew could have broken it. He moved out, chastened. But shortly he realized that the wild one was not wholly aware of what she had done. In her semitutored state, she imagined her warding was inadequate. She was afraid it would break. She kept her attention on it and on those young, prowling anxiously over what she could see of her handiwork, testing its links, watching for him to try to invade it.

Laughably, she had forgotten to ward herself in the slightest. The High Head soon found that, provided he was very cautious and quiet, he could use the wild one just as he had used the young. She was a good deal more informative too, because she was to some extent in her sister's confidence. But she was touchy. She tended to become aware of him if he tried to direct her thoughts in any way—though, so far, she had never connected his presence with "Earth Angel"—and he found it best to nudge up to her, make the most tenuous of contacts, and then hope she would think of what he wanted her to. She very often did. The hope of a High Magus of Arth was a powerful thing in itself.

This time, as he made delicate, delicate contact, she was fortunately musing alone. There was the usual sadness. There had been a very unfortunate love affair. It was to be supposed that her present unhappy musings were about that.

. . . the emptiness. That time there was nothing there— horrible—like looking down a long, long well. But there *was* something at the bottom. He was down there and seemed the way he *should* be for the first time. Once I'd seen how he *should* be, what he let me have was almost as horrible as the well. Like a dead thing. But *she* was down there with him. *She* did it . . .

The High Head had not much idea what this was about. He waited. His subject went on to her mother next. This was an equally unhappy topic and seemed to inspire some of the wild rage he had encountered himself.

. . . I could *kill* her sometimes. If she makes Amanda cry once more, I really might. Nasty thought. Stupid, though, two grown women cringing when the phone rings in case it's their mother. She never ought to have had children—except she needed something to hate, and besides, we were both accidents anyway. Had Amanda in her teens when she thought life couldn't *do* that to her, get her pregnant like common girls—and me late on when she thought she was too old for it to happen. But I'll kill her if she gets at Amanda *once* more—for being

kind to *me*, for God's sake! Poor Amanda—when she's
got enough on her plate keeping this country safe . . .

Ah, here it comes! thought the High Head.

. . . No, it's the whole world this time, isn't it? Or is
it the universe? I get muddled. Are there really lots of
other ones? Amanda seems to take it as proved there are
lots. Or do I mean the cosmos? Cosmoses? Cosmodes?
Anyway, lots. It wouldn't take me long to step over into
one just to get away from the bottom of that well—but
I don't think you can do it just like that, and anyway, I
don't want to muck up their greenhouse plans. And I bet
I would. Born with two left feet, that's me—as Mother
likes to point out. Anyway, they wouldn't choose me
because of Marcus, bless him! But if I could find out
how I'd—

Unfortunately, at this point she became aware of the
High Head.

—Oh, bugger! There's that bloody demon sniffing
around again! I can feel it. Out, you! Get *out*! OUT!

Just as if he were a mongrel after scraps! The High
Head retreated hastily. Her strength was such that his
face stung with it and a vile vibration shook him from
neck to coccyx. He had to sit still for a moment, recovering. But it was worth it! They knew they lived in a
multiverse, though they had showed no sign of knowing
that before this. As he picked his way through her ram-
blings, he gathered they were choosing a team—surely
of those with the strongest magics—and about to take
some action that must somehow involve the whole cosmos. Blowed if he could see what action, but otherworld
could be relied on to take some bold, wild way—perhaps
something on the lines of manipulating the tides between
universes? This could well be it. Anyway, Observer Horn
would soon be able to tell him. And meanwhile there
were the new servicemen to talk to. Jovially he picked up
his wand and his mitre and left for the exercise hall.

3

The two sparse rows of young men hastily came to attention as the High Head swept in, smiling, in all the awesomeness of the uniform of his office. Blue and silver glittered on him. The short cloak flared gracefully off one shoulder, jutting over the silver sword-wand, half concealing the great moon-badge on his chest. On his head, the great horned mitre raised him a kingly foot above men of mere mortal stature. Even the centaur felt this, and shifted his hooves, thinking he was looking up into a man's face for a wonder, instead of the other way around. The High Head of Arth was a legend to all of them. Therefore they all looked carefully, trying to see the man within the legend.

He was tall and moved with a brisk grace which carried the uniform well. They understood that grace. It came from a lifetime of the exercises they had just been put through. Most of them were still panting. The High Head looked a heavy man, but moved as if he were not. They were impressed by that and by the authority living in his face. It was a round-featured face, but not fleshy or commonplace, and seemed genial. They were impressed that he could smile, and even more impressed by the way that smile died away as he ran his eyes across them. His eyes were remarkable.

Loving Goddess! the High Head thought. Edward
didn't tell me half of it! His eyes raced over spindly
legs, narrow chests, feeble chins, at least one potbelly,
a stoop, several thick, brutish faces—one with a broken
nose—and a lad with glasses. The only normal one was
the short, square-built young man who had to be the
Pentarch of Frinjen's son. That one wore his new blue
uniform quite naturally, as if he were used to regalia,
and he was the only one not panting. Quite an athlete
from his build—though to judge by his shoulder-length
cone of carefully styled hair and his jaunty little mustache,
he tried to conceal the fact. The young man's face, as the
High Head's eyes met his, was neutral, not quite casual.
He showed nothing of the discontent Edward said he felt.
But Edward seldom got men wrong. I think we may have
a troublemaker here, the High Head thought. He was
speaking his usual words of welcome as these thoughts
went through his head, and would have been very much
surprised to know that the Pentarch's son was thinking
much the same about him.

Ay, ay, I think we have a sticky one here! Tod thought.
(He had a whole string of names and titles, including that
of Duke of Haurbath, but he was Tod to himself and his
friends.) In fact, his thought continued, our High Head
looks a right swine!

"As you know, you'll be here for the next year, training
with the cadets and the regular Brotherhood, eating with
us and sharing our duties. This, of course, means sharing
our rules," said the High Head. "I know the rules have
already been read to you, so I won't bore you with them
again. I would just like to impress on you that these rules
are here to be kept."

His eyes passed on to the gualdian lad, standing gawki-
ly beside the centaur. The boy looked like the runt of his
race, fragile, white, uncertain. His new uniform stood
around him like drainpipe he had got into by mistake,

and chin-high though it was, it somehow revealed that this lad had none of the usual thick body hair. The High Head's eyes moved involuntarily to the boy's feet. *Had* he two left ones? Something was odd there. The boots were huge. So were the great white hands. And gualdians usually ran to thick red or chestnut hair, but this one's hair was mousy blond, and thin with it. Perhaps the only true gualdian feature about the boy was the eyes. Here their eyes met, and the gualdian boy's great shining eyes widened and lit with amazement as he saw that the High Head had gualdian blood too.

The High Head hastily switched to the centaur instead. Maybe spavined was too strong a term. But the youngster was swaybacked, with the horse ribs showing. And the front legs were knock-kneed, each knee with a large callus showing where they knocked. The equine coat was a mealy gray as mousy as the gualdian's hair, and the boy-body as skinny as the rest. A charcoal dapple, which ought to have been on the equine barrel, was splattered across the boy's face and pale hair instead. The king may have thought this some kind of joke on Arth, the High Head thought, but I don't find it funny. Not funny at all.

"We don't go so far as to ask you to take the Oath we of the Brotherhood all swear," he was saying meanwhile, "but we do require you, while you are in Arth, to keep to the terms of the Oath as if you *had* sworn it." Before the uneasy movements of the lads could amount to a real protest, he went on swiftly, "We honor the Goddess by our Oath. We take Her seriously here in Arth, and we worship Her regularly. She rewards us by giving us greater powers than we would have in the Pentarchy, by which we control the rhythms that hold this very citadel in place. So you see that the Oath—"

Here the centaur boy, rendered thoroughly uneasy by finding the High Head staring straight at him, was unable to control his bowel. His droppings fell with a most audible *splat*. There was smothered mirth. The young centaur shifted from hoof to hoof in hideous embarrassment, and his dappled face was scarlet. He clearly had no idea whether the rules required him to clear the mess up, as he would have done instantly at home, or to go on standing to attention and pretend nothing had happened.

This was a frequent problem with centaurs. The High Head solved it by briskly conjuring the long-handled covered pan and broom from the side of the room into the centaur's hands. "There you are, Galpetto. Clear it up."

The mirth rose to a glad roar, much of it rather jeering, and the centaur hastened to turn himself around and set to work, looking as if he wished the floor would open. No bad thing, the High Head thought. There needed to be some kind of joke after the solemn talk of Oath, though this was not quite the joke he would have chosen.

He spoke for a short while longer, outlining the tutoring they would have, the recreations and the duties. And it was typical of this substandard group that none of them were attending. The joke had been too much for them. He could feel their minds wandering, cloacal quips building up, and, in some of them, a resolve to make a butt of Galpetto. Usually the High Head ended his speech with a genial wish to them to enjoy their year of service. You may have come here because you were obliged by law to come, the usual ending went, but there is no reason why doing your duty should not be fun as well. Now he found he had not the slightest desire to say this.

"One last thing," he said. "I spoke of Oath and I spoke of rules. When I said you must observe both, I meant it. May I remind you that you are under Brotherhood law

while you are on Arth, and the Brotherhood's punishments for lawbreakers are severe. If you break our laws,
you will be punished, by us, in our way, and you will
not enjoy it."

He swept out, hoping he left them considering this.

III

Earth

1

"**T**he capsule's nearly ready," Amanda said, looking up from the student essay she was marking. "Do you want to come and see it?"

"Who else is going to be there?" Zillah asked. She managed to keep her manner entirely neutral. I'm getting good at that, she thought.

"Nobody, I hope," said Amanda. Zillah relaxed, unhappily, and dabbled one hand in the large bowl of crumble mix on the table beside her to show both herself and Amanda she was truly relaxed. If Mark had been going to be there, she dared not go—and yet the hope, the horrible hope, attacked her that he *might* be going and she *might* have a chance of seeing him again. Even after two and a half years, she could not trust herself.

"Nobody?" she said.

The sisters were sitting in Amanda's kitchen, a comfortable, light, spacious room, in which every detail was planned for convenience and beauty together, and in which every detail was also slightly battered from having been used by children. To Zillah's mind, this added to the comfort. Without the battering, she was sure the place would have been as soulless as a magazine advertisement for a kitchen.

Amanda reached for the cup of tea beside her and took off her glasses. "Most of the people making the thing can only get there at weekends," she said, "but the ones who live nearest work on it in the evenings when they get out of their jobs. I usually drop in by bus on my way to the university—to make sure it's going right and to check the wards on the warehouse and so forth. But I make sure to keep my visits as random as possible. Today I'm at home. So I thought I'd go there by car at a totally different time."

Zillah reached a floury hand for her own cup of tea. "Security really is that tight then?"

"*Lord*, yes!" said her sister. "All the people working on the capsule think we're taking it up into space to meet UFOs. They think we're a bit mad, but they trust us. Some quite skeptical ones are seriously rethinking their position on aliens. And I'm the only one of the Ring who ever goes near the capsule. We don't want the pirates noticing we're all interested in a certain warehouse."

Zillah relaxed further. Mark was never likely to have been there. She let the devastating misery of that discovery ebb away and laughed a little. "Isn't the Ring taking a bit of a risk, leaving it to you? You know what you're like with machinery. Jerry swears the dishwasher blew up last time just because you looked at it."

Amanda's eyebrows peaked in that stare of hers. It must *terrify* her students! Zillah thought. "I was being deliberately negative then, Zillah. When I monitor the capsule, I'm entirely positive. If things blow up when I look at it, it's because our designer got them wrong. I know what I'm doing. I've studied the plans until I know them backwards."

And really! Amanda thought as she stared at Zillah, Zillah could be unspeakably irritating at times. They were very alike, she and Zillah. This was probably the reason why they got on so well most of the time and clashed so furiously for the rest of it. Zillah had the same clear features as Amanda, but hers were softer and tawny. Where Amanda's hair was straight and raven black, Zillah's sprang into a cloud of wiry tendrils, with red lights. Both had the same strangely luminous eyes, though Zillah's eyes were blue. And Zillah had, Amanda was positive, at least as strong a talent for magic as her own, but—Amanda sighed, and drank tea to cover the sigh. One of the irritating things was that she was always having to look *after* Zillah and always failing. Over and over again. Knowing, from her own bitter experience, what Zillah's life was like, Amanda had rescued her from their mother as a teenager and made sure she went to college. Result: Zillah dropped out, saying apologetically that university was not her scene, and disappeared. A year later Amanda had found her making baskets for a living somewhere in Yorkshire and fixed her up with what she herself considered a proper job in London. Result: Zillah disappeared and turned up working in a record shop a few months later, saying she felt that suited her more. By this time, Amanda had resigned herself to the fact that Zillah had an extremely low opinion of her own worth. Mother's fault. Amanda let her get on with the record shop and tried instead to induce her to train that magic talent of hers.

"It gave me tremendous self-respect," she told Zillah over and over. "I know you'll find the same. And what you've got is *strong*. But as it is, it's wild. You really could do damage, to yourself and other people, unless you learn how to use it."

Zillah, as always, meekly agreed to Amanda's plans. For a while she did study, almost diligently, with a circle of witches in outer London. Amanda encountered her at one or two ceremonies and felt proud whenever they met, because a number of people—Mark and Gladys among them—told her that her little sister had at least

the potential of Maureen Tenehan. Amanda harbored
fond notions of seeing Zillah selected for the Ring.
Result: Zillah vanished again, saying she was not sure
she had any talent at all. When Amanda next traced her,
she was eight months pregnant. She said, in her usual
apologetic way, that she had decided she needed to be
a single parent.

"Oh, don't talk nonsense!" Amanda had almost
screamed at her. "How are you going to support the
child? Who's the father, anyway? Can't he help?"

"Not really," Zillah explained. "He's happily married,
and I didn't want to upset him, so I didn't tell him."

She had obdurately refused to discuss the child's father
any further. Amanda, to this day, had no idea who was
responsible for Marcus. The only thing to do seemed to
have Zillah and the baby to live with her own family.
It was lucky the kids liked Zillah and that Amanda's
husband, David, was so easygoing, because there were
times when—

The bowl of pastry mix tipped, pivoting sharply on the
edge of the table. Both sisters shouted with one voice,
"*Don't*, Marcus!" Zillah shot a hand out and grabbed
the bowl. Amanda, with a swift gesture, halted the ava-
lanche of dry crumble in midair and guided it back into
the bowl.

"Gladys would approve, but everyone else would call
that a waste of magic," she remarked.

Zillah lifted the bowl high, and Marcus was revealed
below the level of the table, lightly dusted with flour
and still with both hands raised to grab the bowl, gazing
at them blandly. "Little devil," she said. "Did nobody
notice you for five minutes? Is that it?" She lifted him
up, absently checking the stout denim seat of him for
damp, and dusted the flour from his hair, which had the
same reddish tone as her own.

Marcus gave utterance. "Bond jewry," he said, stretching a hand like a plump pink starfish toward the bowl.

"It's *not* jelly," Zillah said, translating expertly. "And you're not having it. Amanda, if we go to the warehouse, we'll have to take him too. Will that be safe?"

"Honestly, Zillah, the way you've got that child warded, I don't think even Gladys could touch him," Amanda said. "I doubt if a nuclear missile could."

Zillah checked a need to cry out, *Because he's all I've got!* and also to explain that most of the protection was so that Mark—and therefore Mark's wife—should never know that Marcus existed. "Well, it's not so much what it might do to him, but what *he* could do to *it*," she said. "But if you think it's all right, let's go, shall we?"

With Marcus safely strapped into the backseat, Zillah drove—ferally, as she did many things—while Amanda crouched down in the passenger seat and invoked protection from several different pantheons, wishing she had remembered the way Zillah drove before she suggested this. Amanda did not care for driving herself. It was useful that Zillah enjoyed it. Besides, she had sensed that Zillah was having a resurgence of unhappiness lately and needed a break. But this—they hunted down a lorry and overtook it on a bend; luckily there was nothing coming the other way—this was enough to make Amanda wish she had left Zillah by the wayside two years ago. If she killed them, what became of the capsule, of their plans, of the world?

The road opened up straight. Zillah stalked a motorcycle down it at ninety miles an hour, only dimly aware of her sister's growing panic. She always hoped that driving dangerously would take her mind off the ceaseless tramp of misery inside it, but it did not. Nor did having Marcus. It was not that he was a constant reminder of Mark: he was another thing again. When Marcus was born, she discovered it was quite possible to love two people with the same intensity. It was as if her mind opened up another lobe, and there was Marcus in there, passionately precious. Alongside him, her feelings about Mark remained, exactly the same. They said you got over things in time, but it was just like her, Zillah thought, to have missed the trick of that somehow. Two years had made absolutely no difference. Maybe it had something to do with the weirdness and intensity of that moment—

She caught the motorcyclist where the road bent, passing him well over to the right, and absently dodged the Bedford van coming the other way. Beside her, Amanda uttered a faint, brave gasp. Marcus turned his head calmly to watch the van driver waving two fingers about. He liked the way they always seemed to do that.

—the moment when she had seen Mark as a shadowy reflection of himself at the bottom of a deep well. And Paulie down there too, drinking him. The horror of it was that she clearly knew Mark was *allowing* Paulie to do this to him. He was *letting* Paulie have all the eager, interesting, vital parts of him—the parts that laughed, or cried—and Zillah was only going to be allowed the pale, decorous, serious Mark. Prim, she had often thought, when she first met him. *Priggish* was a better word, she thought now, as old, gray factory buildings began to flash by.

"Next left," Amanda said faintly. "Then the first big gate on the right."

Zillah turned the wheel and they howled left into a side road. She slowed to sixty, not to miss the gate. If ever she could bring herself to tell Amanda about this vision of Mark in the well, she was sure Amanda would tell her it was a true Seeing. Amanda always said Zillah's talent was enormous, but Zillah had never noticed it herself, except just that once, when she *knew* she had seen the most important fact about Mark there was and—

There was gate. She swung through it. And there was another car parked just inside it, no time or space to miss it.

—left him. Zillah thought that something picked the car up and lifted it bodily sideways. At all events, they were stopped, facing the warehouse, side by side with the other car, and not even scraped. Just a little shaken.

"I'm grateful to rather a lot of gods," Amanda said.

"Whose bloody car *is* that?" Zillah demanded.

"I'll see." Amanda swept out of the car. Zillah unbuckled Marcus and ran after her, carrying Marcus, ready to lend her weight to Amanda's fury if necessary. And it might be necessary for once, she saw. The warehouse door slid aside under Amanda's angry hand, evidently unlocked. "*And* they took the wards off!" Amanda snarled. "Who *is* this fool?"

They clattered inside, into semidark. Zillah at once felt that, for some reason, everything was probably all right. She could see the capsule, a shrouded, nearly oblong thing almost the size of a bus, bulking in the center of the space, and she could tell it had not been tampered with. There was more than that. A kind of strength grew up around her from the floor. Doubtfully, she conjectured that this warehouse had been chosen because it happened to have been built over some place of power. She felt quite unworried as she followed Amanda around to the far side of the capsule.

A limber brown-clothed figure swung its long legs down from the crate it had been sitting on. "At *last!*"

"Maureen!" Anger, relief, and surprise made Amanda's voice turn high and chilly. "What the *hell* are you doing? We nearly hit your damn car! You know perfectly well that none of the rest of you are supposed to come here."

Maureen shrugged. "Where's the harm? This place is warded sky-high—and I just had to consult you over our final list for people to go. Whatever time they go, it has to be *soon*. Don't you understand? And I've got teams training in separate batches all over the country. None of them know if they're going or not, or anything about what they're really going for, and it's not fair on them or their families, Amanda. It's putting me under a lot of pressure, not being—" She stopped as she saw Zillah behind Amanda and continued looking at Zillah over Amanda's head, meaningfully.

Zillah lowered Marcus to the floor. She did not like Maureen, and she knew Maureen did not like her. This could be rather unfortunate.

"I still fail to see why you had to come *here*," Amanda said. "You could have phoned me, or consulted one of the other two. They both know all the people as well as I do."

"It's your baby—you made the first selection," Maureen said, strolling back and forth with her hands in the deep brown pockets of her coat. "And Gladys isn't doing anything but watch Laputa-Blish these days. Mark's up to the armpits calculating those tides Gladys found and matching them with sidereal tables, trying to find us a window." Her eyes flicked across to Zillah. "I went and tried to see Mark twice, as it happens. The first time all we did was have this long, long argument, because he said it wasn't possible for them to go at full Moon, and I said it had *got* to be."

She knows! Zillah thought. She fancies Mark herself and she's letting me know.

"I managed to persuade Mark in the end," Maureen continued, "but it was so late then, I had to leave. The second time I went, that wife of his was there, and it was all cuddle up, cuddle up, and she wouldn't let me have a moment alone with him—"

She stopped as Marcus plodded forward and stared up at her. He pointed with a starfish finger. "Do bitch," he stated.

"What?" Maureen's head jerked downward, and she bent over him like a vulture.

"He says you're a witch," Amanda translated hastily. "It's amazing how they know."

"Oh," Maureen said.

It became imperative to Zillah to get away from Maureen. She scooped Marcus up and carried him away through the porthole-like door of the capsule. Inside, it was suddenly all right again. Immense safety had been built into the thick walls of the thing—strong Amanda safety, which reminded Zillah of Amanda's house, particularly of her beautiful, battered kitchen. There were no windows. The only light came from the round door. Soothed and calm and quiet, Zillah carried Marcus along the central gangway, hearing nothing but the metallic ring of her footsteps and seeing nothing much but bent, wriggly reflections of herself and Marcus in the silver metal welded over the walls, ceiling, and floor. The thing *had* been a bus once. The seats were now reduced to twenty or so. The rear end was partly blocked off with more silvery metal, and Zillah conjectured that the machinery she could dimly see through the places where the metal was missing had to be a life-support system. At the front end, the drivers' seats faced television screens instead of windows, and there were controls of a sort, though not many. Zillah paced back and forth. As she went, she detached a long, coiling gingerish hair from her head and then quietly removed a short, fine one from Marcus. Why she should do this, she had no idea. When she had both hairs, again impelled by reasons she did not understand, she tucked both, the long and the short one, well down inside the upholstery of a seat near the back.

Meanwhile, Maureen said ferociously to Amanda, "Why is *she* here? How much have you told her? You talk about *me* breaking security, but *honestly!*"

"Don't be stupid! I've only told her the most general outline," Amanda said with equal ferocity. A certain amount of guilt lay behind her fierceness. While she had not given Zillah any real details, she knew she had talked to her more than she should. It had been so hard, never telling David or the children anything about this other, hidden side of her life; and when Zillah came to live with them, who knew all about this hidden side, the relief of having someone to talk to had certainly led Amanda to say far more than was quite discreet. "I've told her almost nothing!" she snapped. "Far less than you did by babbling about windows at full Moon! And what do you mean about Gladys not listening to you?"

"That was a *smoke screen*, you idiot!" Maureen retorted. "Besides, she didn't listen much."

"But what about the attack-magic? It doesn't matter how many teams you select, if they're going to arrive in Laputa-Blish without anything to—And don't you *ever* mention Laputa-Blish in front of Zillah again! All I've told her is that there are hostile magicians in the next universe. I haven't said a word about where!"

Maureen shrugged. "I assumed you'd told her the lot. All right. You needn't glare. And Gladys *has* got the attack-magic ready. She's calling it virus-magic—that was Mark's idea—and they're both dead chuffed with it actually, and they say it'll go through Laputa-Blish like wildfire as soon as it touches anyone there."

"Good," said Amanda. Both were cooling down a little. Both found themselves looking around and behind them. Their anger had been interacting with the delicate magics of the capsule. They could feel it building elemental things that could be disastrous. They smiled at each other, like bared teeth. "Well, let's have a look at that list," Amanda said.

"Okay." Maureen plunged a hand into her pocket. Before she took the list out, she said, "I'm sending Flan

Burke. I can't really spare her, but I think the team needs her vitality. And I think Roz Collasso will have to go. I hate the woman, personally, but you can't deny she's got a strong character. Then Tam Fairbrother is a must—"

"Tam?" exclaimed Amanda. "He's a *man*! It's unlike you not to notice, Maureen!"

"Jesus, Amanda! You are a prig!" Maureen said heatedly. "We *discussed* it. I thought even *you* agreed that an all-male world is likely to have a fair share of gay men. I'm sending two of our best looking boys. Even *you* must have noticed that Tam is bloody good-looking!"

This was hopeless. Around them on the dim floor, dust was beginning to rise in little dancing fountains. Maureen's copper hair and Amanda's straight black locks were lifting, and there was a smell of ozone. "Maureen," Amanda said decisively, "you'd better get into your car and trail us back to my house. We'll discuss the list there. If we argue anymore *here*, this capsule's going to be possessed." And, so that Maureen should have no chance to argue, Amanda strode to the open door of the capsule, calling ringingly for Zillah.

"Sorry I spoke!" Maureen muttered, plunging her hand back into her pocket, where the typewritten list was already half-materialized. "Back into hiding for now. Mother knows best!"

Amanda took the wheel this time and drove slowly and considerately in front of Maureen—which probably made Maureen even madder than she was already, Zillah thought. Maureen drove a fast car, new and expensive. Zillah could tell she hated crawling. Zillah sat in the backseat of Amanda's car, because Marcus seemed to want her there, and kept her thoughts carefully on Maureen raging in third gear behind. It served to push that curious, primitive piece of magic she had performed in the capsule right down to the bottom of her mind. It was necessary not to know about that, though she had

no idea why. She wished that the sight of Maureen's
furious face could push the misery out of her mind
too—but nothing did much for that. And I'm so sick
of it! Zillah thought. I'd like to be shot of it for good,
though that's a sort of death, and not fair on Marcus.
She found her mind repeating this. A sort of death . . . a
sort of death . . . Anyway, back to Maureen. I think she's
a bitch. Swaggering into the warehouse and behaving as
if she's in charge of the whole operation. Thinks she's
plenty officer quality, doesn't she? I can just see what it
would be like if she really *was* in charge. Zillah let her
mind run on this. It was better than thinking of death.
Maureen strutting, sauntering, hitching her long, limber
legs about, taking all the best men for her own use . . .

It was during this flight of fancy that the High Head
of Arth made his routine, delicate contact. He smiled.
Then he hooked Maureen's boyfriend out of the ether
and told him to get off his haunches and get to work
on Maureen.

2

M ark found a window for the next full Moon. It was a very small one, but it would serve, provided everything was synchronized to the second. Laputa-Blish would then be, as far as Gladys could tell, at a high point in one of its eccentric, wobbling circuits of its parent universe, and slightly inclined toward Earth. In this position, the capsule could clear the pirate defenses and reach Laputa-Blish without spending too long in the dubious interstitial stuff between universes. That was important. The moment it left Earth's universe, the circles of magic users sending it would lose touch with it. It would have to rely on its own inbuilt defenses, and no one wanted it to have to do that for too long.

According to Mark, who had been strenuously calculating for most of a month now, the window was all right, but the other influences were iffy. Much that was good was streaming in the inner spheres, but there was strong, obscure opposition too. "Perhaps we should wait for a more favorable Moon?" he said doubtfully.

The others vetoed this. There was, no one quite knew why, a general feeling that it was now or never. Mark, even as he gave in, admitted to having the feeling too—as if the pirates were breathing down their necks and would read over their shoulders what they were doing if they left the attack to wait any longer.

Gladys and Maureen, with occasional crisp interventions from Amanda, devised a very strong double ritual, whose purpose was cleverly hidden from all but the four of them. After that, as Gladys said, they had reason to be glad that the Ring was so well organized. The Outer Ring accepted the ritual without question and went to work on the mass of detailed arrangements whereby it was distributed and timed to synchronize all over the country. Gladys, as always, gave marveling chuckles. The groups of magic users were so various. The circles of serious, educated witches were only a small part of them, and to them the word could be handed down openly; but there were hereditary covens, who required secret negotiations; groups of amateurs who thought they were playing independently at magic, who needed to be nudged to do the right thing at the right time; spiritualists to be hinted at to meet and perform a specially adapted rite, which they did not see as a rite at all; individual magicians who did not know they were being organized; prayer groups, mediums, dowsers, meditators, and also numbers of people who imagined themselves to be charlatans and cheats, all of whom had to be induced to put forth power in a certain direction at the same time; and last but not least, there were the several mighty Orders of trained magicians, who needed very careful handling indeed. A few of these did acknowledge the authority of the Ring, but most regarded themselves as independent priesthoods and would have been utterly outraged to know that the ritual they had ordained for the next full Moon was not ordained by their own need and will.

"Bless their hearts," Gladys chuckled, when the last major Order made it known it had decreed a Grand Rite for that night. "They do know their job, those Outer Nine."

The real disappointment was that there had not been time to organize witchcraft in the rest of the world. Only where some of the great Orders were international was there any hope of cooperation. The witches of the continent had already planned a propitiation of their own. Australia and New Zealand were working on the rising sea. Asia gave vague answers which were not easily understood. The witches in America replied regretfully that they were having hell's own job holding down a major earthquake, but assured the Ring of their goodwill. Africa did not reply at all.

"Damn!" said Maureen. "I wish we dared explain what we're really trying to do."

"Most of them are using power that night anyway," Gladys said, "and that should help. Goodwill is a power on its own. Don't fuss, Maureen, and have you got down the exact minute we want each of those Names said? Well, don't look like that! I only asked."

"I'm *sorry*!" Maureen said irritably. "I've a lot on my mind, what with Flan leaving to go on the capsule. Joe's behaving strangely too. I'm under a lot of pressure. I—"

She was interrupted by Amanda telephoning to say that there was a hitch in the capsule's directional jets, and could someone get hold of that strange girl who had worked on the French space programme, quickly please!

Zillah felt the mounting excitement, although she knew nothing of the details. It's going to take off at full Moon, she thought, quite calmly, and then I shan't have this misery anymore. On the rare occasions when she let herself think of those two hairs she had planted in the capsule, it seemed to her that they were designed to carry her unhappiness out of this world with them. In fact, it was as if her misery were already there, installed in those two hairs. She cooked, cleaned Marcus and the house, washed clothes for Amanda and her children, shopped for socks for David, and talked cheerfully with everyone, all without the dark background of misery she had been used to for so long. A sort of death, she thought, by substitute. She felt rather empty.

The night before the launch, those who had built the capsule tested everything carefully and packed up their tools for the last time. Each in his or her way gave it a blessing. Some simply patted the stained metal skin. Some said things like, "You're awful, but I love you!" or "Hope you make it, bus!" Others were more serious. One prayed. Another poured champagne from a mini bottle. Then they departed, to journey to the various sites of power where they had to be tomorrow.

Amanda kept vigil there, just in case.

In the morning the finally selected team arrived, eighteen of them, very cheerful and healthy, with their bags, lunch packs, woolly hats, and knapsacks. None of them knew quite what to expect. The rumor most of them believed was that they were to storm a monastery in Greece. Most of them were very surprised to see who the others were.

"Well, fancy *you* as a shock trooper!" Roz Collasso said to Tam Fairbrother.

They were even more surprised when Amanda locked the warehouse door and told them why they were there, adding that none of them were to leave the building from then on. They saw the point of that. It would be fatal if the pirates were to learn of the plan *now*. Besides, they were all dedicated. Each of them had, at Gladys's special request, made their wills before they set out. But they still did not quite believe it, and they spent a lot of time laughing. Tam doing his gay walk made them fall about.

Sobriety set in during the early evening when someone suggested that the capsule ought to have a name. Somehow, discussing *what* name made the whole thing seem more real.

"It used to be a bus."

"What does that make it? The Magical Mystery Tour Coach? Hold very tight, please, for your tour of the multiverse!"

"Call it Omnibus."

"Try again!"

"Well, omnibus does mean *everything*."

"Sky-High Bus?"

"What about the Flying Coach?"

"*I* know!" said someone. "The Celestial Omnibus!"

That name pleased them all, so they christened it with coffee, unaware that it had already been done with champagne, and ran through yet again the routine for using the virus-magic when they got to Laputa-Blish.

A little before moonrise a motorcyclist roared up to the warehouse door and, when Amanda opened it, carefully handed her four packages, two blue and two red. Gladys had insisted on there being four. "The two halves have to stay apart until the last minute," she had said. "It's too potent to handle any other way. And just two packets is daft. I'm going to send a backup pair."

Amanda gave a telephone number to the motorcyclist, and he roared away, first to phone through a code word and then to join his own coven. The packages Amanda gave to Helen, Judy, Francine, and Laura, all of whom were stable, proficient adepts who were unlikely to panic. After that, she had to leave herself, locking the door behind her, to fling herself into her car and to drive in a manner not so unlike Zillah's to a secret site of great power about forty miles away.

Her going was the signal for the storm troopers to climb into the Celestial Omnibus and sit there, tense and ready. Judy and Lynn settled at the controls, and Roz stood by the door to seal it. Tam and Solly tested the oxygen supply yet again and found to their relief that it still worked. After which they only had to wait.

By this time, not only were innumerable apparently unconnected small groups gathering in rooms all over Britain, but dark-clothed persons were assembling in stone circles, woods, and other places of power from Land's End to John o' Groat's, whispering and occasionally flashing a flashlight to make sure that things were where they should be. Lights were not supposed to be shown at this stage.

The Moon rose as Amanda arrived at the secret site. It gave her enough light to see Mark in the pale majesty of his robes, preparing to begin. Paulie was with him. She had chosen glittering black robes. Well, she would, Amanda thought. Maureen was there, in white and green, looking very lovely. And there stood Gladys, bulging out of a disgraceful maroon Burbery, with Jimbo scratching himself in the grass at her feet. Nothing would ever persuade Gladys to dress up, but Amanda sometimes suspected her of dressing *down*. There, too, were the nine of the Outer Ring, who had arrived commendably promptly, considering they knew nothing of how tight the schedule really was.

"I do think we should tell them what it's all about," Amanda had objected when they were discussing the schedule.

"Afterwards," Gladys said with great firmness. "The traitor's in there with them. We don't want to give her or him a chance to ruin everything."

The four of the Ring drew together to begin. "Christ! I'm nervous!" Mark whispered. "Suppose the capsule just vanishes into the void!"

"Or blows up," said Maureen.

"Hush. It'll get there," said Gladys.

Amanda said nothing, but her private fear was that the Celestial Omnibus would still be there in the warehouse when she unlocked the door in a few hours time. But the ritual had started. Almost at the same instant, other groups joined in all over the country. Amanda felt the building of power as she carefully cleared her mind.

Zillah, at home in Amanda's house, felt the build of power as a great void, waiting to be filled. In some strange way, she *was* the void, and ached with it. Then, as the first Name was spoken, nearly in chorus, from the lands all around her, it brought her a sudden vision of Mark. He was not as she usually remembered him, but dressed in robes with the Moon shining pale on his hair. Idiotically, this hieratic image carried with it an acute sensory memory. Mark's body hair. Mark had a surprising amount of hair on his body for such a pale, slender man, and it was not fair, like his hair, but dark like his eyebrows, and all of it kitten-soft. Remembering the feel of it gave Zillah a scathing wrench. The misery was back, thundering in her head, worse than ever.

"Cut it *out!*" she said aloud, because it made her furious not to be able to forget. And her furious exclamation made her see what she had to do. She had to cut it out properly, make it a sort of death, the biggest and cleanest break possible. Only that would lance the boil. Call it what you like, only *stop* it.

She wrote as much on the back of an envelope for Amanda. Then she went upstairs and picked Marcus up out of his crib, he mumbling sleepily and slobbering a little against her neck. She stood with him in her arms, facing the direction she sensed the capsule to be in. The rituals were building now, and she could feel the power. It was as if she stood in a large, faintly glowing space, where, twining toward her, she could see two misty filaments of her own hair and of Marcus's. She waited. Power grew. It grew in Zillah, too, rising to surround and fill her, as it always seemed to do when she had real need. She had so much, in seconds, that she knew she could do whatever there was need for. She could choose not to do this. But she chose. She hooked the two filaments to her with a little finger, which was all she could spare from holding Marcus, and made them draw her in.

There was so much power there that it was easy. Quickly, coolly, without stress, like sliding around a half-open door, she found herself, still holding Marcus, standing in the aisle of the capsule, quite near the back. Behind her, the metal that held the machinery was now a complete silvery wall, with a sound like an electric fan coming from it. The space in front of her was full of people, many of whom she did not know. They all looked very tense. Marcus felt something had happened and sleepily uttered a small inquiring noise. Several heads turned. Zillah slipped into an empty seat quickly and apologetically, like someone arriving late in church, and drew the sense of her own insignificance tightly around herself and Marcus. She was nothing, nothing to bother about at all. It was something she had often found useful, this sense of not being worth anyone's trouble. It worked again here. The heads turned away. Nothing there after all.

Outside, the gale of power being raised was translating into a physical wind, beating around the warehouse, causing hair and robes to stream, all over the country. The Names had mostly been spoken. The time was coming when something should happen—if it was going to.

The Celestial Omnibus jerked.

"I think we're away!" whispered someone.

Nothing else.

It isn't going to work! Zillah thought. What a fool I shall look! Oh, go, go, go, *go*! She pushed, urgently and wildly in her mind, at the solid lump of the bus. Again some wild part inside her rose to her need. She felt it flare around her as she pushed. But this tin box full of people was so *heavy*! Oh, go, go, go, *go*! she told it.

Then came the heart of the ritual. Lights blazed in many hundred circles, and fire streamed in high places. Inside the capsule, there was a sudden definite sense of floating, almost of weightlessness.

"This is *it!*" someone said.

As the last great effort went out, Gladys, wearing her Aspect of the Old Woman, turned to Amanda in her Aspect of the Mother and gave a slight nod. The effort was double-phased. The first was intended to send the capsule off—and there was not a soul participating who did not feel that *something* had moved, been sent, gone— and the second phase was to raise the Great Wards around the British Isles and—if possible—around the world. Mark felt the Wards of Pridain rise. He, too, nodded at Amanda. Now nothing of evil intent could penetrate the country; but no one could tell if the world was warded. It had never needed to be done before.

3

It was an exhausting night. Maureen was tottering with weariness by the time she climbed the stairs to her London flat. Dawn had come already. Unnatural-seeming sunshine filled the street. A few hours sleep, Maureen thought, setting her keys into the locks with unsteady hands, and she *might* be all right for dance practice this evening. It ought to be all right. Her weariness was mostly the weariness of elation. That great gale of power that had lifted the capsule and the wards together kept blowing through her mind, exultingly. What a *feeling*! It was the feeling that she dwelt on, though it had been good, too, arriving at the warehouse to find the capsule gone. Maureen was rather pleased that she had had the forethought to visit the place when the capsule was still there. She at least knew that there had been something there to vanish. It was not so with the nine of the Outer Ring.

They had gone there in a procession of cars. The nine had been very annoyed. And hurt. And incredulous. Koppa's strident voice still rang in Maureen's ears. *Why* had they not been told? *What* traitor? They were welcome to take her to any sphere of truth they pleased, and they would see she was At One with the Ring. Etcetera. And to be shown an empty warehouse convinced nobody of anything. Maureen kept remembering Paulie standing beside Mark in a white fury. Luckily Amanda had had the sense to take some photographs of the capsule, but what with Amanda's total incompetence with a camera and the emanations of power in the warehouse, the prints she handed around were both blurred and crooked, and they mollified no one. Amanda had further irritated Maureen by the way her head went up and an expression of woe and worry kept crossing her face whenever she thought no one was looking. Amanda thought something had gone wrong. *Did she now?* Amanda *would* claim this special sensitivity— and most of the time when Maureen checked up on her worries, she found Amanda was just making a great fuss about nothing.

In the end Maureen left Mark and Amanda to deal with the Outer Ring and drove home. She absolutely had to sleep. Not even a cup of cocoa first. Just fall into bed.

She opened her door into a blue cloud of cigarette smoke. The curtains of her living room were drawn and the lights on. Faugh. And there was bloody Joe sitting on her sofa leering at her with a can of beer in his hand and a loaded ashtray between his feet. He's been drinking again, she thought. She hadn't the energy to cope.

"Out," she said, holding the door open with one hand and gesturing with the other. "Come on. You're going. I need to sleep. How did you get in here anyway?"

He shook his head. "No. I'm not going. Neither are you. We're staying here together."

"Don't give me—" Maureen was beginning, when the door moved heavily under her hand and shut itself with a dull boom. She whirled toward it. There were wards down on it, preventing her from touching it. Strong wards, *weird* ones, ones she did not know. She whirled back.

Joe continued to grin. There was something odd about his face. "You won't find you can break those wards. They're the wards of Arth. I've got them all around this flat. Nobody's going in or out, and nobody's going to hear any kind of call you make for help. So you might as well tell me all about this project of yours now. It'll save us both a lot of trouble."

I don't *believe* this! she thought. She was so tired. "What the hell are you talking about?" As she spoke she realized he was right about the wards round the flat. She could feel them hemming the place in, thick and heavy and strange to her.

Joe stood up. He was thickset, black-haired and with black stubble on his chin, but he was not as drunk as she had assumed. Perhaps not drunk at all. She wondered how she had ever fancied him. "This project of yours," he said. "I waited until you'd done whatever it was, because I knew you'd be easier to catch then. Now I want you to tell me exactly what you've been doing so that I can report to the High Head."

"You're raving," said Maureen.

"No way," he said. "And don't try any tricks with witchcraft. I learnt my mageworking on Arth, and I know things you've never even dreamt of."

"The same goes for me!" she snapped. "You've no idea of half the things I know!" And, as he took a heavy step toward her, she added, "And don't think you can over-power me physically, either. I'm a professional dancer, remember. I'm much stronger than I look."

Joe gave her a look of contempt that somehow deep-ened the strangeness she had seen in his face. "I know that. I came prepared to wait it out. Look. Take a look." The sharp smell of his sweat mingled with the smoke-fug as he moved sideways away from her, always making sure not to turn his back, she noticed, and kicked open the doors to the kitchen and the bathroom.

Maureen moved, equally warily, to the center of the room. She was so tired that she seemed to be functioning on animal instincts alone. Her main feeling was exasperation and outrage. The kitchen was piled with boxes of groceries. She could see fruit, vegetables, potato crisps. The bath was full of packs of lager. How typical of Joe!

"See?" he said. "We'll be quite comfortable while we wait for you to tell me. I got all this stuff mostly so that you'd see I'm in earnest. But it would be much easier if you'd tell me everything straightaway." Still keeping himself facing her, he retreated sideways and settled himself back in the corner of the sofa. "Well?"

There were reserves of strength in everyone, Maureen told herself. She ought still to have a charge of power from the ritual too. She drew on both, or tried to, and told herself she felt better for it. "Piss off," she said. "I don't know what you're talking about."

"Yes you do," he said. "You've just performed a very big ritual of some kind. I want to know what it was supposed to do. The *real* world needs to know. They sent me over here to find out what you were doing, and find out is what I'm going to do. I don't want to be stuck in your stinking world for any longer than I have to be."

He's a spy from the pirate universe, Maureen thought. She was beyond either surprise or alarm. The thought came to her simply as a sort of summing up of all the things she had seen since she first unlocked her front door. She thought of the capsule. It might be in Laputa-Blish by now, or it might not. No one knew how long a transition between universes should take, or even whether they had got the transition right. Even assuming the very best, that the capsule had got there almost instantly and the team had succeeded in entering that fortress, the virus-magic needed time in which to take effect. They had had six hours. They needed at least six more. I'll just have to wait it out, she thought. "Damned if I tell you anything," she said.

"Really?" Joe said. "You have to sleep sometime. I can work on your head then."

"So do you have to sleep," she said. But her spirit sank. She was so weary. There was a sort of hollow weakness under her breastbone that she suspected was despair. "It seems to be deadlock," she said, and seated herself grimly facing him at the other end of the sofa. He gazed at her jeeringly. And she realized what the odd thing was about his face. There were all sorts of foreign thoughts in it. She could see the alien consciousness behind his face pushing the features she had thought she knew well into a completely new shape. She tried to tell herself that this did not scare her—not at all. She was just so tired.

IV

Arth

1

Tod was not happy. It did not make him feel any better to know he had not expected to be happy in Arth.
He was only there because his father had insisted on it.

"It's your legal obligation, I'm afraid, son," the Pentarch
told him. "I wouldn't bother you with it if it wasn't. Hated
my stint in the place. Stupid rules and out-of-date notions.
They say it's even more of a back number these days. Lost
its point, to my mind, as soon as all the new technology
came in. But the law still says that the heir to a Pentarchy
has to have his year in Arth. If you don't, you don't qualify
as my heir, son, and the king could roll me up as well as
you. He might, too. I've had several polite inquiries from
the Royal Office about you. You'll have to go."

Tod liked and trusted his old father. He got on with
him, even though the old man behaved like a swine to
Tod's mother. So he did not make the fuss he might
have done. He gave up his lovely, happy, easygoing
life—his expensive car, his good-looking girls, his racing
and antiques collecting, his first-class food—he was an
adult, for the gods' sake, and could afford to have these
things!—and entered the austere regime of Arth without
doing more than grumble savagely to himself.

Now, nearly two months later, Tod kept wondering
how his father had been able to stand it, even as a young

man. Poor old August! he kept thinking. How had he
stood the soldierly bunk rooms, for a start? Not to speak
of the food. Drink—forget it! Anything but weak passet
beer was against the rules because it disturbed the vibes,
so they said. There was a rule against almost everything
enjoyable on these grounds. It irked Tod almost to fury
at times, even though he had been prepared for it.

What he had not been prepared for was to find his fellow servicemen were—with two exceptions—complete
louts. Stupid louts, too. That had surprised Tod, because
he had heard that only the best young men qualified for
Arth. But these were not only stupid, but the kind of
louts who resented Tod for his high birth and got at
him for it whenever they could. They did not seem to
grasp that Tod's birth was nobody's fault, or that Tod
could have melted them to little pools of body fat if he'd
wanted. So far Tod had refrained from doing anything
to them. But it was severe temptation—all the more so
because the servicemen were never out of one another's
company. The cadets and the qualified Brothers kept
themselves priggishly separate and would barely speak
to Tod and his like.

Well, that was no loss. Except that it probably made
the days in Arth even more boring—though nothing
could be more boring than the mageworks servicemen
were required to perform. Take this very moment. They
were all ranged along the wide window of the lowest
observation room, sighting the specula for patterns in
the ether. This was something Tod had been trained
from the cradle to do, like almost everything else in
the curriculum. Old August, having made sure that his
son indeed carried the birthright, had had him tutored
by experts from the moment he could walk. But nobody
took any notice of that. The reverse, in fact. Their Mage
Instructor, a po-faced fellow called Brother Wilfrid, told
Tod on the first day, "We're going to treat you just

like everyone else." When people said that, in Tod's experience, they meant *worse than everyone else*—and so it had proved. Brother Wilfrid, just like the louts, resented Tod's birth and smugly punished him for it. While the louts struggled with mageworks that ought, in more intelligent hands, to have been at least slightly interesting, Tod was stuck with base calculus and childish observations like the ones he was making at the moment. These were so easy that Tod could do the whole thing in his mind without the help of specula. He could even spot a growing disturbance in the ether, off to one side, troubling several bands of the Wheel, which nobody else seemed to have noticed. He was going to have to render himself odious to the louts by pointing it out soon. Brother Wilfrid would, of course, regard this as showing off.

Tod sighed, and bent over the instrument he did not need. Dreary, boring days of schoolboy exercises and mass rituals, and still ten months to go. The rituals were perhaps not as bad as Tod had expected. This latest High Head—little as Tod liked him—seemed to have done quite a bit of work bringing the ritual side of things up-to-date, even though he had done nothing at all to change the archaic rules of the Brotherhood. Take the celibacy rule, now. That was idiotic, because no one had any chance to break it. Tod had expected to find that particular rule the hardest of all, but in fact, without any girls passing daily before him, he found he missed them far less than he had supposed he would. It was not as if he had left behind someone he was passionately in love with—that *would* have hurt. No, the irksome part of that rule was the inevitable advances one got from mages and brethren alike. Ridiculously, Tod had not been prepared for that; but he had, from very early on, learned to carry in his aura the message *I am heterosexual* at all times, day and night. It was a pity Philo, the gualdian boy, could not seem to learn to do that too—or maybe Philo's incredible politeness stopped him—anyway, Tod suspected that Philo was building up a horribly large list of senior folk out to get him, either because Philo had politely told them no, or because they were scared rigid that Philo was going to report the passes they had made to higher authority.

All right, Tod thought. So I'm not the only one having a hard time. I still don't have to like it.

He had been rather thrown together with Philo and Josh, the centaur lad. They were the three different ones, and they were all finding it tough here. Poor Josh— he went around perpetually bewildered. Up to now, Tod had not realized how much centaur magework and teaching differed from human. The Arth system was human-based, and Josh could not grasp it at all. Everyone thought he was stupid. The louts made fun of him all the time. They were laughing at Josh at the other end of the room at the moment. It sounded as if there was another practical joke starting.

Ah gods! Tod thought savagely. This was all I needed! He had many times tried to conjecture why in hellspoke's name the law required him to come to this armpit of the universe. It was a very archaic law. The only modern justification he had been able to come up with was that all this adversity was supposed to toughen his soul. To Tod's mind you did not make a soul tough by walking all over it: you just made dents.

And all the time he had this nagging anxiety. The time rate was so much slower in Arth that nearly three years would pass before he could get home, years in which his father would get even older. August Gordano was not young: he had been nearly sixty when Tod was born. Tod was terrified he would get home to find his father dead. Then . . .

Yells and laughter erupted at the other end of the room. Tod looked. There was poor Josh inside a ring of louts, the ringleader as usual being Rax with the broken nose. Josh was standing helplessly up to the withers in a pile of horse manure—or it looked like horse manure, but it was evidently as hard as concrete. Josh was trying to buck his way out, but much to the mirth of his tormentors, the stuff was holding him fast. As Tod looked, someone took the joke further, picked up a ball of the stuff and flung it at Josh. Josh was quite unprepared. He screamed and put both arms over his face. The next second he was being pelted, bowed over, with blood streaming down his face. It looked as if one of his eyes was smashed. Tod left his instrument and ran. Philo, who was nearer, ran ahead of him. Tod shouted to him not to, but he saw Philo plunge up the pile of concrete dung and try to spread himself out in front of Josh. Tod heard the thud of concrete hitting his body.

"Right! That bloody does it!" Tod said. Still running, he called up his birthright. It was intensely strong, here in Arth, as they had warned him it would be. He took hold of the big, dynamic rhythms of the citadel and used them to thrust Philo away to the far wall. Then he hurled that concrete dung in all directions in a near-explosion, scoring a hit on a lout with almost every ball. Josh burst loose from the pile and staggered about with his hands to his face, only half-conscious. Tod took further energies, formed them into spears of healing, and beamed them at Josh in strong thrusts. But at this point the other servicemen turned on Tod in a pack, and he had to leave off to defend himself.

He didn't dare kill them. He fought them instead. He felt like a fight anyway. He made sure each one he hit got a fair voltage of electricity with the blow. For a joyous few seconds he was inside a pandemonium of fighting bodies, blows, screams, and swearing, with stinking cobbles rolling about underfoot and electricity crackling and arcing all over the place. Then, as was to be expected, Duty Mages and Senior Brothers stormed into the room from all directions. A fair amount of stasis was cast. Tod could have broken it, had he tried, but someone had hit him in the stomach the instant before, and he did not feel like trying anything just then.

When he felt more himself, he was—as he supposed he should have expected—being blamed for everything. Rax had run the street gangs of Praslau before coming to Arth. He was an expert in shifting blame. Besides, after the healing Tod had thrown at Josh, nobody thought there was too much wrong with his eye, and Philo, though dazed, was only bruised. They were marched off to Healing Horn. Tod, licking a swelling lip, had to stand and endure a po-faced lecture from Brother Wilfrid. He stood. He endured, wondering anxiously throughout whether he had been in time to save the sight in Josh's eye, and controlled his temper while Brother Wilfrid lectured on about the damage done to the vibrations of Arth. Tod might have got away merely with that lecture had not Brother Wilfrid then said, "And thanks to your folly and aggression, Galpetto could well lose an eye."

"I *saved* his eye, you fool!" Tod roared at him. "Don't give me that po-faced rot!"

Brother Wilfrid's breath went in. His eyes and his mouth became vicious lines. "You don't speak to people like that here. No one here is your servant."

"No, thank the Goddess," said Tod. "If you were my servant, I'd sack you for sanctimonious stupidity. Plus incompetence."

That did it. Tod was marched off in disgrace before the High Head himself. And naturally the system was that Brother Wilfrid nipped in through the veil and had his say before Tod got near the High Head.

"Well, what have you got to say?" the High Head asked. He was in worn blue fatigues at that moment, and his office was spread all over with tide charts, but Tod found him unexpectedly impressive even so.

"As what I've got to say is probably the opposite of everything Brother Wilfrid told you," Tod said angrily, "I think I'll pass on that."

The High Head surveyed Tod's incipient black eye and swollen lip, his disordered hair and aggressive anger, and tried to conquer his prejudice against Tod and be equitable. "Servicemen are always brawling," he said. "I'm prepared to believe your cause was just. But you're not here for fighting, or the damage to the centaur's eye." Tod ground his teeth audibly at this. "You are here for causing acute disturbance in every band and spoke of the Wheel. Can't you feel what you've done? If not, look." The High Head gestured to his large mirror, which was boiling and tumbling with the mixed rainbows of a large cosmic disorder. "You did that, Gordano, by raising wild magic."

The injustice of this was almost too much for Tod. "With respect, sir, I did not do any such thing. First, I did not use wild magic, because I have been very well trained from as far back as I can remember. What I did was to draw on my birthright in the ways I have been taught. Second, sir, that cosmic storm was brewing at least an hour ago. I saw it on the speculum quite clearly."

"Then why did you not report it?" asked the High Head.

"Because I assumed Observer Horn is full of highly trained Brothers who would report it long before I did," said Tod.

"There is no need to be insolent," said the High Head.

"Yes there is," said Tod. "If I speak normally in this damned joyless place, some po-faced prat ups and tells me I'm being insolent. So if I'm insolent, it ought to work the other way round. Sir."

They stared at each other with considerable dislike, while the High Head wondered which of twenty scathing things to say. And which of thirty condign punishments to order. None of them seemed nasty enough for this nasty piece of work, who could nearly put a serviceman's eye out and then show no contrition whatsoever, who refused to acknowledge he had caused a cosmic storm, who—

The upper off-center mirror spoke, blazing the sigil of Observer Horn. "Sir, there appears to be a supply capsule out of control outside the atmosphere."

The Observer sigil was almost instantly joined by sigils in every other mirror. That of Housekeeping blazed, Defense, Maintenance, Observer again, Healing, Calculus . . . Each sigil brought a new voice, speaking in crisp sequence.

"Housekeeping here, sir. There's a capsule outside the air that's definitely not one of ours."

"Defense Horn, requesting permission to explode a strange capsule, sir. We divine some kind of foreign life aboard it which could be dangerous."

"This is Maintenance, sir. There's a capsule plunging straight at our atmosphere. If it gets any closer, it could breach us, sir."

"Sir, we are now in contact with a mind in distress inside the supposed supply capsule. Person seems human and says the controls don't answer."

"Healing, Healing. Be wary. There are dead humans aboard a capsule outside. Be wary. It could be plague."

"Calculus Horn reports, sir, with some shame, that the cause of the current cosmic storm appears to be a rogue capsule that entered Arth from elsewhere in the multiverse some twenty seconds ago."

"Ritual Horn, sir. Be wary. Alien magework is affecting our efforts to damp the storm."

Tod gazed from sigil to sigil, almost admiringly. What a display of order and efficiency. No sigil occupied a glass already in use by another. The voices spoke precisely in turn. It was all so cool that he had to force himself to realize that this must be an emergency, that there must be people in bad trouble outside the citadel.

The High Head snapped an order to Defense Horn to hold off their attack for a while and drew in the air the symbol for the emergency rescue of a transport. As artificial elementals sped howling down the corridors, screaming their orders to the heads and other ranks of the Horns involved, he swung around to Tod again. What those people out there thought they were doing in this capsule, he had no idea, but Edward's message had not been lost on him. Corpses. Possibly plague. Good. "Gordano, you go to the upper rescue port and tell them to put you into a safety suit. I want you to be first man to board that capsule. Your punishment is to deal with whatever you find inside it."

2

They had not expected the weightlessness. It happened after the second heavy jolt. Zillah found herself rising above her seat and grabbed for Marcus as he floated away from her, still asleep. The space ahead of her was full of floating bodies, lying in the air at all angles, some threshing about, some clinging to seats. Something was on fire down there, in four different places. People were making frantic efforts to beat flames out with hands that suddenly worked to different rules, and rebounding to the ceiling—which was now a side wall to Zillah—with the force of their efforts.

"I told them—I *told* her so!" Roz Collasso was crying out. "The place *does* have defenses! They've gone and burnt our virus-magic! *Now* what do we do?"

Along the sideways ceiling Zillah had an upside-down glimpse of Judy's arm, ridged with straining tendons, shaking and shaking at the woman beside her. It was Judy's voice doing all the screaming. "Something's wrong with Lynne! Somebody *help* me! None of these controls *work*!"

A small, energetic person swooped down to Judy. Flan Burke, Zillah thought. Judy's screams redoubled. "Flan, Flan, Lynne's *dead*! I don't know what to *do*! Somebody hel—!" There was the sound of a smacking blow. Flan's

110

body came arcing up again with the force of it.

"Shut up, Judy!"

The fires must have gone out. The metal space was murky with smoke, and a lot of people were coughing, including Judy, who was coughing and sobbing together, but there were no flames anymore. Everyone was sinking slowly toward what had been the right-hand wall. Some small pull of gravity seemed to be coming from there.

"We're falling," said the big black girl, among coughing and retchings.

"Falling *where*?" demanded Roz.

Judy's voice was now low and grinding. "How the hell should *I* know? You can hit me all you like, Flan, but it won't do any good. This screen's no use at all. *Look*, if you don't believe me!"

Among the crowding bodies, Zillah had a slowly rotating view of a screen over the two empty drivers' seats, alight with meaningless colored whorls. Whatever they were receiving, it was not in the usual manner of VDUs, but in wide-spaced, wavy bands which changed width perpetually.

"And our viruses are gone," Judy said dully. "And we don't know where we are."

"What do we do, supposing we *are* in Laputa-Blish?" asked a girl with a stiff, gangly body.

"Do what we came to do without the virus, of course, you stupid bitch," Flan Burke said as she rotated, knees to chin, through Zillah's view. She looked both fierce and comfortable. "Do you think we came for a holiday?"

"Flan's right," Roz proclaimed. "We mount an attack regardless."

The walls, seats, and ceiling had been rotating spirally about them as they talked, spinning everyone into a kind of plait along the length of the Celestial Omnibus. Now the motion changed again. Zillah found herself falling, gently and inevitably, together with half the floating company, toward the rear of the capsule.

"What's going on *now*?" someone squawked from the other end of the aisle. That aisle now stood up from Zillah like a tube, and people hung there at the other end with outspread arms, inexplicably.

"Rotation, that's all. We must be flipping over and over. Gives us gravity at both ends."

Whoever said that must be right, Zillah thought, as her feet landed on the silvery wall that concealed the life support. She could hear it hissing beyond the metal. She hoped it was meant to hiss. It sounded nastily like a gas leak. She had a vivid vision of the capsule turning over and over in space, perhaps endlessly. She had been *mad* to bring Marcus. He was stirring and mumbling against her shoulder, disturbed by the hissing and the changes of gravity—perhaps also by Zillah's own rising panic. In a moment she was going to be screaming like Judy, and that *would* wake Marcus.

She soothed him and she rocked him, trying to throw her panic into the distance, out, away, into whatever appalling emptiness surrounded the capsule. Marcus calmed. He slept steadily again. Zillah tried to convince herself that she was calm, too, by turning to the young man who had landed curled up on the backrest of the seat sticking out of the wall beside her. He was nice-looking. She did not know him well, but she thought his name was Tam—Tam Fairbrother, or something like that.

"Excuse me," she said. "I know it seems silly, but I only got here at the last minute. What *is* the attack Roz and Flan were talking about? Can you put me abreast of the plans?"

Tam did not answer. This puzzled Zillah at first. It took her a long, difficult minute to realize that Tam was dead. So was everyone else at this end of the capsule.

3

Tod was given an all-over gossamer-thin suit with smickering suction-soles. The soles were the only things that impeded him as he walked into the big, tranparent bubble of the rescue port. The rest of the suit was Arth's secret, some kind of time-tested magework that allowed a man to breathe and move normally while protecting him from vacuum, germs, and even fire. Exploring it as he walked, Tod thought it was simply a hundredfold thickness of any mage's usual protective circle—in which case, it must have taken years to make. However it was done, it was a wondrous efficient thing. The High Head may have intended this as a punishment, but Tod felt like a schoolboy on a treat. He stared out and around into the cerulean blueness beyond the port's bubble and finally detected the silvery flash-flash of the rogue capsule turning over and over as it fell toward the citadel from about the ten o'clock position.

"This is something like!" he murmured. Up till then he had hardly believed there really was a capsule.

It was coming fast, too, enlarging rapidly as he watched it. Behind him, safe inside the walls, a monitoring mage murmured reports of what he was able to gather from the shocked minds inside the thing. Another, from Calculus, spoke crisp figures about speed, position, and deflections due to the storm the thing itself was arousing. Some other higher Brother was relaying orders to ranked mages from Ritual Horn, who were supposed to apply the brakes to the hurtling object. Tod could also hear various kinds of rescue teams gathering in the bubble at his back, but they kept away from him because, of course, he was in disgrace.

"Now!" said the higher Brother. Tod felt the force go out.

They had done it, too! The rotating silver shape swept to one side and whirled out of sight beyond the blue wall of the citadel. But they had cut it fine to Tod's mind. The thing had surely all but impinged on the nearly unseeable veil that held Arth's atmosphere. Still, why grumble? They had deflected it. Now presumably they had to slow it down enough to maneuver it into the funnel of veiling that led to the rescue port.

4

It was close and fuggy inside the Celestial Omnibus. *That hissing,* Zillah thought. *We're all going to die.*

A voice spoke, from somewhere in the central part where no one could go. "Be calm," it said. "Please attend."

It was a deep male voice that struck ringing echoes from the walls in a way none of their own voices did. Marcus stirred at the sound of it and came awake quite peacefully. Even Judy stopped whimpering.

"I speak for the Brotherhood of Arth," the voice continued. "Have no fear. The Goddess has permitted you to enter Arth. Our skills will bring you safely to the citadel. Be calm and you will see."

The accent struck Zillah as Scottish at first, but it also had a burr to it that suggested Cornwall. Whatever, the deep, measured speech was decidedly soothing. *Thank you! Bless you!* she thought.

And thinking that, she found she could see the citadel the voice spoke of, in a sort of round white viewport that floated just in front of—or maybe just behind—her eyes. Marcus had no doubt that the sight was in front of him. He stretched out a starfish hand and made his pigeon noise. The place—building?—lay below like a toy, an improbable blue castle sprouting hornlike turrets in all

115

directions from a flat base. Turrets and central block had windows of all sizes, but there seemed to be no doors. Some of the turrets supported open gold devices like crowns, multiple ladders, and many-petaled flowers.

A babble of exclamations greeted it from down the front end of the Celestial Omnibus, and Judy's voice demanding, "What is it? What are you all *looking* at?"

He means just what he says—the voice—Zillah thought. If you don't panic, you can see. Poor Judy.

She watched the castle enlarge with incredible swiftness. We are going *fast*. Will they ever stop us?

The thought had hardly entered her mind before something caught the Celestial Omnibus and steered it sharply away sideways. Gravity altered too, not so sharply, but inexorably. Zillah found herself able to stagger forward up the aisle and guide herself and Marcus into a seat not quite halfway along. Behind her, bodies of people she did not want to look at subsided to drape over seat-backs or flop into the gangway. Up front, Flan and Roz were forcing Judy into a seat.

None of this interfered with the vision of the castle. They were sweeping over it, above it, and down the other side.

"They've put us in a braking orbit, I think," the gawky girl said very coolly from up front.

Must be that, Zillah thought, watching their dive to the flat base of the building and around underneath it. But here something decidedly odd happened. Instead of finding the Celestial Omnibus speeding along above the flat base, which surely ought to have appeared as a large disc, there was the merest blink of darkness, after which they were soaring up past the great blue walls of the fortress on the other side. It was as if the castle had no bottom at all—or one only a few feet across. There were exclamations from everyone about this, and then further exclamations as they all realized they were now much nearer the fortress and traveling at less than half the speed. As they swept over and above the multiple turrets this time, they were near enough to see several gardens, some in deep wells between turrets, and others niched high in among complex hornworks. A great open space appeared, beside the central block, and a tiny group of people hastening across it, who looked up and pointed. Then they were going down again, past blue walls and a hundred windows of many shapes.

This time, when they came up the other side after the blink of blackness, the Celestial Omnibus was virtually crawling. Now they were being maneuvered. The force that had sent them into that swift orbit had them again. This time it pulled. The Celestial Omnibus turned nose forward toward the vast building and jogged docilely inward.

Vast, Zillah thought, was too mild a word. The thing on a tower she had thought was like a golden flower must have been nearly a quarter of a mile across. It now— slightly—resembled a radio telescope dish. The multiple ladders on a more distant tower proved to be a structure several times the size of the Eiffel Tower. The walls of the outjutting horn-shaped tower they were approaching were built of square blocks of bluish stone that were each nearly the size of a house. Some of the windows were enormous. A slight shiver blurred her view as she wondered if the burring voice had belonged to a giant. Now they were approaching a medium-enormous bubblelike window.

"They have to be friendly after this," Roz said. "Don't they?"

"As long as they don't find out where we come from," Flan answered. "Let's hope they believe our story."

5

N ice work, Brothers! Tod thought, as the battered metal thing glided to a joggling halt between calipers that were the wrong shape and size to hold it. Whoever had made the object, on the other hand, had not done nice work at all. He could see welded plates starting apart all over it. More ominously, atmosphere was steaming in white clouds both from the rear and from the hatch, or door, in one side. The thing looked as if it had never been meant to withstand the forces between the worlds.

Tod sensed barriers go up behind him. The Brothers were protecting themselves and the rest of the rescue team from whatever was steaming out of the capsule. After that, veiling fell over capsule and calipers together, isolating Tod in with it.

"Can you manage to open that door, serviceman?" a telepathic voice inquired coldly.

No, Duty Mage, I am but a poor fool from the Pentarchy and only a seventh child at that. "I'll have a try, sir," Tod replied. Up with the old birthright then.

It took only the slightest shift of the Wheel to spring that leaking hatch cover right out and send it spiraling down the citadel wall below. As it clanged loose, Tod found himself gagging in the air that gusted forth. Someone had thrown up in there. Someone else was definitely

dead. The rest had sweated like pigs. The veiling over
his face cut none of that out at all. Why can't they design
it like a Frinjen wet suit? he wondered as he climbed
inside. "Here comes the help! Anyone home?"

He met a chorus of thanks and relief. Two women
thrust a third at him, who was blubbering and weep-
ing. "Can you help Judy out? She's gone to pieces."
Tod helped her to the platform with a will. Hysterical
and red-eyed as she was, the girl was a good-looking
blonde. Tod had not had his hands on a blonde for two
months now. He discovered he missed the feeling after
all. And missed brunettes too, he thought, as Roz and
Flan jumped to the platform after Judy. The tall one in
boots looked a bit masterful and strident, but the little
'un struck him as a sweetie. What fun! And what an
embarrassment for the Brothers!

Tod was grinning, despite the stench, as he jumped up
inside again and helped another woman down—this one
a thin, staid creature who said gruffly, when he asked
her, that the name was Helen.

"And I'm Roderick. Call me Tod," he said. He turned
to help the next, who was shaking all over, and found
her, to his perplexity, to be an Azandi. "Hey! What are
you doing here, my lady?" he asked.

"Wish the hell I knew, man," she answered, in an
accent that was most definitely not Azandi. "If I'd known
this was going to happen, I'd have stayed safe in London.
I'm Sandra. And the rest are dead. The crossing killed
them. Believe me."

She was right there. Just beyond the hatchway, the
corpse of a good-looking boy lay half-across that of
a comely young woman. Tod stepped over them and
took a look along the capsule to make sure. And found
Sandra had made a mistake. The best-looking one of all—
an absolute wow-wow!—was coming slowly down the
metal gangway carrying an infant.

"Not dead after all then?" Tod said to her. The infant responded with a broad, companionable smile.

"Ike boo how," it remarked.

Zillah saw with interest that this cheerful young man, whose face gave her a feeling it was encased in an invisible nylon stocking, only hesitated an instant before correctly translating Marcus. "Like the blue house, do you, laddie? Well, that makes one of us. Your son, is he?" he asked Zillah.

She nodded. "Marcus. I'm Zillah. We were up the other end."

There was more to it than that, Tod suspected. Why, he hadn't even *seen* her until she was most of the way down the gangway. Nor, it seemed, had the other women. When Zillah climbed out through the doorway, she was greeted with astonishment.

"Good Lord! It's Zillah—and Marcus!"

"Zillah, what the *hell* are you doing here? Why are the others dead?"

"Who is she?"

"Zillah Green, Helen—she's Amanda's sister."

Zillah mumbled some reply, sounding so embarrassed that Tod turned away to the nearest corpse and began hauling it along the floor. But a man does not have six elder sisters for nothing. He did not make nearly as much noise dragging the dead young man as the castaways thought. He clearly caught the rapid whispering between the two brunettes and Zillah.

"Look, Zillah, how much do you know?"

"Well, the outline—What killed them? I don't know—"

"Not the cover story and all that?"

"Obviously she doesn't. Suppose they question us?"

"They're bound to. Zillah, keep quiet and play dumb, there's a love!"

"We'll talk a lot. You just follow our lead."

Ay, ay! Tod thought, backing from the door with the

dead young man's ankles in his hands. What are you up to, sisters? If you're up to no good in Arth, then that's fine by me. I won't say a word to stop you!

It amused him the way they all sprang to help him, to allay his suspicions just in case he *had* heard anything. Flan and Roz jumped to the corpse's arms, while Helen and Sandra raced inside to collect the girl. Zillah put Marcus down beside Judy. "Marcus, look after Judy. Mum's got to go and help. Judy, have a go at holding Marcus—he's awfully comforting to hold." As she climbed into the capsule, she asked Tod, "Are you all on your own? Isn't there anyone else in this castle to help you?"

Tod shot a look at the dark, filmy screen between them and the Brothers. They were all watching in there, and it looked as if they were now doing some kind of decontamination work. They were not going to risk plague. The platform was alight with small flashes, each representing the death of a microbe. "Oh, I'm in disgrace," he said cheerfully, struggling rather to drag the dead young man to one side, out of Judy's line of sight. He did not look plague-ridden to Tod's eye, but why crossing to Arth should have killed such a healthy specimen was beyond Tod to say.

Here the Brotherhood condescended to lower the weight of things out on the platform. The heavy bodies suddenly became quite easy to handle. Tod found he could manage the next on his own, and Judy, sitting cross-legged with Marcus in her arms, was hanging on to the child as if she thought he might float away. In fact, had it not been for the sad gruesomeness of the work—which Tod saw was upsetting all the women—he would have enjoyed himself. Here were six new people to talk to, and females at that—with all the while the chuckle welling up inside him at how *wonderfully* awkward this was for Arth.

But of course, it was over quite soon. Five minutes hard work later, Tod's suit became a fizzing scintilla of dying germs. Oh, so they *did* get around to me! he thought angrily. Simultaneously the dark screen cleared and busy, blue-clad Brothers rushed forth to deal with the capsule. Others swiftly shrouded the sad row of corpses, speculating in murmurs as to whether the cosmic storm or oxygen-loss could have killed them. Tod and the living ones were ushered through ranks of staring mages and goggling cadets, to where the High Head was standing, cloaked and mitred and stately.

The look on the High Head's face, Tod thought he would never forget. It was almost horror, as the High Head realized all the survivors were women.

V

Arth

1

Tod was told to take the party straight to Healing Horn. *Our High Head wishes for time to think,* he told himself in considerable amusement as he led the women there.

He was quite right. The High Head was forced to retreat to his workroom and think furiously. What *do* you do with six women (and one infant) of uncertain origin and social status, when you are an all-male community under Oath of Celibacy? The worst of it was that the problem, however he solved it, would be with him for the best part of a year. The tides that permitted travel between Arth and the Pentarchy were two months past. The next were eight months off. Otherwise the High Head would cheerfully have decanted his unwanted guests to the Orthe and let the king deal with them.

There was always otherworld, of course. The ritual for sending people there was at everyone's fingertips. But these people had already burst from another universe into this one, and a lot of them had died inexplicably on the way. A second transition would probably kill the survivors. Pushing them off to otherworld was the equivalent of allowing Defense Horn to explode the capsule when it first appeared—as well as a waste of a perfectly executed rescue operation. And the Goddess had permitted these women to come here.

This was a strong consideration. The High Head, although he presided daily at the most reverent worship of the Goddess, took a wholly pragmatic view of Her—some might even say cynical. She was the Power in the Wheel upon which Arth drew: therefore, you did not run counter to this Power. And the rogue capsule had passed through several hundred subtle and strong defenses set up in the name of the Goddess, designed to keep hostile intruders out. It followed that the intruders who survived were under the protection of the Goddess and harmless to Arth. It was in Arth's best interests to treat them politely.

On the whole, the High Head favored pitching the women back to wherever they had come from as soon as possible. There were, however, two difficulties about this. First, as in the case of otherworld, was the Law of Altered Reality. This stated that the changes brought about in a person in order to permit him to pass from one universe to another were—particularly in the case of worlds of high reality like Arth and its parent the Pentarchy—so great as to allow a person only one such transition. In other words, these women might be stuck here. Going back might kill them in the same way that sending them to otherworld might. But, since the hasty scan the High Head had made while the women were in front of him suggested they were as human as he was, he had hopes that he might find a way around the Law. It was just possible they came from a universe of equivalent reality to Arth. This was his main reason for shunting them straight off to Healing Horn. Edward was presumably checking on the women's humanity at this moment. If it tallied enough with Arth's standard, they could be returned whence they came.

This brought him to the second difficulty. Where exactly *were* they from? The High Head was not sure he followed or quite trusted the explanation given by the one who called herself Roz Collasso—standing very straight and speaking with brave schoolgirl openness—that they were a sport team from somewhere called Middle-Earth who had been on their way to compete in the Highland Games by strato-cruiser. They had, claimed this Collasso, hit sunspot turbulence and found themselves in Arth in free-fall. The High Head doubted this. Even allowing for the fact that the woman was in shock, his study of suns had never come up with a similar accident, and her manner had too much in common with that of one of his cadets trying to conceal the truth from a Duty Mage. He intended to question them separately until he got at the truth.

But what was he to do with them meanwhile, until he found out?

The measure of the difficulty was Brother Dewi, Horn Head of Housekeeping, and his assistant Brother Milo, standing in his outer office waiting for a decision. It was unprecedented. Housekeeping prided itself on knowing the precise social status of every visitor to Arth and providing accommodation for that visitor's exact rank and degree without ever consulting anyone. But Brother Dewi had no idea what these women were. Nor had the High Head. All he could tell Brother Dewi after his brief survey was that, although one woman had the black skin of a highborn Azandi, neither she nor any of the others merited being housed in the Rooms of State where the Ladies of Leathe had spent the night.

He had no wish anyway to treat these women as important. Even though the Goddess had allowed them to reach Arth, strong twinges of foreknowledge suggested to him that they meant trouble, and his impulse was to lock them up, away from everyone else in the citadel. But Arth had only three solitary-confinement cells. It would mean draining a fish-cellar for them. Besides, this was the sort of solution one would expect of otherworld—all Arth knew that otherworld locked refugees up as a matter of course. Arth could not do that. Arth was civilized.

Edward's sigil appeared in his glass at last. Thank the Goddess!

"Just my first impressions, you know," Edward said in his most apologetic way, "but I'd say these—er—people are every bit as human as we are. The black one has nearly all the Azandi traits, and some of the others test out as quite markedly gualdian—specially that very pretty one and her little boy."

"Fine," said the High Head. "Then we can send them back where they belong before long."

"What do you want me to do with them when I'm through?" Edward wanted to know.

Gualdian traits did not mean gualdian status. The decision was not all that difficult after all. "Put them in the servants' hall attached to the Rooms of State. They can sleep and eat there. It's convenient for Kitchen."

Feeling considerable relief, he gave the same order to Brother Dewi.

2

"I saw a centaur," said Flan. "I know I did. Just after that Tod boy took his skin off."

"Don't be silly." Roz glanced at Judy. Judy was sitting quietly in one of the few hard, upright chairs, which were all the furniture the room had, and she seemed calm enough. That doctor fellow, even though he seemed to be scared stiff of all six of them, had worked wonders there. Now it looked as if Flan was going bonkers too, and that could set Judy off again. "You can't have seen any such thing."

"Centaurs are a physical impossibility. I read it somewhere," Sandra said. "Hey! Is that why they're all so respectful of *me*? Do they think I'm a physical impossibility too?"

"Perhaps black women are, in this universe," Roz agreed repressively. "But centaurs can't exist anywhere."

"I tell you I *saw* one," said Flan.

"You saw someone riding a horse, maybe," Helen suggested pacifically. "They must ride horses all over the fortress. Why else do they have ramps instead of stairs?"

"For centaurs, of course!" Flan said angrily. "Why would anyone ride a horse in the *sanatorium*, idiot?"

Zillah, who was sitting against the wall trying hopelessly to amuse Marcus in this bare blue hall, said, "Flan *did* see a centaur. I saw him too."

No one gave her much heed. She was an outsider among them. Roz looked at Judy and at Flan, then expressively at the other two, and changed the subject. "Odd, wasn't it, how that doctor fellow never really came near us? But he saw my bad tooth and spotted Sandra's allergies."

And cured Judy, Zillah thought, by tentatively touching her head. And there *had* been a centaur, but it had only appeared near the beginning when the doctor's assistants were all down the other end of the room somehow causing warm water to gush out of the ceiling. The chief doctor—Edward, he'd said his name was— had been trying to shepherd them all down that way to have a shower behind chastely thick veiling. Zillah followed the others. But Marcus had rushed the other way, shouting, "Eeh awe!" and she turned and chased him. That was how she had seen the centaur tiptoeing— as far as knock-kneed horse legs *could* tiptoe—around the corner from another part of the health center. He looked pale, and he had a dressing over one eye. Tod had seemed delighted to see him. Tod had been in the act of removing his all-over invisible covering—Zillah had been glad; by then she had been wondering if the sort of squashed look to his face was some kind of deformity— and he had flung it aside in order to seize the centaur by both hands.

"Josh! Did they save that eye?"

"Oh yes—it's really only a cut," the centaur replied, in a wholly human, though rather resonant, whisper. "Tod, I heard you got all the blame. What's going on?"

Here, however, Edward had approached, causing the centaur to back hastily out of sight and Tod to look nonchalant. Edward, it seemed, wished Marcus to have a shower on his own and not with Zillah and the others. As soon as Marcus grasped this, he clung to Zillah's leg and

protested lustily. Zillah pleaded. Edward replied that
Marcus was male, and therefore it would be unseemly
for him to stand in a shower with six naked females, and
he tried to drag Marcus off her.

"Oh, look *here!*" Zillah shouted, flaring up. "He's only
two!"

She saw Tod shoot a sharp look at her and step forward.
"Excuse me, Horn Brother," he said with crisp politeness,
"but the little fellow's still only really a baby—far too
young to be separated from his mother—and in a strange
place and all."

It had seemed reasonable, and yet Zillah had been
sure something very strange was going on. While Tod
spoke, she felt as if the whole angry tangle of her feelings
were being deftly sorted into a strong and orderly chain,
stretching down from somewhere far, far overhead, and
that this chain was then being firmly bound around
Edward. Edward's look of bewildered hauteur bore out
this feeling, particularly when it turned to alarm, possibly even fear. At any rate, his small, pale features red-
dened slightly, and his eyes were as wide and hurt as
Marcus's. "All right then," he said. "If that's the way it is,
I've no option. The child shall stay with his mother."

I like Tod, Zillah thought gratefully. Tod's strange help
stopped her feeling quite as lost as she might have done.
She had made her complete break. She and Marcus truly
were in quite another universe, she had no doubt of that.
But, in her usual unforeseeing way, she had not bargained for being alive and having to live in this universe.
Maybe she was in shock. It had been plain terrifying in
that capsule. She felt she ought to have been dead from
whatever it was killed all the others at her end of the
capsule. Now she had a dreamy, raw, invalid feeling,
like you do when you have passed the crisis in a bad
illness but are still far from well. Frankly, she had no
idea what to do next.

This citadel was causing some of her disorientation. It was queer the way it was all blue, inside as well as out. The floors throughout were of ribbed rubbery stuff which was not rubber—it had a smell more like stone. The walls were those huge blue blocks. They had been led through passages and under veiled archways of queer proportions but many different shapes. Veiling seemed to be used for doors everywhere. And it was all blue, blue, blue, and brightly lit, including the mad Escher-like ramps. On a ramp, bringing up the rear with Marcus, Zillah had looked up at the top of Tod's head, or at Roz standing out at right angles into space at the front of their group. After that it had been ramp after ramp, with everyone at crazy angles, all blue, but without ornament, chaste and bare. Not a trace of decoration anywhere. It was, to look at, a serious, clinical place. The cells they were to sleep in were monastic. Yet—this was what was muddling Zillah—for no reason she could see, the fortress was not cold or joyless. If the place were a person, Zillah would have said it was itching to spring up and do a mad dance, because it was full of health and delighting in that health, but it seemed to have been too well trained or severely brought up to do anything so frivolous. Perhaps *repressed* was the best word for it.

There I go, fantasizing again. Trust me!

Her companions seemed to be fantasizing too. "All these men!" Flan was saying, stretched on her back on the ribbed floor, grinning like a hyena. "Some of them real good-lookers too! Did you see that little dark medical one? Yum-yum-oh-yum!"

"There were two in those short-horn things," Sandra concurred. "You know—when we first got inside. I can't wait to get to know either of them!"

To which Judy, looking much more her normal self, added, "You can't have Edward. He's mine. I love him. He's so shy."

"Pleasure with business!" chuckled Flan, kicking her legs up.

"Talking of business," Zillah said, "will you fill me in on the Highland Games story a bit? I don't want to say the wrong thing."

"Zillah, for goodness' sake!" said Roz. "Walls have ears. Put a sock in it—huh? Now, I tell you who I'm going after," she told the others, "because I always make straight for the top, and that's the great panjandrum himself—the one with the *big* horns!"

"You mean the High Head," said Helen.

It was at this moment the High Head chose to sweep through the veiling at the door. Zillah was hard put to it not to laugh. Roz, caught with her hands to her head to illustrate the horns she meant, pretended hastily to be stretching. Flan rolled into a ball and bounced to her feet. The rest just looked guilty.

"Good evening," said the High Head. He spoke with the same pleasant firmness he used to the Ladies of Leathe. Judging by what he had overheard, what he had to say decidedly needed saying. "I hope you are settled in comfortably. These are only temporary quarters—I want you to understand that. We will do our best to get you home. I came to assure you of this. Or, failing that, we'll send you over to the Pentarchy in a few months time when the tides are right, where you'll be much more at home. But until then you will, of course, be guests of the citadel, and there are one or two things I have to make clear to you about Arth."

Looking along their faces, he had a sense of *déjà vu*. This felt just like his speech to the servicemen, except none of these women struck him as second-rate. They all gave him a sense of quality. But what *was* the same was that they were all—he *knew* it—potential troublemakers—including the child, who was raising his voice in some kind of complaint.

"Please silence your infant," he said politely.

Zillah's face flushed all over. There was a sense of anger. Of powers. But the child stopped his noise.

"Thank you," he said. "Now, Arth and its Brotherhood were founded a thousand years ago on the king's orders, for a double purpose: first, so our charter states, to protect the Pentarchy and, by our researches, to strengthen the realm; and second, to provide the young men of the five provinces with proper teaching in magework. This citadel was made so that the Brotherhood could employ its arts in peace and seclusion, and a very holy ceremony was performed to create it. A piece of the Sanctuary of the Goddess was raised and moved to this place, which afterwards became Arth. Now, you will understand from this that Arth is in a special position: not only is it in existence solely by favor of the Goddess, but it is also at once very potent and very fragile. We in Arth have to be very careful that, while we take advantage in our mageworks of the special vibrations of this citadel, we do not in any way unbalance them. If we did, Arth would be destroyed. For this reason, all of us in Arth—" He paused impressively. They were listening patiently, waiting for him to stop. "All of us in Arth," he repeated, "take solemn vows of total celibacy. The Goddess exacts extreme penalties from those who break those vows. Now, you are all women. I must therefore ask you to understand, and to respect the oath we take." Ah, that got to them! They were looking alarmed—shocked, in fact—and impressed. "I believe you take my point," he said. "Thank you. Someone will be along with food for you shortly."

He swept out. He did not hear Flan say, "Obvious, isn't it? Work on these vibrations with a bit of kamikase sex, and who needs virus-magic?"

"Tantric," agreed Roz, and cackled hilariously.

3

The food was appalling. What was not tasteless and tough, swimming in some weak liquid, appeared to be some kind of cereal—large, off-white mounds of it—that looked like rice but, as Flan said, tasted like overcooked potato. They were none of them hungry after their experiences. Most of them could not eat it. Marcus deliberately overturned his bowl on the floor and smacked the resulting sloppy heap severely and often.

"Ardy poo," he stated. "Dummy ay." No one asked Zillah to translate.

But after a night under one thin blanket on a hard wooden bed, every one of them was ravenous. They were given a jug of brown liquid that—possibly—partook of the nature of both tea and coffee, and, to their dismay, the cereal again, this time cold but fried. ·

"Oh, looky, looky!" said Flan. "Potato Krispies!"

"Snap, crackle, sug," Zillah agreed.

"And I like my popcorn hot," Roz said morbidly. "Is this drink toffee or kea, or neither?"

"Cooking's not really my scene," Sandra observed, "but it wouldn't take much to make me go in that kitchen and try. Even I could do better than this."

"You wouldn't be allowed," said Roz. "This is the way they mortify their flesh for the Goddess. This is not food, it's religion, friends."

"Not religion—magic," Helen said in her quiet way.

"Oh, you mean we're supposed to transmogrify it into bacon and eggs like they all do?" said Flan. "Abracadabra—*kippers!* No, still the same old ardy poo."

Zillah was not surprised that Marcus spat the stuff out. She was scooping it off the floor when they were summoned by two solemn young mages. "They go in pairs, to chaperone one another," Flan said in a stage whisper. Both young men went scarlet, but pretended not to hear. They guided the party decorously along corridors and dizzy blue ramps to the outer office of the High Head. There an elderly mage told them to wait. The High One wished to ask each of them some questions.

The High Head meanwhile was looking at the full report Edward had handed him over breakfast. All the survivors were in good physical condition, it seemed, but none, except for Flan Burke, appeared to be athletes. The child was healthy too, but Edward was at a loss to think what sport a child so young might compete in. So was the High Head. He intended to find out.

He had them in one by one, starting with Judy. Edward had stated that she was the least stable and most likely to give the real truth if pressed. But Judy simply and doggedly repeated the story Roz had given, and then burst into tears. "All my friends are dead!" she sobbed. "And I don't know *why*. Lynne just died. She was talking to me, and then she was dead—just like that!"

The High Head was not used to people crying. He got the woman out of his room as fast as he could and called in Roz.

It was a trying half hour. *Why don't I like this woman?* the High Head kept thinking. She stuck long legs in high boots out across the floor of his office with a confidence that would have reminded him of Leathe had it not also seemed so masculine. If he had let her, she would have got up and strode about. He judged it prudent to keep her seated, but her aggression still came out—Leathe-like—in strident little phrases tacked on to the end of everything she said.

"Tossing the caber is immensely satisfying to a woman—but female satisfaction will be outside your experience, I imagine," she remarked; and later, "female athleticism is largely a matter of mind and emotions, you know. Muscle tone isn't hugely important to us. But I don't expect an all-male community to grasp this sort of fact."

He knew she was lying, over these Highland Games of hers and almost everything else, but there was in her aura a background of sincerity almost as strident as the rest of her, which he was at a loss to account for. Somewhere, at some level, Roz cared deeply about what she was saying. It kept reminding him she was alien, with alien notions of truth. There was magecraft in her aura too, though not much of it, and that little as alien as the rest of her. That did not surprise him, since she reminded him of Leathe anyway; but, annoyingly, that and her sincerity kept her mind warded from him. He looked her in her frank and self-confident face and thought of cracking her open with raw power. That would destroy her mind, and one did not do that to a guest under the protection of the Goddess. A pity.

The last ten minutes of the interview was rendered even more trying by an uproar in the next room, where Marcus was becoming steadily more unhappy. The High Head shielded, and warded, and blocked, by every method he knew, and the child seemed to slide his noise past everything put in its way. Irritably the High Head realized that he had better see this infant next or it would disrupt every interview until he did.

"There was a time in my life when I contemplated being gay," Roz announced through the din. "Do you know the term? It means homosexual."

The High Head had had enough. "I'm not interested in the history of your life. Go to hellband, Lady Collasso," he said cordially. "Kindly go away. I will see the small child next."

He made the last two sentences performative, rather forcefully. The mages in the outer office responded. Roz, without quite knowing how, found herself walking forth from his office into the outer room, with the curtain wall folding and dilating about her to let her out and to let Zillah and Marcus pass her on their way in. She directed a look at Zillah to *Play dumb!* and wished there had been more time to brief the woman. The others, waiting in the outer office on high stools, evidently felt equally anxious.

This was not lost on the High Head. The veiling of that entry was designed to give him sight of such things. But he was mostly taken up with exasperation. "When I said I would see the child, I meant the child on its own—er—Lady Green."

"I think I'd better stay with him," Zillah answered diffidently. "He's a bit difficult when he's upset like this." In her arms, Marcus turned wide, accusing eyes on the High Head and was shaken with a huge gasp of a sob.

It was, the High Head recognized, primitive magic he was up against, the bonding between a mother and a small child. It was something he had only read about up to now, and he was astonished at its strength. Zillah, for all her apologetic manner, was immovable. It had nothing to do with her own magic gifts. He had Edward's report to show him these were strong indeed. According to Edward, this woman had actually adapted young Gordano's birthright for her own use and held Edward pinned to her desire. These were not gifts you meddled with lightly. He sighed and gave in.

"Little boy, what is your name?"

Marcus looked up under his mother's chin, a stormy blue glare, and gave another body-shaking sob. "Barker."

Odd name. "And where do you live?" asked the High Head.

"Idanda how," said Marcus. "Dilly bool." He turned his face away.

"And how did you travel here?" persisted the High Head, with a strong sense of getting nowhere.

"Bud," said Marcus, with his face pressed into Zillah's shoulder. "Jidey bud. Didden lie bub. Go bub. Doe lie did how. Wan hoe, wan hoe, wan *hoe*, Dillah! Wan gorblay, wan bregia, wan barberday, wan *doad*!" By this time he was bawling desolately again. "Dillah, I need DOAD!"

"There, there, honey," Zillah said, rocking him.

There was a sort of helpless concern to her rocking the boy, and a meekness before fate—the High Head had read this described—but he nevertheless discerned that her meekness was a blind. The wretched woman knew he could not make head or tail of the infant. She was trying not to laugh.

"What is wrong with him?" he said, giving in again. "Why is he crying?"

Zillah swallowed. She was rather good at concealing her frequent unseemly need to laugh, and she was fairly sure this High Horns had not noticed. "He's hungry," she explained. "He was frightened in the capsule, and this place is strange, and he doesn't like the food we were given." She added, in her usual placatory way, "I'm afraid."

The High Head saw a way to break this partnership without a clash of mageworks. "In that case we must find him something to eat. If I get someone in from Kitchen, would the child consent to go there while I ask you a few questions?" It was not the way around he wanted things, but the other way was hopeless.

"I think—well, he *might*," Zillah conceded.

"Good." The High Head gestured, crisply and precisely. Marcus took his head out of Zillah's shoulder and gazed with tear-filled but interested eyes at the sigil of Housekeeping forming in the air, then dissolving to that of Kitchen, but he hid his face convulsively again when the sigil gave way to the flesh-and-blood figure of Brother Milo, with a list of stores in his hand.

The High Head explained. Brother Milo nodded and seemed rather relieved that this was all the High Head wanted of him. He held out his free hand to Marcus. "Coming with me, sonny? Come with Brother Milo and we'll find something to eat."

It was not as simple as that. The High Head contained his exasperation while Marcus hid his face again and Zillah placed him on the floor and then knelt down to explain that the kind man would find Marcus some toast, and that Mum would stay here for just a *bit*, and Marcus would be happy with the kind man. Then there was further delay while Marcus turned and examined Brother Milo, with his thinning hair and wiry body, and while he made up his mind that maybe he rather liked the way Brother Milo's face hung in nervous folds like brackets around his mouth. Finally, with some condescension, Marcus held out his hand for Brother Milo to take and trustingly vanished with him.

Zillah gave a little sigh. It was not relief. She hoped High Horns did not realize how much she had spun all this out. She was dreading this interview. No one had *told* her what she was supposed to say.

Luckily, the High Head was too inexperienced in the ways of children—as far as he knew, Marcus was the only child ever to visit Arth—to do more than conclude that Zillah was an overprotective mother. She was bound to be, he thought irritably. Love beamed from her aura. Here he realized, with something of a jolt, that Zillah was the one whom the Goddess had been most concerned to protect in that madly plunging capsule. He looked at her in this light, wonderingly but warily. She was, he had to admit, very comely—not in the highly wrought cosmetic fashion of the Ladies he was used to, but in a direct, untreated way which, again he had to admit it, spoke directly to the austerities of his soul and no doubt pleased the Goddess too. But she was also tiresomely humble and probably very devious. He told her curtly to sit down.

"Tell me the reason for your journey in that capsule."

"It—it was on the way to the Highland Games," said Zillah. This at least she knew to say.

"But you were not taking part in those games yourself," guessed the High Head.

"That's right." Zillah found she had agreed before she was aware. Panic. She sat twisting her hands between the knees of her jeans and wondered what the hell to say she *had* been doing. Inspiration flushed through her—thank the Lord! "But it was a charter flight, you know, and Marcus and I got the two spare tickets at the last moment because I—er—had to get away."

The High Head watched the power rise around her to answer his suspicions and was not surprised that the Goddess had singled this one out. This woman was important. He began to suspect that whatever business the occupants of the rogue capsule had been on, it concerned Zillah and her child somehow. Maybe they were her bodyguard. Yes, that might fit. Roz would lie to protect her. Well, that was no concern of his, so long as it did not threaten Arth. But he needed to be sure.

"Had to get away?" he asked, using the time-honored technique of simply throwing the remark back.

"Oh—yes," Zillah invented. "The courts had given me custody of Marcus, but his father wants him. He was threatening to kidnap Marcus, so I had to get away quickly to somewhere where he wouldn't find us."

"Where is that somewhere?" the High Head inevitably asked.

Zillah wished she could remember whether Roz had
named a place. "Lyonesse," she said desperately. "Near
where they hold the Highland Games." And, striving for
local color, she added, "Logres is near there too, just
down the road from Camelot. Marcus's father wouldn't
dream I'd gone there. Camelot's politically unsound."

"And Marcus's father is who?" came the next question.

Oh my God! Zillah thought. "Someone very important—whose name I'm not at liberty to reveal." Which,
she thought, was not so far from the truth.

A ring of truth there, thought the High Head.
"Where—"

Brother Milo rematerialized in the middle of the
room, still holding Marcus by the hand. Saved by the
bell! thought Zillah. Tears were rolling dolefully down
Marcus's cheeks. "What *is* it, Marcus?"

The High Head lifted his chin and expressed his irritation in a venomous look at all three. "Why are you here
again, Brother?"

Brother Milo was harassed. "I do beg your pardon, sir.
The little fellow is getting very upset. I'm afraid none of
us can understand what he's asking for. He keeps saying
he wants damages."

Zillah bit the inside of her cheek in order not to laugh.

"Damages?" the High Head said irately.

"Damages, sir," said Brother Milo.

Both of them looked at Marcus. Marcus was exasperated at their stupidity. "Damn bitches," he enunciated,
his whole body shaking with the effort to communicate.
"*Damn* damn bitches."

The High Head's astonished face turned first to Brother Milo, then to Zillah. She unclenched her teeth from her

cheek. "He's asking for jam sandwiches," she said, rather impressed to find her voice was quite steady.

The two mages of Arth stared at her much as they had stared at Marcus. "Could you perhaps explain what a sandwich is, my lady?" Brother Milo asked helplessly.

"You take two slices of bread," said Zillah. "You do have bread, do you?" Both nodded. "Then you spread butter on each slice and a lot of jam on one—Do you have jam?" They looked blank. "Marmalade? Preserves?" Zillah asked, beginning to see how Marcus had become so upset in the kitchens. They looked enlightened at "preserves." They nodded. "Then you put the two slices together and give it him to eat," she explained patiently.

"*Oh!*" said Brother Milo and looked at the High Head, who said almost simultaneously, "Oh! She means a buttie—or that's what we used to say in Leathe. Didn't you call them that in Trenjen?"

"No, sir. We used to call them slathers," said Brother Milo. Jolly with relief, he looked down at Marcus. "Come on, my fine fellow. You shall have a red slather and a yellow one and see which you like best."

"Dyke *dead* buds," Marcus announced confidently as he was led away into nothingness.

The High Head took a second to recover from all this. Zillah looked up at the thick-framed window while she waited. He's not so bad, she thought. Just not got a clue about toddlers. They all seem to *mean* well here— I don't understand it. Amanda was sure everyone in this place was out to destroy the Earth. I'd expected to find a whiff of downright evil somewhere at least, and nothing's even sinister. If you look at him without that costume, High Horns is more like the director of a big company, or perhaps a cardinal—one of the worldly ones. I'm sure he thinks of himself as a good man.

Through the window, apart from the corner of a blue tower, she could see only clear pale blue sky. No birds of course. Insects? How do they pollinate those gardens I saw? Come to think of it, what do they use for a sun? I must find out. And how funny that they didn't know what a sandwich was. At this point she remembered that sandwiches were the invention of the Earl of Sandwich, who ate them rather than leave the gaming table for a meal—which surely had to be something entirely local to Earth.

So much had her confidence been restored by the incident with Marcus that she said, before the High Head could ask her further awkward questions, "Please could you tell me why it is we both speak so much the same language? We don't even come from the same universe."

He answered with surprising readiness, "It's fairly simple. This cluster of worlds develops in parallel, with parallel influences—this applies to many other things beside languages. It is clear that you come from a world in this cluster, or we would not be able to understand one another." He was happy enough to explain. It was a surprise—he could almost say a treat—to deal with a woman who was simply asking for information, as a cadet might do, instead of using questions to trip or manipulate like the Ladies of Leathe.

Zillah realized she had stumbled on a way to divert him whenever his questions became too difficult. Thereafter, whenever she needed time to think (what kind of place *had* she implied Logres was?), or when he pressed too hard (why did he keep asking what kind of work she did?), Zillah simply asked the High Head some of the things she genuinely wanted to know. She learned in this way that plants had to be pollinated by hand or by magecraft, depending on type; that Arth's light source was a small star, maintained by mageworks and veiled by a special ritual each evening; that atmosphere was contained in a mage-net; that most research in Arth was directed toward otherworld, because it was a debased image of the Pentarchy; and that the starchy potato-rice was called passet.

Here the High Head confounded Zillah by projecting, with a gesture, a dazzle in the air like a Rorschach blot. She blinked at it.

"This is a map of otherworld," he explained. He was perfectly aware that she kept trying to divert him, and it amused him. He simply answered her questions and went on. "I'm showing you otherworld first because it's one of the three main types of land distribution in this cluster of universes. Look at it carefully and tell me whether it in any way resembles your own world."

"It's a *map*?" It resembled to Zillah more the lights and lungs of an animal hung in a butcher's shop. "Sorry. It means nothing to me."

Another gesture. The butcher's shop dazzle was replaced by another, mostly a large pear shape with a crab wedged against it, trying to eat it. Zillah was already shaking her head when she recognized a sort of Africa in the pear shape. And could the crab be a version of Australia? Antarctica? High Horns was using some form of map-projection that was squashed and sideways and alien to her, and showing her a world not really anything like Earth, but—The moment she saw this, Zillah realized what the butcher's shop had been. Earth! *My* world! The one he calls otherworld and a debased version and they all do research on! It had all been there, dangling and sideways, Europe, Asia, Greenland, the Americas, Africa, and Australia masquerading as the meat hook. *Now* she understood what Amanda had been talking about, and the reason all the other women were here. Guilt flooded her, along with shock and anger. How could she have been such a fool as to blunder in on what had to be a commando

action? How could the mages of Arth so coolly tamper
with Earth? How *dared* they?

To cover up her feelings, she kept shaking her head.
The High Head dismissed his second projection with
something of a showman's gesture. He was unable to
resist the flourish because, if her world was like neither
of these, it had to be even closer to his own than he
had realized. The pear and the crab vanished, and with
panache, blue on white—like the United Nations! Zillah
thought—two new shapes came to hang in the air. The
larger, if you stripped away outjutting lands like Britain,
Spain, Greece, India, Japan, and then tilted the whole lot
downward, was not so unlike Europe and the bulk of
Asia. The smaller was—somewhat—like North America,
if you turned it sideways and south.

"That's it," said Zillah. This projection was almost
saying *Choose me!* anyway.

"Then we must be very near neighbors," said the High
Head, rejoicing. It should be simple to get these castaways home before long. He used his sword-wand as a
pointer. "This larger blue mass is the Pentarchy, where
everyone on Arth was born, and this other is Azandi.
If your home looks anything like this, it must be quite
close."

Zillah could see the idea pleased him. She could not
think why. Her mind was still roaring with shock and
anger, which she knew he would notice unless she was
careful. She could feel her hands shaking. She tried to
disguise her feelings as excitement. "Well, fancy that!"
Lord, how artificial that sounded! She clasped her hands
together and clamped them between her knees to stop
them shaking. She leaned forward as if eagerly. And
spoke almost at random. "I'd never have believed it—
never for a moment!—because my world is so much
more creative than yours."

"How do you mean?" asked the High Head.

He was offended. Zillah realized that her anger had fooled her and somehow slipped out sideways. She bit the tip of her tongue. Otherwise she was going to give the obvious answer: *Because your world sponges on mine.* "Well—I suppose I meant—well, this fortress is so bare. Don't any of the mages paint or sculpt or—compose music or anything?"

"If we do," the High Head answered austerely, "it goes into our work. Magework is creative and leaves us little room for hobbies." He was taken aback. Zillah's power had risen about her until she appeared to him to be enfolded in golden, feathered flame. He could not understand why a trivial thing like artwork could be that important to her. But there was no accounting for alien ideas. His main thought was that he had been right about Zillah: she was the important one among the castaways, and it behoved him to treat her with respect, or her world might become a hostile force on the Pentarchy's doorstep. "Why," he asked, with as much courtesy as he could muster, "does this trouble you so much?"

There seemed no way on but honesty. Zillah blurted, "It—it seems so sterile. And—I get the feeling that this fortress *needs* something more creative."

"Ah no," the High Head politely corrected her. "What you have sensed is that all Arth, and particularly the citadel, is precariously balanced. It certainly has needs. Our work is performed very carefully to supply the needs without upsetting the balance." He stood up to show the interview was at an end. "Any extra activity—music, artwork, and so on—would influence the vibrations in a way that might destroy the balance."

Zillah wanted to say that in that case, they should redesign the whole thing—anything to show she was at odds with him without giving away the real reason why she was so angry—but he was showing her to the wall, or door, or whatever, bowing her out and asking for Helen. All she managed to say was, "How do I find Marcus?"

"The child will be brought to you," he said.

Then Helen passed her and disappeared, and she was in the anteroom under the severe eyes of the elderly mage. Roz looked the old man in the eye and demanded, "How much longer do we have to kick our heels in here?"

He pursed his old lips and did not answer. It was obviously a battle that had been going on for some time.

4

By the time it was Flan's turn to be interviewed, the High Head was in no good mood. Zillah's accusation had eaten away at his serenity. Helen did not help by sticking doggedly and colorlessly to the Highland Games story. When faced with projections of the three worlds, she pointed to the second—the one Zillah had thought of as the pear and the crab, and known to Arth as Postulate—and declared the whole party came from there. Insipid liar, the High Head thought. Postulate and its people were known to Arth. The two universes guardedly traded objects of magecraft, talismans from Postulate for specula from Arth, and its mauve-skinned traders in no way resembled these female castaways. Sandra he treated with respect, as a quasi-Azandi, and was puzzled to find she seemed to think he was mocking her in some way. She claimed otherworld as her home, and he could tell it was a random guess.

So then he came to the small, chirpy woman with the bright, dark eyes, determined to discover why they were all so intent on concealing their origin.

Flan's chirpiness was verging on bad temper by this time. Waiting about always gave her a headache. Or maybe it was Roz, sniping away at that old man. Poor old fellow, in his slightly shriveled blue uniform! You might as well make rude remarks to a Chelsea Pensioner because of your income tax. Flan herself wanted to get at High Horns. She wanted to get on with the job they had come to do. But careful! she warned herself. He's quite capable of locking us all up.

"The Highland Games?" she said. Curse Roz for landing them with that stupid story! Amanda had invented a perfectly reasonable tale of a strayed strato-cruiser, and bloody Roz had to go and embroider it! "Oh yes, Roz tosses the caber, all right. It's a dirty great tree and she staggers around with it. Me, I'm a dancer. The Games has every kind of competition you can think of. I'm in the Eisteddfod section, which is singing and dancing and weaving, but if you could have talked to the others on the Celestial—the stratobus, you'd have found every kind of competitor. Pity they're dead." To her annoyance, Flan found she choked up here and tears came to her eyes. Poor *Tam*. One of the nicest boys you could hope to meet.

"Healing Horn will, of course, be examining your dead companions," the High Head told her.

"What do you *mean*?" Flan squawked. "Autopsies? Oh, well, I suppose we'd have done just the same at home. But I hope you'll have the decency to tell us— tell us *why* they died." She choked and broke off again.

"Of course," he said. "Was Zillah Green a competitor too?"

"Zillah?" Flan found she was furious with Zillah. What did she think she was doing, bringing not only herself but her *baby* along on what she must have *known* was a dangerous mission? Flan had been simmering about this from the moment on the rescue platform when she had realized Zillah had got herself on the Celestial Omnibus; but now she was so angry that, for a moment, she wondered whether to say Zillah was a pole-vaulter and get High Horns to make Zillah prove it. No. Zillah undoubtedly must have told him something. Flan did her best to make it awkward for her. "Oh no, Zillah just came along for the ride because her husband was competing. He's a pole-vaulter."

To her annoyance, High Horns simply accepted this, with a bit of a look as if it confirmed something someone else had said, and then went on to show Flan three sets of floating colored shapes he said were worlds.

"Worlds?" said Flan. "I never saw a world that shape. Worlds are round where I come from. But if it makes you happy, this one." She pointed to the one that struck her as strangest.

Otherworld. The High Head tried to suppress his annoyance. Another transparent lie. "Very well. As you probably realize, I have a pretty fair idea of what your party was doing by now." He was glad to see that this terrified her.

"What is that?" Flan asked. She was so scared, her voice almost went.

"You were escorting one of your number to a meeting of great magical importance. I do not think your arrival here was a simple accident. I suspect some enemy on your own world tried to eliminate you all."

There was a short silence while Flan wrestled with both relief and incredulity. The High Head watched red turn to white in her face, and then the pallor change to a surge of red, and believed he had struck home. Eventually Flan gave a short, wild cackle of a laugh. "Oh no!" she said. "Oh no, what we were *really* doing, of course, was coming to attack and destroy your citadel." Hearing herself say this, she wondered if she had gone mad.

She could barely credit her ears when High Horns laughed too. "Indeed? Sarcasm apart, what was your meeting about?"

I don't believe this! Flan thought. I must be in shock. She heard herself say solemnly, "That's something I'm not at liberty to say." And as if that were not enough, she heard herself adding, "But I don't doubt you could read my mind if you wanted to."

He looked decidedly shocked. "Great gods, I wouldn't dream of that! There are very strict laws against reading the mind of a fellow human. But," he said, standing up to show her the interrogation was finished, "I wish you could all bring yourselves to be a little more open with me. You must see that it is very difficult to restore you to your own world when we don't know which it is."

Flan leapt to her feet too. "But we don't know either!" she babbled. "I thought you knew that. We just call it the world—you know, the way one does—and none of us have the slightest idea how to tell you where it is, because none of us has ever been outside it before, and we don't even know what it looks like."

She had no idea if he believed her or not. She tottered forth through the veiling of the wall with a feeling of having diced with death and unexpectedly won.

5

The preliminary reports from Calculus Horn came in later that morning, and they were somewhat confusing. It seemed that Arth had arrived at a node of fate which, although only a minor node giving rise to low-probability outcomes, prevented a fully satisfactory long-term forecast. Calculus had attempted long-term casts, but these were woolly. Two suggested disaster. One of these gave Arth as completely destroyed by the castaways, and the other suggested far-reaching changes; but since all eleven of the other casts gave the situation as largely unchanged by the refugees, High Brother Gamon had written off the two minority casts as the lowest probability and ticked the majority reading. Looking them over, the High Head had no hesitation in countersigning Brother Gamon's conclusions.

When it came to short-term readings on the castaway party itself, the confusion was even greater. Every single reading was different. Most balanced out into precisely nothing. Looking along the charts, the High Head saw love, success, and stability jumbled with death, disaster, and change in both major and minor readings. "This looks like the Powers of the Wheel saying, 'pardon us, what was your question?' to me," he said wryly.

"My opinion too," said Brother Gamon. "If you take the disaster to refer to whatever accident befell that capsule, then there is nothing to suggest that their stay in Arth will be anything but peaceful and happy. But of course, I shall have to take detailed individual readings on all the survivors before I can be quite sure."

"Start those as soon as you want," said the High Head. "Meanwhile, for horoscope purposes, look at all the close analogues to the Postulate worlds, and if those don't fit, try analogues to ours. It's going to be one or the other. As soon as you get a match, tell me."

He discounted otherworld and its analogues. Flan and Sandra had so plainly been lying. All in all, he sent Brother Gamon forth with considerable optimism, both of them confident that the castaways' home universe would be discovered in the next day or so. And as far as early readings could be trusted, it looked as if these people were pretty harmless to Arth. You only had to compare these readings with the sharp indications of disaster read on the Ladies of Leathe, to see how little there was to fear. Tentatively he ordered that vigilance on the party be relaxed. He would be interviewing them all again anyway tomorrow.

This done, he turned to Edward's preliminary report on the dead in the capsule. So far, Edward was puzzled. All seemed to have died of total heart failure without any evidence of violence at almost the same instant. Edward conjectured that this instant of death was the moment when the capsule broke through into Arth and encountered the first wards. He simply could not account for the fact that death had been selective.

The High Head's decision was conveyed to the castaways along with an execrable lunch. Two young mages arrived carrying a large platter mounded with passet, which steamed overcooked vegetable scents and seemed to have uncertain-looking dark gobbets embedded in it.

While they placed this unsavory heap on the only table, the higher mage who chaperoned them stood tapping his boots with his stick—officer's baton? wand? none of the women were sure which it was—and gazing at some point above all their heads.

"Vigilance upon you is relaxed," he announced. "You will not any longer be closely watched, and you may go anywhere in the citadel within reason. You will be told if you overstep the bounds. And you will be careful not to interrupt any mage in his work." So saying, he summoned the two young mages with a flick of his stick and departed, conveying them before him with the tip of it pointed at their backs. It was as if the young men were marched off at gunpoint.

As the doorway folded shut, feelings inside the room were divided between suspicion that this announcement was a trick to get them to talk, and disgust at the nature of the lunch.

"At least we can talk about this food," Flan said. "What *are* those horrible-looking black bits?"

"Burnt meat," said Sandra.

Helen put forward a long-fingered hand and squeezed one of the gobbets in a cautious finger and thumb.

"Oh, don't!" Zillah said. "It looks like a slug."

This earned her a startled look from Judy and a reproof from Roz. "There's no need to be disgusting," Roz said. "Well, Helen?"

"Someone burnt the meat and then soaked it in water to make it soft, I think," Helen said. "It may be the way they do things here."

None of them could manage much of the stuff, and Marcus refused to eat anything at all; although this, Zillah suspected, was because he had spent most of the morning eating bread and jam. "Oddie *dug*!" he shouted. Encouraged by Flan's shuddering laughter, he threw a handful of black gobbets across the room.

"Marcus has it right," said Flan. "Ardy poo for break-fast and oddie dug for lunch. What a gift with words your child has, Zillah." She might be angry with Zillah herself, but she did not feel Roz had the slightest right to treat Zillah so peremptorily. Having, she hoped, made that clear, she said, "Well, Roz? What say we test out this permission to go anywhere we like?"

"Suits me," said Roz. The two of them departed without another word. The veiling of the door opened to let them through without any difficulty, and no mage appeared, either to stop them or escort them.

Sandra said unbelievingly, "It looks as if that mage meant what he said. In that case, I know what I'm going to do. I'm going to find their kitchens and I'm going to tell them a thing or two."

"I'll come with you," Helen offered quietly. "Suppose we take the plate of stuff back with us? That will give us an excuse to go there."

Sandra thought this was an excellent notion. The two of them set off, carrying the large platter between them; with everyone's forks stuck into it at random and Marcus's handful of gobbets reposing on top. This left Zillah with Judy and Marcus. We're the two shell-shocked ones, Zillah thought, looking at Judy sitting very upright against the wall. Judy's eyes filled with tears from time to time. Otherwise there was almost no expression on her slightly droll face. She looked like a sad Pierrot. Zillah did not feel like crying. It was more that she had a blank, disconnected feeling, rather light and feverish— the way she had always thought a person might feel if they were coming around after a lobotomy. She sim-ply could not get used to the fact that she was not missing Mark any longer. By coming here, she had put it out of her power to hope, and her misery was gone. Oddly enough, it did not seem to make her feel relief.

But there was Marcus to look after. "Do you want to go for a walk, Marcus?" Zillah said dubiously. As far as she could work out, he should have been resting—or was it getting ready for bed? She felt more than a little jet-lagged herself. Every rhythm in her body was telling her that, though it was afternoon in Arth, it was quite another time on Earth. If Marcus was feeling the same, he would be restless and irritable.

He agreed, "Awk," at once and held out his hand to be taken.

"I'll come too," Judy said, somewhat to Zillah's surprise.

The three of them went out through the almost unfelt folds of the doorway into the blue corridors beyond. Judy said nothing and seemed to rely on Zillah to choose a direction. Zillah let Marcus tug her the way he wanted to go. She rather thought he was making for the kitchens.

If he was, Marcus had made a mistake. He stumped doggedly up one of the circling ramps, towing Zillah, with Judy sleepwalking behind, and plunged through a wide area of veiling at the top. The brightness and blueness on the other side made Zillah blink. There was a smell of asepsis. In great busy quiet, mages in pale blue gowns were working beside a sort of bier on which lay a young man with a handsome, friendly face, evidently dead. Because his fair hair was trailing backward, it took Zillah a second to recognize Tam Fairbrother.

Marcus knew him at once. "Dib!" he cried in desperate sorrow, and advanced with one hand out and his face crumpled for crying. "Dib dead!"

The tallest mage whirled around. Before Zillah could move, he had fielded Marcus with large, gentle hands—hands from which a blue shimmering stained with blood rapidly disappeared as they met Marcus—and turned him back toward Zillah. "I don't think this is quite the right moment to bring the child in here," he said, looking down on her with awkward shy firmness.

Zillah recognized the curiously small, boylike face of
the head doctor-mage. What was his name? Edward. He
was nice and he seemed to like her. This made her feel
truly bad about bursting in here. "I'm so sorry. Marcus
just—just brought us here. I didn't know—I didn't realize you'd be doing autopsies. I'll—I'll take him away at
once."

"For now. You're welcome to bring him back in a day
or so," Edward said. He made it sound as if it were
all his fault. Then, as Zillah started for the door with
Marcus, and Judy turned dumbly to go with them, his
large hand fell on Judy's shoulder, stopping her. "She'd
better stay," he said. "She needs more healing than I
knew."

Before Zillah was aware, she was out on the ramp
again without Judy, rather taken aback at the power
of this medical mage. At another time she might have
been almost destroyed with embarrassment—blundering
in on an autopsy like that!—but Marcus claimed her full
attention. He was very upset. "*Dib!*" he said desolately,
over and over, as he stumped downward.

Zillah had not realized even that Marcus knew Tam,
and she certainly had had no idea that he liked Tam
enough to give him a special name. As far as she knew,
Tam had twice, but only twice, briefly visited Amanda,
but evidently that had been plenty of time for him to
make a hit with Marcus.

"Dib's all right," she explained as they stumped she
knew not whither, except that Marcus firmly led her
downward. "He doesn't hurt, Marcus. It's like being
asleep, only better," she said, and found herself saying
all the things adults do say to a child confronted by
death. And they were so inadequate. Marcus had known
instantly that Tam was dead. He always knew so much
more than she gave him credit for.

They came down to another wide veiling, blue fluting filling a sizable archway, which gave way into a sudden open space. Zillah was relieved. Here was something that might distract Marcus. The large, open square she had seen from the orbiting capsule stretched in front of them. It was possibly a parade ground, for it was nothing but a stretch of gravel with one carefully tended strip of grass around the perimeter. Here, sure enough, Marcus forgot his sorrow and ran gleefully out into the large, sandy space. Zillah followed, pretending to chase him—"I'll catch you, I'll *catch* you!"—to keep his mind on other things. She had to quell an attack of some kind of agoraphobia as she ran. Blue sky was overhead. The blue buildings around the square, reduced by distance to the height of cottages, *might* have concealed landscape beyond, except that she knew they did not. The blue sky was all there was beyond them. She had to keep her eyes on Marcus's small trotting figure, and even that became the center of vertigo. For a moment the whole flat space swung upside down, and Marcus was trotting across a ceiling.

It *was* a parade ground. With immense relief, her eye caught a disciplined group of blue uniforms over in the right-hand corner. They were just breaking ranks after some kind of exercise and streaming toward another of those veiled archways. Some were detaching themselves in twos and threes and making for other exits. The sight helped a little. She now saw everything at a steep slant. No, it was worse. She was absolutely going to *fall*. But Marcus had changed direction and was now running toward three of those detached figures, arms stretched out, for some reason in an ecstasy of delight. Zillah swerved after him. Her knees bent and she had to restrain an urge to trail her knuckles along the gravel.

"Ort! Ort!" Marcus was shouting.

It was the centaur again, now wearing a smart blue
jacket on his human torso. The degree of illusion in this
place became apparent when Marcus pounded up to the
centaur and his companions in remarkably few strides.
Or maybe the centaur moved swiftly to meet him.

"Ort! Ort!" Marcus cried, relief and joy all over him.
Zillah realized that it was in hopes of meeting the centaur again that Marcus had gone to that medical place.
Perhaps he had even been afraid that the centaur was
dead too.

The centaur reached down and swung Marcus up level with his face. "How did you know I came from the
Orthe?" he asked, through Marcus's squeals of pleasure.
He was quite as delighted as Marcus. His pale, mottled
face was shining.

Zillah, as she sloped up, decided it would not be
tactful to point out that Marcus had been saying something else.

"You've got it wrong, Josh," Tod said, with his arm
affectionately over the centaur's flank. "The little fellow
was actually calling you a horse." Josh laughed. Tod nodded cheerfuly at Zillah. "Nice to see you again. What's
wrong? This place giving you the slopes?"

Zillah came upright again in the greatest relief. "Yes,
but I'm all right now." Tod had made it all right, by
being so normal.

"It does that to me too," said the third one of the
group, leaning on Josh's other side. "All the open places
give me the slopes. That's because space really is bent
here, you know. The more of it you can see, the more it
shows."

Zillah looked at him with interest. He was not as odd
as the centaur, but she could not help feeling he might
in fact be even odder. He looked human, skinny and
fair, but there was a sort of inner shining to him, and his
eyes were tremendous—as were his hands and feet. Like

an undernourished version of Michelangelo's David, she thought.

"Let me introduce," said Tod. "The fellow keeping Josh upright on the other side is Philo. He's a Peleisian gualdian, if that means anything to you. The centaur is Horgoc Anphalemos Galpetto-Cephaldy, or Josh to his friends."

"Pleased to meet you, lady." Josh deftly swung Marcus around to sit astride at his back, where Marcus nestled against the blue jacket looking blissful, while Josh held out a large, pale hand to Zillah. It was warm when Zillah took it, horse-warm. The young-man-seeming part of him was all over larger than human. It would have to be, she thought, to match the horse part. The patch that had covered his eye the day before was gone, showing healing cuts above and below, although the cuts were hard to see for the big liver-colored horse-mottle that crossed his face and spread into his hair.

"I'm glad you're better," she said.

"I'm fine," he said. "Thanks to Tod."

Philo came forward and held out a hand almost as big as the centaur's, but not as warm when Zillah grasped it. He seemed shy. But when Zillah smiled, he smiled too, and his smile was big and sly and confiding. "We should add that Tod's full name is Roderick Halstatten Everenzi Pla—"

"No, don't!" Tod said, wincing. "Tod will do."

"He's heir to a Pentarchy," Josh explained. "It bothers him."

Since it evidently did bother Tod, Zillah said to him, "How come you're the only person in this place who understands what Marcus says?"

"I have six elder sisters," Tod said wryly. "My parents kept grimly on until they got the required boy-child. Apart from being brought up in a houseful of hysteria and general henpecking, this means I have nephews.

And nieces. Dozens of them. Some of my earliest memories are of having to understand baby talk so that I could tell the little bleeders that I was their uncle and they couldn't have my toys."

They began to walk as Tod talked, to another of the archways, all in a group in the most natural way. It was clear all three young men assumed Zillah was one of their number. And she was too, in some strange way, she thought, looking up at Josh's laughing face and over at the prattling Tod. Something eased within her. She had friends. This was something she had seldom found possible before. She had never been able to fall easily into a relationship, the way other people could—yet here she was, chatting away as if she had known all three of them for years. She felt as if she *had* known them for years. Each of them felt familiar: Josh's awkward strength, Philo's slyness and sweetness, Tod's insouciance. She smiled at Philo, and in the most natural manner, he came around Josh to lean against her.

6

R oz halted in a large unveiled archway and struck an attitude, feet apart, hands on hips. She felt good. Every line of her said *Woman!* And it worked. Without her needing to project her presence at all, the heads of the blue-clothed mages bending over their work in the room beyond were turning toward her, one and one, then hurriedly and guiltily turning away. She could almost see the flickers of lust playing across them. Good. This was doing what she had come to do.

After a moment one of the higher brothers hastened across to her, self-consciously adjusting his short-horned headdress.

"Am I somewhere I shouldn't be?" Roz asked as he opened his mouth to speak.

He shook his horned head and looked flustered. "Not at all. This is Observer Horn. Where did you wish to be?"

She knew this was not what he had been going to say. He had meant to turn her out. Good. "Mind if I look round then?"

"Not at all, not at all. Let me show you around." He led the way toward the rows of busy mages. Roz followed, stalking high, knowing he was conscious of every movement she made behind him. She felt like the cat that had the cream.

7

Sandra and Helen, bearing the large platter toward where they thought the kitchens were, were intercepted by two mutually chaperoning young mages. Politely, deferentially, they told Sandra her presence was required in Calculus Horn.

Sandra popped her eyes at Helen. "Okay. Sure you can manage this plate-thing on your own?"

"Of course," Helen said quietly. "I'm far stronger than I look. Which way are the kitchens?"

The way was pointed out. Helen arrived there to find the place in that afternoon lull that occurs in all kitchens. She set the platter of half-eaten food carefully on the nearest table and surveyed the long, vaulted chain of rooms. Ovens she located, pans, work surfaces. The business of cooking varied very little from world to world, evidently. This place reminded her of a monastery kitchen she had once visited.

Having acquainted herself with the various arrangements, she walked quietly to the far end, where dishes were being washed by two weary-looking young mages. "Do you two do the cooking here?" she asked them.

"We're only cadets, ma'am," they told her, "on scullion duty. Brother Milo's in charge. Do you want him?"

"Not yet," Helen said, thoughtfully. "What's being

planned for supper? Do you know?"

Passet casseroled with lamb, she was told, with baked passet on the side. When she inquired how it should be made and for how many, they looked somewhat blank. They were only cadets. The mysteries of cooking had been withheld from them. But they were ready enough to talk. There were, after all, two of them and they felt they were chaperoned. And Helen's looks had a cool angularity that amounted almost to gawkiness, and almost but not quite to unattractiveness. People always assumed she was a virgin. She carefully accentuated this quality for the benefit of the cadets. They felt she was safe, even if she *was* a woman. Besides, she was kind enough to help with the dishes. While she did so, they explained, more and more eagerly, that cadets with less than average ability were sent to work in the kitchens and that this made them feel slighted, the more so in that almost none of the mageworks—such as those were—that were used in the kitchens had yet been shown to them.

"It's not so much magework," Helen said carefully, "as artistry that one uses in cooking. Would you like me to show you what I mean?"

Would they! But what *on*?

"We could always make a start on that casserole."

They liked that idea. Brother Milo would doubtless commend their zeal.

Shortly they were scurrying about fetching ingredients from great cupboards primed with stasis spells. Helen learnt that the magecraft which prevented food from decaying was simple and easy to operate. It had to be, she was told, because so many people handled the food. In one cool corner of her mind she toyed with the idea of simply breaking those spells and then putting blocks on against anyone renewing them. A suicidal act—like this whole foray was, she suspected. Soon everyone in the citadel would be down with dysentery or starving. She dismissed the notion. It was not creative, it was too easily detected and, besides, she liked to cook.

Meanwhile the two boys had heaped the long tables with daunting quantities of provisions, very short on the meat, despite the quantity, and as usual high on the passet. Helen surveyed it, stretching and flexing her thin fingers. When she had talked of artistry, she had been quite sincere. What she had in mind was very artistic indeed, not exactly a weaving, more an insidious campaign to bend the inhabitants of the citadel to the ways of Earth. It would not be as swift as virus-magic, but it ought, in the long run, to be just as effective. And it suited her better, as one whose gift for witch-craft had always been bound up with practical things. In the meantime, the food itself should divert attention from what she was doing—*surely* someone in this citadel would appreciate better food!

"The first art lies in the choice of herbs," she told the cadets. "What herbs are there?"

There were gratifying ranks of them, under stasis in glass jars. Clearly the cooking in Arth had not always been so plain. Not all the herbs had names Helen was used to, but touch and smell told her which was which of the ones she knew, and which of the unknown ones might prove useful as well. And, thank goodness, there were masses of garlic.

As she worked, the older kitchen staff began to filter back from their rest period. With quiet, cool requests for this or that, she soon had them busy too. When Brother Milo came back on duty, he was outraged to find his entire staff hard at work and supper well under way, all at the command of this long, calm, gawky young woman—who smiled coolly at him.

"I'm showing them the way we cook in my world," Helen said. Her composure was wholly unruffled by her instant recognition that Brother Milo was going to prove her chief difficulty. "It seems to have ended up as cooking supper. I hope you don't mind."

Brother Milo did mind, but he could hardly throw good food away and start again at this hour.

8

"**W**hat I want to know," said Sandra, "is why you're all being so *polite* to me!"

High Brother Gamon bowed yet again. "We think of you as Azandi, ma'am," he explained. "Azandi is the other continent of our home world. The people there look like you. They inspire respect."

"Whatever for?" said Sandra.

"They are," Brother Gamon told her ruefully, "somewhat dangerous adepts, even the least of them."

Sandra began and then bit back—just barely—an angry description of the status of black women on Earth. This was a mission, for God's sake! It might still be possible to do what they had come to do, and she had not been chosen for stupidity. "Explain. I think it might be a bit like that where I come from."

"Azandi specialize in types of mageworkings that we have never succeeded in mastering," the man in the horned headdress explained. "They can handle the hidden side of the Wheel. This naturally makes them, in addition to other things, experts in divination. Since we in Calculus, in our laborious way, work at divination too, this is bound to make us treat someone of your appearance most respectfully."

"Oh," said Sandra. "Ah."

"Though I hasten to add that we pride ourselves on treating *all* ladies with respect," Brother Gamon added.

What a windbag! Sandra thought. "Okay. So what do you want to do with me?"

"We're about to try various techniques to discover the whereabouts of your homeworld and how soon you may safely be conveyed back there. There is no need to feel the least alarm, ma'am. A full birth horoscope is, of course, impossible at first, but we are drawing up one for the exact moment of your arrival in Arth. And we shall scry in various ways, based on information Observer Horn imparts—we shall need your age in years, months, and days for all this, a hair of your head, your hand on one or two implements of calculation, and we should like you to cut the cards for our readings of—"

At last the man had got to something Sandra knew about. "Cards? You mean tarot?"

"What is that?" he asked. "Atala is our usual system, but we also use—"

"Show," Sandra said imperiously. "Cards."

He led her to a velvet-covered table. Sandra swaggered after him, acting what she hoped was an arrogant Azandi as hard as she knew how. I have power. I work the hidden side of the Wheel. I am *arrogant*. Bloody hell, I feel like Roz! She looked haughtily down her nose as Brother Gamon spread a pack of cards on the velvet with an expert sweep of his palm. Hm. Quite like tarot really. The old, really weird decks. Sandra picked up what seemed to be the Magician. "What do you call this?"

"The Archmage. That is a most potent and revealing card, which—"

"Piffle. Weak and ordinary—but then he's only one of the unnumbered trumps: all those count low." Sandra sensed gasps from all over the great room. "Honest. Does he count high with you then? He counts low with me,

where I come from. It seems to me you ought to read me
the way it goes in my country, or you'll get it all wrong.
Want me to show you my way?"

There was a long murmur of assent. Mages left
what they were doing and drew in around the velvet
table. Sandra kept as sober as a judge, but inside she
was doing her grin-and-hug-yourself-Sandra. She loved
fooling people. Here we go then. Back-to-front tarot. This
should mess them up some. After that I'll have a go at
upside-down horoscopes. I'll never get a better chance at
sabotage, not if I look all over this mad blue building for
a month!

9

Flan had wandered into a tine of Ritual Horn. *But I'm still not sure how we got from there to here!* she thought as she swung and bent and sidestepped in front of a grave, dark young mage, who most faithfully echoed what Flan did. *Except he's so good-looking. Perhaps that had something to do with it.*

"*From* the waist, now! *That's* better!" she told the young mage. Dip arm, dip arm and up. As far as Flan could recall, she had happened on this dance room, with its smooth blue floor and full-length mirrors on two walls, to find a Brother Instructor attempting to put a team of mages through some kind of movement routine. Swing around *and* swing. What the purpose of the routine was, Flan still had no idea, but she had hung around at the door fascinated at first, then disapproving, then exasperated. Most of them were so *bad* at movement. The Instructor didn't seem to have much of a clue either.

"You in the second row—red hair—you're *still* missing the beat! One and *two* and, one and *two* and! *That's* better!" Somehow, with her total exasperation, the professional had arisen in Flan and taken over completely. She remembered herself suddenly in the middle of the room, clapping for attention. Music came jangling to a startled halt, faces had turned, gaping. "That was *awful*, people,

171

just *awful!*" Flan had found herself telling them, in the full, carrying voice of a dance teacher. "You can all do much better than that. I'll show you. Let me just get these shoes off my feet . . ." And then she had shown them how and worked them and worked with them. Faces by now shone with sweat. The Brother Instructor's face was twisted and gasping. Honest! He should be fitter than that. He didn't know what work *was!* Tomorrow she was going to take them all back to basics, but now it was probably time for a little simple yoga.

"All right, people. You can rest. You have the makings of a good dancer," she told her handsome mage. His grave face lit with a besotted smile. She knew that if she'd asked him to lick her toes, he would have lain down on the floor and done so.

But Brother Instructor was bustling up to Flan, limping a little and very angry. "My good woman, it is not our purpose here to *dance*. This is a Ritual of the Goddess."

"Then you *should* dance," Flan told him. "She likes it. Anyway, dancing is the basis of all good movement, whatever you think She wants. All right, people, if you've got your breath, we'll have a little yoga now."

10

As two dozen mages tried to force their unaccustomed legs into lotus position, the High Head received an urgent summons from Edward.

"Couldn't it wait until I met you at supper?" he asked as he arrived in Healing Horn. One of the women, the blond hysterical one, was lying on the outermost bunk, pale and comatose. Though the High Head was sure she was unconscious, her presence made him uncomfortable. He was not used to the outline of breasts on a sleeper under a blanket.

"No, it couldn't be then," Edward said, in his most apologetic way. "It had to be here." He was hovering beside a more distant bunk that reeked of stasis mage-work, and he seemed to be concealing something in one hand. "She's in healing trance," he said, seeing the High Head's attention on the woman. "I didn't realize how upset she was when her friend died. My fault. But I think I've discovered the reason for those deaths now. Will you come over here?"

The High Head approached the further bunk and found himself staring down at a true corpse, a fair young man lying lifeless and, oddly enough, looking in death much less deathlike than the unconscious woman. A nice young lad. The pity of this death wrung him, like a pain in his chest.

"Look at him carefully," Edward said. The High Head did not want to, but for Edward's sake, he looked. "Does he remind you of anything?" Edward asked.

"Death," said the High Head. "Life. Waste."

"No, I meant does he make you think of anyone?" Edward said. "Anyone you know?"

Now Edward mentioned it, the face of the dead lad did seem familiar, a little, but the High Head could not, for the life of him, place the face. Was it Edward as a youngster? No. Edward's face was longer and his features smaller. "Not—that I can think of, I'm afraid."

"Then does *this* ring a bell?" Edward said. Eagerly, precisely, he let unfold the thing in his hand. It was an irregularly shaped sheet of purplish plastic—probably the backing from a dressing—with random holes cut in it. Edward spread this with great care over the right half of the young corpse's face. "Now look."

Suddenly the young man was mottled with purple dapples that extended into his hair.

"Great Goddess!" said the High Head. "The centaur—Galpetto!"

"Yes," said Edward. "And no proper cause for death. He's the centaur's analogue in whatever world they come from, and I'm afraid the two of them couldn't exist together in the same universe. The centaur was nearly killed at about the same moment that capsule got into Arth. I'm willing to bet that the analogues of all the other corpses had bad accidents at that instant too. I'm going to tell her." He gestured toward the unconscious woman. "It might make her feel better about her friend."

The High Head had certain difficulty with some of this. "But most of the corpses are *women*, aren't they?"

"Yes. Their analogues will be people over in the Pentarchy, I think," Edward said.

Not a good thought. "I'd always supposed Arth was

better separated from the world than that," the High Head said ruefully.

"So had I, but I think we must be more closely connected than we'd realized," Edward said. "Anyway, this means I can enter the correct cause of death in my records."

11

S upper that night was unusually and surprisingly
good.

VI

Earth and Arth

★

1

"**I** canceled the milk," said Joe. Maureen jerked awake, very much amazed that he had attacked her only with this. "But there's enough milk in the fridge to keep us going," he said. "Do you want some cocoa?"

"No," she said, and yawned ostentatiously. She needed to yawn anyway, so the only thing to do seemed to make it look like boredom. She was so *tired*.

"And of course, I cut off the telephone," Joe continued, "though not physically. Don't imagine British Telecom's going to come here wanting to repair it. No one's going to find anything wrong with it, but anyone who tries to get in touch with you is going to get wrong numbers—unless they persist, in which case they'll get your answering machine with your voice saying you'll be away for a while."

Maureen blinked at him. He was lounging at the other end of her sofa, creasing the chaste oatmeal cushions with his weight and looking extremely smug. "Very clever," she said, "to think of taking all the obvious precautions." She could not understand why he had not attacked her while she dropped off into a doze there for a moment. Or—she met his eyes. They were heavily, almost pruriently surveying her. Could it be that what she had here was a hunter getting a buzz off entering into

the feelings of his prey? She thought so. It would be just
like Joe. He wanted to play cat and mouse for a while.
If so, could she use it? Keep him occupied while she
counterattacked or called for help. There were several
Names that should answer her call.

"Don't even think of it," said Joe. "I've got it fixed so
that not even your pet entities are going to hear you.
Take a look." He gestured with his can of lager.

Maureen looked. He had brought his wards to vis-
ibility: there was no doubt that he was a truly skilled
operator. They hung all around the room, tenuous as
cobwebs, roiling a little like clouds, and hard as concrete.
She reached up to the nearest. Her fingers met a chilly
hardness that she knew she had no hope of penetrating
while Joe was awake and aware. She trailed her fingers
across its rough, icy surface and thought. He had to
sleep, too, in the end. She only had to wait it out. She
only had to wait until the raiding party released that
virus-magic into Laputa-Blish, and then Joe's precious
bosses would all be disabled, and anything Joe learned
would be no use to anyone. It would give her great
pleasure to tell him that when the time came. So, how
long before it came?

Maureen let her hand trail back into her lap, hopelessly. Keeping the look of blank dismay on her face, she
felt for her precognitive powers and let them fill her,
gently and surreptitiously. What she found chilled her
worse than Joe's clammy wards. It had gone wrong—
would go wrong. There was—would be—death. Future or
present death, she had no means of knowing because—
this was the fact that truly dismayed her—there was a
time difference between the two worlds. The difference
might be years, or months, or only minutes. It was not
regular. Now she saw this, Maureen remembered Gladys
muttering something about time not running the same
in Laputa-Blish. She had not paid much attention then.

Gladys had muttered in her most senile manner, something about "Long or short, short or long, who knows?" and *nobody* attended to Gladys when she went like that. Now it occurred to Maureen that this was a mistake. When Gladys was acting fretfully gaga, it could be that she was functioning at a level none of the rest of them could reach.

Death, delay, things gone wrong, but still a blink of hope. Someone was—or would be—still trying, though Maureen could also see opposition and great evil from a quarter no one expected. This could ruin everything: it would certainly cause further delay. Good God! It could be that she would be shut up with Joe, never daring to sleep, for the next year! There was no question of waiting it out. She would have to defeat him, and soon. And how was she to do that when she was so goddamn *tired*?

2

G ladys paid off her faithful taxi driver and shambled up her path, muttering fretfully in the foggy white of coming dawn. "Tired, Jimbo. I'm too *old* for this all-night ritual stuff." Around her were the mushroom scents of wet garden. Things grew. A trill of birdsong swept across the trees. "Thanks," Gladys muttered. "Pretty. Too tired to appreciate." Jimbo clinging to her skirt was as draggled as she was. She stumbled over him slightly as she went into the house, which was unusual; but then an unusual effort had been put out by both of them. And the capsule had gone off safely and the Wards of Britain were up, so it had been worth the effort. "Tea," she mumbled, shuffling among the jungle plants to the kitchen. "Hot. Wet."

She had it brewed. She had her hands wrapped around the warm belly of the mug. She was sniffing its fragrance and putting it to her mouth to drink when the phone rang.

"Curse. Thought I'd disconnected." She took the tea with her and shuffled off to hunt through the jangling jungle for the phone and answer it.

It was Amanda's voice, high with agitation. "Zillah's gone! She hasn't slept in her bed. So's Marcus. Gladys, she's taken Marcus and *gone*! I can't feel where she is. All I get when I try for her is nothing. Gladys, where *is* she?"

Gladys held the tea mug against her ear, warming it

against Amanda's insistence. "Lovely bell-like voice," she muttered. "Clear and high. Like a damned carillon or an alarm clock."

"Oh, *sorry*," Amanda said without much contrition. "You must be so tired after last night—but, Gladys, can't *you* try for Zillah? Can you get any idea where she is?"

"Just a moment." Gladys sighed and took a warm, warming gulp of tea. Zillah. Amanda's younger sister, the one with the little boy—Mark's child, Gladys had always suspected. "Damn it, Amanda, I only met your sister twice." Reddish hair. Sense of unrealized abilities about her that could be even stronger than Amanda's. In fact, Gladys recalled, where Zillah's abilities were concerned, the sky was the limit, if only the silly girl could bring herself to realize it! At least someone with that kind of strength ought to be fairly easy to trace. She drank more tea and put her mind to it. The trace was there. It led—"Oh, all the powers, Amanda! She went in that capsule and took the child!"

A sharp silence on the other end was followed by an even sharper cry of horror. "*Gladys!* Are you *sure*? Are you still in contact with the capsule?"

"No." Gladys sighed again and tried to explain. "They went out of contact as soon as they crossed over, Amanda. All I know is that the trace leads to the capsule and stops."

"But she was inside the capsule the other day—and so was Marcus. Mightn't that be what you're feeling? I mean, she definitely *wasn't* there, or in the warehouse, when I left the team there. I *know* she was at home with Marcus. I could feel. There was no way for her to get there. The team wouldn't have let her on board if she did go there."

Hope, Gladys thought, was a heavy thing and would do no good here. "Amanda, I'm sure. I don't know how

Zillah did it, but that is what she did."

"Really sure? Gladys, *please* try and trace her further! I have the strongest precognitions of disaster for the capsule anyway!"

So had Gladys. Some of the foreknowledge was, to her regret, the result of calculations she wished she had not had to make. "I can't try to trace her now. For one thing, I'm tired to death. For another, I know I was lucky to make contact with the Laputa-Blish thing anyway. I got in on them when they were exchanging messages and people with their home universe, and I'm going to have to wait for them to start doing that again before I can see anything clear about our folk. Don't worry. I'll keep trying. I'll let you know as soon as I find them again."

"And can we fetch her back? Gladys, I don't know what Zillah thought she was doing, but if she did go there—! Gladys, she hasn't a clue—really. She didn't know it was supposed to be an attack."

"Well, obviously, or she wouldn't have taken Marcus. Amanda, do try to get some sleep. There's nothing you can do until we know more."

It took a while to persuade Amanda. Gladys put the phone down at last and made her way back to the kitchen, rolling like a badger from foot to foot out of weariness. "Nothing we can do," she repeated to herself, pouring more tea. It had gone strong and orange and tepid by then. She drank it all the same, full of guilt and sorrow. Cats were appearing, on windowsills, on the draining board, out of cupboards, treading warily with sympathy. "Don't tell Amanda," she said to them guiltily. "Nothing we can do." It was something Maureen had accepted— but then Maureen was like that—but they had both tacitly agreed that there was no point in telling Amanda that the only way for the raiding party to get back was to force the inhabitants of Laputa-Blish to tell them how. Which meant they had to win first. Now, with this feeling of disaster she had, winning did not seem likely. "Did it ever?" she asked Jimbo, crouching beside her aching feet. Never had she felt so weary and old.

"I'll get onto it first thing tomorrow," she said. "Not now, not now."

3

For two days, life on Arth proceeded in its usual pattern, apparently undisturbed by the survivors from the capsule. The capsule itself had been consigned to Housekeeping and Maintenance, who could use the metal, and it was almost as if the women had always been there. When the High Head, as part of his routine duties, sampled the vibrations, they seemed normal and healthy. There was, it was true, the occasional accelerando in the rhythms, in which everything seemed to pulse several degrees faster, but he was able to discount that. A small tide was coming up, when communication would once more be possible between Arth and the Pentarchy, and these sudden quickenings were quite often associated with tides. The High Head was able to discount the phenomenon—in fact, he would readily have forgotten the tide if he could, since the opening would certainly bring renewed demands from Leathe to hurry up the work in otherworld. And here was a mystery. The experiment had succeeded: he was sure of it. Otherworld had done its usual lateral thinking and taken action of some kind, quite recently too. But of his three main sources, only one was reporting, and that in the vaguest terms. The agent watching the young female had cut off completely. And, to his exasperation, so had his wild native contact. He had to conclude, after unprofitable hours spent trying to raise both, that otherworld had become aware of them and taken steps to silence them. It was imperative to get another agent on the scene as soon as possible. But this was going to take time and planning.

Meanwhile, the women seemed to be settling down to wait for Arth to send them home—as if Arth *could,* when they were all so ignorantly vague about where they had come from! At least they were causing surprisingly little trouble. There had been one complaint, from Brother Instructor Cyril of Ritual Horn, that the woman Flan Burke had attempted to undermine his authority. But when the High Head asked High Brother Nathan to investigate, Nathan reported that Brother Cyril now unreservedly withdrew his complaint, saying that the young woman was sent by the Goddess to perfect Her rituals.

If the High Head was inclined to think Brother Cyril's retraction was rather suspiciously fulsome, his doubts were set at rest when he interviewed Flan. He questioned the women once a day at first, trying to sift their vague answers for clues to their home universe, though he became increasingly sure that he was going to have to rely on Calculus to find it.

"Brother Cyril and I had what you might call an eyeball-to-eyeball confrontation," Flan told him. "And," she added cheerfully, "he came around to my point of view."

As for the others, Brother Gamon of Calculus Horn soon asked for permission to interview Sandra himself so as not to interrupt the work he was doing with her. He fancied he was close to discovering a new and improved procedure. Observer Horn made a similar request about Roz. She was, they said, giving them some aspects they had found they were missing up to then, and they wished to continue working closely with her.

Very commendable, the High Head thought, although he wished the other one whose name he always forgot—Helen, that was it—had not decided to work closely with Kitchen. Mealtimes were steadily becoming a distinctly sensual experience. The High Head, who preferred to eat in the same way that one stoked an engine, and then forget the matter, found this distracting. It surprised him that so few Brothers agreed with him. Even Brother Milo raised no objection. He said, rather obscurely, that Helen was a challenge to himself and his Oath.

"Don't you at least . . ." the High Head asked Edward, as the two of them breakfasted on little fish from the reservoirs, mushrooms, and honey pancakes, "don't *you* at least miss passet for breakfast?"

"No, I don't," Edward said heartily. "I don't mind if I never taste the stuff again."

The High Head sighed and stared at the blue wall of his private dining room. It was becoming clear to him that he must be the only person in the citadel who actually liked passet. "How is the woman you had in the trance?" he asked, to change the subject.

"Coming along very nicely." Edward poured himself more of the excellent coffee—the best thing, in his opinion, that ever came out of Azandi. "As soon as she came out of shock, I discovered she was a natural-born healer. So of course, I asked her to stay and help us in Healing Horn. But," he added, with an odd, wistful little smile, "I'd still much rather have had the pretty one."

"Zillah," said the High Head. There was somehow no doubt which woman Edward meant. He knew a sudden surge of annoyance, even actual anger, that Edward had presumed to want Zillah, when it ought to be obvious she was—was what? In some discomfort, the High Head realized that he had been, in some odd way, regarding the woman Zillah as *his*. He seemed—he could not think how—to know her extremely well, in a special way, and he was certainly not going to let any other Horn Head take over the job of interviewing her. No, this was absurd. He should not be thinking this way. He had better let someone else (provided it was not Edward) speak with her in future. But he still thought he should ignore Brother Wilfrid's complaint that Zillah was harming the vibrations by corrupting the servicemen. Brother Wilfrid was, in his way, a fanatic. Nor was there anything amiss with the vibrations. "I do, of course, lock their quarters with the strongest possible wards every night," he said, possibly changing the subject again.

"I'm sure," Edward said rather dubiously, "that is very wise."

4

The women knew perfectly well they were locked in at night. "I can tell a ward when I see one," Roz said, "even if I hadn't tried to get past the veiling and found I couldn't." She paced up and down past the rows of sleeping cells. "What I don't know is if they listen in on us or not."

"Oh, they don't," Judy told her. "I asked Edward, and he was shocked I thought they would."

"You *asked*?" Roz said. "You *fool!*"

"Why not? He's nice. In fact," Judy said, with rather tremulous defiance, "he's so innocent, I feel a beast most of the time, knowing I'm here to undermine him."

"We're not here to be nice!" Roz said disgustedly. She marched to stand looming over the others as they sat about on the floor. "Okay. So we're here trying to do the best we can without the virus-magic. It's obvious from what we've all heard them say that the best way to undermine this place is to spoil the vibrations by getting as many of them as possible to break their Oath. I've been working on that principle anyway. I'm up to twelve. Two High Brothers and ten mages. How about the rest of you? Sandra? Flan?"

"Who made *you* leader?" muttered Flan. She hugged her knees and rocked like a Kelly clown. This gave her repeated little sights of the smug smile playing over Roz's face. Confronted by that smile, she had not the heart to add Brother Instructor Cyril to Roz's string of scalps. The look on the man's face when she kissed him to shut him up—no, it was too much. And then Alexander, the dark young mage, was something very special. But Roz was impatiently tapping a foot. So what *could* she say, except that her movement class somehow doubled every time she went near Ritual Horn? And dozens of other brothers crowded hopefully in the veiling of the doors. "Dozens," she said.

"Yes, but how many?" Roz demanded.

"I've lost count," Flan said airily, "except that they're queuing up."

"You can't have managed more than fifteen in the time," Roz said suspiciously. "Let's call it fifteen. Sandra?"

Sandra seized gratefully on Flan's lead. "They're queuing up for me too, Roz." Something surely was going to happen with High Brother Gamon soon; though, windbag as he was, it was going pretty slowly—so slowly that she didn't kid herself that the other mages in Calculus had not made bets on whether it would happen at all. And Sandra was enjoying it, in a way she had never enjoyed it before. He was so courteous, so considerate. It was courtship, that was what it was, in the old-fashioned sense, and all the while there *she* was sabotaging his divinations. It was a shame. Sandra was aware that she might be beaming and that her eyes were a trifle misty. "Say fifteen," she said hurriedly.

"Forty-two," said Roz. She was looking rather less smug, now it seemed that Flan and Sandra had both exceeded her score by three. "Helen?"

Small, wry brackets grew around Helen's mouth. She was well aware that Flan and Sandra were—at least— exaggerating, and she thought she understood why. She supposed she ought to shut Roz up by explaining what she was doing with the food, but she was fairly sure that Roz would dismiss it as too slow. Roz's mind was not adapted to fine-tuning of this kind. And Helen was absolutely certain that Roz would not understand for a moment the way she had chosen to distract Brother Milo from what she was really doing. She had seen at a glance that Brother Milo was incorruptible. So she had told him that she had come to Kitchen to seduce him. Brother Milo had at once, and with great glee, dropped all his complaints about her lavish cooking and dared her to try. As far as he was concerned, Helen could do what she liked to the food as long as he kept his Oath. By now they were locked in this slightly strange contest, in which Brother Milo had to win without suspecting that Helen was letting him win, while Brother Milo tacitly ignored the fact that Helen was now ruling Kitchen. But Roz would certainly think this was just silly.

The brackets deepened round Helen's mouth as she considered what to say. "You have to remember we're all quite busy most of the time," she said, with her mind on the bustle in the long chain of rooms, the heat, the smells, and attacks of hysteria from Brother Feno or Brother Maury, one them chasing a cadet with a ladle, and everyone else in fits of laughter. Flan looked at her with respect and wished she had thought to say that. "Say six," Helen said judiciously, and allowed her mouth to spread in a wry smile. Why was it, she wondered, that a great long creature like herself always, unfailingly, fell for small men like Brother Milo?

"Forty-eight," said Roz. "Judy?"

Judy colored up. "Just the one. And," she added tremulously, "that's all there's going to be."

While Flan, Sandra, and Helen carefully kept their faces noncommittal, Zillah looked from one to the other and began to feel as desperately innocent as Edward, or even

Marcus. Marcus—probably luckily, given the nature of Roz's interrogation—was fast asleep across Zillah's legs, clutching his new bag of toys. While Zillah had simply been enjoying herself, it seemed that the rest of them had been making a cynical attack on the virtue of the citadel. Well, it stood to reason. They had come here to make an attack of some kind. But it made Zillah see that she was a complete outsider here. And I bet Roz doesn't even bother to ask me! she thought.

Sure enough, Roz said, "Grand total of forty-nine! Not bad for two days. If we keep this strike rate up, enough mages will have enough fun to spoil every vibration going. A week ought to bring the fortress down."

"Oh, but it won't," Zillah said. Five faces turned her way, Roz's irritated, the others surprised, questioning and perhaps even faintly pleased. She tried to explain. "It *likes* fun—the citadel, I mean. Can't you feel? People keep repressing it, and it's just sort of *itching* for something to enjoy."

Roz turned away. "Do try not to talk nonsense, Zillah. You just don't have the training the rest of us have had. Everyone knows this is a serious, evil place."

Zillah was somewhat consoled for this snub by Flan, who rolled over to whisper, "I like fun too. But don't tell teacher."

5

Tod found himself with sudden, immense popularity. Every serviceman and nearly every cadet was overnight his firm friend. Tod was amused. The speed of it amused him. So did the various approaches. Cadets in their second year, who were total strangers, came up to him with the serious, haunted look of those who were having strong second thoughts about being mages at all, and either chatted about Frinjen or offered to help with Tod's work. Cadets in their first year bought Tod drinks at the buttery—Arth passet beer, as Tod informed Zillah, was far worse than the food—and tried to find out from him what might please Zillah. So did nearly all the servicemen except Rax. Rax, being Rax, simply asked what Tod would take for giving him an hour alone with Zillah.

To everyone except Rax, Tod said that Zillah would like toys for Marcus. He told them this because it displeased him that Zillah had apparently rushed aboard that capsule without even thinking that Marcus might need something to play with. It was one of several faults Tod found in Zillah. But to Rax, he said in a dark whisper, "I don't advise it. She's worse than the Ladies of Leathe. Five minutes with her could well blow your mind—it comes close to blowing mine, and I've got my birthright to help me!"

This, he thought ruefully, could almost be true. Whatever peculiar magecraft it was that Zillah possessed, he
sensed it was very strong indeed. He was glad that she
chose to exercise it so seldom. And anyone would defend
Zillah from a lad like Rax. But he sometimes wondered
why he held the rest off her. It was pure dog in the
manger. That first afternoon when Zillah had been so
pleased to see him, Tod had had great hopes. Then, the
next day, he had come upon her sitting in a blue window
embrasure, looking out into Arth's blue empty sky, and
realized that his hopes were just wistful phantoms. One
glance at her sad profile, and he had known there was
a wall around Zillah and that someone else was inside
the wall with her.

"Did you come here to get away from—someone?" he
had asked her, almost literally out of the blue.

"Yes," said Zillah. The sadness of that one word was
terrible.

"Then you've come to the right place," Tod answered
cheerfully, watching his hopes swirl away down an imagi-
nary plughole. "You've got Josh and Philo and me to take
your mind off it."

He did wish she had not given him that particular
grateful, friendly smile.

All the same, he and Philo and Josh spent every available spare minute with Zillah. When Marcus was not too
restless, she sat in on classes with them, despite Brother
Wilfrid's sour looks, and seemed surprised at how much
she learned even when she had to carry Marcus out
halfway through most of the time. This was another
thing about Zillah that irritated Tod. She was so plumb
ignorant of magework. It was almost as if she refused
to learn on purpose, and possibly encouraged Marcus
to make a noise so that she could leave. He allowed
that this was partly due to lack of confidence—someone,
way back in Zillah's history, had evidently sapped her

confidence pretty badly—but he also suspected it was due to arrogance. In some secret place in her mind, Zillah felt she had no *need* to learn.

Josh had detected this too. Centaurs had somewhat the same arrogance. "Come on. Admit it. You're proud of not knowing," Josh said to her. And Zillah laughed guiltily, proving Josh right.

Tod knew he was finding faults in Zillah as a defense against falling in love with her. It was not only her looks. She was such good company too. They wandered about the citadel, talking of everything under three suns, and Tod found himself prattling to her as he had not found himself able to prattle since he left home.

"What *is* passet?" Zillah asked.

All three of them groaned. "A grain, lady," Philo told her. "I'm told the centaurs used to live on it."

"Only when desperate," Josh protested.

"It grows dreadfully easily, particularly in the north of the Pentarchy," Tod prattled. "It used to be what poor folk had to eat. When there was a passet famine, that was *real* famine. So the government tried to prevent famines by putting up a reward for growing passet—that was a few hundred years ago, and naturally no one ever remembered to repeal the law. There's always a huge passet mountain. They make a lethal spirit out of it in Trenjen. But until I got to Arth, I always wondered what they did with the rest of it. Now I know. They just send it all here."

"There are grain cellars full of it," Josh said, pointing downward.

"We'll show you if you like," Philo offered.

"Oh, *would* you?" Zillah said. Her delight at the thought of going into the bowels of the citadel was so sincere that Philo wrapped his arms around her. Philo was one of those who was always embracing people he liked. This was what had caused him such trouble with the Brotherhood. But Tod suspected, from the look on Philo's face, that it was not just friendship where Zillah was concerned; and he had a notion that Philo had discovered, like himself, that Zillah was only open to friendship.

No one else in the citadel believed it was just friendship. Philo and Josh were petitioned as often as Tod was for Zillah's favors. Arth was filling with rumors and randy stories. Chief among them was one—which Tod thought might be fact—that the woman in boots had slept with every soul in Observer Horn and was open to any other offers. There was known to be some kind of bet on over the black girl in Calculus, and though the stories varied about the small, lively woman, there were jokes about the way Ritual Horn literally danced attendance upon her. Meanwhile Maintenance had opened a book upon the virtue of Brother Milo and the High Head. You could only get 2–1 on the chances of Brother Milo, but they were offering 100–1 that the High Head would not keep his Oath until the end of the week. There was some bitterness about the way the High Head seemed to exploit his position. He kept calling the women to his room. Zillah confirmed that she had been called in twice, and she confessed to Tod that High Horns terrified her.

"You're not the only one," Tod said. "I do dislike that man." And he went off to collect toys for Marcus in a sack that Josh had filched from Healing Horn. Tod called it the Charity Bag. He took it around with them and watched with pleasure as it filled with mascot dolls, cubes and prisms and other hardware from Observer and Research, a wonderful model train made by a lonely Brother, a boat, and wax images from everywhere. It gave him enormous pleasure to watch Marcus tip them all out, crying, "Ooh! Doy!"

Tod turned to Zillah. "There. You see? I'm a truly expert uncle."

By the third day, all of them except perhaps Marcus were sick of the blaze of attention. Instead of attending a parade in the square where Zillah got so giddy, Tod planted Marcus and his Charity Bag on Josh's back, Philo took Zillah by the hand, and they all descended the ramps into the lower parts of the citadel to show Zillah the stores. Tod saw afterward that he should have persuaded Josh at least to stay for the parade. A solitary centaur is noticeable, present or absent. But at the time they thought no more about it than to laugh with guilty pleasure.

"Playing hooky," said Tod. "I used to be an expert at it. Life in this citadel takes me right back to school."

They went slowly. The blue ribbed surface of the lower ramps was steep for Josh's hooves, and the light, away from living quarters, was kept dimmer. When they reached the first of the huge grain cellars, there was hardly light enough to see the mountain of passet, heaped up into the distance.

"It looks almost like wheat," Zillah remarked.

"Bed," Marcus announced.

"Quite right, infant," Tod agreed. "It smells vile. Just look at it all! Enough to feed a thousand Brothers for at least a year, even if they ate nothing else—which they almost didn't until that life-saving Helen person got into Kitchen."

"They grow mushrooms in it when it goes bad," Josh said.

"And then it smells even worse," Tod said, starting to move on.

Philo, however, hung back at the grainy foot of the mountain, sniffing wistfully. "It reminds me of home," he said.

"I was forgetting you came from the Trenjen Orthe," Tod said. "Rather you than me!"

"I wish I was back there," said Philo.

He sounded so yearningly homesick that Zillah asked sympathetically, "What is the Trenjen Orthe?"

"My bit of the Pentarchy," said Philo. "The Fiveir of Orthe is all over the place."

"In order to understand our friend," Tod prattled, leading the way on down the next ramp, "you must realize that the Pentarchy consists of five onetime kingdoms, or Fiveirs, now united into one. These are Frinjen, Trenjen, Corriarden, the Orthe, and Leathe. Apart from Leathe, each Fiveir is governed by its own Pentarch—one of these is the old buffer who happens to be my father. The king governs the whole country, but he is also Pentarch of the Orthe—which is quite a job, because, apart from a lump in the middle of the continent, the Orthe is scattered over everywhere else but Leathe, in lots of little enclaves. I think it's where the Other Peoples happened to live. Philo's lot of gualdians—who no doubt had their reasons—chose to take up their abode in the north and put up with the weather and the passet, so that became part of the Orthe, instead of being part of Trenjen."

"But I'm from central Orthe," Josh said, following Tod downward with braced hooves and little mincing steps, "which is much more sensible. Most of my people are."

"Sensible? Or just from the Center?" Tod called back.

"What exactly makes you a gualdian?" Zillah asked as she and Philo followed Josh.

"It's hard to explain. I'm not typical," Philo replied. "Most of us have a great deal of body hair—in fact, the usual way to tell a gualdian-human cross is that they look rather furry."

"Not our beloved High Head, though," Tod shouted up irrepressibly. "Unless he shaves all over daily, that is. He's vain enough. He might."

"No, but you can tell he's a cross from the eyes," Philo said. "That's the main sign usually." He turned his great wide eyes toward Zillah. She looked at them closely. In the dimness they seemed very penetrating and luminous, as well as large, but they looked like human eyes to her. So, come to think of it, did High Horn's eyes. "But most of the time," Philo went on, nuzzling closer to Zillah as his way was, "it's quite hard to tell, particularly with gualdian women. And look at *me*. The only hair I have is on my head, and I was born with these enormous hands and feet. My parents took one look at me and consulted the Gualdian. And he said, a bit helplessly, that it was to be hoped that I'd grow into something special—which I didn't. But I think they kept on hoping. It was the Gualdian who sent me over to Arth. Maybe he thought *they* could bring something out in me."

"Did they?" Zillah asked.

"No," said Philo as they rounded the ramp into the next level.

"As if Arth could bring anything out in anyone!" Tod said. "The Gualdian must be senile to think it could. Here, Zillah, we have the first of Arth's main reservoirs. Enough water to last the citadel for years. And, since the Brotherhood sometimes amazes the rest of the Pentarchy by being practical from time to time, they use their reservoirs to breed fish in."

Zillah was already staring at a high glass wall behind which, in nightlike gloom, swam a shoal of small silver fish. Other bigger fish stirred in the dimmer distance. The lighting down here was just bright enough for her to see their five twilit reflections murkily mirrored in front of the fish, Philo all hands and feet and clinging, limber movements; herself and Tod both neat and quick; and Josh's great silver body, which seemed to draw all the light to itself and focus that light on the small, vigorous figure of Marcus on his back. Marcus liked the glass surface and the fish. He made Josh go close so that he could push the boat from his Charity Bag across it.

"Voom-voom," he murmured, happily ignoring the fact that his boat had sails.

At intervals along the glass wall were curious faucets, which Tod explained were fish traps. You drew the fish into them by magework. "I'd show you, if I only knew what we'd do with the fish once we got it," he said. "But no one's going to notice if we pinch some mushrooms for Josh on the next level."

"I'd kill for fresh mushrooms!" Josh told Zillah. He moved slowly along beside the glass for Marcus to push his boat. It was warm and secret there, with only the half-seen fish and their own reflections, and it made Josh as confidential as Philo. "It was the same for me," he said, "as it was for Philo, really. They said a weedy centaur with knock knees has no excuse for existing unless his natural magecraft is something unusual. Mine isn't— but I'm sure that's why the king ordered me to Arth. I was lined up with rows of really good specimens, and he chose me. He said he expected great things."

"Only after your year's up," said Tod. "This place is inimical. I wish I was anywhere else most of the time. The only good thing to happen here is Zillah."

Zillah laughed, but she had never been able to handle compliments, and she had to change the subject. "Is the king the same as the Gualdian?"

"Good gods, no!" the three native Pentarchans cried out together. Philo explained, "The Gualdian is only for gualdians."

And Tod added, "Clan chief, sort of. The king is for everyone. He's an odd fellow, our monarch, very modern type. Wears thick glasses and likes to trot out shopping with a string bag. To look at him, you wouldn't think he had an ounce of birthright."

"But he must have," said Josh, "or he wouldn't be king."

"At least," Philo said, with his chin resting on Zillah's shoulder, "our Gualdian looks the part."

"And renowned for his silver tongue," said Tod. "They say he once sweet-talked an archangel—or was it Asphorael?—into fetching his newspaper every day!"

Philo shot straight beside Zillah. "That's a lie!" She could feel his body almost twanging with anger. And though there was no apparent change to that body, in the glass of the reservoir, Philo's reflection blurred. It seemed to be flaring and shimmering around the edge. Was this what made him gualdian and different?

"You still haven't said," she interrupted hurriedly, "what makes a gualdian a gualdian. How would I tell a gualdian woman, for instance?"

"She'd be stunningly beautiful for a start," Tod said, and Zillah had no idea if he knew how offended Philo was. "One of my uncles married a gualdian lady, and she's still stunning, even though my cousin Michael's the same age as me. Otherwise you'd think she was human. She's not the kind to go round telling everyone she was born with second sight. She—"

Tod *had* known, Zillah saw. Philo forgot his anger and inquired with great eagerness, "Which branch of us is she?"

Josh winked at Zillah. "Now, that's typical gualdian. Family, family."

"Frinjen," said Tod. "Town-gualdian from the estate at Haurbath. But you might just know her. Her family has estates in the north too. Hang on a moment. With all this glass to reflect off, I can easily project you a likeness." He stepped back and drew upon his birthright.

To Zillah, still wondering at the way everyone here took magework so much for granted, it looked as if Tod shook his shoulders a little and then—possibly—thought hard. Josh shifted a hoof, sparing it, quite unconcerned. Even Amanda, Zillah thought, never took witch-craft so calmly, and it had been part of her life for twenty years now.

"Look there," Tod said, pointing.

An image grew in the glass, brighter than their own reflections and somewhat above them. It was the head and shoulders of a radiant woman with long black hair and the most striking dark eyes—all so dense and real that the shoal of pinkish fish swimming behind the image was all but hidden.

Marcus's hand became a starfish, pointing. "*Badder!*" he shouted. Zillah, equally astounded, first looked around to see if Amanda was standing somewhere behind and above, and then, finding nothing but dark blue wall, had to struggle with tears. Oh *Lord*, I miss Amanda! Why did I leave? That really might be *her*.

Philo added to her shock by saying, "Oh, *Amanda*. She's my second cousin. Is she really your aunt?"

"By marriage," said Tod. The way he said it made it clear to Zillah's shocked, heightened senses that this Amanda had somehow conferred an honor on Tod's family—which surely, unless she had gravely misunder-stood, was itself one of the highest in the land—simply by marrying into it.

"She's been a widow for years," Philo said, as if this excused the lady. This made Zillah struggle to replace Philo—and perhaps the whole gualdian race with him—in a social bracket above Tod's.

"Yes, but she just remarried, did you know?" said Tod.

"I did. The second man was not gualdian either," Philo answered, with unmistakable strong disapproval.

Marcus all this while continued to bawl, "*Badder!*" at the bright image. Josh swiveled his torso around in the way that was natural to a centaur but which made Zillah's vertebrae ache every time she saw it, and silenced Marcus

with a small shake. "What's the matter with him?" he
asked Zillah.

The tears in her eyes ran off down her cheeks. Her voice
cracked as she answered. "That—that lady's the absolute
image of my elder sister. She—she's called Amanda too,
would you believe?"

Something belligerent vanished from Tod, and so
did Philo's stiffness. They both turned to Zillah. "Oh,
great Goddess!" said Tod. "Analogues! What a pity
my Amanda doesn't have a sister, or you might get
to meet yourself." Philo, seeing Zillah's tears, started
to put his arms around her. Tod pushed his reaching
hands aside. "No, you clinging vine! It's my turn this
time." He wrapped his own arms around Zillah in a
hearty embrace. "It's quite all right," he prattled. "You're
the sister of my favorite aunt—or you would be if she
had one. Don't cry. Please. I'll take you to see her as
soon as this horrible year's over and we can get on a
transport."

Distress, homesickness, the relief of being comforted,
caused Zillah to put her head on Tod's shoulder and
cling to him. Her tears leaked into the prickly blue cloth
of his uniform. The warmth of him suffused her. She had
not felt this warm since Marcus was born—as if she had
been perpetually two degrees in arrears.

Tod found her frank leaning on him a decidedly sexual
experience. Her body was the most satisfying shape to
have his arms around and to have pressed against his. At
the edge of his senses, he noticed Josh moving away with
Marcus, probably so that Marcus should not be upset
by his mother's misery. Philo followed him, shrugging,
rather annoyed. Tod waited until both his friends were
out of sight on the next downward ramp and then fell
to comforting Zillah like anything. Though he was quite
aware that comforting was all Zillah would let him do,
this did not stop him kissing her ear and her cheek, and

then moving her around, gently but forcibly, so that he could at last kiss her mouth.

He had reached this stage, and the image of Amanda that had caused the kiss had faded away—Tod having forgotten entirely by then how he came to start—when Brother Wilfrid advanced down the ribbed passageway, accompanied by his own righteously triumphant reflection in the glass of the reservoir and, with a flick of sanctimonious fingers, froze Zillah and Tod in place while an image of them was transmitted to the mirrors in the office of the High Head.

"I knew this was what I would find!" said Brother Wilfrid, and his voice trembled with what Zillah and Tod both detected to be a variety of unhealthy emotions.

VII

Arth

★

1

The High Head felt put upon. Breakfast had been too rich. Maybe it was the nagging of an overtaxed stomach, or maybe genuine anxiety, but he knew today that things were not right in the citadel. Those quickening vibrations bothered him. If they had been caused by the onset of the tides, they should have stopped when the tides began, late in the watches of the night. But the tides now ran full, message channels were open to all parts of the Pentarchy, and the rhythms still continued to quicken.

He was inclined to blame it all on their six unwanted guests. The sooner they could all be sent back wherever it was they came from, the better it would be for everyone. But Observer and Calculus Horns, though professing to be hard at work, were producing only increasingly obscure and contradictory results. As for the women, he began to suspect that Flan and Helen at least had unexpectedly expertly shielded minds. All they gave him was the same inane story. Zillah now seemed a dangerous mystery. Her child—well, he had long ago given up there.

To add to his troubles, Edward, on whom he was accustomed to rely for sane and self-effacing advice, seemed thoroughly out of sympathy with any of his worries. Take breakfast that morning. The two of them had

as usual arrived in the spare blue room to find it reeking
of coffee. Edward had sniffed the stuff as if it were
nectar, poured himself a great mugful, and announced,
"It's even better than yesterday! Goddess, it's *years* since
I tasted good coffee!" After this he had eagerly snatched
the silver cover off the heated dish on the table to reveal
a great mound of buttered mushrooms, nine-tenths of
which he had eaten as if he actually enjoyed the things.
Then he had set about the hot bread, wrapped in a crisp
blue napkin. "Reprimand Brother Milo?" he said, with
evident astonishment, when the High Head suggested
it. "Why? He's working miracles! Try some of this ginger
conserve."

Nor did Edward seem to feel any urgency about the
women. "They're doing no harm," he said, and then,
leaning forward eagerly, with his face slightly flushed,
"Besides—did I tell you?—the live ones have rather
interesting physiology. I haven't by any means got all my
results yet, but it's beginning to look as if all of them have
what *we'd* call gualdian blood. The pretty one—Zillah—
would probably count as eighty percent gualdian in our
terms. That's quite unusual, you know—or it would be
in the Pentarchy. Gualdians make a great thing about the
purity of their race, but the fact is that they've been inter-
breeding with humans for centuries. You hardly get one
who's as purebred as he likes to claim. In fact, the nearest
thing to a purebred gualdian I've ever come across is that
latest serviceman—what's his name?—Philo, and I think
he may be some kind of throwback. He doesn't look like
modern gualdians at all."

And to the High Head's suggestion that half a doz-
en well-shielded alien gualdians might be more than
enough to disturb the vibrations of Arth, Edward simply
laughed and advised his friend to center himself.

The High Head had no leisure to do that. Once in his
office, he found his daily routine constantly interrupted

by urgent calls from the Pentarchy. Everything poured in with the tide. Trenjen reported that the passet crop had failed and required an instant review of expected climate changes for next season's planting. The King in Council sent majestic formalities and, embedded in them, a disturbing request to Arth to match the observation made by the Orthe surveyors which suggested that the energy flows of the Pentarchy were becoming seriously deranged. And of course, there was Leathe. Leathe Council came on the ether several times in the persons of various High Ladies wishing to know if there was any progress yet in the experiment with otherworld.

The High Head answered the ladies politely and wished he knew too. It nagged at him increasingly that he must plant another agent there, and soon; and, since otherworld seemed to have located at least two of his best, this agent would have to be both exceptional and cunningly planted. But naturally he did not betray this anxiety either to the ladies or to Lady Marceny. Lady Marceny wanted to know as badly as the rest—probably more so, because her aim was transparently to get him to tell her ahead of the rest of the Pentarchy. She gave strong hints that she might impart the secret of her private experiment with otherworld in exchange. But since she left the talking to that wretched son of hers, the High Head doubted if she had any such intention. What Lady Marceny knew, she always kept to herself. This was just as well, because the High Head knew he would have been sorely tempted by now. He looked with disfavor at the vitiated face of her son in his mirror and promised him results soon. Rumor had it that the young man was half-gualdian, but if so, his mother had put him beyond sympathy.

To meet the various demands of the Pentarchy, he was forced to draft more mages to Observer Horn, rearrange schedules, interrupt and curtail routine rituals—He worked through lunch, dourly ordering himself a plate of the parched passet he so sorely missed. It came with honey on the side, which he ignored, with contempt. His temper was already very badly frayed when the news came from Brother Wilfrid.

He stared at the simulacrum of Tod embracing Zillah. Behind them a small, lazy shoal of fishes swam, fluttering gauzy fins, opening foolish mouths, and for a moment the fish seemed to have all his attention.

He pulled himself together and gave the required orders. "Bring the serviceman here at once, and use the strongest mages for the guard. Remember the man has Pentarch birthright and could be dangerous. Keep the young woman apart. I'll see her when I've dealt with the serviceman."

That Zillah could stoop to make love to Tod really hurt. The High Head was not aware of hating Tod particularly, but he saw—with passionate relief—that here was his chance to get rid of him in a way most profitable to Arth.

The real stumbling block was the inevitable reaction from the Pentarch of Frinjen. The High Head was careful to keep abreast of affairs at home. He was well aware that Tod's father, August Gordano, despite being a fool, had, if he chose to use it, enormous clout in the Pentarchy. Even Lady Marceny referred to August as "that bluff old sweetie" and seemed—surprisingly—to value his opinion. Furthermore, Roderick Gordano was Frinjen's only son. Even Arth was not free to deprive a Fiveir of its sole heir. That would bring the king in, heavily, on Frinjen's side.

With thoughtful eagerness, the High Head contacted Records Horn and had them send the Gordano family tree through to his main mirror. It was headed by *August wed Amy Adonath* and followed by no less than six daughters preceding young Roderick into the world.

The High Head shuddered a little at such crude per-
sistence. The good Amy must be nothing more than
a brood mare. He moved the display with a gesture,
searching for males to whom the birthright could also
descend. Five of the daughters had sons, any of which
were likely—but Pentarchs never did favor the female
line. The High Head was in sympathy with that, though
he could at a pinch argue— Ah! This was better. Going
back a generation, August's father had married twice.
One son survived from this second marriage (though
with the symbol alongside his name that suggested dubious personal morals). The younger son of this marriage
was long dead, having wed a gualdian woman. Interesting. *His* son, however, survived: Michael Gordano, born
within a month of Roderick.

That settled it. Tod had a cousin supremely well qualified to hold the birthright. August Gordano could shout
all he liked, but no one could say Arth had left Frinjen
without an heir. Arth had its laws. Gordano had been
caught breaking them. No one could bully Arth into false
leniency.

He banished the display as Brother Wilfrid entered,
breathless but very ready with his version of the matter.

"And that's about the size of it, High One. I've known
all along the fellow was subversive. He's been brought
up to think himself entirely above the law—and for that
we should pity him, of course—but his total levity is all
his own. He regards Arth as a joke, High One. As for
that unclean woman—!"

The High Head looked into Brother Wilfrid's pale face
and saw it quivering with prurient hate. "Center yourself, Brother Instructor!"

Brother Wilfrid did so—or at least contrived to control himself a little—with obvious effort. "The centaur
and the gualdian servicemen are down there, too, somewhere, sir. We don't know their exact role in the affair,

but they certainly connived at it. They missed parade without excuse and are now hiding. We're looking for them now."

"Scared, I suppose," said the High Head. In the normal way, a centaur and a gualdian would form a powerful combination. But—he thought of the pallid horse-man, birthmarked and knock-kneed, and skinny Philo with those enormous hands and feet—not those two. "Send them to me as soon as you find them. I'll see Gordano now."

Before Tod was marched in, the High Head made efforts at least as strenuous as Brother Wilfrid's to center himself. He thought he had. Therefore, it was quite a surprise to him that the mere sight of Tod's jaunty figure and cool gaze brought him ablaze with anger— though why the anger should be accompanied by deep hurt puzzled him more than a little.

"Well, serviceman," he asked, "what have you to say for yourself?"

"Nothing," Tod said frankly. "I was doing what I was doing, and Brother Wilfrid came along and saw me, and that's all there is to it really." There seemed very little else he could say. But he did not deceive himself that his frankness pleased the High Head. He could feel anger beating off the man, like the heat when you open an oven. He saw that the result of this anger would be an even heavier penance than he had been expecting: fasting, compulsory prayer, maybe a very stiff term of solitary confinement—or perhaps worse. There were whispers, he remembered, of extremely horrible punishments of a secret nature—but here Tod found he had lost all desire to speculate and simply composed himself to receive whatever it was.

The High Head thought, You think your birth makes it impossible for me to touch you, don't you? "In short, you admit to being taken in oathbreaking."

The angry grind in his voice caused Tod to jump slightly and find he was not as composed as he thought. "Only after a fashion, sir. With respect, I'd like to point out that as a serviceman, I haven't taken any Oath to break."

"But you were made aware that you are legally required to follow the laws of Arth during your year of service, *and* that the Oath is an important part of those laws," the High Head stated. "You must also be aware that your sensual dallying has seriously disturbed the rhythms by which Arth survives."

Damn it to hellspoke, I only *kissed* her! Tod thought. For a base moment he thought he would tell the High Head some of the rumors that were going around about the woman in boots—and she *could* be disturbing the vibes, even if only half of it was true—but the next moment he rightly concluded that the angry High Head would only see that as a whining attempt to incriminate others. "No," he said. "At least, I suppose the rhythms must be wrong if you say so."

"I have," said the High Head, still in the flat, grinding voice of anger, "heard enough. And since you come before me without the slightest sign of contrition, your punishment will be the utmost reserved for those who trouble Arth's fabric in this way. You will be banished to otherworld—"

Tod looked up, astounded. "But—"

"Silence," said the High Head. "I'm well aware that you are heir to a Fiveir and consider yourself immune to punishment, but I have acquainted myself with your family tree, and I know you are not the only heir. You have a cousin and four nephews who can easily take your place. Am I not right?"

"Yes, but," Tod said feebly, "I was only going to say this will kill my old father, sir."

"You should have thought of that before," the High Head told him, with considerable triumph. "It is now too late. Your banishment begins as soon as the necessary ritual transposes you. And, since you are so amorously inclined, I am going to place you in otherworld as the lover of a certain female. You will use your relationship with her to obtain information which you will then pass on to me. The weave of the ritual will leave your mind linked to mine so that you may do this. Have you understood?"

Tod nodded, although in fact his mind seemed barely able to grasp more than the sounds the High Head was uttering. He could scarcely think. Feeble little phrases rotated in his head: It's not fair—I only kissed her— He can't *do* this—It's not fair— Around and around. His mind seemed to have given up. Dimly he wondered if the swine in front of him had put some kind of clamp on his intellect.

"Right," said the High Head. "High Brother Nathan will instruct you further in your mission, and if you have any questions when you get to otherworld, the present agent can answer them." He turned aside and summoned High Brother Nathan by sigil. When the Horn Head of Ritual duly appeared, somewhat flushed and disheveled, the High Head said, "Take this man away and prepare him for immediate transposition to replace agent Antorin. I'll be along in ten minutes precisely to officiate."

He turned back to Tod and gestured. It gave him strong satisfaction to watch Tod's trim figure be snatched away backward out of his presence, with the most uncharacteristic expression of stunned dismay on his face. So satisfied was he that he did not realize until Tod was gone that he had not, as he always did with his agents, privately told him the lie that he could come back if he behaved himself flawlessly. He found he did not care. He could dangle

that bait when Gordano reached otherworld. "And he
can't come back!" he said aloud. "That broke through
his self-possession a bit, I'm glad to see!"

He turned again and summoned Zillah.

She was ushered in, looking distressed and puzzled.
"Look," she said. "I don't quite understand—"

"Silence!" he snapped at her, and it pleased him that
she stopped speaking and quivered as if he had hit her.
"While you are here in Arth, you are subject to Arth's
laws, and you have just seriously transgressed these
laws."

Zillah was as incredulous as Tod. She could not bring
herself to take this seriously. "Oh, come!" she said, tremulously half smiling, "Tod was only—"

"I told you to be *quiet!*" the High Head more or less
roared at her.

Zillah quivered again and pressed her lips together.
She could see he was in a rage, and she hated people to
rage at her. She drew into herself, shrinking into a corner
of her mind and pulling strong walls around the corner,
as she used to do when Mother screamed at her, while
she tried to understand why he was so angry. When she
thought of the boasts Roz and the others had made, she
could not believe it was simply because Tod had kissed
her. She was hurt, because she had thought until now
that High Horns, though frightening, was a fair man.

The High Head glared at her, breathing heavily, and
promised himself he would break down the wards he
saw her building, just as he had broken Tod's composure. "You—"

The room filled with call-chimes, and the master mirror lit with the sigil of the double rose, the call sigil
of Leathe. Leathe had yet more to say. It caught the
High Head off balance. He was still trying to turn his
mind from Zillah, and sign the call to the outer office
on *Hold,* when the double rose vanished and the face of

Lady Marceny's nasty son filled the glass instead. "Good morning, High Head of Arth."

The High Head whirled on the mirror. "Oh, what is it *now?*"

The young man was not in the least perturbed. He smiled malicously. "Caught you at a bad moment, have I? Well, this won't take long. It's only an ultimatum."

"Ultimatum?" repeated the High Head. "What are you talking about?"

Behind his back, Zillah leaned forward, staring, frozen into a stiff bend, with the word *"Mark!"* on her lips, frozen too. She knew it was not Mark. It had to be another analogue like Tod's image of Amanda. But God! He was like him, whoever he was! This man seemed younger than Mark, in spite of bagging under his eyes and seams on his cheeks, and where Mark was clean-shaven, this one sported a little curl of mustache and a small, pointed beard. Rather like a goat, Zillah thought dispassionately. Unlike Mark again, this one's face was full of malicious glee, with a suggestion of much great-er viciousness hidden behind the satyr's smile. But the voice was identical—and somehow the very differences in him served only to show how like Mark he was. Zillah's frozen heart banged until her chest ached with it. And the misery of her loss poured through her again like a flood through a lock-gate. It had only been in abeyance after all.

"Ultimatum *is* the word," the face in the mirror agreed. His hand, long and elegant and white, and very like Mark's, appeared and gave the little beard a mischievous tug. "There's been a great deal going on here in the three days since I last spoke to you, Magus. The upshot is that we in the Pentarchy are going to give you six weeks—six of *our* weeks, Magus—to get some results. If you don't have something to stop this flooding by then, Arth is going to be discredited and disbanded."

"Nonsense," said the High Head, pulling his mind around to the point. "Leathe has no right in law to threaten Arth. Go and tell your mother that she's making a fool of herself."

"Ah, but it isn't just Leathe." The young man chuckled—no, *giggled,* Zillah thought, like a particularly vicious schoolboy. "This is the whole Pentarchy, High Head. The Ladies have consulted with all the other Fiveirs. Frinjen and Corriarden joined us at once—they're both getting swamped, Magus, while you sit in your fortress doing nothing—and Trenjen came in when the Orthe did. The *king* agrees with us, Magus. If you don't make a move, he'll use his powers."

"Oh indeed?" said the High Head. This had to be a bluff. "Then why haven't I heard from the king direct?"

"I'm sure you will," answered Lady Marceny's son. "But you know how slowly Royal Office moves. Red tape. Protocol. Leathe decided to give you advance warning so that you can get a move on *now.*"

"My humble thanks," the High Head retorted. "Now, do you mind leaving me in peace? I happen to be very busy."

"But certainly," said the young man and vanished from the glass.

His insolence, the High Head thought, was beyond even Tod's. Goddess! How he hated the ruling class! He turned back to Zillah, fueled with additional anger and prepared to break her. To his further annoyance, she was staring at the master mirror with eyes that had become wide and large. Around them the rest of her face seemed pinched in and bluish white, as if she were suddenly near death from exposure.

"Who was that?" she said. "On the screen."

"Only the chief Lady of Leathe's despicable son," he said. "I'm told it's not really his fault he's like he is. His mother has steadily perverted him from the cradle up."

"What's his name?" Zillah asked, in a strange, breathless, unhappy way.

"Herrel—Herrel Listanian, I suppose—he'd take his mother's name since the gods alone know who his father was, though it's rumored the poor wretch was a gualdian—" The High Head stopped himself, exasperated. What was it about Zillah's peculiar powers that always caused him to be sidetracked into patiently answering her questions? No more. "Let us now return to yourself and the way you broke the law," he said coldly. "Arth's laws were not made lightly, you know. By your amorous seduction of young Gordano, you have seriously imperilled the stability of the citadel. I explained this when we first took your people in—and yet you still behave like a whore! What are you—a rutting bitch?"

Zillah had gone back to her first meeting with Mark, the night when he dropped in to speak with someone in the witchcraft circle in Hendon. She had been so bored with them by then. Then she had looked up and there was Mark, speaking in his serious, confidential way with— what was his name? Never mind. It was as if the sun had come out. In the same dispassionate way she had noted Herrel's beard just now, she had noted then that Mark seemed very repressed, probably rather a prig, and realized that it made no difference at all to what she wanted. She remembered the artless, almost greedy way she had made sure she was included in the party that went to the pub afterward. The first opportunity she got, she asked Mark back to her bed-sit with her . . .

"Yes, I think you're right," she said, and looked up at the High Head almost judiciously. "There are times when I seem to behave like that—as if I can't help it. If I *could* hate myself for it, I would, but I can't. You're quite right to call me names."

He gaped at her. Once more she had contrived to send this interview down the wrong track. It was typical of her. Ridiculously, he had an urge to leap to her defense and assure her she was not a whore at all. Nor a bitch. Oh—*women!* "Well," he said, after a pause, "as you seem to have a proper sense of contrition, you had better go away and—er—think about it. But remember: if you do anything like this again, you will be in very great trouble indeed."

What got into me? he wondered as Zillah passed through the veils of the doorway like a sleepwalker. He shook himself and stalked off to Ritual Horn to supervise Tod's departure.

2

66 I must go," said High Brother Nathan, mopping his
flushed face. "So must you. There's going to be a
ritual."

Flan watched him attempt to push the streaks of gray
hair back over the bald center of his head. "One I can't
see?" she asked, composedly zipping herself back into
her trousers. On the whole, she was rather sorry about
the interruption. True, Brother Nathan had shamelessly
blackmailed her. He had found her near as dammit
undressed with Alexander in this very same gallery
and swiftly made his bargain. He had not needed to
say much. The sight of Alexander's face when Brother
Nathan said the word "punishment" had been enough
for Flan. She would have agreed to anything. And she
had gone to the assignation with clenched teeth, only to
discover that Nathan could be quite sweet after all. And
the poor old soul was in a real dither now. I'm getting
quite soppy! Flan thought.

"No, you can't see—you mustn't be seen!" he said.
"Goddess, girl! It was only the merest luck the High
Head didn't have most of you naked in his mirror!"

"All right then," Flan said equably.

But High Brother Nathan had had second thoughts,
evidently not unconnected with the unfinished business

between them. "On the other hand," he said, firmly smoothing gray strands of hair to his scalp, "I don't see that it would do any harm for you to watch, provided you keep well out of sight behind the wall of the gallery. It wouldn't do at all for the High Head to see you were here." He shook his uniform straight and picked up his headdress. "I'll see you," he said, hurrying toward the doorway at the side of the gallery. There he paused, artistically. Flan, who knew a studied movement when she saw one, wondered, What's the old villain up to now? Brother Nathan turned around. "This ritual," he said, "is to punish a serviceman, as it happens. It's the same punishment I mentioned to you in connection with Brother Alexander. Though, of course, we both know Brother Alexander to be blameless, don't we?"

You old bastard! Flan thought. More blackmail! She had no desire at all to see anyone punished, least of all in the way that had brought that look to Alexander's face. As soon as Nathan's stout figure had faded through the veiling, Flan dived after him, only to find herself brought up short with such force that she was bounced back into the gallery. "Bastard!" she shouted. "Blackmailer! I'll give you female harassment!"

She would have shouted a great deal more, but by then, feet were hurriedly and hollowly shuffling in the great rituals room below. Evidently when the High Head ordered a sudden ritual, people jumped to it. Not knowing whether or not the High Head was there in person, Flan decided not to draw attention to herself. But she was still damned if she was going to watch this ritual. After plunging twice more at the veiling without the slightest effect, she sat down on the raked steps of the gallery with her face obstinately between her fists. Out of sight below her, objects clanged, feet continued to shuffle, two voices called off lists in a low murmur, and she could sense the room filling up. This ritual was big.

Incense or something abruptly clouded the air, thick
and sharp as woodsmoke—pine smoke, Flan thought. By
this time she was feeling more than a slight tug of curiosity. She had spent the last two days professionally trying
to improve the way these mages moved, and yet she
had still no idea what the movements were needed for.
When music struck up, the wavery, jangly sort favored
by Arth, she yielded to her curiosity. Just one look, she
told herself. She bounced to her feet and ran downward
to crouch by the balustrade at the edge of the gallery.

She got there just as the High Head swept into the room
through the archway opposite. Flan dared not move. His
eyes were moving all over, now high, now low, checking
up on everything, and the look on his face scared Flan.
She stayed in a crouch, with her chin on the plain cold
stone of the coping, and cursed Brother Nathan all over
again. At the same time, she was frankly fascinated.

She was looking down into blueness, a hundred or
more blue-uniformed mages in a blue stone room clouded
with rising blue smoke. The nacreous metal of the incense
holders ranged in a double star around a space in the
center was the only thing that was not blue, apart from
hands and faces. Around the central space, the Brothers
were standing in a complex zigzag pattern, some facing
the center, some lined up sideways to it. As the High
Head raised his sword-wand, they sang, long bass notes
that vibrated through Flan's knees on the floor and her
chin on the coping, while the musical instruments, still
out of sight underneath, jangled a bewildering shrillness
around the song. The effect was to make Flan decidedly
dizzy, and for the first time, she found she was ready to
credit all this talk of vibrations in Arth.

She did not at first notice the young man being hustled
through a narrow corridor between the standing mages.
She saw him only when the blue-clad men leading him
thrust him out into the star-space in the middle and

hurriedly retired. Even then she had trouble recognizing him. He seemed dazed and his face was slack. As he staggered into the very center of the space, Flan saw that he was the young fellow who had been so cheerful and kind when they first arrived. Zillah's friend. She forgot the name. She wondered what he had done—no, that was silly. It was just a question of who *with*. Zillah?

The mages began to move. Again Flan became fascinated. Each line of men took its own path of difficult curves and strange zigzags, wheeling smartly at the corners, emerging from the complex of movement at the edges to gesture, bend, and sidestep, then plunging back into what seemed a living, walking maze. They were making, Flan was astonished to see, actual, living sigils of power on the floor of the room. Signs she knew well and signs she had never before seen formed before her eyes, were marked by the deep notes of the song, ratified by the gestures of those mages at the edge, and then re-formed to a new sign. No doubt to the mages down there it was just a muddled sort of dance they had to learn, but from up here she could see lines and patterns of pure power. She could also see, quite as clearly, the mages who slipped up and muddled a gesture or muffed a turn, as many did. They were so *slack*. Tomorrow she would—

The young guy in the center fell heavily to the floor. Flan looked at him almost irritably, for distracting her from the faults of the dance. But what she saw stretched her eyes wide and kept them that way, strained open and staring as if they would never shut again. Blood ran from a knuckle she did not know she was biting. He was melting. No, changing. Under her stretched eyes, he rose into gray, jellylike hummocks, heaving and mounding and shifting, trickling pulpily, until he was a big, slug-colored shape like a frog or a toad, except that, like a slug, the surface of him ran with some kind of slime, glistening stickily in the blueness.

The creature lay humped and pulsing faintly while the dance went on around it, quicker now, with fewer pauses between the deep, sung notes. Smoke gusted upward and stung Flan's staring eyes. Her hair moved and crackled, and she smelled ozone mixed with the smoke. Through the blue wreathing haze, she saw the reptile shape writhe. The slime on it was oozing to big, frothy bubbles, which burst and re-formed and burst again. It flung one desperate paw-thing out as it writhed, clutching for a hold on the smooth flagstones. God, he was in agony! It was like pouring salt on a slug. He was twisting all over.

He was gone.

Just like that, there was an empty, stained space on the floor. Oh my God! What a way to kill someone! Flan's legs jumped straight, ready to carry her away, quick. She knew she was going to throw up. But the ritual was by no means over. Like the rituals she had taken part in at home, it had to be wound down. She was forced to wait there, retching, gulping against her bloodied knuckle, while the lines of power were drawn in reverse, and the music stopped and each mage relaxed and turned to his neighbors, chatting, laughing a little, as if this were all in a normal day's work. Normal! By Flan's watch, the entire ritual had taken a bare twenty minutes, but it felt like a lifetime. She scrambled up and ran. When the veil still did not ler her through, she was sick on the veil, uncaring, and it parted with a shiver as if it were disgusted. Flan bolted forth and ran again.

3

Zillah went like a sleepwalker through bare blue halls and down impossible ramps. Marcus, she could feel, was a long way below and quite safe. She would go there presently. For now her mind was straining to contain that dissolute image in the High Head's mirror. When she tried to put Mark as she had known him beside this other, this Herrel, it seemed almost more than she could do. Mark's image, like a pale moon, would keep sliding behind Herrel's bearded face, and only appearing dimly through. She supposed it must be that they were both only half the person they should be. Mark was all solemnity, seriousness, and responsibility, and the face in the mirror had nothing but humor, wickedness, and sly malice. Both half the person—both halves of a person. Well, there was no knowing about analogues, of course, but if you thought of them as identical twins— Analogues were like twins in a way—twins brought up apart from each other—the same person put in a different environment, so that different aspects of his personality were enhanced. No, because it was known that identical twins turned out quite alike all the same. With these two, Zillah thought that each must have repressed at least half of himself. Mark certainly had. Zillah bitterly recalled her vain search for humor in Mark—the sheer fun that

instinct told her was really part of Mark's character—
and her frustration when he seemed to be constantly
withholding it from her. With Herrel, she suspected she
would search equally vainly for any kind of seriousness—but it *must* be there! Yet now Zillah could not
rid herself of a feeling that there had never been any
humor in Mark to find. She was sure of it, having seen
this Herrel—as if she had stumbled on the missing half
of Mark.

At this, it came to her like a bolt of electricity, *Why
not?*

The question jolted her out of her sleepwalking state.
She looked up and around the curved blue corridor where
she found herself, to find it ringing faintly, as though the
bolt of electric thought had somehow struck it physically.
She could smell ozone.

And here, around the corner, just as if the striking
bolt had called her up, Flan Burke came hastening.
Or maybe a better word was fleeing, or scuttling.
Flan's face was pale, and her manner uncharacteri-
stically dithery. "Oh, thank God!" she said. "Zillah!
I thought I felt you around. Zillah, something awful's
happened to your friend—I've just seen the nastiest
little ritual—he *was* your friend—I mean that dapper little fellow with the slightly smart-ass air—you
know—"

"Tod," said Zillah. "You mean Tod?"

"Yes, I think I mean him—the other one you go round
with apart from the centaur boy and the kid with big
feet—"

"Yes. Tod," said Zillah. Flan's eyes had dark bags
under them and she reeked of sweat. What *was* the matter with her?

"Yes, well, High Horns and my Ritual boys have just
disappeared him," Flan said. She gulped back a retch and
leaned against the wall, shaking. Her teeth chattered. "It

was—awful. They dragged him to the middle—he was looking absolutely stunned—I don't know what they did to him—not before, I mean. The ritual was all living lines of power—I saw that—and it was quite short really— it just felt like several lifetimes. But, Zillah, first he— sort of changed—he kind of melted into something gray and lumpy and slimy—and they boiled him—I knew it hurt—and then he *went*. He wasn't there anymore, Zillah. Then they all packed up as if it was all just one more job in the day and left. After that I didn't care if High Horns saw me. I ran. But, Zillah, what did they *do*?"

"I don't know." Anger scoured Zillah—a different form of electricity. So High Horns had punished Tod. He has punished Tod and turned me loose with just a caution! The injustice of it filled her with rage, and the clean blast of that rage seemed to make a whole lot of things clear to her. She had wondered that this place did not seem evil. Now she knew that evil *was* here. How stupid—how *innocent*—of her not to have remembered that evil seldom appeared to *be* evil! "I'm sorry, Flan," she said. "I've got to go. I must find Marcus."

"*Go?*" Flan wailed. She did not want to be left alone. "Can I come with you?"

"No, you stay here and go on spoiling the vibrations," Zillah said. "From what High Horns said, the place is practically rocking on its moorings. Push it right over. Have fun. Now I have to go." She sprinted away down the nearest ramp with a speed that surprised Flan.

"Damn!" Flan said, sinking to a crouch against the wall. "Have fun, she says! I could cry. I want to go home. I think I hate magic."

Zillah ran. She fastened her mind on that place where she had always been conscious that Marcus was and continued downward towards it, ramp after ramp. She was aware, as she ran, that this did seem like her usual habit of ducking out as soon as things got nasty. But it was not, not this time. Perhaps all the other times she had ducked out were simply a preparation for this time. She could do nothing about Tod, not here, not now, but she could help his friends, and after that she could go on to fight her own battle.

Down she went, where the lights got dimmer. Among the *pat-pat* of her own feet, she heard the beat of others. Brothers in search parties seemed to be everywhere. Blue uniforms hurried past below the next ramp. There were more in the distance at the end of a corridor. A further ramp down, blue uniforms milled in a storeroom beside her. They bothered Zillah not in the slightest. She was somehow aware that there was a path, twisting and intricate, between all these searchers, and timed to miss every single one, and she took that path. It led her, a breathless ten minutes later, to a corner behind a deep fish reservoir where Philo and Josh lurked with Marcus.

She heard Philo's whisper before she saw them. "No, it's only Zillah, Josh." She rounded a corner and found them. Josh was backed right into the corner, more or less wedged into a space only just big enough to contain him, with Marcus crouched between his front legs and Philo behind, right underneath. They all relaxed as they saw her.

"Dare Dillah dum!" Marcus proclaimed. The tone of his voice was *I told you so!*

"What's happened?" Philo whispered, peering out above Marcus. "The place is full of Brothers hunting for us. Are we in big trouble?"

"I think you may be," Zillah said, and she told them what Flan had told her.

Their faces twisted into almost identical worried horror. They were quite at a loss. Philo crawled out from under Josh and mechanically planted Marcus on Josh's back. "Goddess!" he kept whispering. "We *are* in trouble!"

Josh protested, "But I've never heard—no one ever said anything about that kind of ritual!"

"But it's what they meant," said Philo, "when they talked about punishments."

"Then what shall we do?" said Josh.

"What I'm going to do," said Zillah, "is to leave Arth. There's someone I've got to see, over in your main world. Why don't we all go there?"

Josh and Philo looked at each other and then back at Zillah. "Zillah, I don't think you understand," Josh told her kindly. "There's no way to get to the Pentarchy except by personnel carrier when the big tides are running—and the next tides aren't going to be for months."

"Not to speak of the fact that Josh and I would be breaking the law if we go back before we've served our year out," Philo added.

"But if you stay—" Zillah began. There was no point in going on. Along with the mere words, Flan had put into Zillah's mind a strong image of what she herself had seen—Tod melting into something alien and obscene. It was as if Flan had not been able to help conveying it. Zillah knew that both Josh and Philo had received that image in turn, from her. What Zillah found almost impossible to convey to them was the fact that the twisting, intricate path she had seen leading to Marcus was still with her. It led on from Marcus to Herrel. But it was such a strange and delicate thing that there was no image of it that she could convey. It would be like asking them to look at an invisible thread. She simply knew it could be traveled. And she could only try to explain. "Have you been right under this citadel? I mean, when your carrier brought you here, did it orbit the place the way our capsule did?"

"No. It came straight to the entry port," said Philo. "What do you mean?"

"We went up the walls on one side, and over the middle and down the other side," Zillah explained. "And you know how wide the citadel looks—as if it ought to have a flat base miles wide underneath? Well, it hasn't. We went right underneath twice, and each time there was just a blink—only an instant—before we were rushing up the other side again. I think the fortress narrows to a point there. High Horns—I mean your High Head— told us that the place was made out of a piece of ground that belonged to the Goddess. And I think that just there, just at the narrow point, it could still be joined to your world—anyway, I *know* it ought to be."

Philo and Josh looked at each other again, with a slow, stunned sort of hope growing through their anxiety. "Josh," said Philo, "how do you stand with the Goddess? I've never dared ask, but I hope I haven't offended. It may depend on that, whether we—"

He was interrupted by the echoing shuffles of a search party descending the nearest ramp. Josh started into motion with a curvetting leap that threw Marcus forward against his torso. Zillah saw his arms come back to steady Marcus as he vanished into the dimness ahead. Philo seized her hand, wrapping it completely around with his own hand, and they sprinted after Josh together. Behind them, there was silence. The search party had stopped moving to listen, in order to locate the sounds of their feet. Zillah and Philo both ran on tiptoe to cut down the noise, but they both knew they were being heard. They dared not stop. Josh was moving so fast, ahead in the dimness, that they had to keep running or lose him.

They ran, guided by the soft beat of Josh's hooves and the occasional faint glimpse of his white whisking tail. Behind them they could hear the pursuit closing in a multiple rubbery hammer of feet. Philo was gasping before long. Zillah guessed that fear was making him hyperventilate. She grew increasingly anxious. Josh was not on the path she could see so clearly, and they were deviating more from it with every second. She wanted to shout to him about that, and about Philo, but she dared not let the pursuit guess they were in trouble.

Then, to her immense relief, Josh accidentally cut back into the right path by swinging down a ramp, and they caught him up at last. It was so dark down this ramp that Zillah could only see Josh because of the pallor of his coat. He seemed to have his knock knees braced while his hind legs nervously trampled, and he had been forced to spare a hand from Marcus to hold himself up with against the wall. This ramp was unusually steep. Zillah put a hand out to brace herself, too, and found, to her surprise, that the barely seen wall was rough and dewed with water.

"Philo," Josh said, sliding awkwardly downward, "put a whole heap more protection round us—quick. They're doing some kind of strong location magework on us."

Philo's hoarse breathing slowed down and he whimpered slightly with some kind of effort that Zillah could not detect. But she detected the result almost at once. In the same soft, yearning way that Philo liked to wrap his arms around her, something seemed to wrap all four of them in. The dark and narrow ramp went suddenly safe. They crept downward in a calm stronghold, pillowed by something intangible and rather sweet.

Marcus felt it and immediately became very jolly. "Dart," he remarked loudly. "Diting. Ort go dlidder-dlidder."

"Hush, love," Zillah said.

"Doesn't matter," Josh panted. "Philo's good at this—in short bursts. They've lost us completely again."

Zillah wondered how Josh knew. The result, for her, of whatever Philo was doing was that she lost even the faintest sounds from the pursuers. It was like having her head wrapped in a bolster. They slid slowly downward into what seemed a wormhole that grew darker with every step, and warm and wet. All she could hear was Philo's breathing and the somewhat frantic scraping and backpedaling of Josh's hooves.

They rounded yet another corner, and Josh did not go on.

"Dop!" Marcus announced.

"What's the matter?" Philo asked.

"I don't know," said Josh from below. "There doesn't seem to be anywhere to go to."

Zillah found this hard to believe. No one would carve a ramp out of stone that led nowhere. The path she could see in her mind lay clearly onward down there, below Josh's braced hooves. Perhaps it was too narrow for a centaur. Then they *were* stuck. She unwound Philo's hand from hers, put her back against the rough and curving wall, and pushed past Josh. Dark as it was, she could feel that the passage continued to spiral down beyond him, and it was no narrower than before.

"See?" said Josh. She could feel the panic behind his voice. He would have to back himself upward, and he was not sure he could. "We're *stuck!*"

"Nonsense!" said Zillah. In a surge of irritation at Josh's pointless panic, she snatched the hand he had braced against the wall and hauled him forward. He came with a startled trampling.

"Hey!" Philo called from above, panicking too. In his distress, he lost his hold on whatever was wrapping them in, and the dark wormhole instantly became a noisy, sinister little trap, filled with echoes, scufflings, the trickle of water, and the roaring of an unfelt wind.

Zillah found herself suddenly terrified, and furious with the pair of them. They were being such *wimps!* "Hang on to his tail, you fool!" she screamed at Philo, and "Come *on!*" at Josh. She heaved angrily on his hand. Power rose at her need, and wrapped her round.

In another trampling rush, during which the unfelt wind rose to become the roaring of a gale, the three of them staggered on down and were then, abruptly and briefly, weightless in a vortex, which caught them, whirled them, and then, with shocking suddenness, shot them forth into blazing light.

VIII

Earth

★

1

There *was* a way, Maureen thought. Her eyes were closing, and pricking from the smoke with which Joe was filling the flat. She could turn her own tiredness to her advantage—*use* it, in fact—if only she could get Joe off guard. Then she could sleep as long as she liked. She promised herself sleep, held it out as a reward to herself for doing just this last extra piece of hard work. The trouble was, it was mental work. Even wide-awake, that was the kind Maureen was least adjusted to.

She rubbed her eyes to stop the pricking. Held out the reward. Sleep. Carrot to donkey. "I can't think why you do this dirty work," she told Joe.

He stopped in the act of stubbing his latest cigarette into the loaded ashtray. "What do you mean?"

"I mean, I can't think how they induced you to come here and spy. You've told me how you hate it. And I know nothing would induce *me* to go to your place and pretend to be something I'm not."

He looked at her suspiciously, but she had put just the right amount of contempt and boredom into her voice. He laughed. "You'd do it, all right, if you had no choice. They made sure I had no choice, didn't they?"

"How could they?" Maureen wondered. Her manner suggested he had to be lying. "You're at least as powerful a magician as I am—and you know I'm not one to

239

be caught easily. You had your work cut out to set this up, and I wouldn't be here if I hadn't been tired to death." She pretended to think. "You mean they caught you when you were tired too?"

"Of course not," said Joe. "They caught me with a woman."

She laughed, lightly and incredulously, and admired herself for how well she did it. "Cloak and dagger! Incriminating photos! I don't believe it!" God, this was hard work!

"That's not how they do things on Arth," Joe said, with equal contempt. "Mind you, it *was* a put-up job, I'm sure of that now. There were these two girls who came over with the embassy from Leathe. Antorin and I were both fresh from Oath—you won't know what that means, but you can take it from me you feel—well, caught—boxed up before you've had a chance to look around—and we were the two who were told off to guide the party. And I still don't know how they worked it, but it wasn't long before there was only these two and us two. Fresh young things. Both swore they were scared to hellspoke of all the mageworkings going on in Leathe and said they hardly knew any magecraft themselves. We believed them. We were fools, but Oath takes you that way. You realise it's too late and you wish you'd stayed quietly at home in the Pentarchy."

He was distracted. Behind him, on the arm of the sofa, the half-extinguished stub end smoked in the ashtray, a thin, irritating wisp. Maureen kept her eyes on it. Concentrated on it as an annoyance. I *wish* he'd put it out properly! It kept her awake. It also kept a trivial idea at the front of her mind in case he started to notice what she was doing. Very slowly, she started to edge her mind forward to his. "Oath? What Oath?"

"You swear celibacy. It makes sex illegal," he said irritably. His eyes were fixed on misery a universe away. "I see now I was never cut out for it. I fell for that girl—I was like a rutting bull—well, *you* know how I get—and I swear to the Goddess I'll never forget until I die the way they all came bursting in, her Lady, my High Brother— loads of people—and the High Head walking through the lot of them. You feel a right fool. You want to be sick. And of course my sweet little girl who doesn't know any magecraft obliges them all by holding me helpless just as I am. If I ever get back, I'll find her and I think I'll kill her."

Maureen's mind continued to stalk forward, softly as a cat. "And what happened?" she said, still with her eyes irritably on that rising trickle of smoke.

"Trial," he said. "Dragged in and both told we'd earned the death penalty. That was true. Then the High Head visits me in the death cell—I never heard what happened to Antorin, maybe they killed him—and he tells me I could commute my death sentence to exile, by coming here and serving the Brotherhood another way—the way I seemed to be good at, he points out—if I wanted." He laughed, staring into the distance. Maureen crept on. Sleep soon. Soon now. "You know, I was disgusted! I refused. I said I'd broken Oath and I'd rather die. Would you believe that! So he went away. Then he came back and said if I behaved well and got him the information he wanted, Arth wanted, then I'd be allowed to come back—he'd reinstate me in the Brotherhood."

"So you agreed?" Maureen said, inching on.

"Life is sweet," Joe said. Maureen, as she crept, spared an exasperated little thought for the way Joe always had to speak in clichés, even when he was sincere. Go on, go on talking, she thought. Nearly there. Then sleep. "Yes," he said. "I agreed. They put me through the transmutation ritual and I arrived here. And I did my best to be obedient. It was better than being executed, even working in that music shop. But if you ask me—Hey! What are you doing?"

But Maureen was there. Her mind sprang and leaped on his and twined with his and dragged him down with hers like a nixie, wrapped tight together. Sleep, sleep, sleep. On the sofa, both their bodies lapsed slightly and remained utterly still, barely breathing. After a while, the burning cigarette end smothered in the rest of the ash and went out.

2

G ladys had sensed that things had gone wrong. Next day, when she attempted to trace Zillah, she realized how badly.

She withdrew her mind from Arth and considered. The deaths of some of the party, she and Maureen had agreed, were probably inevitable. It had seemed likely that there would be analogues of one or two of the strike force in the pirate universe, and most theories held that two versions of the same person could not exist in the same space.

"Though I did hope it would turn out to be like twins," Gladys remarked to Jimbo, as usual, crouched by her feet. "No reason why not, on the face of it."

What shook her was the evident number of the dead. She had simply not been prepared for two-thirds of them to die. The virus-magic—well, she had no hopes for that really. It stood to reason that those wizards up in Laputa-Blish had ways of protecting themselves from outside magics. She had made them as a psychological device mostly, so that the strike team would not think it was being sent without a weapon. And now, not only were they without a weapon, but both boys and eleven girls were dead. Thirteen analogues.

"I never bargained for *that* number," she told Jimbo.

"It means that the place must be more like here than we'd realized. But *thirteen*, Jimbo. I feel so responsible."

Most dreadfully did she wish that there had been some way of telling who had an analogue in the pirate world and who had not. But when they were selecting the team, neither she nor Maureen could think of any way of finding out. And now what could six girls do in a worldlet full of mages? Except there were not six. When she looked for Zillah, Zillah was—gone. Not dead. Just not there—though there were traces enough to show Gladys that Amanda had been right. Zillah *had* gone with the strike force, even if she was not with them now.

"It's too bad!" she said to Jimbo. "She took that child, and that child's not safe at all. Silly, irresponsible girl. What do I do about that, Jimbo?"

There was no response from Jimbo. She got the impression he was rather carefully keeping quiet. She considered some more.

"It's like this," she said. "Am I, or am I not, making allowance for it being what I want to do? Come on, Jimbo. You know me. Shall we take a hand ourselves?" She found she was grinning as she spoke. The same grin was resonating off Jimbo too, purring and fibrilating through her. Jimbo liked a joke and a bit of excitement as much as she did. "And why not, Jimbo? Someone has to take a bit of thought for that poor child—but the truth is, I've been so *envying* those girls. What did you say? Yes. Well. If there turns out to be another Auntie Gladys over there, it's just too bad, isn't it?"

She heaved out of her chair and shuffled among the jungle for the phone, where she dialed a number in Scotland.

"Aline?" she said, when it was answered. "It's me. It's that emergency at last. I'm going to have to ask you to have the cats for me."

While she spoke, the cats began gathering in a circle

around her, staring accusingly.

"Well, cancel it then," she said. "I'm not having you go off and leave them. They'll feel strange. And they know. They're all here now—except that Jellaby. She knows too, but she's hiding. Just a moment." Gladys broke off to make a brief mental search around the house. Ah. Under the spare bed. After a struggling moment, tortoiseshell Jellaby landed in the midst of the other cats, glaring, distended, and angry. "Stupid," Gladys said to her. "Aline's nothing *like* the vet's." To the phone she said, "That's all of them now, and you'll find they're no trouble. They all look after themselves, except they can't open tins. I'll send the cat food up with them. And you know what to do about the message, don't you? Thanks. 'Bye."

This important matter being settled, Gladys shuffled to the strangely empty kitchen to pick up her fat black handbag. "There's no point in traveling anything but light," she told Jimbo, who still scuttled at her heels, "but I still don't trust that place to make a proper cup of tea." She took up her box of tea bags and emptied two-thirds of them into the bag. "Amanda's going to need the rest when she comes," she murmured, snapping the handbag closed. It was one of those that shut by twisting together two knobs the size of marbles. She stood considering what else she needed. "Nothing for Maureen—she's not coming here at all," she muttered. Then the grin spread on her face again. "And why not?" she said. "It'll be far more fun if I dress up in style."

She shuffled out of the kitchen and upstairs to her dark and cluttered bedroom, where she opened cupboards and chests and proceeded to array herself. She put on first a wondrous cocktail dress dating from the twenties (which had belonged to her great-aunt: Gladys was by no means as old as she liked people to think), an extraordinary creation of limp blue chiffon covered with swags and dangles of glass beads all over. The beads clacked gently with her every movement. To this, after some thought, she added a white feather boa and a flame pink scarf for warmth. To her head, with some puffing and critical grunting, she attached the crownlike headdress that reputedly went with the dress. Apart from further blue beads, its chief feature was a curling blue feather—somewhat crimped with age—which rose from the center of the creation in the middle of her forehead. With this nodding over her face, she bent to consider her feet.

Her normal tennis shoes did not seem to conform with the rest of her. "Got to be comfortable, though," she observed, "and warm. And look expensive."

Bearing these criteria in mind, she fetched out and laboriously trod into her most treasured footgear—a pair of large white yeti boots. She had never worn them much because she had always feared that someone had killed and skinned at least four persian cats to make those boots. But there was a time and a place for everything. She looked at herself critically in the mirror.

"Yes, I know, I know," she said to Jimbo, who appeared to be crouched on her bed, probably surveying her finery with considerable astonishment, "but I don't want anyone to take me too seriously, do I? *You* should know all about that. Besides, *you* may be all right, but *I* need to take my mind off that other Auntie Gladys over there."

It only remained to consider what was the best way to take. Gladys half closed her eyes, cocked her feathered head on one side, and contemplated the defenses surrounding the pirate universe. The window Mark had found was no longer available to her. But there was one spot in the defenses she had had her eye on from the beginning. A careful person could use that spot, provided she had Jimbo to help. The plainest way to use it was to summon her faithful taxi and have it take her to the nearest place of power.

"No, no," she said irritably. "Too much hassle, too obvious, too easily traced, and it's not fair to mix Jim Driver up in this anyway. I'll have a go at getting in from the garden, Jimbo. All we need is a wood of some sort."

She gathered Jimbo in her arms and went downstairs, where twilight had arrived at midday with low, bruised clouds and a storm building. "Hm," Gladys said as she hid the key in the usual place. "Something *is* brewing, isn't it? This looks like a *disturbed* storm to me. But it can wait. Amanda can probably see to it when she gets here."

3

Tod came to himself. He was sick, disorientated, and rather cold. Some of the chill seemed to be due to the garments his uniform had been transmuted into, which left his arms largely bare and struck him as decidedly tight in the crotch, as well as inadequate for the climate of wherever this was. He seemed to be lying face downward on cold, varnished boards listening to the chilly patter of rain. There was a pair of shoes hazily within his line of vision, and he wondered querulously why. As he turned his face to focus on them, the shoes moved—an impatient sideways shuffle. A man's voice from above them said, "Are you with me yet?"

Tod groaned. "Oh, probably," he said. He sat up, considerably increasing his wretchedness.

He was in a cheerless alien room. Everything in it was *like* the contents of rooms he was used to, in that he could recognize a sofa, a table, a cooking stove (Why? Did aliens cook in their living rooms, the way all the shops in Leathe sold lipstick?), a yellow mat on the varnished floor, and a chest of drawers; but each item was subtly and distressingly *different* in its proportions, its color, and the substance of which it was made. It all added up to something that seemed to belong to another dimension entirely—which, he realized miserably, was exactly what it did. He thought he might be going to be sick.

To take his mind off it, he raised his eyes from the impatiently shuffling shoes to the man who was wearing them. He was fair-haired and a total stranger. He was wearing what Tod recognized as an alien version of a sober formal suit, and his blond hair was cropped in a manner that even Brother Wilfrid would have found excessive, since it left the man only with an interesting golden wave drooping across his forehead. Despite this, he was undeniably good-looking. Behind him was the window against which the rain pattered.

"Who are you?" Tod said. At the sight of that cold, wet window, his teeth began to chatter.

"I *was* Brother Antorin—I'm called Tony here," the other answered. "Drink this."

Tod bent dubiously over the mug that was thrust into his chilly fingers. To his surprise, it contained coffee—coffee thin and unfragrant and no doubt subtly shifted from the drink he knew, but drinkable all the same. He drank, and his teeth clattered on the rim. "Where is this?"

"Pengford, Surrey—in what you call otherworld," Brother Tony replied. "These are my lodgings, but they'll be yours from now on. The High Head tells me you'll be taking over from me. I've been posted to Hong Kong instead, thank the Goddess! It looks as if all my obedience has paid off at last. What's your name? You're new since my time in Arth."

"Tod," said Tod. Shaken though he was, he did not want to antagonize this Brother by confessing he was heir to a Fiveir.

"Lucky," said Brother Tony. "I'm fairly sure that's a name here too, so you won't need to get used to a new one. Now, what else do you need to know?"

Probably everything, Tod thought. At the moment all

he could think of was how wretched and how cold he was. Anxious inspection showed him that his feet were in light, laced shoes, but at least they were still feet. The crotch-clutching lower garments were heavy blue cotton, inside which his legs were icy, but still legs; and above those he proved to be wearing a short-sleeved yellow thing of much thinner cotton. Below the little sleeves every hair on his arms stood up with chill, but he still recognized his own arms when he saw them. Funny. On Arth they had given him a distinct impression that he was about to be changed into something quite other. "Have you," he said, "anything warm I can wear?"

"I expect so." Brother Tony went and rummaged in a lower part of the chest of drawers, saying over his shoulder, "You'll find the climate in this sector averages a good ten degrees below what you're used to—unless you're from North Trenjen, of course. That's one of the many reasons why I'm so glad to be going to Hong Kong. Here. This should do."

He tossed Tod a heavy woollen floppy thing made of gray-brown knitting. The maker of it had industriously twisted the stitches into an ornate plaited pattern. It looked ethnic. After turning it around several times, Tod discovered it had sleeves. Possibly it was a wool-work smockfrock. When Tod put it on, it came nearly to his knees, but at least it was warm—although he had a shamed moment when he was glad his parents could not see him in it.

"It's called a jumper," Brother Tony told him. "The people here have queer names for things, but they're actually much more like real people than the experts of Arth seem to think. Are you feeling better now? We've not got much time if I'm to show you the ropes before my flight leaves."

Tod cautiously stood up. The ethnic garment showed no signs of jumping, and to his increasing relief, the messages coming through from his body seemed to be all the usual ones. His left big toe cracked when he put his weight on it, the way it always did, and the ragged edge of his top back tooth caught his tongue in the usual way. His hands putting the empty mug back on the alien table were his own square hands—though they trembled a bit—and his height in relation to Brother Tony was what he expected: quite a bit shorter.

Brother Tony looked at him critically. "You look rather foreign at the moment," he said. "We'd better get your hair cut and perhaps shave off that mustache too."

Tod located a mirror over a white sink-thing. Despite the rainy dimness of the light, it was himself looking back out of it. He had seldom been so glad to see anyone. "Oh no," he said. "My hair stays as it is—all of it. I want to recognize myself when I see me."

Brother Tony did not argue. "Well, I've only got a couple of hours," he said, stooping and picking up a bundle of booklets and papers that had been on the floor beside Tod, "but you'll find you'll want to rethink that hairstyle after you've been here a day or so. These are yours. They came through with you. Arth's getting quite good these days. They're all here—credit cards, bankbook, insurance, checkbook, and they even remembered a driving license. You're better off than I was. I had to get most of this stuff for myself. What do they mean by putting you down as Roderick Gordano?"

"Because that's my name," Tod said. He took the bundle from Brother Tony and sorted through it bemusedly. Otherworld script was balder than that of the Pentarchy, but much the same. Someone had scrawled his name on the various cards and documents without even attempting to imitate his signature. He was going to have to learn to forge his own name. And on such a lot of things. Tod had often complained about the number of documents he was required to carry about at home, but they were not a tenth of these. "My friends call me Tod," he explained to Brother Tony.

"Great. Well, I don't have time to be friends, Roderick," Brother Tony said briskly. "My job is just to make sure you've got it straight in your head what you're here for before I leave for Hong Kong. How much were you told?"

What had that sod—the High Head—said? "I'm supposed to be the lover of some female and report back what she says."

"That's right as far as it goes," Brother Tony said. "Actually, Paulie's the wife of the equivalent of the High Head here in this country, and you're supposed to report about *him*. Paulie's very communicative—you'll see—but Mark's a complete clam. Doesn't let his own wife know what he's up to most of the time, and quite possibly misleads her when he *does* tell her. Paulie and I both know he's been up to something lately, but that's all we know, and that's all I've been able to tell the Head. Did he—our Magus—explain that the ritual gives him a thread to your spoke in the Wheel, so that he comes through direct to your mind?"

Tod shook his head, or nodded. He could not remember. All he knew was growing rage. How had Arth the right to do this to him?

"Well, he does," said Brother Tony. "It can be damned awkward if he comes on at the wrong moment. What else did he tell you? Did he explain that if you behaved yourself and reported faithfully, they'll bring you back to Arth when you've worked out your sentence?"

Tod shook his head.

"No? I suppose they left that up to me to explain. He's told me that often enough—and I assure you, Brother, it pays to be as obedient as you damned well can. Look at me. I asked to be relieved here, and they sent you almost at once. My sense is that I'll be fetched home after this stint in Hong Kong. I've behaved myself, see."

Tod nodded glumly, wondering why Brother Tony seemed so joyous at this idea.

"So if you're ready," Brother Tony said, "I'll take you out and make sure you know where everything is."

"Out?" Tod looked at the window, where raindrops were now pattering less fiercely, but still pattering. "Won't we get wet?"

Brother Tony laughed. "Takes getting used to after Arth, doesn't it? Don't worry. You can wear this." He unhooked a limp blue garment from a hook behind the door and flung it to Tod. It seemed to be a waterproof jacket. Tod put it on and wrestled with the unfamiliar zip, while Brother Tony took up a smart gabardine raincoat from a nearby chair and put that on over his suit. He picked up a shiny leather grip. "Ready?"

Tod gave the zip up as hopeless. The garment was too big anyway. He gathered it around him and followed Brother Tony through the door and down some dingy stairs. "I'd introduce you to the landlady, but she's out at the moment," Brother Tony said over his shoulder, "but you can take it she'll accept you as the new lodger without question. Arth's quite good at that kind of thing." Outside the front door of the house, he ceremoniously handed Tod a small, flat key. "There you are. It's all yours now."

While Tod worked the key into the tight pocket of the cotton trousers, Brother Tony led him briskly down a street lined on both sides with striped brick houses, small, stingy, and ugly. The fact that the rain was now passing into weak, watery sunlight only seemed to make the dwellings look more dismal.

"This is the shabby area," Brother Tony told him blithely. "You'll find it's all you can afford. Costs are high here."

They rounded a corner into a larger road. Here the

buildings were larger and flat-faced and full of windows and constructed either of raw red brick or raw gray concrete. The place was full of people and traffic, but Tod found he could only concentrate on the buildings. Seldom had he seen anything more ungracious. He thought of the small Residence he had inherited in Haurbath, and of the town beyond it, all of it quiet, old, and beautiful, and was stabbed through and through with the homesickness he had somehow managed to avoid on Arth.

"Is otherworld all like this?" he said miserably.

"Most of the towns. It's a crowded world," Brother Tony said. "Some of the coutryside is almost worth looking at, but of course, they build on more of it every year. No idea of space."

"Oh," said Tod. Almost he could have believed he was simply in a bad dream, except that the rain had left the sidewalk full of puddles, and his canvas shoes were now soaked until his toes squelched. They reminded him at every step that this was no dream. And if he was tempted to imagine still that it was a dream, there was Brother Tony's trim and cheerful figure beside him, dressed like the smartest of the passersby, to make sure he knew it was true. Tod himself looked like the shabbiest of the males who passed. As for the females, Tod found he was too depressed even to be astonished at the short skirts the young ones wore. Bad. Female legs usually interested him rather a lot.

"Hope you don't mind my asking," Brother Tony said confidentially, "but what exactly were you sent over for?"

"Eh?" said Tod. "Oh, I kissed a woman."

"Really?" said Brother Tony. "They're punishing just for that now, are they? Where was she from? Leathe?"

"No, she was from here, I think," Tod said. Looking at the style of the females they passed had made him quite certain of this.

"Here? Otherworld? Come off it! She couldn't have been! They don't know about Arth here, let alone how to cross over!"

Tod had transferred his attention from the pedestrians to the traffic and was watching cars rushing through sprays of water from the wet road. The cars, he thought, were probably the only things worth looking at in this place. Although none of them were as handsome as his own wonderful old beloved Delmo-Mendacci, some of them were almost comely. He wondered if the controls for driving them were anything like the same. But Brother Tony's incredulous outcry recalled him to what he had just said. He had spoken without thinking, and yet, now he considered, he knew it was true. He had all along picked up from Zillah pictures of a world he knew was this one. Hm, he thought. And a great deal fell together in his head—most of what the women might have been doing in Arth, in fact, although he found he was still a little puzzled about what Zillah herself was doing there.

"I was joking," he said, and hastily laughed. "She was Leathe, of course." One of the things that fell together in his head was that Zillah's safety depended on his not letting Arth know where she came from. This was going to be a little difficult if the ritual had indeed given the High Head a thread through into his mind.

To his relief, Brother Tony laughed too. "Leathe from whence all our troubles come!" he said. "Are you quite sure you don't want a haircut?"

They were level with a large window behind which several young men were having things done to their heads by other young men. The aim seemed to be to get their hair to stand upright. "Yes, I *am* sure, thanks," Tod said firmly.

"Then we'd better get to the bank before it shuts," Brother Tony said. He led Tod to an establishment a few

doors on, where he showed him how to obtain money
and pay it in. Tod looked at the small wad of blue papers
he received. Money? Astonishing to think Arth was able
to do this. It didn't do to underestimate the power of
Arth. "And this is how you use a cash-point," Brother
Tony instructed. Tod watched and nodded. His head felt
far too full of new things.

But there was more. Brother Tony marched him into
a side street lined with more of the windowed buildings and showed him a glass door leading into a concrete place called Star House. "This is where you'll be
working."

"Working?" said Tod.

"Yes, you have to earn the money to live, you know.
It's not difficult. It's only a firm of accountants. Get
there just before nine on Monday—today being Friday,
of course—and go up to the fourth floor to Garter and
Sixsmith and just walk in. You'll find they'll accept you
as my replacement as soon as you give your name. Have
you got all that?"

"Fourth floor at nine on Monday, Gutter and Sick-
smith," Tod repeated like one hypnotized. He had never,
ever in his life, worked for wages. Perhaps the gods had
decided it would be good for his soul. He knew numbers
of people, back in the Pentarchy, who did work. His
cousin Michael did. But Tod had never, ever had the
slightest curiosity to know how it felt.

"Right. Then we'll go and get the car," Brother Tony
said.

"Car?" Tod felt a certain brightening. There was a car
went with this? His eye fell on a vehicle standing by Star
House, large and sleek and gray, clearly a thing of power
and beauty, and otherworld at once seemed a slightly
better place.

"Yes, I'll be leaving it with you," Brother Tony joyed
Tod's heart by saying. "It belongs to Arth and I can't take

it to Hong Kong anyway. This way."

They went briskly around a few more corners, and
Tod's step was nearly as jaunty as Brother Tony's, until
they came into the other end of the road from which
they had started. It was lined with cars, parked closely
on either side. Halfway down the line, Brother Tony
stopped and felt for keys. Though none of the cars near
was as beautiful as the gray one, there was a red one and
a white one which were trim and passable. Tod's spirits
were quite high until he saw the car which Brother Tony
was actually unlocking. Up to then, his eye had passed
over it because he had not thought it was a car.

It was small. It had a domed top, like the head of an
amiable but stupid dog, and a curious posture, down at
the front and up at the back, as if the stupid dog were
engaged in sniffing the gutter; and to make it more
remarkable, it was not one colour but several random
ones. The domed top was orange. One flimsy-looking
door was green. The down-bending bonnet was sky-
blue. The rest was a rusty sort of cream. It was like a
jester—or someone's idea of a joke.

"This," Tod said, "is a car?"

"Yes," Brother Tony answered, flinging wide the green
door of the motley monster. He threw his leather bag in
upon a smart pile of luggage on the rear seat. "It's a Deux
Chevaux. That means two horses, by the way. Get in."

But it's not even one horse! Tod thought, dubiously
opening the other door, which was pink and appeared to
be made of tin. It bent about as he moved it. He climbed
in upon a seat made of the cloth they wiped dishes with
in the kitchen of his Residence in Haurbath and gingerly
sat. "Watch carefully," Brother Tony was saying. "You'll
have to drive it back here. So watch the way too."

"Where are we going?" Tod asked.

"To meet Paulie. The ritual will transfer her affec-
tions to you as soon as she sees you, don't worry,"

Brother Tony said cheerfully. "I just have to bring you together."

Arth seemed to have thought of everything. Tod sat in wordless misery watching his companion insert a key into the shaky fascia of the little monster. In response, the monster growled and produced a tinny chugging which caused it to shake all over. Loose metal flapped. Tod shut his eyes. Then forced them open again because he was supposed to watch.

A few seconds were enough to show him that the controls were identical to those of his own superlative Delmo-Mendacci. He wondered if one was not borrowed from the other, and if so, which world had borrowed from which. He was inclined to think otherworld must have stolen the idea of cars from the Pentarchy. This thing Brother Tony was driving was so clearly a debased copy of a dim notion of a car. It went with the same disgraceful chugging with which it had begun, in what was probably a westerly direction, slowly and with obvious effort, toward the outskirts of the town. Tod hoped they were going right beyond the town, but those hopes were dashed when they had chugged into a wider, quieter neighborhood and Brother Tony announced they were nearly there. Fawn-colored houses, these were, or delicately reddish, standing individually at the back of little pieces of grass and driveway, each one a slightly different shape from its neighbors to show that it was the residence of persons who could afford to choose.

With the verve of long habit, Brother Tony swung the wheel of the motley little monster to chug down the sloping driveway of the most fawn-colored house of the lot. The little piece of grass in front of its clean new prim facade was adorned with sparse mauve-flowering bushes. "Here we are," he said, and before Tod could move, he was hauling his smart luggage out of the rear seat. Having done this, he presented the keys of the subcar to Tod. "She's all yours." Leaving his luggage in the driveway, he went with jaunty steps to the front door—which was labeled with a tastefully crooked 42—and pushed a button there. Tod could hear the result inside. *Ping-pong* it went, dulcetly. Tod stood on the doorstep, resigned, as little tripping footsteps approached the door inside.

The woman who opened the door was plump and about Tod's own height. Her hair was most carefully done in a sheeny, close-fitting way, with burnished fair highlights evidently applied afterward. Her face was exquisitely made-up, and the same care had been applied to the rest of her. The triangle of skin revealed above her bosom by her long floral robe was soft and white; the hand that held the door was equally soft and white, adorned with oval shiny pink nails and gold rings with diamonds in them; her small feet in high-heeled floral mules were as soft and white as the rest of her visible skin.

"Tony?" she said. Immaculate black eyelashes lay wide around her eyes as she stared at Tod.

Brother Tony leaned over Tod's shoulder. "Paulie, let me introduce my good friend Roderick," he said, and clapped Tod on the shoulder he was leaning over. "I just *know* the two of you will get on like a house on fire. Now I must fly—taxi's here." He retreated briskly and picked up his luggage. Tod looked around to see him climbing into a square, high black vehicle which had drawn up beyond the drive.

"Where's he going?" Paulie said—not unreasonably, Tod thought.

"Hong Kong, I think," Tod said.

"Oh." The lash-rimmed eyes turned back to Tod. Paulie's carefully pink mouth smiled. Behind that, she had an air of being slightly bewildered. "Well, won't you come in, Roddy?"

Arth knew its stuff. Tod reluctantly advanced into a

small, shiny hallway as Brother Tony's taxi pulled away, where he stood smelling the several perfumes emanating from Paulie. She had certainly been waiting, all prepared to meet Tony, he thought while she was shutting the front door, but she was accepting a scruffy-looking substitute without a blink. Fear and hatred of Arth grew in him. She led him forward into a sitting room as carefully decorated as she was herself, with not a shiny cushion nor a little brass ornament that was not evidently placed exactly so. She induced him into a soft, clean chair and sat beguilingly on a tuffet at his knees. Tod's misery increased.

"Do you want a drink, Roddy?"

"No, thanks." It was not that he did not like plump women, Tod told himself. His taste ran to all sorts. But this Paulie's plumpness had a solid, sorbo-rubber look to it, and looked hard to dent. As one who had had his arms around Zillah only—yes, it really *was* only a couple of hours ago!—Tod felt decidedly off plumpness. But there was more to it than that. Paulie was so carefully got up, perfumed and coiffured and jeweled. He found he kept remembering the time, a year or so ago, when he had accompanied his father on a state visit to Leathe. The Ladies who had met them there were all equally carefully dressed and perfumed and lacquered. And they had talked to him in the same soft, high, charming voices that Paulie was using at this moment.

"Tell me all about yourself, Roddy."

One of the Ladies of Leathe—Lady Marceny it was— had said almost exactly that, in the same sweet, condescending tone, and Tod had been very scared indeed. Afterward August Gordano had opined that he was quite right to be scared. "Always trust your instinct, boy, where those kind of women are concerned. If they notice you, they want something. They eat men for breakfast—and never forget it!" While Tod did not give this Paulie credit for being quite as dangerous as Leathe, the memory of Leathe came to him so strongly with her that it made him thoroughly uneasy. And it was fairly clear to him that she, too, ate men for breakfast. He understood now why Brother Tony was so cheerful about going elsewhere.

"All about myself," he said. "Well, actually I'm an exile from a pocket universe called Arth where all the residents are mages. Most of them are in the business of spying on you people, as a matter of fact, but not being able to get a really close view, they sent me to be a spy in your midst. My real home—"

He stopped because Paulie was swaying about with laughter, her arms plumply clasped around her knees. "Oh, Roddy! Tony told you to say that, didn't he? He spun me just the same yarn when I first met him! Tell me what you really do before you make me die laughing!"

And not even original! Tod thought sadly. Paulie's laughter, he noticed with foreboding, had served to unwrap the floral gown from around her. At the top, a good deal of plump black bra was showing, and below, much of a smooth white leg. Depression seized him, because these sights were not without their effect. His recent brush with Zillah had most strongly reminded him that he was missing women badly.

"The truth is that I work at Sick and Guttersnipe, just like Brother Tony," he said.

"Oh, is he your brother? You don't look a bit alike!" Paulie leaned forward, and more plump things showed.

"Now you tell me all about yourself," Tod said hastily.

"Nothing to tell really," Paulie said lightly. He could tell her lightness hid deep discontent. "I'm just a housewife married to a computer expert. Mark's in computers now, though when I first met him, he didn't seem to be anything. A friend of mine—American—found him wandering around London, and he didn't seem to know

who he was, even, beyond his name. Koppa thought it
was drugs, though I still think it was something more
interesting than that. Anyway, she took him in—I was
sharing a flat with her then, so we both looked after Mark
until Koppa moved out. I tell you, I looked after that man
like a mother and taught him magi—well, taught him all
sorts of things, everything I knew really, and I was even
fool enough to pay to get him retrained in computers.
You know, Roddy, I've done everything for that man,
given up luxuries and the best years of my life, and he's
given me nothing in return. *Nothing!*"

"He married you, didn't he?" Tod said.

"Only when I *asked* him!" She leaned toward him.

Tod leaned defensively back. "And this looks to be a
nice house."

"It's a nice *prison!*" Paulie declared. She smiled, still
leaning forward, with her chin almost on Tod's knees.
"But you won't want to listen to my troubles, will you?"
Her hands came out and clasped Tod on either side of his
head, a grip hard to break. "A nice boy like you, Roddy,
doesn't want words. You want action." She stood up,
arched over him, and the floral gown fell apart.

Here we go! Tod thought resignedly.

But it seemed they did not. His hands had barely
grasped the proffered plumpness when it was whisked
away from between them. Paulie was suddenly standing
a decent three yards off, not a hair disarranged, and
was swiftly retying her gown. Tod was gaping at her,
as much injured as relieved, wondering what kind of
teasing this was supposed to be, when he was aware
of footsteps in the hallway. His head shot around—he
was sure he looked the picture of guilt—and he saw
a pale and serious man entering the room. "Maureen's
still not called me back," the man said as he came. "I've
called her answer phone six times now. I suppose she's
still asleep."

"Hallo, Mark love!" Paulie cried out. "You're back early, aren't you?"

Mark, in a measured way, laid his broad hat on a table and removed the spruce raincoat he was wearing over his dark suit. Not till then did he look at his wife. Giving her time to get her sash tied, Tod thought, uneasily recognizing the signs. Tod himself got to his feet, but was ignored.

"Yes, I am a little early," Mark said, "but there's no need to be so surprised. I did warn you. I hoped you'd be dressed. Do you spend all day in your dressing gown?"

"It's a *housecoat,*" Paulie said petulantly. "I've told you before. And what do you mean, you warned me? Was that phone call about Amanda fussing supposed to warn me? I thought you meant she was coming to supper."

"I made myself quite clear," Mark said, mildly, but with an air of speaking through clenched teeth. "I wish you'd listen. Amanda's sister has gone missing, and Amanda was in such a panic when she realized that she asked Gladys to find her. Now she knows she shouldn't have asked, because Gladys is old and tired out, so she's asked us to go with her and help Gladys. If we all—"

"But you were on about supper and Amanda precogging all sorts of dire stuff," Paulie interrupted. She was standing very upright and carefully straightening the bow of her retied sash, as if the annoyance in her voice had nothing to do with her body. "How am I supposed to sort all that out?"

"You only hear what you want to hear," Mark observed, with the same teeth-clenched calmness. To Tod, listening, it was as if neither Mark nor Paulie was able, for some reason, to show the anger they felt. What stopped them, he had no idea, but whatever it was, he had a growing feeling—quite apart from the awkwardness of his own situation—that it was strange and wrong and terrible.

Tod had been in this situation once or twice before. He had also, many times, stood in the margins when his numerous brothers-in-law quarreled with his sisters. But he had not felt so threatened by anything since he spent that time in Leathe. He could not understand it. "I told you," Mark went on, in the most calm and domestic way, "that I am worn-out too, and I asked you to drive us both to Herefordshire because I'm tired enough to have an accident. I thought you agreed. The idea was that you'd have some food ready to take—because you know how I hate Gladys's pies—and we'd pick it up and be on our way. I'm ready. I left the car running. And I find you aren't even dressed."

"You may have had all that clear in your head," Paulie retorted, motionless as a statue, "but you didn't make it clear to me. I don't read minds, Mark. If you'd made yourself clear, I wouldn't have invited Roddy round. Mark, this is Roddy."

Mark turned to Tod and looked at him, truly, Tod thought, as if he had not noticed him until then. Tod's sense of danger increased tenfold. The feeling of Leathe grew. Mark was, as most men were, considerably taller than Tod, and Mark was, after all, the husband Tod had been about to injure—which was awkward enough and put Tod at a disadvantage enough—but, as Mark's gray, dispassionate eyes met his, Tod saw that the man was also a powerful mage. It was enough to make Tod, by reflex, call up his birthright. To his slight surprise, the birthright was half-roused already, waiting for his call. Maybe the feeling of Leathe, lurking between these two people, had been enough to trigger it.

"Don't I know you from somewhere?" Mark said.

"Oh, I doubt it," Tod replied merrily. "I'm a total stranger in these parts. I—"

"Roddy is Tony's brother," Paulie interrupted. "You remember Tony, Mark? I've just been telling Roddy how

Koppa and I found you wandering around London and took you in."

That, Tod thought, was unneccessary. It was the remark of a complete bitch. His birthright felt Mark wince at it, though Mark gave no outward sign. The man was probably bleeding inwardly from a thousand such snide, wounding things. A great desire came upon Tod to be away from all this, out of the cloying poison of Leathe, not have anything more to do with these people.

"If you don't mind," he said firmly, "I'll be getting along now. Nice to have met you—Paulie—Mark."

Neither of them suggested that he stay. Neither even made a polite noise. They were locked in combat with no time to spare for Tod.

"Well. Good-bye," Tod said. He left them standing there and got out of the house with long strides. His birthright told him that, in order to do so, in order just to make it through the front door, he went bursting through wards and barriers of truly formidable magework. The space in front of the house door was blocked now by a car that was presumably Mark's. More barriers. Tod burst those too, dodged around the car, and fled to the pavement at the head of the short drive, where he stood breathing deeply and trying to recover what Arth and otherworld between them had left of his poise.

The footpath, and the road with it, was slightly raised above the ground where the houses stood. It was as if Tod were for a moment standing with his legs astride on top of otherworld—his birthright tended to give him this effect when it was roused. Now it served to show him that he had had enough of the place. He hated everything he had seen here, and Paulie most of all. There was no way he was going to do the High Head's bidding and become Paulie's lover. He would be sick. He *was* sick. He had to swallow. The homesickness that had overcome him in the center of town rose up in him and clamored.

"Damn it all to hellspoke!" Tod said. "I'm going home."

To make this quite clear to himself, he fished the key to Brother Tony's lodgings from its tight pocket and deliberately dropped it down a grating at his feet. Some kind of drain, he supposed. As the key clattered away, he felt nothing but relief.

"That settles it then," he said.

Nobody had told him the thing was impossible. Nobody had even told him he was forced to serve out the rest of his service-year here—though the High Head had evidently intended that. But the High Head had clearly forgotten the little matter of Tod's birthright. Tod had forgotten it himself. Brainwashed by Arth, he thought. Arth preferred not to know about magework outside its own control, and Tod had tried to be a good citizen of Arth. He was a little astonished at himself now. He had tried to be good. They would not let him. So he had better go home and put himself under August Gordano's powerful protection. August would fight tooth and nail for his heir if necessary.

When he thought about it, Tod was slightly ashamed of running and hiding behind his daddy's coattails. He always was when he did it, but it never stopped him doing it. And to justify him on this occasion, there was the peculiar business of Zillah and his realization that she came from this place. If that ritual really had given the High Head a line through to Tod's mind, then the sooner he got where this information was not available to Arth, the better. But let's see.

Tod let his birthright gather and then reached out and examined this thread. Reaching into the Wheel was curiously difficult to do. Either he was out of practice or otherworld was not a place where magework came easy. But the thread existed, all right.

Tod recoiled as the High Head himself took up the

thread and came through to Tod's mind. Damn. So delicately set up, I jogged the swine's mind. *Your report
please, agent.* Tod had the sense of another day at least
having passed in Arth—time did indeed run strangely
between universes—and the High Head well rested but
slightly irritable from a rich breakfast, and exceedingly
worried behind that in a way he was careful to keep
hidden from Tod. Whatever this worry was, it served to
distance Tod's affairs. The High Head was now able to
regard him as just another agent in the field.

My report? There was no reason in any world to tell the
sod the truth. Tod instantly set about misleading him.
*Contact has been made, sir, satisfactorily to both parties, and
I've also become very friendly with the husband. By the way,
sir, the man has powers rather in excess of yours.* Tod had no
idea if this was the case, but he saw no harm in usettling
Arth a bit.

I suspected as much, the High Head's thought came,
heavy and irritable. *So what's he up to?*

Something very crucial, Tod thought back glibly. *There's
a being called Gladys I haven't met yet, who's even more
powerful, and we're all just off to do important magework
with her. I'll let you know what when I've seen it, sir.*

*Good work, agent. The old female is of great interest to us.
Was there any mention of another called Amanda?*

I don't think so, Tod lied, while his mind made rapid
connections. Mark had been talking about her—Zillah's
sister.

*When you do come across her, I'd like a report on her too.
My usual source on her is temporarily out of action.*

Of course, Magus, Tod thought unctuously, while vow-
ing that no one who was an analogue of his favorite aunt
was ever going to be given over to Arth.

To his relief, the High Head dropped the thread then.
Tod felt him turn to pick up another, belonging to some
other poor Brother in the field. He felt unclean. Hateful to

have that fellow in your head. But quick. Now, while the swine was complacently turning elsewhere. Tod reached into the Wheel again and carefully, delicately, nipped that thread apart. The effort left him quite unusually drained, but it was worth it. Let the High Head try looking for him now. The next thing was to consider the best way to get home before the High Head started looking.

Tod raised his birthright in a new direction and was more than a little daunted to find how well defended the Pentarchy was—it was as if a great thorny wood filled with booby traps grew between here and there. But the luck of the Fiveirs was with him. His mind's eye caught what looked like a possible way through, accessible from here. The real problem was the strange difficulty there seemed to be in mageworking. Tod felt exhausted just looking. He began to see that otherworld was in fact much less benevolent to magecraft than his own world. Perhaps that was the main difference between them. In order to get through that wood, he was going to need to be in, or near, a place of power. He ignored the weariness and searched for such a place.

There was none near. The nearest he could feel was miles away, north and west of here. That was all right. He had transport, courtesy of Arth. He jingled the car keys in his pocket and looked down the driveway with disfavor. There stood Brother Tony's motley little monster, nose-down beside Mark's sleek gray job. Mark's was a real car. It might not have been in the same league as the beloved Delmo-Mendacci, but it was a good, classy vehicle all the same. The contrast was pitiful.

Tod walked slowly down the drive, tossing the keys of the subcar in his hand. He was between the two cars when he realized that the engine of Mark's car was running. So quiet! Marvelous. Of course, Mark had said he'd left it running. And considering the barriers of magework around it, there was probably no fear of someone making off with it. But Mark must, all the same, be incredibly heavily engaged in that family row of theirs, not to have come out to remove the keys, just in case. Tod himself would have done that first thing. Mark would get around to it any second now. In which case—

Tod did not hesitate. There was absolutely no moral struggle. He simply jammed his own keys into the ignition of the motley subcar and slid behind the wheel of Mark's real one. An exchange, if not a fair one. Wards and barriers fell apart around Tod like so many cobwebs. The car smelled clean and new. Bliss. The seat adjusted to Tod's shorter build with a sigh of power. It took him a second or so to discover how to get reverse, but he was backing smoothly up the drive by the time Mark arrived at the front door. Seeing the sober, pale figure emerge, and stand aghast, Tod gave him a cheerful wave as he swooped backward into the road. Then he put the lovely car into forward gear and surged away.

4

I t could not really be sleep, not if she was to hold Joe for the length of time they might need in Laputa-Blish. Maureen continued to drag downward, into a place she had only heard of and never yet experienced, deep in the ether. Down and down.

Some time later they were hanging, still tightly wrapped together, in a place full of whorls of feeling and shadows of color, where everything seemed a sick sepia to the taste, and motes like sticky dust rained into their hearing. Things wrong and bad lurked in the corners of the senses, or made little scuttling rushes, trailing gelatinous disturbance over the floor of the mind. Some of the things—Maureen had an image of just such a disturbance, with too many legs, nestling in the lap of a fat old woman, which was surely wrong, and bad. Nightmares, she thought. Perhaps this was a mistake.

Joe roused when she did—they were that closely involved. Oddly enough, he finished the sentence he had started when she caught him. "If you ask me, that was a con job too. I don't think they *can* bring me back. What did you want to bring us down here for? This is a very bad part of the ether."

"I know," she said, or rather communicated, being bodiless here. "But tell me a better way to hold you. I had to get some sleep."

She could feel panic writhe in him and be controlled. "It'll be more than sleep you'll get unless you know the way out. Our bodies could starve to death. *Do* you know how to get out?"

"No," she confessed. "I was desperate. I—"

"You never *think*, do you? You're worse than I am." She felt him consider. "I had lessons in this. I should remember. Yes. The first thing to do is we make ourselves bodies here, or we lose what little we've got left. Come on, woman, concentrate! Imagine you've got your usual body."

Maureen did so. Joe's carefully controlled panic assured her it was urgent. She pushed her answering panic away and thought of herself, her body, as she knew it. Long legs, slender, shapely back—particularly nice firm buttocks— thin, strong arms, small breasts, her neck, the sweet line of jaw, her hair, which she loved for its color, her own freckled, wide-eyed face. Toes. Long fingers. Elegant flat belly.

And it came into being, nebulously, as she succeeded in visualizing it. Joe also assumed a form, almost at the same time, but she noticed that he had edited himself so that he no longer had that heavy, coarse look to his face. She could see little else but his face, for they were still entwined, because that was how their minds were, arms around each other, leg wrapped into leg, as closely as lovers.

"You've made yourself prettier," he told her. "Your face usually looks much more like a camel's."

"So have you. You usually look like a thug," she retorted. "What now?"

"Unwrap me."

"No way! You'll scoot and leave me here."

"You're dead right, you bitch! Unwrap, or neither of us moves."

"Stuff that!"

It was another deadlock. They hung there in the senseless sepia nowhere, gazing each over the other's shoulder at scuttling whorls of nightmare. When a disturbance
came uncomfortably close, one or the other would push
or pull or tug sideways, and their combined bodies would
drift away in a new direction. It was timeless. They could
already have been there twenty years. Our bodies are
probably long dead, Maureen thought.

"Of course they aren't. You never did have a sense of
time!" Joe snapped at her.

My thoughts are not private anymore, Maureen realized.

"That's your own stupid fault—Hurl's balls! Look out!
Upwards!"

Maureen looked and found a huge and regular disturbance approaching. Overhead, the fabric of everything
was dented and pounded inward, as if a company of
four-legged giants were marching towards them across
a hammock made of thin veiling. The sepia was trod-
den to sick pink in bulges. And whatever the giants
really were, they were striding straight for their two
enwrapped nebulous bodies.

Both pushed and pulled frantically to get out of the
line of advance, but the striders seemed to sense their
presence and altered their course to follow. Closer and
closer, until Maureen caught a whiff of their nature—
something wild, but harnessed by a malevolence that
had its origin in this place. Closer still. The malevolence almost unbearable, right on top of them. As the
leading monstrous dent came bulging down upon them,
Maureen freed her arms, scarcely knowing what she did,
and pushed, hard and desperately. Joe's arms were free
too. He stretched up and heaved at the thing's underside.
Between them, they caught the strider at one side. That
seemed to unbalance it. It, and the bulges that followed
it, appeared to stumble and tip, and then veer ever so

slightly. Maureen tilted her head and watched the whole train of striders pace off into sepia distance at an angle to the two of them.

As the striders went, a vision came to Maureen, not of this place, and not of anything she knew. Things were striding in the vision, too, but these things were metal towers, giant sized, that were marching over grass against a stormy sky. As they strode, the metal things trailed a wild, unharnessed malevolence that seemed akin to the striders, but with that they also trailed arcing, crackling blue violence. Killing violence.

She threw her arms around Joe again, not holding him now, but hugging him for what comfort she could get. "What the *hell* were those?"

He was scarcely articulate and clung to her as hard as she clung to him. "A sending—bad one—really strong—ye gods! Wild magic—the size of it!—right down through half the Wheel—How have we made someone *that* angry?"

5

"**Y**our lover," said Mark, "has just stolen our car." Paulie, now hurriedly dressed in stretch-nylon trousers and an Arran sweater, paused in filling the thermos. "He is not my lover. I never saw him before today."

Mark discerned that she was telling the truth. "Then why did you have him in the house?"

"He's Tony's brother—I told you." Before Mark could make any comment about Tony, Paulie swung to counter-attack, with the thermos clutched to her sweater as if it were her injured name. "You *watched* him steal the car, and you didn't try to stop him! I suppose it didn't occur to you that you're the most powerful magician in this country. You could have stopped him in his tracks if you'd thought to use your power."

"I did think," said Mark, "and I did try. Whoever he is, he turns out to have more power than I have. By some way. He brushed me off like a fly—along with all the wards on the car."

"But he's only *small!*" Paulie said naively. "Though I suppose he is chunky."

"Size doesn't enter into it," Mark said contemptuously. "Some children have more power than *you* do."

"Then I suppose you'd better call the police," she said.

"I already have," Mark replied. "They may just catch him—but what's really worrying me is that I mentioned Gladys in front of him, and I can feel him heading her way. Do you know anything at all about him—what his intentions are, or whether he's into the black stuff in any way?"

Paulie put the thermos to her mouth in dismay. "No. I told you. I only just met him."

"Then we'd better follow him," said Mark. "Quickly. Get that food and come along."

"How? Do we hire a car? Or walk?"

"As he's had the extreme generosity to leave us a Deux Chevaux in exchange for the BMW, we might as well use the thing," said Mark.

"Oh, not *that* car!" Paulie said as she turned away to the fridge, thus inadvertently admitting to more knowledge of Tony than she had ever admitted before.

Mark pretended not to hear, in order not to have to remind her that she always said of Tony, "I hardly know the man—I don't even know what car he drives!" He hurried about finding biscuits and apples and adding them to the basket of food on the counter. And he felt cold, and lonely and empty.

Five minutes later, locking the house and making sure the wards of protection were back in place, he wondered why he was bothering. The house was a heartless shiny box. He did not care if someone broke in. He did not care if he never saw it again. But he supposed Paulie would mind, and so he made it safe, meticulously.

Paulie meanwhile inserted herself into the dishrag seat behind the wheel of the motley car, bemoaning her fate. "This is an *awful* car, Mark, even awful for a Deux Chevaux!" She turned the key and wailed as the thing began to chug and clatter. "Christ! Pieces are falling *off*, Mark! Next door's looking at us—I'm *ashamed*! Where to, if it will move?"

"Make for Herefordshire the usual way. He's still heading there."

Paulie slammed the little monster into reverse and went grinding backward up to the road. She made further piteous cries as soon as she got it into forward gear. "God, Mark, we'll be lucky if this gets us to Gladys by *tomorrow*! It won't *go* above forty! I'm not sure it's *intended* to!"

"Just keep going," he said patiently. "Your acquaintance doesn't know we're following him, and he may not hurry. He thought too little of me to notice I got a link to him."

"I don't understand how you can be so *calm*!" Paulie said. "When I think how much that car of ours *cost*—!"

She repeated these remarks at intervals over the next thirty miles. The little car got caught in the beginnings of rush hour, and it took them an hour to cover that much. Mark sat with his arms folded, and endured. Most of the time he was wondering, and not for the first time, why he had come to marry Paulie when he disliked her so much. He could not remember ever liking her. But she had looked after him in those early days, and it had seemed quite natural, as if she were what he was *used* to . . .

And from there to Zillah, who was and always would be the only one he wanted. Up to now he had not dared to let himself consider how easy it would be to find her. He had not even dared to ask if Zillah was indeed the sister Amanda had living with her, though he had suspected it for some time. Somehow he had known it would do no good. For no reason that he could fathom, Zillah had closed him out, dropped the bar on him as if he were a game of pool in a pub, and he knew she was not about to reconsider. But now it was out in the open. Amanda, in her agitation, had said Zillah's name on the phone. He could let himself think of her and of her habit of ducking out and of Amanda's precognitive fear that Zillah was in deep trouble. If he could find her and rescue her, then he might for the first time have some hope . . .

The little car chugged on like an ineffectual terrier running at a rathole. An hour later, luck turned Mark's way.

"Ah!" he said. "Your friend's stopped. He's run out of gas. I was hoping for that."

Paulie put her foot down. The small monster roared. "Tinker with our car then. Make sure he can't start it again."

Mark sat back after five minutes of effort. "No good. He's got protection on it I can't break."

"We'll *never* catch up!" Paulie wailed. "Oh, I *hate* this car!"

Five minutes later, Mark said, "He still hasn't gone on. We may be in luck."

"Probably seducing the cash girl," said Paulie. "I hope she gives him *AIDS!*"

For whatever reason, Tod remained stationary for the next hour and a half. By this time, Paulie had entered straight roads in the chalk country, which she knew well. And the little car seemed to have warmed to its work. Though its sloping hood showed a tendency to rise and then clang back into place, like a terrier snapping at flies, and its parti-colored wings kept up a continuous rapid flapping, as if it entertained the illusion that flight was a possibility, it attained sixty miles an hour and kept that speed up. Mark watched a stormy yellow sunset gather among big indigo clouds against the wide western horizon and began to think they might actually catch the man. He blocked out a buzzing headache, which was probably due more to the gathering storm than to the noise of the little car, and concentrated on drawing in all the power he could muster. He was going to have to use

Paulie's power, too, in order to defeat Tod. This part of
England was a network of old, strong places. Mark could
draw on those, but by the same token, so could Tod.

It puzzled Mark that someone of this man's power had
not made himself known before. It was as if a sudden
wild magic had come into their midst from somewhere
else entirely. And he could not understand his own reaction to it. Why had he, Mark, who was normally secretive
and circumspect to a degree that irritated everyone, not
only Paulie, even himself at times, felt compelled to babble of Gladys and Amanda in front of this man? When
he saw the fellow cheerfully stealing his car, he had felt
a jolt of horror that had nothing to do with the theft. He
had known his nemesis. He had known that if he could
not stop this rogue magician reaching Gladys, he, Mark,
was finished. And that was hard to understand too.

Tod was moving again, though not so fast. "We're
closing on him," Mark told Paulie. She nodded. They
roared along a nearly empty road that seemed at the
top of the world.

"Do I need lights yet?" she said. "I've no idea how
they go on."

The yellow sunset was being sucked away inside the
advancing storm clouds, leaving a twilight trying on the
eyes, gray road merging into gray-green downs on either
side. "I'll get them on for you," Mark said.

He was leaning forward, fiddling with a knob that
turned out to be the heater, when Tod suddenly and
inexplicably swung northward, perhaps mistaking the
route. Mark sprang upright.

"He's turned off! We can cut him off! Take the next
right. Here—*this* one!"

Paulie swung the wheel. The little car dived around
and plunged into a narrow road running uphill. It was
going too fast. Paulie's effort to brake sent it into a series
of skids, swooping from hedge to hedge, wilder and

wider, as Paulie lost her head, swore at Mark, and turned
the wheel against the skid. They ended nose-down in a
ditch at the top of a hill.

"You stupid *wimp!*" Paulie said. "This is *your* fault.
What did you have to shout at me to take this road
for?"

Mark cursed. He could feel Tod accelerating away into
the distance.

They disentangled themselves from the tilted seats
and climbed out into a half-dark landscape bare of anything but a line of pylons against the sky. A keen wind
moaned through the hedges, flapping hair and plastering
trousers to legs.

Paulie shivered. "This *beastly* little car! The steering's
shot to blazes. Is it badly broken? I'd hope it *was*, only
that'd mean we'd be here all night."

Mark squelched down into what proved to be a very
muddy ditch and took a look. The motley car had both
front wheels and its snout plunged into the mud, a terrier
digging out a rat, but he could see no obvious damage.
Lucky Deau Chevaux were so light. "I think if we both
got down here," he said, "we could lift—"

Paulie said, "*Mark!*" She sounded calm, but there was
a strident note of panic underneath. "Mark, something
very odd is happening."

"What?" he asked, heaving at the buried bumper.

"Those pylons," she said. "They *moved*—they're moving *now!*"

The wind took her voice. Mark could not believe what
he thought he heard her say. He stood up irritably. The
line of pylons, dark against the lead-dark sky, stretched
away out of sight over the hilltop. They were just pylons—
skeleton steel towers with stumpy arms at the top to carry
the cables—standing like a row of stiff giants across the
fields. But as Mark looked, ready to ask Paulie not to
add to their troubles by imagining things, he saw another

pylon rise into sight from behind the hilltop. *What?* he thought. His eyes shot to the nearest, halfway across the field on the other side of the road. And he saw it take a waddling stride nearer, and another. Behind it, the whole line of tall metal towers swayed in unison as they strode, and strode again.

He watched without believing it for a second. Then it got through to him that a line of metal monsters—and they seemed to be bearing God knew how much voltage of live cable—was steadily and unstoppably marching toward him. He leaped around the car's buried hood, seized Paulie, and dragged her away down the road. He felt the foremost pylon turn slightly to reorientate on him as he ran.

"*Down!*" he yelled at Paulie.

They dived into the ditch together, treading on each other, wet to the knees, almost waist-deep in mud as they crouched around to watch the nearest metal giant arrive in the road in one clanging, swaying stride. Mark could feel it search for him. Not Paulie, for some reason, just him.

"Protection," he said. "Put up protection for both of us. I can't. They're homing on me."

Paulie was uttering small, yammering sounds of terror, but she did her best. With his senses heightened by terror, Mark saw the warding grow around them in a gentle blue haze, glowing faintly in the half-dark. In the road the foremost pylon took another crashing stride and then stood, towering, at a loss. With the same heightened senses, Mark felt the strength and nature of the sending that activated it. God in heaven! It was wild magic. Someone hated him enough to harness that which no one should have been able to control at all.

"Turn it—turn it away!" he whispered.

"I can't—it's wild—it's *strong*!" Paulie whimpered. He could feel her pushing weakly, so weak against the mighty thing, and wished he dared help. But he knew without a shadow of doubt that if he used the slightest power himself, those things would know and home in on it.

Clang. Paulie's push had been enough to start the thing moving again. Or perhaps it was the pressure of the pylons advancing behind. The line continued stalking forward, curving slightly now from its former course, striding solemnly and mindlessly across the road, through the hedge, and on downhill. The first passed twenty yards away, the second ten. The third tower strode straight upon the motley car with an appalling tinny rending, and swayed, held up only by the cables strung from its stumpy arms. This brought the rest striding so near that Paulie and Mark both lay flat, faces in their arms, feeling the earth vibrate, the crunch of tarmac torn from the road, and the wail of wind in struts and cables. With that was mixed the acid-blast of magic full of violence and hatred, which in turn mingled with heat and thick fumes as what was left of the motley car caught fire and blazed against the hedge.

"They've stopped," said Paulie. "They've lost you."

Mark risked standing up. The blazing car cast orange light along the ditch, showing it steaming, and it was hard to see beyond. He could just pick out the line of giants standing slanted downhill toward the main road. One stood like a sentinel against the fading light of the sky not far away. "They're waiting," he said. "Thanks for turning them."

"I had help," Paulie said gruffly, "but I don't know whose. Why is Roddy after you like this?"

"No idea." It took a mere flick of power to trace Tod, and Tod was, to Mark's surprise, very far away and quite unconcerned with Mark. Then why—?

The nearest pylon lurched and began to advance on Mark.

"Oh God! They found you again!" Paulie staggered up. Mud sucked and she exclaimed with disgust. "Sorry, Mark, but I'm off. They're after you, and you can cope on your own."

Mark caught her arm as she set off downhill. He needed her for protection. It shamed him, but he dared not let her go. Their whole marriage was like this. "Don't be a fool. No one's safe from the wild magic. There's a small stone circle quite near. It's strong. It might help."

Her eyes rolled sideways to the metal giant. "Which way?"

He pointed, and they fled that way, leaving the car burning, bursting through rolls of smoke, clumsily jumping the torn-up tarmac and then the broken hedge. They ran, panting and choking, up beside the deep-gouged tracks the advancing pylons had made in the turf. Paulie stumbled trying to look back. Mark jerked her upright, wrenching his arm. The foremost pylon was looming past the flames, towing a crescent of more distant striding giants with it. Paulie's breath came in shrieks as they reached the top of the hill, and Mark could barely breathe, but neither dared slow down. They careered down the slope beyond, mostly rough grass, and crashed through the narrow end of a black, spiny coppice.

Below them lay a small meadow, hard to see in the near dark, with the white ribbon of a hedged lane, and a gate into the lane beyond that. The small stone circle was a warm emanation in the center of the meadow, faintly seen beside the dark blot of a parked car. They pelted for the ring of stones, invoking—imploring—assistance if any was to be had, and threw themselves within it, each clinging to a separate stone and heaving for breath.

"That car," Paulie gasped. "Could we?"

Above came crashing as the first pylon marched into the coppice.

Mark looked at the dark, deserted car. A BMW. He looked again, unbelievingly. It was his own car. He could sense it, feel the habitual little protections he always used around it in traffic. Beyond it, the gate was shut. There was no sign or feel of Tod anywhere near. With the warmth of the stone under his hands and its safety suffusing him, he was free to see that the things waddling down the hillside at him had nothing to do with Tod. They were a sending from quite another quarter. The unknown was angry and drawing on an associate who came from somewhere very dark and low indeed.

Mark was sprinting toward the car as soon as he saw this. It was a godsend—too good to be true—there *had* to be a catch! Christ, I hope he left the keys in it! At the very least, it was bound to be locked. But when he seized the door handle, the door opened. When he grabbed for what he *knew* would be an empty keyhole, his hand encountered the dangling tab of his own keys. Thank God! He hurled himself into the seat and thrust it back to its usual position, turning the keys as he did so. And—another miracle—the engine purred, and the gas gauge swung around to *full*. He almost blessed Tod.

"Get that gate open!" he bellowed to Paulie.

Paulie ran again, a weary, rolling trot, as soon as she heard the engine. She dragged the gate wide and left it that way, regardless of cattle. Mark threw the door open for her as he bumped past into the lane. Somehow she scrambled in and somehow she got the door closed as he accelerated back to the main road.

"Don't *ever* let me in for anything like that again!" she sobbed.

The pylon halted in front of the stone circle like a cat faced with water. But the line was pressing downhill on either side of it. Slowly it moved again, sideways, giving the circle a wide berth, and seemed to set off striding mechanically. It had reached the lane when it stopped, and stood trailing cables, as the sending left it and moved on after its object.

6

It was an awful journey. They could feel the sending pursuing them, taking on other forms as it came. The storm howled around the car, purposefully, and brought rain increasingly heavy as night fell. Once a tree came down in the road just after they had passed it. Mark had to ask Paulie to keep up constant protection, and she was soon tired out and angry.

"*Must* we go all the way to Gladys's?" she demanded.

"Yes," he said. "Even if I hadn't promised Amanda, that house is the one place I know that can keep out this sending."

Paulie could not argue with that. When they finally arrived under Gladys's storm-torn trees, to find another car parked on the verge and the gate fallen down, she refused to move. "I'm past caring about *any* of you," she said. "Leave me be." Mark had to drag her out of the car. "I just want to lie down and *sleep!*" she wailed as he hauled her through the pelting rain and up the muddy path. But she cheered up at seeing dim lights coming from the house. "There! She's perfectly okay in spite of all your fussing!"

When Mark tremulously clattered at the ring on the verandah door, it was opened by Amanda. She was carrying an oil lamp, which she held high to see who they

were. She seemed pale by its light, and her eyes very
big and dark. "Good Lord!" she said. "You two look as
if you've been through it!"

"We have," Mark said. "Let us in and shut the door
quickly. There's a sending after me. And is there any
coffee? Paulie's about had it."

Amanda stood back to let him guide Paulie through to
a seat in the jungle room and then shut the door—both
doors—with firm claps. There was a sense of something
wrong. Mark realized that the dim light in the room
came from a row of candles on the mantelpiece. He
could have done without the shifting, clawing shadows
they made among the jungle.

"The power's out again," Amanda explained, casting
more shadows, huge, walking ones, as she came back
with the lamp.

"That figures," Mark said, thinking of the pylons.

"Oh, does that mean there's nothing hot to drink?"
Paulie moaned, putting her draggled head in her muddy
hands.

"No. She's got those gas cylinders," said Amanda.
"The kettle's just boiled, but there's only tea bags."

"That'll do," said Paulie.

There was still a sense of something not right—a sort of
silence and emptiness that was there in spite of the frus-
trated storm roaring around the house. "What's wrong?"
Mark asked. "Maureen?"

"Gladys," said Amanda. "Vanished. And she seems
to have taken the cats. Have you noticed there isn't an
animal in the place?"

That was it, of course. Mark had never known this
house without the soft prowling of cats—and usually the
rhythmic scratching of the beast Jimbo too. If Gladys had
removed her animals, she had indeed gone. "Didn't she
leave a message?"

"No. I've only been here half an hour, but I've looked

everywhere I can think of," said Amanda. "There's nothing, unless you know any secret place—"

"Oh, damn that! Let's get warm and dry first!" Paulie cried out.

"Yes, yes, of course." Mark seized one of the candles and forced himself to hurry about looking for dry clothes, while Amanda lit a fire and made tea.

Half an hour later, they were feeling much better. Mark had discovered various strange garments thrown around the bedroom that seemed to belong to Gladys. He selected a flowered kimono for Paulie and got her into it. For himself he found a gown of scarlet flannel, which Amanda, with great surprise, identified as a Cambridge doctoral gown. Now he and Paulie sat side by side drinking tea and staring into the fire, looking as if they were taking part in some new ritual. The sight amused Amanda. She was sitting on the hearth, being too tense to take a chair.

"What happened to you?" she asked.

Mark started to tell her, but Paulie, as she so often did, interrupted him. "Where's Maureen? I thought she'd be here too."

"No idea, and she's not answering her phone," Amanda said.

On cue, the telephone rang, hidden somewhere in the jungle.

"That'll be Maureen, I bet." Amanda leaped up and made the usual search among the plants. When she located the phone and answered, however, it proved to be yet another puzzle. "It's for you," Amanda said, holding the receiver out through the leaves toward Mark. "Sounds Scottish."

"But no one knows I'm—" Mark began. Then he remembered that there was both a sending and a rogue magician abroad, and simply and grimly took the phone. "Mark Lister here."

The voice was female and, as Amanda said, slightly Scottish. "Mark Lister, are you? I'm sorry to seem to doubt you, but I'll have to ask you to identify yourself by your title. I was told to do that, you see."

"Told? Who told you?"

"My mother. She told me particularly that I—"

"Your mother? I'm sorry. I think you may have the wrong—"

"My mother," said the woman, "is Mrs. Gladys Naismith."

"*Gladys!*"

"That's right. I'm her daughter, Aline McAllister, and I live in Dundee. I have a message for you from my mother if you can prove you have the title to it. The secret title, mind. She was most particular."

"If you really need—" Mark gave in and gave her his full titles.

"Thank you," said Aline McAllister. "She said you would be in her house before midnight, and I see she was right as usual. She sent the message up with her cats, you know. I have them all here. Making fifty-two, along with my own, I may say. Dearly as I love my mother, we do not get on, and this is why. Long ago I told her that only in a real, genuine crisis will I do any other thing for her, and this is what I get. Fifty-two cats. So you may take it the message is urgent. This is it. I am to say that my mother has gone after Zillah, partly because of the child, but mainly because you and all the rest of British Witchcraft are in serious danger. In order to find out the nature of the danger, you would do well to consult the girl she and you visited in hospital. End of message. I hope you have it. It's clear as mud to me."

"I—I have it," Mark said. "Thank you."

"Don't thank me, thank my mother's cats," said Aline McAllister, and rang off.

"Who on earth was that?" Paulie said as he came out through the jungle.

"Gladys's daughter," he said. "With a message from Gladys."

"*What?*" exclaimed the other two. Amanda added, "I never knew she'd been married—or—or— Anyway, how extraordinary!"

"The poor girl must have had a terrible childhood," Paulie said feelingly.

Mark was inclined to agree. "She said they didn't get on."

Amanda gave that stern little frown of hers. "Never mind that. What was the message?"

Mark told them and astonished them a second time.

"Gone after Zillah!" said Paulie. "Why should that make a crisis? That girl is always dropping out. She's probably just joined a squat somewhere."

Amanda frowned again. "What is this danger? Where is this girl who'll know? In hospital?"

"No," said Mark. "She's dead."

"*Dead!*" shrilled Paulie. "Gone after Zillah, and she tells you to consult a dead girl!"

"How long ago?" Amanda asked intently.

"About six weeks now," said Mark. "Gladys is right. She should be over the shock now."

"Or she could be dissipated," said Paulie. "Gone after Zil—!"

"Shut *up*, Paulie!" Amanda snapped. "Be helpful or be quiet. Mark, we'd better get in touch with her at once, don't you think? What was her name?"

"We never found out," Mark explained. "The hospital had no idea, and she didn't—"

"And you don't even know her name!" Paulie said disgustedly.

Amanda stood up and advanced on Paulie like an avenging queen. "Paulie—"

"She's tired and overwrought," Mark said hastily.

"No she's not," said Amanda. "No more than I am. My sister is missing, and I spent the whole sleepless night receiving warnings in *every conceivable way*, and yet *I* can still behave reasonably! Paulie is just strutting into the center of the stage in her usual *selfish* way, and you, Mark, are conniving with her to let her. As you both always do. Paulie, you behave or I'll *make* you! This is serious."

They stared at her like injured children, such was her majesty. At length, Paulie whispered, "Sorry."

"Good," said Amanda. "Now, Mark, what made Gladys think you'd be able to contact this girl's soul?"

"Because she was desperate to tell me something when she died," he admitted. "I'm sorry—it was so peculiar that I've rather avoided thinking about it, but I should have told you. Apart from anything else, she was probably from the pirate universe. Gladys was sure she was. I think that was what made Gladys see I was right."

"Then," said Amanda, "let's get on with it. Are you helping, Paulie? Good—get over there then. Mark, you take the north and do the invocation. How many candles?"

"Just one in the middle," said Mark.

There were few other questions. They all knew what to do. Shortly, with the solitary candle casting dark leaf-flickers over ceiling and faces, and gusting occasionally from the wind that still roared outside, they stood in three-quarters of a circle, and Mark, standing with his back to the fire so that the glow of it shone red through his gown, spread his arms and began the strange, simple call that summoned a dead soul.

By fire and flete and candlelight, to hearth and house and warmth, he called, and called three times. The sound of the wind dropped away. None of them heard anything but the light breathing of the others and the gentle whickering of the candle flame.

He spread his arms to call her to earth and air and flame, but she was there already. She had been yearning for the call. Her gusty voice filled the room.

Oh, I'm so glad!

They had all expected her to manifest, if she was visible at all, somewhere among the plants where they had left space for her to come, but she manifested instead in the middle, hovering over the candle like a tall, streaming nimbus, causing the skin of them all to prickle with the haunting energy of her. She had not been, perhaps, very beautiful in life, but she was beautiful now. She had, Mark remembered, manifested like a flame at her death. She was all flame now.

I knew you'd call, her voice gusted. *I waited. I had to tell you. I knew you didn't know.*

"Which of us are you speaking to?" Amanda asked quietly.

The man I came to this otherworld to find, she said. *The one who called me. Herrel Listanian.*

"His name is Mark Lister," Paulie said. "You mean he's an analogue?"

No, the gusty voice insisted. *The man who called is Herrel Listanian.*

Paulie drew breath to argue. Amanda's eyes caught the candlelight and glinted off the substance of the ghost as she stopped Paulie with a look. "Please explain," she said.

His name. His mother gave him a new name when she broke him in half and sent this half here to otherworld, the dead girl gusted. *Forgive me. I helped her. I thought it would save him. But she used both halves as her puppets just as she always did.* Mark could feel her presence orientate on him. The candle flame streamed toward him, imploringly, and guttered with the flickering voice. *Forgive me. I helped put you here to spy for her, and now I can feel her pursuing you with a sending. You must have disobeyed her. Forgive me. The only good that came of it is that she stopped punishing you like this for a while.*

"His mother is who?" Amanda asked.

Marceny, chief Lady of Leathe, the reply came, but the candle flame still streamed toward Mark. *She sent you to rule the magework here and tell her what you knew. I helped because I thought it would save you. It was done for pity and love. Forgive me.*

"How would it save him?" said Amanda.

To have the best half of yourself free, the voice gusted pleadingly. *And you were free, and I saw you didn't know. So I had to come to tell you, to atone, but I died too soon. Forgive me. Let me go.*

Mark could hardly move. His face, and his tongue, were stiff, but he managed to croak, "I—forgive you," and the words of release.

She gave a small, gusting sigh. The nimbus faded away, and the candle flame burned straight.

"Mark!" squawked Paulie.

Amanda gave her another quelling look. "Who was she, Mark?"

"Colny Ventoran, my mother's best assistant," he answered without thinking. "She always was rather an intense little—" He stopped, seeing the way they were both looking at him.

"Then you're from the pirate universe?" said Amanda.

"I rather fear I must be," he agreed.

IX

Arth and Pentarchy

1

"You *what?*" said Edward.

"Come from otherworld," Judy repeated, speaking very muffled, with her head down to twiddle the tapes of her medical gown. "We all do—the whole capsule did."

Edward, as always, did not react in any way she expected. Instead of demanding to know more, exclaiming, repudiating her, or racing off to inform the High Head, he simply turned away to the blue embrasure of the window, where he stood gazing out at the blank blueness and tapping the fingers of his large, agile right hand on the sill. Judy waited, long, long minutes. Before the wait was over, she was fighting herself not to say—in what she knew would be a girlish whine—Don't you love me anymore now? Edward had this ability to make her behave—and feel—like an insecure schoolgirl. Perhaps, she thought, this was because it was what she was deep down and naturally. Before she knew Edward, she had never, not once, felt natural with any man.

She managed not to speak and was glad she hadn't when Edward turned back to her with a look of mild exasperation. "This just shows," he said, "how important it is to keep questioning our reasons for believing things. It's particularly important with traditional doctrines. Here were we in Arth all assuming, without question, that otherworld is a debased copy of ours, and the inhabitants of it some form of reptile—and why? Because some High Brother or Head Magus made inadequate observations centuries ago and decided it was so. And we acted on this assumption, and did our experiments, and never once thought to examine otherworld as we examine other universes. And now you tell me that you're as human as I am. Judy, I'm ashamed—for Arth and for the Pentarchy—I truly am."

Judy stared at him, feeling that radiance was breaking out all over her. She had hardly dared to believe that even Edward would take the news this way. "Edward, you're amazing."

Edward put a hand on each of her shoulders and gripped with the gentle grip that Judy, from the start, would have walked through fire for. "Why have you only told me this now, though?"

She hung her head again. This was the question she could not answer honestly. How could she tell him that this was the result of agitated planning in the women's quarters? Roz demanded action. Flan and Helen wanted firm news about Zillah. Knowing Edward, Judy could not believe there were any hidden horrors in Arth and said so, whereupon Flan, to everyone's surprise, burst into tears, and Roz loudly expressed her contempt of both of them. And Sandra surprised Judy, and Roz too, by telling Roz to shut her mouth until she knew what she was talking about. "See here, Judy," Sandra said, "something's wrong. No one's seen Zillah or Marcus since yesterday, and no one will talk about them. Everyone's suddenly busy with rituals all the time, and they're beginning to look funny at me in Calculus. Suppose they found out about us? We need to know. Edward is High Horns's friend. You go and ask him about Zillah and see what else you can pick up while you're at it. You *have* to. It's urgent." The rest had agreed—though Judy felt that there was no need for Roz to add, "If you can conquer your passion enough to remember your mission, that is."

Because of what Roz said, Judy resolved—in this newly discovered schoolgirl way of hers—that she would only ask Edward if she gave him important information herself first. That made it fair. And it did seem, from what the others said, that it was only a matter of time before someone in Arth guessed where the women were from. But not being able to tell Edward any of this, she hung her head and told him something else that happened to be true.

"Because I love you. I didn't want to be under false pretenses anymore."

Edward kissed her. It was reverent and wondering. He had told her that if he had even suspected what it was like to love a woman, he would never have thought of joining the Brotherhood.

Eventually, still not feeling honest, Judy said, not sounding as casual as she would have liked, "By the way, have you any idea where Zillah and her little boy have got to? Nobody seems to know."

The slightly austere look Judy had dreaded seeing came over Edward's face. Much of it was guilt. He had once quite lustfully thought of Zillah before he came to know Judy. That felt like retroactive infidelity now. "I'm afraid I can't tell you anything about that," he said. As far as he knew, Zillah, Josh, and Philo were still wandering about in the depths of Arth, somehow parrying all the magework used to find them. The only other explanation for their disappearance was, he had agreed with the High Head, plain impossible. So search parties were still looking. And for fear of the alarm and despondency it might spread, he could not tell Judy what havoc the truants seemed to be working upon the fundamental rhythms of Arth. But being reminded by this of his friend and his duty, Edward added reflectively, "I suppose I must tell the High Head that you all come from otherworld."

"Oh, *need* you?" Judy said. She must, after all, have been relying on Edward not to react like any other High Brother, she saw. Roz was not going to forgive her for this.

"I do need to," he said. "Arth has been laboring under false assumptions for centuries. The Magus will be glad to put that right."

Glad, Judy thought, was not a word anyone but Edward would have chosen. In a dither of panic, she said, "When—when are you going to tell him?"

"Oh, when I next see him, I suppose," Edward said vaguely. It had occurred to him, too, that *glad* might not properly describe his friend's reaction. He might find Judy snatched away from him. Perhaps it would be better to wait until the vibrations settled down and Lawrence was in a better humor. "I shan't see him until this evening anyway," he said, consoling himself and Judy.

2

To Zillah, it felt as if they all spilled out feet-first as though Arth were a giant helter-skelter. So strong was this impression that, when the light ceased to dazzle her, she looked upward, expecting to see Arth hanging above like an enormous blue tornado, or at least the twisted tail of it joining them to wherever they were now.

Blue was certainly what she saw, but it was the clouded blue of sky appearing through dark, shiny leaves. Among the leaves were small white flowers and round golden fruit. They were in a grove of fruit trees, and the light was, in fact, only bright after the darkness in the base of the citadel.

"What did you do?" Josh asked. He was collapsed on the grass with all four legs folded. Deep dents in the soft turf showed where he had landed and staggered before folding. Even so, he was keeping a firm arm around Marcus, who was struggling to get himself and his bag of toys off Josh's back.

"Daddle," Marcus announced.

"I didn't do anything," Zillah said.

"Yes you did," said Philo, who was clinging to the nearest fruiting tree. He looked as if he might fold like Josh without it. "I never felt power like it!"

"Daddle!" insisted Marcus.

There was a small lake, or large pool, of an extraordinary fresh blue-green in the center of the grove. A play of mounded water and white bubbles near the middle showed where the pool was being fed constantly by a spring. Zillah could not blame Marcus for wanting to paddle. It was hot in this grove. But the whole of it had a look that was somehow—special.

"Better not, Marcus," said Philo. "This all belongs to the Goddess."

Over the days of their acquaintance, Marcus had decided Philo was the wise man of the party. He did not protest. He nodded gravely at Philo. *"Dow?"*

Zillah helped Marcus slide down off Josh. "Have either of you any idea where we are?"

"It feels like the Pentarchy," Philo said decidedly. "But how far south or north we are depends—this hot, it could be summer in central Trenjen or winter in south Leathe. These orange trees don't give much away. If only we knew what season—"

"Spring," said Josh. He pointed to where, between two orange trees, some small blue-gray irises were flowering.

Philo stared at these in some perplexity. *"Do* those only come up in spring? It was spring when I left for Arth. It ought to be summer if—"

"Or we've been away a whole year," Josh suggested. "I think we'd better go and ask someone—in a roundabout way, of course, or they'll realize we've broken the law."

With Zillah and Philo each hauling on an arm, Josh struggled to his legs and they went cautiously out of the grove. At the far end of the pool, the water ran out in a stream over a carefully built small wooden lock, and a path led beside the stream, out of the grove and into sunlight strong enough to dazzle them all again. They halted nervously, shading their eyes.

There was a woman a few yards downstream. She was coming toward them on the path, halting from time to time to test the carefully turfed banks of the stream with a long tool. She was an idyllic sight. Long coal black hair blew in the breeze around her shoulders, and her faded blue-gray gown was blown to outline her figure. She was a beautiful woman, disturbingly familiar and strange at the same time. She looked around, seeing them, and Zillah could have sworn for a moment that it was Amanda staring at them.

Marcus had no doubt. With a loud shout of *"Badder!"* he set off down the path toward her as fast as his legs could take him. "Badder! Badder! Badder!"

Zillah set off after him, and Philo with her. Analogue of Amanda or not, the woman was a total stranger and might not care for a small boy hurling himself upon her. A dirty small boy. The pyjama suit Marcus had been wearing all their time in Arth was gray at the knees and rear and splotched down the front. The real Amanda would have found it bad enough, let alone this unknown image of her.

The woman, however, darted to meet Marcus even faster than Zillah ran after him. She reached him fractionally first and swept him gladly up in one arm. The bag of toys thumped to the ground and came open, spilling everything over the path. Zillah and Philo stopped, for fear of treading on Marcus's treasures.

"Doy! Doy!" Marcus draped himself desperately over the woman's arm.

"I'm so sorry," Zillah said as she stooped to gather the toys up.

"Leave those," said the woman. It was an absolute command. Her voice was high and chilly, and nothing like Amanda's.

Zillah slowly stood up, staring at her, wondering how she could ever have taken her for Amanda. Her hair was not even very dark, and arranged in careful gleaming tresses which the wind had scarcely power to move. Her dress was indeed blue-gray, but it was of satin as stiff as her tresses, in a high-fashion mode that Zillah thought as displeasing as it was strange—a matter of two huge puffed panniers descending from the woman's armpits around a tight whaleboned bodice that spread into a hooped divided skirt. Against it, Marcus looked even filthier. The kicking cloth feet of his pyjama suit were black and shiny as leather, except where one toe was coming through.

With a fleeting wonder as to however this woman managed to pee in such a dress, Zillah looked into her face. It was nothing like Amanda's, being pretty and heart-shaped, with faint, hard lines of age to it. It dismayed Zillah utterly. It was the woman's eyes, which were dark. They were eyes that greedily, urgently, and softly sought out what was valuable and vulnerable in Zillah and drank it in, without giving anything back. Mother's eyes, Zillah thought. You could easily mistake such eyes for those of a kindly student of humanity, unless you knew Mother.

"Perhaps you'd better give me my son," Zillah said. Marcus was still reaching and crying after his toys, and Philo, after one startled look at the woman, was doggedly picking them up.

"I will not," said the woman. "Gualdian, I said to leave those." The thing in her right hand, which Zillah had taken for a tool, was actually a long rod rather like a scepter, with a strange, ugly little head grinning from the end she held. When Philo took no notice of what she said, she reached out and tapped him with the rod. Philo cried out and dropped the toys. For a moment he seemed unable to move. When he did move, it was to clap one hand to the shoulder she had tapped and turn his face up to the woman in horror. He was whiter than Zillah had ever seen him. His eyes had gone enormous.

Marcus saw it and was shocked into silence. Great tears rolled down his face. Seeing them and seeing Philo, Zillah stepped forward in an access of anger and wrenched Marcus away. "You've no right to do that!"

Marcus's tears had splotched the woman's gown. She let him go with a shudder. "I have every right," she said. "I am Marceny Listanian, and you are trespassing on my estate. You used unwarranted power to come here, too. I warn you that we do not treat such things lightly in Leathe. You are all under arrest. Tell that centaur to come out of the grove at once."

Zillah whirled around to find a number of men and several women, who all wore versions of the hooped and panniered costume, hurrying toward them. They must have been concealed behind the trees of the grove. Now they were jumping the irrigation ditches that crisscrossed the flat field in order to spread out and surround Zillah and Philo. Josh was between the last two trees on the path. All his hooves were braced and he was holding on to the trees as if some compulsion were forcing him forward.

"Stay where you are, Josh!" Zillah shouted.

Josh did not reply, but he slowly retreated backward, handing himself from tree to tree, until he was out of sight in the grove. Somehow, Zillah had no doubt that he was safe there. She turned back to find that the rest of the people had arrived around them on both sides of the stream. The women were of all ages, and all, without exception, finely dressed and coiffured. Their perfume blew on the warm wind in muggy waves. The men mostly wore old-looking, rustic breeches and shirts, but there were one or two among them dressed in bright garments almost as fine as the women's. One in parti-colored red and yellow, like a jester, caught Zillah's eye

as he leaped easily across a little ditch and came to stand
on the other side of the stream.

She knew him at once. It was like a shock—whether
of horror or joy, she did not know—to see him real
and warm and moving, and in that silly jester's suit,
so like Mark and so utterly unlike. He knew her too.
He stopped dead and they stared at each other over the
stream. His shock and concern, his unbelieving glance
at Marcus, made him for an instant look almost like
Mark. Then his jauntily bearded face moved back into
the cynical laughing shape which, she saw sadly, was
habitual to it.

"Well now, Mother," he said. "What do you want done
with these people?"

"Bring them to me in the small audience hall," the
woman in blue-gray replied. "And the centaur too, if you
can get him out." Saying which, she turned and walked
away along the stream. After she had gone a few yards,
her figure appeared to ripple. She became transparent
and, quite quickly, melted out of sight entirely.

The rest seemed to relax a little as soon as she was
gone. Two of the men got Philo to his feet, and—Zillah
could not help noticing—they handled him carefully and
tenderly, as if they had more than a notion of how he was
feeling. Philo was still very pale, and he did not seem to
be able to use his right arm.

"You may as well pick those up," Herrel said to one
of the girls, pointing to the toys strewn in the path.

"Why?" she said irritably, glancing at Marcus. "It's
only a boy child." But she and another woman got down
among their billowing satins and started collecting toys.

Two other women, both older, took Zillah's elbows
and urged her along the path. Zillah resisted. Marcus
was leaning over her shoulder reaching for his toys.
"Doy!" he said urgently.

"And someone had better go and see if they can tempt that centaur out from under the Goddess's skirts," Herrel said. "You—Ladny and Sigry—you'd be best at it."

Zillah felt both the women holding her stiffen. One said acidly, "Don't you speak to me like that. I don't take my orders from you."

"Don't you indeed?" said Herrel. "How shocking of me to suggest you might! All right. Sigry, take Andred and our sweet Aliky and see what *you* can do about my mother's orders."

One of the girls who had been collecting toys nodded and handed the bag into Marcus's eager fists. She even gave him a pleasant smile as she did so. She and the other older woman, together with one of the better-dressed men, set off toward the grove, calling out, "What if he won't come out?"

"Besiege him," said Herrel and leaped across the stream.

The woman called Ligny immediately flounced around and marched away along the path. From the way Herrel leered derisively at her stiff satin back, Zillah suspected that Herrel had got rid of her on purpose.

She became sure if it when they all moved off downstream and Herrel contrived to walk beside her, so near that she could catch the faint characteristic smell of him—Mark's smell. It made her shake all over. She could scarcely carry Marcus, who was anyway writhing violently about in her arms to embrace his rescued toys.

"I'll carry him if you like," Herrel said. "Will he come to me?"

Feeling as if she could barely move, so conscious was she of Herrel beside her, Zillah twisted her head to look at Marcus. Some of his writhings, she found, had been in order to get himself into a position from which he could perform a grave inspection of Herrel. "Ike bad," he remarked to her. "Airy bay."

"Yes, I think so," she said, and was surprised that her voice came out cool and normal.

"Here, then, fellow." Herrel took Marcus out of her arms, making a somewhat clumsy job of the transfer. She could feel him shaking too. Under cover of their maneuverings, he whispered, "What in hellspoke's name made you come *here*? You were safe. You'd left me— him."

It was in a way incredible, that this man she had never met should whisper to her in Mark's voice of things that had happened in another world. But even while she was feeling this amazement, Zillah was whispering back, "Because I couldn't *help* it, as soon as I knew. I *had* to. Fetch Mark back. You need him."

Herrel all but lost the bag of toys, but rescued it with a raised yellow satin knee, while he whispered, "I don't know *how* to! For the gods' sake, don't say a word to my mother! She'd kill!" After which he contrived to gather up both Marcus and the bag and hoist them to his shoulder, remarking in a normal speaking voice, "So you think I'm a nice man, do you fellow, hairy face and all?"

"He must be the only person in the Pentarchy who thinks that then," observed one of the women coming behind.

It showed Zillah that they could easily have been overheard. Herrel had taken a great risk. She blazed with joy that it was this important to him—still, after she had walked out on Mark that way, without even a word— and this joy mixed and warred confusingly with fear and dismay, and her guilt at bringing Josh and Philo into this. It *was* her fault. She was sure of that. In some way, getting them all out of Arth, she had been homing on Herrel, instinctively. She had only to think of the woman Marceny to see that this had been a disastrous thing to do. Yet for a short while this was less to her than the mere fact of being here, walking beside Herrel under the blue sky on the path beside the stream.

Nobody said anything much as they walked. From time to time the path crossed irrigation—or drainage—ditches leading from locks in the stream. Then they walked over carefully made plank bridges where everyone's feet thundered, and, it seemed to Zillah, any amount of whispering could have been hidden in the noise. But Herrel did not say another word to her. The confusion of Zillah's feelings began to sort itself out— as she told herself wryly, the confusion at least was familiar, since it was the way her mother worked, both on her and on Amanda—and she began to have suspicions.

She looked at Herrel frequently, pretending to be anxious about Marcus, who was placidly fingering Herrel's beard as he rode in Herrel's arms. The few words Herrel said were all to Marcus. "Don't pull it out, fellow—it's not grass, it's hair." He smiled as he said it with a sort of inane, contemptuous hilarity, as if life were to him nothing but a continuing silly joke. It was not a reassuring smile. It was possibly not quite sane. Zillah saw that Herrel's face around the smile was even paler than Mark's, and full of habitual creases of strain that had nothing to do with the smile. He looked deeply diseased. It began to be borne in upon Zillah that this fag-end left of Mark was not a man you could trust. Perhaps he had even intended someone to overhear him whispering to her—or at any rate, he had not cared.

But Marcus liked him. Zillah clung to that. Just as Marcus had taken to Tam Fairbrother and then Tod, he had taken one of his calm fancies to Herrel. Perhaps all was not lost.

They approached a stand of tall evergreen oaks. The path led around the trees to a shallow flight of steps, really a set of terraces climbing to a lawn. At the back of the lawn, bowered in the trees, was a mansion. It was built in a style so foreign to Zillah that the most she could have said of it was that it was gracious, and probably a good deal bigger than it looked. *Palladian* was the word that came to her, but she knew that was quite wrong. It was elegant, reposeful, and breathed out a menace so total that she gasped. Something crouched inside there that was implacably hungry and full of hatred. Marcus felt it too. He turned and looked at the building with his lower lip stuck out. But to everybody else it was obviously just the house. Their pace quickened and they crossed the lawn in a businesslike huddle, sweeping Zillah, Marcus, and Philo with them. Philo was carrying his arm and looking as scared as Zillah felt.

Up more shallow steps, among pillars and along a cloisterlike passage, they were swept, and finally into a small, lofty room paneled in some strange greenish wood. There was a dais at one end where Marceny was sitting, strumming at a small, painted harpsichord. As the double doors opened to let the party through, she smiled, nodded, and swung around on her stool to face them.

"Oh, good," she said. "I'll talk to the gualdian first."

While Philo was being pushed toward her, Herrel quietly dumped Marcus on the floor beside Zillah and moved away to sit on the edge of the dais at his mother's feet. Just the position, Zillah thought, that went with his jester's clothing. Marcus leant against Zillah's legs, thoroughly and unusually subdued.

"What's your name, my boy?" Marceny asked Philo in a clear, kindly voice.

"Amphetron," Philo said. Zillah tried not to let her surprise show. Philo knew this world and its dangers, and she did not. She realized she had better watch Philo's responses closely and take her lead from him.

"And how did you come to be trespassing in my Goddess grove, Amphetron?" Marceny asked.

"I've no idea," Philo answered. "We simply all found ourselves there."

"You should call me 'my lady' or 'Lady Marceny' when you speak to me, you know," Marceny pointed out, still in the kind and reasonable manner one might use to a small child. "And I really don't think you should tell me naughty stories either, Amphetron. We all felt you coming for hours and hours before you arrived. One of you was using quite terrific power in order to get here."

"And I suppose that gave you time to set up magework to disguise yourself—that, if you don't mind my saying so, was a low trick," Philo said. Zillah had not realized he could be so bold.

Marceny smiled. "Oh, I don't mind your saying so if you feel the need. It was thoroughly simple mental magecraft, purely designed to fetch you all out of the grove, and it took me no time at all—nothing *like* the power you people were squandering. I notice you haven't somehow confessed about that yet."

"There's nothing to confess. I don't know what the power was," Philo said. He seemed totally frank about it. "It must have come from outside us. We were in one grove and we suddenly found ourselves in yours. I apologize for alarming you."

"One grove *where*, Amphetron?" Marceny asked.

"The king's grove in the Orthe," Philo said.

Zillah thought, from Marceny's reaction, and Herrel's, and the slight murmur from those around her, that Philo had played a bold stroke here and named a very important place. Marceny said, with distinct caution—though her eyebrows were raised ready to disbelieve—"The king is a friend of yours, is he?"

"No, of my father's," Philo said, and his voice rang with truth. Philo, be careful! Zillah thought. She's bound to check!

"Dear me," Lady Marceny responded, with delicate incredulity. "Then the king and your no doubt eminent papa are going to want you back, aren't they? Which of them would you prefer me to get in touch with?"

"The king," Philo said. "If you would be so good."

"Very well," the lady said sweetly. "Meanwhile we shall, of course, keep you safely here. The king wouldn't want to lose you. And of course, we're always *terribly* glad to see gualdians here in Leathe. We suffer from such a *dearth* of gualdian blood. It's such a hardship for us. Gualdians are so much better at magework than mere humans. But luckily, half-gualdians are quite as good. It's a pity you're such a funny little specimen. We'll just have to hope that your offspring turn out a little more normal."

Philo, for all his bold talk, must have known she was playing with him. As he realized the extent of it, his face flushed deep red. Herrel looked up and leered at him. Lady Marceny laughed outright.

"Or with such big feet," she said. "It's going to be quite hard to tempt any of my girls with you. But we can always use artificial insemination. It won't hurt you a bit as long as you're good and do what you're told."

Philo, with his face so dark with blood that he looked ill, started to say, "I—won't—"

Lady Marceny held her hand up gracefully and stopped him. "Won't? Is your arm still worrying you? You got off very lightly, you know. It could be a lot, lot worse. Please remember that you *are* a trespasser on my estate. Now I'm going to let you go away to a nice quiet room where you can think about this. I'm sure that by this evening you'll have decided to be sensible, and if you are, I *might* get in touch with the king about you."

Philo's face drained to white as he was led away through another door. There was a decorous little spurt of murmuring and laughter from all the women present.

It was entirely derisive. "*That* a friend of the king's!" someone behind Zillah said, and the satin-clothed lady beside her said, "Lord of Forests! She'd better not pick me for a mother—not with *that*!" As she said it, the woman gripped Zillah by the elbow and propelled her toward the dais. Zillah hastily took hold of Marcus's hand, or he would have been left behind, staring after Philo.

"Bilo god?" he asked in doleful bewilderment.

"Hush, love." Zillah had known she would be unable to deal with Lady Marceny from the moment she saw those eyes of hers. Now Lady Marceny leaned forward, and those same eyes urgently, deeply, and precisely stared into Zillah's, exploring for the wincing innermost tender parts of her with a power that was almost like tenderness, but was not.

"Now you, dear," Lady Marceny said. "Perhaps you can explain a bit more clearly than the little gualdian. I'm very puzzled about you all. How *did* you arrive in my grove?"

Follow Philo's lead, Zillah thought. Talking about the king seemed to have done no good. But Philo, for some reason, had shown her that he did not want the woman to know they had been on Arth. And she was so bad at lying—and always worse with eyes like that searching into her. Mother could always screw the truth out of her. She had a moment of ridiculous homesickness, wishing she were back in Arth being questioned by the High Head. He had powerful eyes too, but never seemed to use them this way.

"I really haven't too much idea," she said. "We were all in the king's grove one minute, and next minute we were in yours. I really do apologize—"

"Bilo *god*?" Marcus asked again.

"Quiet, love—I'll explain later." Zillah was glad of the interruption. It enabled her to free her eyes from Lady Marceny's and turn them down to Marcus clinging to her leg. It gave her a respite in which her mind might work. Would she tell the story she'd repeated to the High Head in Arth, or—? No. But what, then? Something nearer the truth, perhaps. It was said that the best lies were near the truth. "It all seems to be some mistake—er—my lady."

"Really?" Lady Marceny said, with sweet touches of disbelief. "Well, naturally any young woman is more than welcome in Leathe. What is your name, dear?"

"Zillah Green."

The lady's beautifully arched eyebrows rose higher. "Indeed? What a strange name for a gualdian! You *are* gualdian, aren't you, dear?"

"Oh no, my lady." Being unable to look at those eyes, Zillah looked past Lady Marceny's carefully arranged hair, with what she hoped was perfect frankness. "I come from another country."

"Azandi?" said Lady Marceny. "Surely not? Everyone there is *black*, dear."

"I know—but there are other countries," Zillah said, hoping this was true, hoping some warning might come from Herrel if she went too far astray. He was sitting a yard away—too close for comfort—staring vaguely into space, and she had him in the corner of her eye the whole time. "My country's quite a small island in the southern hemisphere." She looked past Lady Marceny's face and thought limpidly of New Zealand.

"Oh—Pridain or one of those places!" The way the lady said this suggested that such an island counted as Third World—or Fourth World, if that was possible. Marceny turned abruptly to Herrel. "*Isn't* she gualdian?"

Zillah very much did not like the way Herrel's face turned mechanically to Lady Marceny's, allowing his mother to stare into his eyes. Like that, the lady seemed to drink him in, quaff him, in great drafts. He shriveled slightly with it. Zillah did not like that at all. "No," he said. "Not gualdian—a slightly similar strain, but without the power, and no training at all."

Marcus picked up Zillah's uneasiness. "Bilo *god*?" he demanded again. The treatment of Philo was really worrying him—as well it might, Zillah thought.

"It's all *right*, love!" she whispered protectively, and swore to herself—probably, she thought, in her usual far too belated way—that, whatever happened, Marcus was not going to come out of this damaged in any manner whatsoever. That was top priority now, even above Herrel.

Herrel turned away, swung his legs to the dais, and crouched there. He fetched out a handful of smooth pebbles with which he began to play a game somewhat like jacks, throwing from his palm, catching with the back of his hand—his left hand, Zillah noticed: Mark was right-handed. Herrel was very good at the game, no doubt from long practice. It was as if his mother's quaffing reduced him to childhood. I have just seen, Zillah thought in a sort of weak, angry horror, a kind of vampire at work. She faced Lady Marceny again, eyes and all, feeling implacable.

"So if you come from that far away," Lady Marceny said, "I don't understand what you were doing in my grove—*either* of the groves—with a gualdian and a centaur."

Go on with the nearly-lie. No help for it. The eyes tried to quaff from her too. "I came to this country," Zillah said, "to look for Marcus's father." She felt Herrel flinch, although he did not drop a single pebble. "I knew he came from this—the Pentarchy, but I didn't know any more. The king was very kind to me and said of course I must look for him, and he gave me—Amphetron and Josh for guides and let me use the grove." She kept a corner of her eye on Herrel, in case this was an unlikely thing for the king to have done—and it probably was, she thought. He'd have to be a king like King Arthur to do that. But Herrel never paused in his smooth throwing and catching. Maybe it was all right.

To her relief, Lady Marceny seemed to accept this story, although with a certain irony. "Far be it from me to go against the king," she said dryly, "but the dear man ought to know better than to interfere in Leathe. But then perhaps our beloved king didn't know he was. I take it the Goddess obliged, dear, by sending you here. Have you seen the little boy's papa at all?"

I have not seen Mark, Zillah told herself, looking into those searching, searching eyes. "No. I told you. I think there must have been a mistake."

Again her uneasiness communicated to Marcus. He shook her leg and raised a booming shout. *"BILO GOD, Dillah?"*

Lady Marceny frowned, a gracious crimping of pearly maquillage. "What *does* that little beast keep shouting about?"

Marcus might have been a dog. There was no doubt Herrel led a dog's life. Anger fired up in Zillah. "He's reminding me that the god of my country is here with us, my lady."

Lady Marceny turned her eyes to Marcus, who glared up at her resentfully. "Oddy dady bake Bilo god," he told her frankly.

"Dear, dear!" said the lady. "Whatever that means, child, you'll have to learn to put those powers of yours respectfully to the service of ladies, or you'll find yourself being punished. I really can't be bothered with your god. Leathe can always speak to the dark side of him if necessary." Her eyes returned to search Zillah again. "My dear, I can see you're full of wonderfully strong feelings for this man of yours. I'm *so* sorry he seems to have let you down and run away. He must have quite a strong antipathy for you, if he went against the Goddess and got you sent to the wrong grove. But I understand why the dear king took up your cause. He's a sentimental man, of course, but he must have seen as plainly as I can that your child has the most *interesting* potential. How very sad. Naturally we'll make every effort to find your man now you're here—I'll lead the search myself."

Zillah thought that this was the least reassuring assurance anyone had ever made her.

3

G ladys plodded forward through the wood muttering to herself, or to Jimbo—it was not clear to either of them which. At first the trees were wet and spilled gouts of water on her finery, but soon they became dry and tightly packed and thorny. The light was the louring storm light she had left behind in her own garden. It was light enough for her to see the thorns and, with mutter or gesture, set them aside, but it was not enough to see the way altogether clearly. Here Jimbo, as she had suspected, proved invaluable. With a scrabble here at her leg, or a pull at her dress that set all its beads clacking there, he directed her always to the easiest path, where the undergrowth was thinnest and the thorns fewest. The marvel was to Gladys that there was a path at all. Among the fierce thorns and formidable defenses it was always there, as if someone or something kept it there for a purpose.

Before long she thought she could detect hints of brighter day ahead. "Jimbo's worth his weight in gold," she muttered. "But don't pull so—I've got to save my feathers."

Here, quite suddenly, Jimbo ceased pulling or even moving.

"And with good reason, I'll be bound," Gladys muttered, and kept still too.

Somebody else, a little over to the left, was fighting through the woods as well. She could hear the crackle of feet stamping brushwood, the slashing of branches, and the dragging rasp of thorns across cloth. The sounds had considerable violence, and that was increased by a certain amount of swearing. Gladys listened. The voice was unquestionably male. She was not sure she wished to have anything to do with its owner. He sounded angry and exasperated as well as violent. The mere fact of his being here bespoke powers rather uncomfortably equivalent to her own. On the other hand—

"Missed the path, hasn't he?" she muttered to Jimbo. Jimbo, in his own peculiar way, agreed that this was so. Gladys sighed. At her long-ago initiation she had been made to understand that power was hers only so long as she never passed by anyone in need. This was need. Her fellow traveler, though he might not yet know it, was in deep trouble.

"Over here!" she shouted. "Work your way over to your right!"

The threshing and crunching ceased. "Who are you?" the voice bellowed back. A young male voice. It reassured Gladys a little. These young fellows might surpass her in sheer strength, but she could make up for that, every time, in experience.

"Doesn't matter!" she bawled. "Just come on over— the path's *here!*"

He was desperate enough—or trusting enough—to obey her at once. His trampling and threshing changed direction. She kept him going right with a shout or so whenever she felt him veering, and it was not long before he burst out of the thorn brake beside her. He proved to be quite small. The light was not good enough for her to see more than that he was only an inch or so taller than she was, though she could tell he was chunky. But he was not as trusting as he seemed.

"If you're some kind of interworld Lorelei mark-stepper," he told her airily, if breathlessly, "you can just dispel. But I can accept it if you're—" And, quite casually, he spoke a word, called her a name that made Gladys positively jump for its potency and accuracy.

She approved of that. She chuckled. "Well spoken, young man. And I *am*, in my way. We can take it we're no harm to one another. I'm Gladys. Who are you, and what are you doing in this neck of the woods?"

"Trying to get home, of course," the young man answered. His manner was still airy, but a strong quiver of indignation now underlay it. "People have been pushing me about lately, all over the place, and I got sick of it. And what are *you* doing here?"

Gladys replied without hesitation, "I'm on my way to look for the sister of a friend of mine." Her sense was that it was important for her to be open with this young man—although she noticed he was not quite so open with her: he had cautiously avoided giving her his name. "A young woman called Zillah and her—"

"Zillah!" he exclaimed eagerly. "Zillah Green?"

It *had* been important, she thought. "Yes, Zillah and her Marcus. Her Marcus and I took a fancy to one another when his auntie brought him over to tea. He calls me Ardy Baddish. So you're a friend of Zillah's, are you?"

He laughed a little. "Probably—I think I still am, even though I got shoved into otherworld just for kissing her."

"Thereby hangs a tale, I guess," Gladys said, moving forward along the way Jimbo was indicating. "Suppose you tell Auntie Gladys."

He had, as she could see, a lot to get off his chest, and he proved, too, to have a naturally chatty disposition. He talked, merrily and freely, as he pushed through the wood beside her. As he talked, he fended aside, almost absentmindedly, thorns, boughs, and creepers, and went forging through the resistance that although it did not come from trees or undergrowth, was part of the very nature of this place—all almost as if he did not notice it at all.

"Remind me," Gladys murmured to Jimbo, "never to get on the wrong side of this one." His name was Tod, as she soon gathered.

"My misfortune," he told her, "is to be heir to a Fiveir, you see. It's not my fault I was born with this great lump of raw magery. Everyone in my family is, more or less, or we wouldn't hold the position we do. And my old father may be a fool in many ways, but he did make sure I was trained to use my birthright properly—which made it all the more annoying when I got to Arth. I should perhaps explain that Arth is a tiny universe attached to the Pentarchy, full of mages who are supposed to protect the Fiveirs—"

"So Laputa-Blish is really called Arth," Gladys remarked to Jimbo.

He said a great deal about Arth, and a certain Brother Wilfrid. He also talked of various Horn Heads and the High Head who seemed to be set above them. His account was not loving. Gladys sopped up all of it, and extrapolated more, while they edged through the next bank of prickles. So the girls were trying to carry on, bless them! It didn't sound as if those mages of Arth were quite as clever as they thought they were. Centaurs, eh? What were gualdians? And what the flaming hell was Zillah doing, letting this boy make love to her when she was breaking her heart over Mark Lister?

"It was only because I gave her a shock, showing her a seeming of my favorite aunt," he explained, just as if she had asked. Perhaps, in this place, she had. "It seems she's the spitting image of *her* sister—and they're both

called Amanda, oddly enough. Analogues, I think. Zillah
was shaken to hellband, and I tried to comfort her, that
was all, but Brother Wilfrid walked in on it, and I got
marched away and put through this ritual that sent me to
otherworld. I should explain here that everyone on Arth
is positive that otherworld is a kind of degenerate copy
of ours, full of subhumans. With respect to you, madam.
I was totally paralyzed with horror that they'd turned
me into some kind of reptile to send me there, and I
didn't start to think of using my birthright until after
I got confronted with a terrible creature called Paulie.
I was supposed to be her lover, and spy on her. But
there was this strong feeling of Leathe that I couldn't
place—"

So *Paulie* is our leak, Gladys thought. Not surprised.

But Tod paused, hand out to waft aside a long trail
of vicious thorns, and the briar paused too, held in the
shock he was evidently feeling. "Great gods!" he said.
"The Wheel down in hellband! *I* know why I kept thinking of Leathe now! That woman's husband—whatsis,
Mark! He was the very image of a perfectly horrible
creature I met in Leathe—if you take the horrible man's
horrible beard off. Man called Herrel. He's the son of the
Coven Head of Leathe, and he's a sort of evil extra hand
to the woman. Something so wrong with him, it makes
your flesh creep. This Mark man was the same. I suppose
it was another pair of analogues."

"I'm not sure," Gladys said somberly. "Given what I
know of Mark Lister, I don't think so. I'm more inclined
to think someone has been very wicked indeed—not that
Mark ever quite makes my flesh creep. But I know what
you mean. So what did you do? Run?"

She chuckled heartily when he told her how he had
changed cars. "Well, it was a lovely car," he said defensively. "And I miss my Delmo-Mendacci. As soon as
I got it on the road, I realized I hadn't been properly

happy for months. And your world turns out to have decent countryside after all. I sang for miles. Then I ran out of fuel, and I even had plenty of money to get more. There was so much money that I decided to spend the rest on food. I thought Arth owed me a decent meal. The roadhouse there did steaks almost as good as you get in Frinjen—but about the time I was thinking of choosing a liqueur, I realized that they were following me. And there was a big sending coming up from somewhere—"

"There was, wasn't there?" Gladys agreed. "I'm afraid I left that for Amanda to deal with."

They were nearly out of the wood. Daylight streamed around them, making gold-green slantings through the leaves of what were now mighty forest trees.

"Young man," said Gladys, "is everyone in your world like you?"

"No," he said. "Most of them are taller."

"I meant," said Gladys, "are they all so immoral—or do I mean amoral?"

"Well," Tod said, "my father's like me, and my uncle's viler. But my cousin and at least two of my brothers-in-law are quite saintly really. Why?"

"Because," she said, "I expect to fit in quite well."

The next moment they were out, truly into Tod's world, into a wide, moist meadow, where, by the light, it seemed to be midmorning. Gladys looked with interest at the small, chunky young man beside her, with his dapper little mustache and his neat cone of hair. He was looking at her with—well—politeness, and plainly wondering if she could possibly fit in anywhere. Indeed, as his eyes fell on the yeti boots, she could *see* it cross his mind that these were actually her own furry feet and that she might indeed be some kind of subhuman species. Gladys drew herself up. Every bead of her finery rattled. "Young man—"

"You've got an ether monkey!" he exclaimed. "I've never heard of anyone taming one of those!"

Gladys forgot her reproof and looked down at Jimbo. Jimbo, realizing he was in the presence of another person who could see him as she did, stopped his defensive scratching and sat up in the long grass with all his hands held out and his bright black eyes ruefully on hers. *Not my fault, Gladys.* "Is *that* what they're called?" she said. "But he's not tame, you know. He just decided to live with me soon after I was widowed. He never eats. It worries me."

"They live on low-band energies," Tod explained. "He's had plenty. He looks to be thriving." While he was speaking, Jimbo took his revenge on Tod for recognizing him by reciting to his extraordinary bead-hung and feathered companion Tod's full name and titles. "But I'm Tod to my friends," Tod told Gladys hastily. And he told Jimbo, "Come off it, ether monkey. You knew I was bound to suss you. You heard me say I'd been properly educated. You come from a spoke of the Wheel that—"

Jimbo did not want Tod to say where he came from. It was somewhere quite near hell, Gladys had always believed. "Yes, and he wasn't any happier there than you were in this place you call Arth," she said. "He had an enemy. That's why he left. Now, if you don't mind, I have a bit of work to do before we go on."

From the moment she stepped into this meadow, Gladys had been feeling a brightness and exhilaration beyond anything she knew from Earth. There was a cleanness. Some of it was, no doubt, simply the air, which smelled infinitely less polluted than Earth's. Tod, as he stepped back respectfully to let her work, was taking deep, long breaths of the air and smiling. But there was more to it than that. The lines of force, as Gladys tentatively reached for them, were far stronger and easily twice as clear as those of home. It was going to be a pleasure working with them. So why did she feel, at the back of all this glowing strength, that something was badly wrong?

"Hm—more than high time I came here," she remarked. "Let's ask a few questions."

She took firm hold of the forces. They almost fell into her hands, so plain were they and so ready for use. What a world! She envied Tod. He must have been able to do this in his cradle! Selecting the correct line, and holding the others she might need ready and wrapped around the little finger of each hand, she softly exerted her power—gently, not to offend here where she did not belong. There was instant response. Oh, what a world! Politely and deferentially, she requested, "The Being who has care of the physical level here—I apologize for not knowing your name—may we speak?"

There was a slight troubling of the air in front of her, a whitening and ruffling of the meadow grass, and the Being was there, sliding into visible existence as if from a great distance that was at the same time only an arm's length away. He hung before her as a narrow, vibrant man-shape in a robe of kingfisher blue and orange. His wings, like a stained-glass butterfly's, were of blue and vermilion lozenges, outlined in jetty black.

"You are welcome!" he said. His eager voice fell into the brain and rang there, oscillating.

Gladys narrowed her eyes against the vibrancy of his form. It was febrile, it seemed to her. "Are you well, Great One?"

"Not quite," the oscillant voice answered her. "But I am not sure what is the matter. The sea rises and the earth heats, and not according to the usual pattern. There seems no way to stop it."

"Ah," said Gladys. "I've met that problem too. When did it start, here with you?"

This was a mistake. The Being did not measure time in a way it could communicate to Gladys, and vibrated anxiously.

"Put it another way," Gladys said quickly. "*Why* did it start?"

"Your pardon, powerful visitor," the Being belled. "I came to *you* for the answer to that. *Have* you no answer?"

"Hm," said Gladys. "Overtaxed in some way, aren't you, My Lovely? Yes, of course you shall have your answer as soon as I can get it. But first, I need to speak to the One who rules the level beyond yours. Bear with me for a while. And, if you would be so good, put in a word for me with that One."

"Willingly," the Being oscillated.

Gladys gently released the lines from her little fingers, and with them, another respectful request. The second Being appeared instantly and eagerly. He was apparently in the air, several yards above the glowing first one. This Being, Gladys was intrigued to see, had the form of a white centaur, and he greeted her as gladly as his beautiful companion. But he was not beautiful himself— though she rather thought he ought to have been. There was a bloated look both to his torso and to his barrel, and the legs looked thick and stiff.

"Something wrong here too, I see," said Gladys. "And I greet you also, Great One. Tell me what is wrong and how I can help."

Tod looked and listened to all this with increasing awe. *Never* had he seen glowing, butterfly Asphorael appear so clearly. Even Tod's tutor—a better mage than any he had met in Arth—had never conjured Asphorael as more than a colored cloudy shape. But this old woman with the mad jingling robe and the big, hairy feet had done it just like that! And now she had summoned Cithaeron as easily and equally clearly. He wished he knew what the Great Centaur was saying to her—but even Asphorael's voice had seemed to be at some frequency almost beyond him. Raise his birthright as he would, Tod could not reach the Centaur's voice, and he was beginning not to hear Gladys either. He could only watch the Centaur's eager, anxious face, its features curiously small and delicate compared with its bloated body. The face reminded him strongly of another face, a mundane one. Josh? No. Where *had* he seen those same small, fair features? He had it—that mage who had patched Josh's eye, the High Brother of Healing Horn—Edward, that was the name. Now, that was very strange.

Gladys's voice came to him, faint and distant. "So *that's* the way of it! How do you suggest we balance it out then?"

Something is wrong with my world! Tod thought. And I never knew! Asphorael was hovering tenderly, almost imploringly, toward Gladys. "It's all right, My Lovely," Tod heard her say. "We shan't let it go on now we know." And beyond Asphorael, beyond the Great Centaur, in distance that was not the usual distance, or at least not physical distance, Tod was awed to see other shapes. They were faint, mostly manifest as bright, watchful eyes, or great, trembling wings, but he knew them for the Guardians of all the bands of the Wheel, all watching and listening, or maybe adding their words to those of the Centaur.

The Centaur faded. Tod seemed to notice the fact at the moment of his disappearance, when he was simply a white trace against the white clouds of the sky.

Asphorael had retreated, but he was still there, dissolved into the meadow around them, a tremulous presence. But it was not over yet. Gladys looked a trifle disconcerted at what she had started. She turned and bowed as a tall figure with a high head crowned with antlers stalked from the wood toward her. Hurl! Tod thought. And seems damned angry! Another, within an

indigo cloud, was rolling in from across the meadow
like mist from the sea. Ye gods! thought Tod. Now the
gods come! And here was yet another, blazing down the
path of the sun. Tod dropped hastily to one knee, and
in so doing, lost count of how many gathered around
the glittering blue figure beside him. But there was one
more that he did notice, because She noticed him and
came to Tod after greeting Gladys. Tod was aware of
this one mostly as pearl or azure and a light blazing
from the forehead. She was very angry too, though She
was not angry with Tod, and She had good cause to be.
She gave him instructions, without using words. What
the Goddess said to him, Tod could not have expressed.
He only knew that, after She was gone, and the rest with
Her, he stood up again in the bright, empty meadow
with certain things in his head that had not been there
before.

He and Gladys stared at each other. "Phew!" she said.
"What about *that*!"

Tod said, feeling unusually humbled and ignorant,
"How did you *do* it? Everything so solid and clear."

"Do it?" she said. "I only did it the way I usually
do. Your world is a pleasure to work with, that's all.
When I think of mine—well—it's all muzzy and twisted
beside yours. You must have some marvelous magic
users here."

"None as good as you," Tod said frankly. And looked
up in alarm. Someone else was coming, and he was not
sure he could stand any more manifestations.

4

It was only a centaur, real and solid and mundane, cantering toward them over the meadow. He was grizzled and largely black and not in the best of tempers. Tod thought they were probably on this centaur's land and he was coming to order them off it. Tod braced himself, ready for polite speeches. But the centaur stopped short with an angry skid to his haunches and glared down his nose at Gladys.

"You must be the woman," he said. "Damn it to hellspoke! I've lived ninety years and never troubled the gods, and they never troubled me. Now I get a whole spatch of them. I'm supposed to make sure you get to Ludlin to the king."

"I know. Gods are like that," Gladys said. "I've got to see the king and someone else on the way."

"I don't know about the someone else," snapped the centaur. "The king was all I was told."

"The other one's bound to turn up," said Gladys. "It won't take us out of our way."

"Women!" the centaur grumbled. "Can you get yourself on my back? I was told it was urgent, and it's bloody miles to Ludlin."

Tod, with a good deal of difficulty, managed to boost Gladys onto the centaur—who stood quietly enough but made not the slightest effort to help, which Tod thought was decidedly ill mannered of him. But then, this was a surly centaur. When Tod lifted the chittering Jimbo, too, and tried to put him in Gladys's arms, the centaur shied irritably. "I'm not carrying that thing!"

"Yes you are," said Gladys, "or you're not carrying me. And we know what the gods would think about that, don't we?"

The centaur shook both fists in the air, possibly at the gods, but he said nothing and allowed Tod to dump the ether monkey onto Gladys's beaded knees.

"Good-bye, then, Tod," she said. "I think I'll see you again, but they gave me the idea you've got things to do now. It was nice meeting you, dear."

"You too," he said. He waved as the centaur leaped into a racking canter and bore her away across the field. It felt very lonely without her, odd as she was. Tod walked slowly in the opposite direction, wondering how on earth he was going to carry out what seemed to be his part in the gods' plans. There was no centaur for him, evidently, and he did not even know whereabouts this was in the Pentarchy. It looked as if he was meant to steal another car—preferably one with a map in the glove compartment.

The meadow, though huge, did eventually end in a hedge, in which was a gate leading out into a deep country road. Tod let himself out into the road and stood between its hedges, wishing there were some means of telling where he was. The place was wholly devoid of landmarks—although, in looking for those, he did notice for the first time that it was spring here. Spring again, or spring still? Tod wondered gloomily. Have I been away a year? A week? Two years? When the gods leave you, they seem to leave everything low and flat. He was glad to be back in the Pentarchy, but this did not prevent him feeling as lonely and ill-used as he had felt in otherworld.

There seemed nothing for it but to start walking and hope to get a lift with a car or a cart.

Tod determined from the sun that turning right probably took him more southerly than turning left did, and he turned that way because it seemed to be correct. He had not gone more than a few steps when—joy!—he heard a car coming up behind. He spun around. It was a big old car, beautifully maintained, idling along with its top down. It looked to be a Delmo-Mendacci too, of all things, like Tod's own cherished, beloved, beautiful vehicle. It was even the same shade of subtle green. The gods provide after all! Tod thought, as he stepped to the center of the road and waved.

Between hedges bright with new leaf and cow parsley in lacy drifts along them, the car rolled to a gentle halt a few yards from Tod. And behold! it was not any old Delmo-Mendacci! It was Tod's very own car! Tod's cherished Delmo that he had left under wraps in the garage of his father's castle, with strict instructions that it was not to be touched—not by *anyone*—until he returned from service on Arth. Driving it was Tod's mechanic, Simic.

The gods provide indeed! Tod thought. He found himself with both hands on the Delmo's glistening square hood, leaning over the shining eagle on the end, staring grimly at Simic. Simic stared back. Tod saw it cross the man's mind that he could simply drive on, let in the clutch and plow on over Tod—So sorry, Your Grace—devastated—terrible accident—wasn't expecting—didn't recognize the young master—thought him on Arth—squashed him into the road—meat jelly—

"Don't even think it!" Tod said.

Simic had regretfully abandoned the idea anyway. He opened the door, jumped out, and became voluble, in one smooth movement. "Well, this *is* a surprise, sir! You may wonder what I'm doing, sir, but it is a fact—

you know and I know, sir—that machinery deteriorates
something dreadful if it lies unused, and so I took the
liberty, sir, of giving this car of yours regular exercise,
in the manner of a dog, sir, to preserve it, entirely with
your own good in mind, sir—"

"Poppycock," said Tod. "Fish feathers. Most of all
about my own good." And as Simic then became seized
of another perfect excuse and opened his mouth to begin
on it, "I don't want," Tod said, "to know whatever lie that
was going to be. I know you're bent as a centaur's back leg,
and *you* know I only employ you because you're a genius.
The fact is, you've been using *my car* to go cockfighting
or girl chasing, or whatever it was—and last I knew, you
had *two* perfectly good cars of your own—"

"Sold them, sir," Simic said sadly.

"Bad luck," said Tod. "I hope you lost on the deal,
but I bet you didn't. How far are we from Archrest
Castle?"

"About twenty miles," Simic admitted cautiously.

Any figure Simic ever admitted to, you automatically
adjusted. Make that fifteen at the most, Tod thought. In
which case, this featureless but comely road was one he
had raced down countless times in this very Delmo.
Good. They were in central Frinjen. "How much money
do you have on you?"

"Hardly any, sir," Simic said pathetically.

"Show," said Tod. He held out an implacable hand,
and Simic, with a look of real pain, slowly produced and
laid in that hand an extremely fat wallet. "Won on the
cocks, did you?" Tod said pleasantly. He counted himself off a hundred in ten-shield notes, which was about
a fifth of what was there, and held out his hand again.
"Pen and paper, and you get the wallet back. Come on,
a betting slip will do." When Simic produced one, and a
ballpoint pen, Tod handed back the wallet, laid the slip
on the Delmo's hood and wrote:

Respected progenitor,

I happened back unexpectedly early and ran into
Simic—you owe him $100, by the way—and have to
rush south. You can probably get word of me from
Michael this evening, but rest assured that I am fine,
though Arth may have the law on us soon. Love to
Mother.

Yrs. Tod.

August would recognize this as unquestionably from
his son and heir. Tod handed the note, but not the pen,
back to Simic. Given the means, Simic would infallibly
tamper with the sum owed him, in an upward direction. "There. If you want your money back, all you have
to do is walk to Archrest and give this to my father. Are
the keys in the Delmo?"

"Yes—*Walk?*" said Simic. "I'm wearing my driving
boots!"

"Bad luck," said Tod. "Maybe you'll flag a lift."

"But it's occurred to me, sir, that you could be rusty
at driving after a whole year, sir, and if I were to take
the wheel and drive until you became accustomed—"

"Nice try," said Tod, "but you're out of luck again.
It's only been three months over in Arth, and I'm not
in the least rusty—just proved it, actually. So either get
walking or get the sack. The choice is yours."

Leaving Simic standing resentfully among the cow
parsley—his boots were pointed and shiny and probably pinched every toe he had, and serve him right!
Tod thought—Tod swung himself into the warm pol-
ished leather bliss of the driving seat of his own car and
drove away, fast. Simic would certainly get to Archrest
somehow in order to reclaim his money. Mother would
worry—but then she always did. And August would be
warned that Tod had broken his service. He might be

furious, but he would get his lawyers onto it at once. So. Tod gave himself up to the full, throaty purring of the best car in his world.

He hurtled down to a crossroads, which proved to be one he knew well, and turned south. Shortly he turned again, into the main southbound highway, and cut in the overdrive. The unlucky Simic had provided both tanks full of fuel. The gods *were* good. Tod sang—rather badly—as he drove. He bore Simic no real malice. In fact, he had often thought that he and Simic were rather alike, with the slight difference that Tod had been born with gigantic birthmagic, and Simic with an equally large affinity for machines. Simic usually seemed to see it like that too, though no doubt at the moment he was calling curses down on Tod's head.

For all his bliss, Tod was aware that this was the merest interlude. Something was urgent, there in the south. He drove faster, bypassing town after town, some of which, he had to admit, were as ugly in their way as towns in otherworld; but there were also a few places where he would have liked to stop for lunch, peaceful, picturesque places. But he did not stop. Consequently, by the time he reached the coastal marshes between Frinjen and Leathe and turned off toward Michael's manor of Riverwell, he was feeling unreal and time-lagged and as if today had gone on for twice as long as it should. And so it had, he realized. He had been ejected from Arth in the late afternoon, arrived in otherworld in the early afternoon, where he had spent most of an evening too, and now he had had most of a day in the Pentarchy.

The marshes were crossed by a myriad drainage cuts, each of them with its several humpback bridges. Tod took the bridges at speed, so that the big car almost jumped, while he tried to calculate just how many hours he had lived through since he got out of bed in Arth. And it was still only late afternoon here. The sun hung quite high behind him in the west. The car seemed to tread on its own shadow at every bridge. But he was nearly there. There was the stand of mighty old willows in the distance, all a vivid new green, and among them the great peeling yellow manor Michael had inherited. The large new sheds stood out to one side among younger willows. These were where Michael designed and built boats—most of them out of a new and wondrous fabric called fiberglass, the formula for which had been sent down from Arth.

Tod had an uneasy thought here. If some of the things he had half caught from what the Great Centaur was telling Gladys were true, then Arth could be destroying the Pentarchy by milking otherworld for things like fiberglass. It could be that he was speeding toward Riverwell to put an end to his cousin's livelihood. The barony was not rich. He could see the sea now, flat beyond the flat marshes, and a distant golden hump that was the seacoast of Leathe. As always, he wondered how anyone could live somewhere so flat and damp and so infested with Leathe and mosquitoes, and as always, as he whomped over the last bridge and swept in under the willows through Michael's ever-open gates, his heart lifted. Amanda lived here.

Around the corner of the drive, he had to brake hard. The place was full of centaurs. There were crowds of them, milling across the drive and the lawns and seemingly surrounding the house. Tod had not known there *were* so many centaurs in Riverwell. None of them looked happy. It was clear that something was going on that made fiberglass, at least for Tod, a side issue. It was quite a relief. He turned off the engine and shouted to know what was happening.

The centaurs seemed altogether too anxious to notice him, but the nearest somehow crowded aside to let a worried black-haired woman fight her way to the car.

To Tod she looked more glorious than Asphorael. She was—though he could not know the irony of it—wearing blue-gray like Lady Marceny, but her dress was linen and loose, with the merest sketch of the fashionable panniers in the form of flying panels which streamed behind her as she ran toward the car.

Tod gave a great shout of *"Amanda!"* and sprang down to hug her.

She was taller than him—many women were. "Oh, Tod!" she said. "I'm so glad you've got here! I knew you would."

She was, Tod discovered with a quite irrational touch of jealousy, pregnant. After all, it was a year since she remarried. He found tears in his eyes. He was always ashamed of how easily he cried. "What's going on here? Why all the centaurs?"

"They're all terribly worried," she said. "There's been a ghost centaur haunting our grove all day, and it's obviously in trouble, but none of us know it, so we can't hear it speak. Our centaurs keep sending for more and more distant cousins, hoping that one of them will know who it is, and none of them do. But I knew you were coming, and I thought that with your birthright—"

She was interrupted by Tod's cousin Michael trudging through the centaurs in big rubber boots, grinning all over his white, freckled face. Michael was tall and rodlike and had shaggy red curls. From head to toe he took after his mother's gualdian family, with none of the Gordano chunkiness. Seeing him now, Tod was struck by how like Philo he was. He might have been Philo with red hair. "Tod!" Michael yelled, and beat Tod affectionately on the shoulder. Again Tod nearly cried. He had *missed* this. "Mother told you about our ghost?" Michael said.

"Yes, but I don't understand," Tod said. "My birthright doesn't make me a medium—"

"It may not *be* a ghost—" Michael started to say, and was interrupted in turn by Paul, Amanda's new husband, as tall nearly as the centaurs who moved to let him pass. Tod had a moment of jealous dislike, which dissipated as Paul's big, warm hand grasped his and Paul smiled down into his face, slow and kind. Paul was a good man—a good sailor and boatbuilder too, by all accounts.

"They've told you?" Paul asked. "I don't think it's a ghost. It looks more to me like a sending from someone in really bad trouble, but it can't seem to talk."

"Oh, I see!" said Tod. "In that case—"

"I'll take you," Michael said. "Come on." He seized Tod's arm and dragged him among the great, hairy centaur bodies, shouting above the deep clamor of centaur voices, "Let us through, please. My cousin's here. He'll take care of it."

The centaurs seemed to know at once which cousin Michael meant—the one with the birthright. They fell back respectfully, and most of them stopped talking. In near-silence, Michael dragged Tod around to the other side of the house, where there was a narrower lawn—if possible, even more crowded with centaurs—which gave onto the marshes. The grove was a small hill crowned with silver birches, reached by a narrow causeway, about a hundred yards out into the marsh. Pushing among all these silent, staring centaurs, the cousins were embarrassed at saying anything private. Neither spoke until they had passed the last few centaurs stamping and wheeling at the end of the path and had hurried out onto the causeway. Then Michael said, "Ye gods, I'm glad to see you! I simply didn't credit my mother when she said you'd be coming. After all these years! And I *still* don't really believe she has Sight! Silly, isn't it?"

"No," said Tod. "I find it hard to believe too. When did this ghost-thing appear?"

"Midmorning. One of my centaur boat hands saw it and raised an outcry. And you know the way centaurs look after their own—there are centaurs here from the Neck of Orthe now—but I don't blame them. It *is* worrying. You'll see. And by the way, where did you get that peculiar hairy garment you're wearing?"

Tod plucked at Brother Tony's large sweater. He had forgotten all about it. "This—otherworld."

"You're joking!" said Michael.

"I assure you," Tod said, "I am not. I was in otherworld this morning, or last night, or something. Appalling cold, wet place full of beastly buildings. This thing's called a jumper. If you can lend me some proper clothes, you can have it as a souvenir."

"Thank you," Michael said. "It looks perfect for sailing in."

They reached the sandy hill of the grove and scrambled up it. From the time he was halfway up, Tod could see the white transparent figure of a centaur within, among the white boles of the birches. It was weaving and trampling this way and that, distressed, mindless, neurotic—something was wrong, that was plain. Tod hurried. The bodiless state of the apparition made the mad effect worse as he got nearer. The weavings and duckings took the centaur-shape straight through trees and even through the small altar by the pool, although the soundless hooves never once touched the bubbling waters of the spring itself. Mad or not, the specter was reverent. It was, Tod thought as he trod cautiously between the peeling white tree trunks, the shape of a centaur naturally white or gray. There was no dark on it anywhere, except perhaps— The apparition wove around toward him, and he saw that half its face was dappled.

"*Josh!*" he exclaimed. "Josh, what's wrong? Are you dead?"

To his great relief, the transparent eyes focused on him. The face broke into a worried smile, and the misty torso sagged. Josh's voice came to him, faint and far away. "Tod! Thank the Goddess! Can you hear me?"

"Clearly but small," Tod said. "Where *are* you?"

"Just a moment," said Josh. The apparition stood still, closed its eyes, and frowned. As it did so, it became milk-thick, then thick as whitewash, almost solid. Josh's eyes opened again. "That's better," his voice said, and he sounded much nearer and stronger. "I've been sending myself to all the groves I could reach," he said apologetically. "And trying to face in all directions while I did it. I'm nearly worn-out. *No one* seems to hear me. Tod, I'm in trouble. I'm in a grove in Leathe, on the estate of a woman called Marceny—"

"*Marceny!*" Tod exclaimed. "Josh, she's the very *worst*! What in hellspoke are you doing *there*?"

"Zillah got us out of Arth—the Goddess alone knows how she did it," Josh told him. "She used some kind of wild magic, and it was so strong that they all knew and were waiting for us. They're besieging me in the grove now. They keep trying new ways to get me out, and they're damned strong—"

"And Zillah?" Tod interrupted. "With you?"

"No," said Josh, at which Tod's stomach behaved as if he were crossing a hump bridge. "No, they got her, and the baby, *and* Philo—and you know what they do with gualdians—"

"I've heard—ye gods!" Tod was afraid he might be sick. But that would do Josh no good. "Hang on," he said. "Don't waste any more strength with sendings. Just stick in that grove like a leech, Josh, and we'll find some way to get you out. There's half a thousand centaurs here who can't wait to help. We'll do something. Just hang on."

"I will," said Josh. "I'd be all right if I wasn't having

to send. I was praying that they'd recall you. I'm so glad they did."

"Recall me?" said Tod. "They didn't. I came back by myself. I'm thoroughly illegal, and my father's going to have to bail me out, but it won't stop me getting to you."

"You're *not* illegal," Josh said eagerly. "At least, I'm fairly sure you're not. I've been thinking through Arth Service Laws to stop the people outside getting to my mind—and I started wishing I could tell you. Banishment's not legal for servicemen. They shouldn't ever have sent you!"

X

Arth, Earth, Pentarchy

1

The High Head was gloomily aware that he had made almost every soul on Arth extremely unhappy. But, he told himself, he had to do something about the wild disorder in the vibrations, and the only way, with the culprits seemingly still at large in the bowels of the citadel, was to order a massive clampdown. This was now in force. Servicemen and cadets groaned under double parades and compulsory rituals. The lower-order Brothers were required to attend mass meditations and cleansing rituals four times a day, while their seniors, when they were not on duty for these, were under orders to meditate alone in their cells. The buttery was closed, so that even the dubious consolation of passet beer was denied.

As a further precaution, the High Head went in person to inspect each Horn. This, he was not unaware, caused considerable panic. He had uncovered a stupefying number of hastily concealed irregularities. In Observer Horn, for instance, he was forced to order them to reperform all viewings made in the last six weeks.

"Regardless of the fact that we *can't!*" a junior Brother told Helen in Kitchen. For some reason, everyone came and told Helen things. Her cool, accepting manner had come to be regarded as wisdom. No one knew Judy very

341

well, and Roz was wisely keeping out of sight. So was
Sandra, after the High Head inspected Calculus.

There the High Head found such chaos that he concluded High Brother Gamon was insane and demoted
him to the ranks. To do him justice, the High Head
did not at that stage connect any of the disorder with
the women—apart from Zillah, that is. He went on to
censure Maintenance for allowing Rax and seven other servicemen to sit in a storeroom breathing glue and
oxygen. "And we didn't even know they were there!"
a Duty Mage told Helen. Rax and his friends had been
stealing a number of foodstuffs to sell too, which caused
Housekeeping to be hauled over the coals as well. Ritual
Horn was then found to be skimping, cutting corners and
gabbling formulae. "But if we didn't do that, we'd never
get through all the stuff he's piling onto us!" Alexander
complained to Helen. Flan was mysteriously not to be
found, so her handsome young mage came to Helen like
everyone else.

And while Alexander uttered these complaints, the
High Head was proceeding through Records, to demote
two senior mages; and to Defense, where he arraigned
almost everyone for overzealousness and rigidity. Even
Healing Horn did not escape, for Edward had unaccountably failed to make proper records of his healing of Judy.

Finally, having dealt out penances to nine-tenths of the
population of Arth, the High Head advanced on Kitchen.
Unfortunately, he arrived to find Helen surrounded by
an indignant crowd from all over the citadel. He sent
every man of them about his business, with further penances, and then laid a geas on Helen, banning her from
entering Kitchen again. After that, he did what he had
really come to do and ordered a diet of passet henceforth
for every meal. No fried food, he decreed, no spices, no
sauces, no roast. Meat stewed in water only, with passet,
was to be eaten from now on, and bread must be kept

for two days before it was eaten.

Someone told Helen that Brother Milo wept. All the other High Brothers were equally upset, for the ordering of discipline in their own Horns was traditionally theirs. This had been the custom for four hundred years, regardless of the fact that the law was on the side of the High Head. Brother Nathan declared that the High Head had been unpardonably high-handed. Brother Gamon added that the man was a soulless traditionalist without a spark of human feeling. "And without a stomach either," snarled Brother Dewi.

"He has been, at the very least, unpardonably impolite," stated the Horn Head of Alchemy, who was so relieved to have escaped reprimand that he could afford to be angry on behalf of the others. "We have been slighted. We are annoyed."

It would not have cheered them to know that, when the High Head returned to his office and tried to get on with the normal business of the day, he was no happier than they were. For one thing, he had acted like a tyrant, and he hated it. For another, the vibrations continued in unabated wild fluctuations. He promised himself revenge on Zillah, not to speak of the gualdian and the centaur, when the search parties finally ran them to earth. They had been lurking down there for three days now. True, there was unfortunately plenty of food in the depths—but surely it was only a matter of time before *someone* tracked them down! When they did, he would find it a pleasure to make them pay for all this necessary tyranny. The whole of Arth would revile them. And meanwhile, with all this going on, all the experiments with otherworld were in almost complete abeyance. He would have Lady Marceny on his tail any minute now. He groaned at the thought.

In their own quarters, the women groaned too. "*More wasting time!*" Roz strode angrily up and down the bare blue room. "I'm sick of you lot sitting about like a wet week! What are all these rituals about? You realize they're excluding us, don't you?"

"We don't count as mages," Helen said dryly. She was sitting upright against the wall, twiddling her long thumbs.

This irritated Roz. Most things irritated her by then. "I count myself a perfectly good female mage," she said. "When I think of all I've learnt—"

"Have you learnt a way to get home?" asked Sandra, slumped beside Helen.

"Well, no," Roz conceded. "But that's obviously a closely guarded—"

"I've told you," Flan called from her corner. "The only way to get home is to get turned into a reptile. I saw—"

"*Flan!*" Helen said warningly, and sighed. Sandra was in tears again. Tears rolled down her face, across her mouth, and dripped unheeded off her chin.

"I want to go home," Sandra said. "I didn't mean for him to lose his post for being mad. I *liked* him—a lot. He's a nice guy once you get used to—"

"Oh, do please bloody well spare me your nervous breakdowns, you two!" Roz snapped. She was not happy either. It was bad enough to have to hide in here for doing the job she had been sent to do, but she did not deserve the way the cadets were behaving. Whenever any of them saw her now, they fell into lockstep behind her. And they seemed to be whispering something like "Haw, haw, haw!" Roz refused to be paranoid about silly boys, but it was horribly depressing that there did not seem to be any real way home. And—

They all looked up as Judy came in, wandering among the veils looking obscurely nervous. Flan was galvanized, and uncurled from her corner with a bounce.

"At last! Did he know what happened to Zillah?"

Judy shook her head, and Flan curled up again.

"So where have you *been*?" Roz demanded. "It can't have taken you two whole days just to make sure he didn't know!"

"Nowhere," said Judy. "With Edward. And wandering. Thinking. I decided in the end I'd better come and warn you. We may be in trouble when Edward decides what to do. I told him we all came from the otherworld."

"You *what*?" said all four as one woman.

"Told him where we come from," said Judy. "I was sick of pretending. Edward thinks he'll have to tell High Horns."

"*Christ!*" said Roz. "And didn't you even have the nous to swear him to secrecy first? Honestly! What kind of a bunch of women have I got myself mixed up with? Not one of you has a scrap of patriotism. Not one of you even has a spine! Sandra goes and falls in love— in *love*!—with the man she's supposed to be seducing in order to save her world. And our poor world goes out of the window at once. Flan sees a ritual and thinks Zillah's been put through it, so Flan curls up and decides to die. Our world goes out of the window again. Helen gets turned out of the kitchen, so what does Helen do? Helen sits and twiddles her thumbs. Our world goes out of the window a third time. And then, to crown it all, little Judy goes and prattles to her Edward about exactly where we come from. World out of the window for good. Lord! Are you lot *trying* to be traitors? Well, I'm not. I'm a patriot. I love my world. I came here to do a job, and I want it *done*. Thanks to Judy, we've got a real crisis on. So let's have some *action*, shall we?"

"Speech!" Flan murmured rudely. "What a lot of good you did!" Judy simply turned around and walked out of the room again. Sandra got up and bolted after her, sobbing.

Helen unfolded herself and advanced on Roz. "And what action do you suggest? Haven't you noticed that we've all worked like stink in our own ways, and it's all come to nothing? *That's* what's the matter!" She stalked past Roz and out through the veiling too.

Flan was still curled in her corner, so Roz turned to her. "Worked? Who's worked? None of you except me. I'm the only one who seems to know the meaning of the word! I've worked. Good stern work! That's what this fortress responds to. I can *feel* it responding. And it's responding to *me*. Me working. Keeping our mission going single-handed. You don't catch me moping in a corner doing nothing. You don't—"

"Oh, shut *up!*" said Flan. "You're worse than High Horns. Your stern work my left buttock! *Zillah* got it right. What this fortress wants is a little *fun* for a change!"

"I'm not staying here to be insulted," said Roz.

"Go away then," said Flan.

Roz marched out. The door veiled and there was quiet. But not peace, Flan thought. Maybe she *was* having a nervous breakdown. She couldn't seem to get that horrible ritual out of her mind. It sapped her of all desire to do anything but curl up in a corner and listen to the pulsing of the citadel—or it *could* be just the pulse in her own ears. At the moment, citadel or ears, it was a sulky, sick bumping, as insistent as Roz's voice, which seemed to be hating all these rituals, every one of them, and urging Flan to do something to give them both some peace. Flan was fairly sure the sight of Tod turning gray and oozy had sent her mad.

There was a sort of sigh, and a feeling of release, followed by multiple movement like an army breaking step to cross a bridge. Flan raised her head. Yes, there were footsteps and voices in the distance. The latest ritual was over. Good. Roz had called for action. Let's *have* some action then. But better catch them before they all went to meditate or whatever.

Flan sprang up and ran. Burst out through the door veil, raced down blue corridors. Shot past mages in groups and pairs coming the other way. Plunged through the veil into the main hall of Ritual Horn. Her friends from Ritual were mostly still there, either standing about looking jaded or packing chalices away in caskets. Nearly everyone turned to greet her. Most smiled. Even Brother Nathan, far from descending on her with more blackmail, kept over the other side of the hall, where he smiled at her anxiously and rather diffidently. How nice, Flan thought. They all like me!

"Had a good ritual?" she said. There was a glum, dead silence. "And how are the vibes?" There were shrugs. Not good, evidently. "Well then," said Flan, "how about a bit of fun to take the taste away?" The way everyone reacted, they would have liked fun, but they thought High Horns might have forbidden it along with most other things. "There's no harm in it," Flan said. "It's a very simple dance. Here, let me show you." And, quite in her old manner—or perhaps a little more feverishly— she seized the four or five who were always ready to have a go and put them in a line with their arms around one another's waists. She put herself at the head of the line and wrapped the arms of good-looking Alexander firmly around her. "Now, just do as I do. Four bouncing steps—left-right-left-right. And *right* leg out. That's it. And again, people. Let's all do the conga—ah! Again! Let's all do the conga—*ah!*" She led the line around the hall. "Come on, people. You sing too!"

They got the idea. The conga is probably the easiest dance ever learned. *"Let's all do the conga—AH!"* the five shouted, capering and shooting out legs in unison. The others, Brother Nathan among them, took up the rhythm, clapping.

"Join in!" Flan shouted.

They did. It was so easy and harmless and a great relief besides. Before Flan had made one full circuit of the hall, everybody in it was rushing to seize the waist at the end of the line and join in—step and step and step and step and *leg out.* Their trained voices rose lustily. *"Let's all do the conga—Ah!"*

Flan, capering energetically, led them out of the nearest door and up the ramp beyond. "This is what you're supposed to do!" she panted. "Conga, people!"

Halfway up the ramp, she knew she had got it right. She was not sure quite *what* was right, except that she knew it was. Mages were racing down side passages and leaping onto the ramp to join the line, laughing at the absurd dance and seizing the chance to express frustrations by being harmlessly silly. The bouncing, singing line was twice as long when it left the ramp and bounced and shot its legs out into Records Horn. By this time, Flan knew it was more than that. The sullen vibrations of the citadel were changing, rising to meet the rhythm she was making. Bursts of energy came to her in glad gusts. She knew that if need be, she could conga for the next twenty-four hours.

They swept up the mages from Records and congaed on toward Calculus. There Sandra, sobbing inside a concerned crowd of mage-calculators, looked up, saw the line, and shouted, "Yes! Conga him out, man!" And the entire Horn joined in. Warm and rhythmic, they bounced and shot legs out, downward to collect the cadets next. To Sandra, with her arms wrapped around Brother Gamon and her face in the prickly blue cloth of his uniform, it was as if life suddenly became new and clean and simple. By the time the line had collected the servicemen and bounced on to sweep in Maintenance Horn and Defense, the surprising pain of love, of the conflicting loyalties Sandra felt at all times, had melted simply to rhythm and song and to Brother Gamon bouncing in front of her, as if difficulties had never been. Absurd mirth flooded her as they swept down on Alchemy Horn. The cadets and servicemen, like a lusty shot in the arm, were roaring out what they thought the words were.

"Bets and balls and bonkers—AH!"

In fact, since the line was now a quarter of a mile long, there was the usual difference of opinion as to just what the words were. Alchemy Horn was certain they were *"Can't stand it all much longer—AH!"* and Crafting sang, *"Wronger still and wronger—AH!"* while Observer Horn, when the mages there found the capering line roaring through their midst, joined it eagerly under the impression the words were *"The High Head is a plonker—AH!"*

Roz stood for a minute aghast, then for another minute with her arms folded and her lip curled—it was *unbelievably* silly and nonserious—but, as the blue-clad capering line receded from her down the corridor, where the front of it was already jolting and singing up and around the ramps on the next level, Roz was aware she had a choice. It seemed to be handed to her by the citadel itself. For the first time she became conscious that the place did indeed have vibrations, potent and awesome, like a voice. It spoke to her. Either she could join in this unusual and crazy piece of magic and become part of it, or she must stay aside and remain aside forever. She was suddenly aware there were others refusing to join in. She sensed Brother Wilfrid for one, hiding in a cupboard full of spare uniforms, and the obdurate Horn Head of Defense, who was still single-handedly guarding Arth from nonexistent invaders. Roz could be like those, the citadel told her, or— But Roz was always one who could not abide to be out of things. She sprinted after the capering line and flung herself onto the end of it. Step and step and step and step and *boot in!* And yelled out her own individual words. *"If you can't beat 'em join 'em—Ah!"*

On the upper level the line was snaking through dormitories and recreation halls, where it swept up any mages who happened to be there and went snaking on down to Kitchen. Some accompanied the line as outriders and spectators. There were a number of mages up there too elderly to dance, and these followed excitedly, the way people follow processions, limping hurriedly through corridors parallel with the dancers in order to intercept them as they went bouncing and yelling uproariously through the kitchens and gathered in everyone at work there.

Brother Milo fled the line, to an alcove in the corridor beyond, appalled and shaken by the fierce new vibrations the dancers brought with them. But in the alcove he found himself pressed against the angular warmth of another body. He sprang around to find it was Helen. "What are *you* doing here? I thought you were banned from Kitchen?"

"I am indeed," she told him, "and if you notice, I'm not in there. Your bloody High Horns made it physically impossible for me to cross the threshold."

"No doubt he knows best," Brother Milo piously said.

Helen's reply was blasphemous, but Brother Milo was saved from hearing it. The conga was upon them, and past, and still going past, and continuing to pass them, an apparently endless line of blue-clad bouncing, yelling mages, a mere body-width away in the corridor. *"Hellband fall on wrong 'uns!"* Brother Milo heard. But next second the words seemed to be *"Spells are all much stronger—ah!"* or were they really singing, *"Helen's food will conquer—ah!"* or was it again *"Blessings fall upon her—ah!"* Helen, he noticed uneasily, was jogging to the time of the ditty, with her widest, coolest smile. She bent down to him to shout, "I want you to join in this!"

He shouted back, "Are you trying to seduce me again?"

"No!" she bawled. "I gave that up days ago. I know you're a saint!"

"Naturally celibate," he yelled reprovingly. "I told you—I keep my Oath."

"I'm not asking you to *break* your damned Oath!" she roared in his face. "I'm just asking you to *dance*! Is that so bad? *I* want to—I will if *you* will!"

It did look fun, Brother Milo thought, wistfully watching joyous faces prancing past. And nothing in the Oath said anything about dancing. The end of the line was coming past now. He could hear himself speak when he protested, "I don't know the words!"

"Nobody ever does," said Helen. "Make some up."

And here came the end of the line, the two kitchen cadets, out of step and shooting the wrong leg out and roaring, *"Cesspits are for honkers—Ah!"*

"Oh, all right," said Brother Milo. He seized the waist of the hinder cadet and joined in, lustily singing, *"Decline and fall and conquer—Ah!"* He felt Helen seize his waist, but there really was no harm in it. *"And conquer—Ah!"* they both bellowed, dancing toward the main ramp. Some latecomer joined in behind Helen. As soon as she felt her waist grasped, it was clear to her that Brother Milo had given in to more than dancing. He would break his Oath with her as soon as they stopped. She felt as much sadness as triumph—which was ridiculous, since this was one of the things she was *here* for, for God's sake! *"Decline and fall and conquer—Ah!"* She resolved that he should enjoy it tremendously. It seemed the least she could do.

Halfway up the main ramp, bouncing tirelessly at the head of the line, Flan felt as if she were in a dervishlike trance by then. It was wonderful. Almost every mage in Arth was coiling up the main ramp behind her toward

Healing Horn, some upside down, some sideways, each singing for all he was worth, and the whole fortress vibrating with it. She was dimly aware that the rhythms were fiercer. The line of heads apparently jogging above her as they came up after her were singing something different now. Flan changed her own song to match the change. *"I came I saw I conquered—Ah!"* Flan sang, too loud in her own ears to hear that the mages coiling up the ramp were in fact singing, *"Let's pull the High Head's legs off—Ah! Let's finish the old bastard—Ah!"* No one knew where this began, but once begun, it overtook and replaced even the servicemen's new words, which were very dirty indeed. "LET'S KILL THAT BROTHER LAWRENCE!" they roared, and pounded upward to do it.

Edward looked up from Judy's face. The citadel was vibrating very oddly indeed—joyfully, fiercely—tum-ti-tum-ti-tum-tum-TAH, in a way he had never known it to do before. Listening, he could hear a huge, rhythmic roar, from the throats of many people.

"What is it?" said Judy. "It's like a football crowd."

It was nothing Edward had heard before, a strange, uplifting, and decidedly threatening sound. He went and took a look out of the doorway. Beyond the veiling, the words were gigantic and unmistakable.

"Wait here a moment," Edward said to Judy. He wasted no time in efforts to project to a mirror: he ran, ran in huge, long-legged strides, downward and along a corridor that gave him, every so often, arched glimpses of the roaring blue line snaking up the main ramp. The citadel pounded around him like a drum. He threw himself through the veiling of the High Head's outer office, bursting between the two elderly mage-clerks there who had been timidly peering out to see what the noise was, and dived into the sanctum itself. It was, as usual, sunny, quiet, and serene. In here there was no hint of the beat or the roar.

The High Head looked up with placid annoyance. "Edward—I was going to send for you to explain these reports—"

"No time for that now, Lawrence!" Edward gasped. "You've got to get out of here! Those women are all witches from otherworld. They've managed to harness the vibrations against you. Every mage in the place is on the way up here roaring for your blood!"

The High Head found it impossible to grasp the enormity of what Edward was suddenly telling him. If it had not been Edward, he would have dismissed it as a joke. "But the vibrations are normal!" he said. "For the first time for—"

"They've got the citadel on their side," Edward said impatiently. "You have to believe—"

"The citadel's not a conscious entity," the High Head interrupted. "Otherworld? Are you *sure*? How did they change their shapes?"

The vibrations were suddenly with them. The room shook to the enormous rhythm, rackingly. The blocks of the walls ground together, jolting in time to it, filling the room with regular clouds of fine blue dust. The High Head stood up and stared slowly around.

"It *is* conscious?"

"Yes, and they didn't change shape—they're as human as we are!" Edward gabbled. "Go *now*! You can just get to the secret way from your back ramp, if you go *now*!"

The singing became audible, huge and throaty, as if the stones of Arth themselves were chanting. The High Head dithered toward his inner door, still incredulous. "Leave everything? If I were to talk calmingly to—"

"They'd tear you apart!" Edward said, pushing him. "Go! Run!"

The High Head looked yearningly toward his mitre and sword-wand on their stand beside his desk; but the chanting was now so near that he could feel the words even through the grinding of the stones. "What about you?" he said, coughing in the blue dust. "That's murder on its way—I can feel—"

Edward knew with fatalistic certainty that he was now cut off from Healing Horn. "Never mind me. I'm not High Head. Run!"

To his relief, the High Head wasted no further time and dived away through his inner door. Edward, coughing and resigned, ducked his way out into the clearer air of the outer office, where the roaring was louder yet, and joined the two clerks at the veiling. Given luck, the avenging mages would assume he was simply kicking his heels here, waiting to see the High Head. But they would be furious to find the High Head fled, and they all knew Edward was the man's one friend.

That man, friendless now, was speeding giddily down a steep blue stair, with its walls beating the murderous rhythm around him. Ramp was a courtesy title: there had never chanced to be a centaur High Head, and therefore no need to adapt the secret way to hooves. Stairs made unfamiliar going. He knew he dared not waste time stumbling. Every Horn Head was given the secret of Arth's peculiar umbilical connection to its parent universe when he assumed office. With it, in case of emergencies that had never yet arisen, they were given the Ritual of Egress. The High Head saw he dared not assume that the chanting crowd baying for his blood contained no Horn Heads. He had angered them all too much. Therefore he galloped, wondering if his knees would hold out, wondering just how long it would be before some Horn Head discovered the hidden archway in his sleeping quarters and led the baying multitude down after him.

He had just reached the point where the stairway turned to ramp as it was joined by secret ways from other Horns when he knew that they were after him. The steady vibrations broke up. Though the joyful, idiotic rhythm of the conga kept on beneath the rest, there were other rhythms above it, angry and chaotic at first, then steady and trochaic—a sort of yammering double beat that reminded the High Head hideously of some Lady's hounds in Leathe when she had a manhunt on. It filled him with fears from childhood he had hoped never to feel again. He swung into the ramp and sprinted, thankful it was all downward, blessing the memory of the founder-mage who had decreed regular exercise for every mage in Arth, and overwhelmed with humiliation. That he should be the High Head around whom Arth broke up! So shaming. He was even more shamed to think he had been afraid of the wrong group of women. Give me Lady Marceny any day! I'd trade her for that Roz and that Helen! he thought, to the regular slamming of his feet. How many Oaths broken? Edward's for one. With whichever woman it was who had contemptuously told Edward the truth. The bitches had got inside and rotted Arth from the core. What did it matter then who knew?

He swung into another ramp that spiraled down among the reservoirs. The mages were closing. They must have sent the younger ones after him. They were too many for him, even with his superior magecraft, and with the vibrations all on their side—

His feet skidded, and he only just saved himself on the wall. The ramp was awash with running water. Here was a further horror. What those women had done to the vibrations had cracked a reservoir. A crack, with that weight of water behind it, only took bare moments to become a large split. Shortly a wall of water would be rolling down this ramp on his heels. The terror of it was such that the High Head spared effort from running to levitate. He heaved himself up an inch or so and sped on. Goddess, the double effort was tiring! And on the next ramp down, his raised feet were splashing, sending up great gouts of spray. He was forced to send himself up another foot and run crouching through the air under the lowered ceiling. He could feel—hear!—the rumble of escaped water following him now. He cringed against the ceiling and tried to put on a spurt, scrambling like a crab. Down and around. Down in front, the water was dimly banking, dammed by the secret portal, banking higher every scrambling step he took. The following water was close to thunder. Gabbling the Rite of Egress, he dived, praying for safety.

2

Gladys had discovered the centaur's name was Hugon, but their relationship was still far from cordial. Nor was he comfortable to ride. She reckoned that if he had been a real horse, he would have been dogmeat years ago. They were jolting across apparently interminable wide fields. Every time she spoke to him, she bit her tongue, but politeness kept her trying.

"How far—ouch—is it to the king?"

"Four days," he said. "I don't intend to go on through the nights."

"Four days!" The time scheme the various Great Ones had laid on her had not allowed for that.

"What did you expect?" Hugon asked jeeringly. "Even the train takes nearly a day."

What I am, Gladys mused, is insular. I keep thinking this country's only about the size of Britain, even though I can feel it around me, much bigger than that.

The size of Europe with half Asia attached, Jimbo informed her.

So big? "Train?" Gladys asked aloud. "You did say train?"

"Sure. Things that go chuff-chuff," said Hugon pityingly. He added with a surly trace of pride, "That was one of the ideas the Brotherhood of Arth handed down here—before I was born, that was."

"Then," said Gladys, "I think—ouch—train would be quicker. Why didn't you mention it before?"

"Because," Hugon snarled, "I'd have to pay, wouldn't I? Or do you have money?"

Gladys fingered her handbag. There was only a handful of change in there. Naturally it would not look like this country's money—though she was strongly tempted to put an illusion on the tea bags and tell him it was her train fare. But to do that, she needed to know what *his* money looked like. "No," she said regretfully, "but I'm— ouch—the king would pay you back."

"That stingy sod?" said Hugon. "Forget it."

They argued. Gladys persuaded. Bit her tongue. Gave up. Was on the point of deciding simply to put a compulsion on this obstinate creature when he said grumpily, "All right. Who else can you get money off if the king won't pay me?"

Easy. "Tod," Gladys said thankfully. "The young man who was with me. Roderick Something. He told me he was heir to the Fiveir of Frinjen. That do? It sounds wealthy to me."

"Garn!" said the centaur. "That makes him Duke of Haurbath and the gods know what-all. And he'd have to have birthright magic. He show you any?"

"Plenty," snapped Gladys.

That seemed to work the trick. Hugon grudgingly changed direction and began to fumble defensively with the pouch slung from a belt across his shoulder. "I may not have enough," he said, "for both of us."

"You can put me on the train, then, and go back to whatever you were doing," Gladys pointed out.

"Not likely," he said. "I stick to you until someone pays me."

Gladys sighed, bit her tongue again, and listened to her beads rattle with the uneven rhythm of his pace.

They had been going for about five minutes in the new direction when they were suddenly in a strong shower of rain. Pelting water obscured the featureless fields all around them. Jimbo whimpered. Hugon's somewhat greasy hair was wet through in seconds. Gladys pulled her pink shawl around herself and Jimbo. The centaur slowed, trotted, walked, stopped.

"I don't like this," he said. As Gladys was about to agree and urge him on, he added, "I've never known it rain out of blue sky before. Those gods don't want us to take the train. I know."

Gladys looked up and found that beyond the fierce slant of rain, the sky was indeed bright, cloudless blue.

"Raining fish too," Hugon said disgustedly. "Alive. What in hellband *is* this?"

Gladys bent forward and stared at the large trout flopping and twisting in the grass beyond Hugon's gnarled front hooves. "Does this happen ofte—?"

She and Jimbo and Hugon were all hit simultaneously by something heavy traveling at speed. There was a good deal of noise, mostly from Hugon and Jimbo, but among the shouting and squealing, Gladys heard another voice crying out too. She let her natural defensive magic take over and landed on her feet in the wet grass. When her confusion had passed, she realized that the person who had hit them must also have natural magic—well, he would have, she realized—because he was also standing unhurt, towering over her. He was tall and well set up, though not young, wearing a blue uniform of some kind. Across his wet forehead and streaming hair she saw a habitual dent, as if he usually wore a headdress of some kind. But how well she knew the features beneath it!

"Leonard!" she exclaimed. "Oh no, you can't be!"

The High Head stared at this dumpy elderly female, at the damp and drooping feather on its head, at its beaded gown the color of Arth, and particularly at its great white furry feet. The edge of his vision took in an irate centaur with an ether monkey crouching beneath its belly, and the shower of water receding across the meadows. "My name is Lawrence, madam," he said, and wondered why she was staring at him as if he were a ghost. Probably because he had seemingly fallen out of the sky. He sensed she had power. Therefore he asked politely, "You are a Goddess Priestess, perhaps?"

"In a way." Gladys still had her face tipped up, staring. "I'm from the place they call otherworld here." The eyes of the High Head sped involuntarily to her white, woolly feet. "No, they are *not* my feet!" she told him crossly. "I'm as human as you are! And you're the very image of Len—my husband. But Len died years ago now, so I reckon you're just his thingummy—analogue—aren't you? Where did you spring from?"

"Arth," said the High Head with grim dignity. "And I take it you are another piece of the otherworld conspiracy?"

The girls, Gladys thought, have managed to pull something off, bless their hearts! "In a way," she admitted. "But there's no good in glowering like that at me, my friend. Len never could get the better of me, and I've learnt a lot since then. So who are you? Your gods and Powers set me to meet someone on my way, and you must be the someone."

He shot her a grimmer look still and turned to the centaur. "Centaur, I'm the High Head of Arth, and I need to get to the king urgently."

"Oh no, not another one!" Hugon growled. "Have *you* any money?"

"Well, naturally, not at the moment—"

"Then go whistle!" said Hugon. "I'm paying her train fare because the damn gods will have my guts if I don't, but I'll be *raped* if I pay for you too!"

The High Head, to his exasperation, was forced to look pleadingly at Gladys.

"Yes, I've got to get to the king too," she said. "That's gods for you. I've never known them be entirely practical. Hugon—"

"No," said Hugon.

Surly brute, thought the High Head. He could argue all day and the centaur would probably still refuse. And he knew he had to get to the king and have him raise his royal power on behalf of Arth *today*. Given the time difference between here and Arth, those alien witches would have pulled the citadel apart by tomorrow. The High Head dithered for a moment, contemplating knocking the centaur out, putting the woman under stasis—which might not work, because she need not have been bluffing that she could best him—and running for the nearest train with the centaur's pouch. But there was that ether monkey crouching between the centaur's hooves. Its round black eyes were fixed on his, knowingly. He was not sure whose side it was on, except that it was probably not on *his*. No one in Arth or the Pentarchy had ever been able to fathom the powers of an ether monkey, but they were generally suspected to be considerable. He saw he would have to stoop to negotiation.

"Madam," he said, selecting Gladys as marginally the most rational of the three, "since it seems we have the same destination and somewhat the same problem, would you agree to some measure of cooperation?"

"I might," she said. "It depends what you want."

"There is," said the High Head, "an alternative means of reaching the king which, being from another world, it is possible you do not know. I would be willing to instruct you in this method, provided you would agree to perform no hostile act until we stand before the king. I would, of course, agree to the same truce on my part."

"Suits me," Gladys replied readily, "though I don't see why you should be on about hostile acts. I bear you no malice, Mr Lawrence. I need to see your king about both our worlds, as it happens."

"Then you agree?" he said.

"I do."

"In that case," said the High Head, "perhaps this good centaur could guide us to the nearest grove of the Goddess?" He turned to the centaur in his most majestic manner, which hid both hope and apprehension: hope because it was always possible the centaur would show a little belated patriotism and offer him the train fare; apprehension because Hugon might realize what he was up to and give him away.

The centaur, however, merely looked relieved at not having to spend his money. "If you want," he said. "The nearest grove's a good mile over that way. But you'll have to walk it."

"I'll walk too," Gladys said. "I need to talk to you," she explained to the High Head. Besides, she was tired of biting her tongue.

"I fail to see what we have to talk about," the High Head said haughtily as they set off toward a gate in a distant hedge, with Hugon jogging ahead and the ether monkey silently scuttling behind.

"Oh, come *on!*" Gladys said. "You're not stupid! But I can see you've had a shock, dropping out of the sky like that, and you may not have taken in what I said. You did hear me mention your gods and Powers, did you?"

"Of course," said the High Head. "People tend to mention the gods when they wish to persuade someone that their argument is important."

"Ah," said Gladys. "Then you've never seen them?"

"It is a very rare privilege which I confess I have not had," he told her stiffly.

"Asphorael?" she asked.

"Not for years." He felt irritable. He had a feeling he was failing some kind of test. "Madam, you must remember I have been on Arth for many years, and Arth is not this universe. Asphorael does not manifest on Arth. But in my youth my tutor did once or twice cause him to appear mistily before us."

"What does he look like?" Gladys asked sharply.

"As always—brightly colored and somewhat anxious," said the High Head. "I fail to see—"

"And the Great Centaur?" Gladys pursued.

He looked down at her in astonishment. "I am not sure he has ever been seen."

"Fair enough," she said. "I don't see my lot that often in my own world. I always think we may be too used to them to notice them. Can you do me a favor and make an effort to see the Great Centaur now?"

He stood still and stared at her. "My good female, that would take a daylong ritual even to—"

"No it won't," she insisted. "Not when he needs to talk to you. Go on. Go for it. Jimbo will help you."

He glanced at the ether monkey. So it was with *her*. He would do well to remember that. Meanwhile he supposed he had better humor the woman. He braced his feet and began to summon the threads of the Wheel. A little way off, Hugon had reached the gate and was holding it open for them, pawing with impatience. The High Head sympathized. He was quivering with shock and desperate to reach the king—and now he thought about it, bruised all over—and yet here he was instead somehow at the beck and call of a fat little—little *dame* covered with beads like a savage. And Edward had said the folk of otherworld were one hundred percent human! If Edward had met Gladys, he might have doubted that.

Gladys watched the strange gestures he made and tried not to shake her head. He was working beside the lines of force instead of along them, and on a level she would never have chosen. But then, Len had always done things his own peculiar way too, she thought affectionately, and Len nearly always got results. This one was just the same. His gestures—with some extra manipulation from Jimbo—had caused a troubling in the air above their heads. Gladys sighed. She was only able to see white filigree whorls. That reminded her of Len too. But it was clear that the High Head, for a few instants, saw. He whirled around on her, his face pulled into a grimace of awe and anger.

"What is this? What have you done? The Great One is dying! What has otherworld *done* to us?"

"Nothing. It's not *our* doing. But come along and I'll try to explain." Sadly and sedately, Gladys went through the gate and turned the way Hugon pointed up the rutty road beyond. The High Head hurried after. Hugon banged the gate shut and strode ahead again.

"You have a great deal to explain, woman!" the High Head panted, catching up with Gladys in the cloud of dust Hugon raised. "The Great One—the Pentarchy—is drowning in poison from *your* world! And you say it's not your fault!"

"I didn't say that," Gladys said. "I do blame myself. If I'd known, I'd have done something earlier. I just hope it's not too late now we do know. The trouble is, it's been going on for centuries now, ever since those magicians up in that pocket universe of yours—Arth, do you call it?—spotted that my world had a lot of ideas theirs *didn't* have. I expect at first they just took a look, then copied what they saw. But then they got the notion of *making* us get ideas for them. If they made us uncomfortable, or worked us around into having a war, or needing a new way to get about, then we set to and invented things to help us out. And they took the inventions and the ideas and sent them down here for people to use here. I reckon they've had everything from steam trains to penicillin and magic, for years and years now. No doubt they justified it by telling themselves that otherworld people weren't really human."

Heat flooded the face of the High Head. "This is certainly true," he said. "That is—we *were* accustomed to rely on otherworld to initiate methods of supplying the needs of the Pentarchy. But I assure you that the whole matter was studied and the experiments most carefully controlled. It was understood from the outset that what we took from your universe must be balanced by something from ours. I was always particularly careful to do this. It was my custom to plant men from Arth in otherworld, whose real physical presence—"

"So I gather," Gladys said dryly. "And they acted as spies for you. And they sent ideas back. Didn't any of you *think*? It's the *ideas* that do the damage. Magic is mostly ideas—they're the strongest thing there is! And you took ideas, a lot of them *magical* ideas—so many, they fair *poured* into your world—and you never once gave a single idea *back*. Now you wonder why your seas are rising and your lands are getting poisoned!"

"This is one idea we certainly put back," the High Head retorted. "I personally supervised a scheme to make the same situation arise in your world."

"So that you could learn—you *thought*—from something that isn't the same and doesn't have the same causes," Gladys said. "What you did to my world was physical, and it's not going to help *you*, whatever we do. One idea takes the-gods-know how many physical *tons* to balance it—" She broke off and thought, with her face wrinkled gloomily. "Oh, Mother!" To the High Head, it sounded like a prayer. "Oh Mother! If none of you had that idea before, then I've just fed this world another dose of poison. Let's hope someone did."

"I—" the High Head began to say, and then stopped. He did not believe a word of this. The whole physically based teaching of Arth was behind *him*, not *her*. And Arth *worked*. Or it had, he thought angrily, until six alien witches arrived in a rogue capsule. "I take it, madam, that you had some hand in the recent invasion of Arth."

"Well, we had to do something," Gladys said. "Did you expect us just to sit there while you played games with our climate?"

And she blandly admits it! the High Head thought. I rest my case! His anger grew, but he centered himself and controlled it. Meanwhile Hugon turned off into another lane, this one without hedges. The High Head saw stretching ahead of him the familiar straight causeway that led to a Goddess grove. The grove itself, a small, gracefully rustling clump of birches, was a bare hundred yards off. What a glad sight, he thought—a first real touch of home! Soon he would be rid of this creature. He looked at it, trudging along with its extraordinary woolly feet stained with grass and mud and its beads clacking, and permitted himself a thought as to where he would send it. Somewhere in north Trenjen where the white bears roamed. It would fit in there. And the ether monkey could go with it.

They reached the small clump of trees in silence. Hugon backed aside as they came up. "I'm not going in there," he announced. "I've had my fill of gods."

"That's all right, dear," Gladys said. "They only used you because you were the nearest one. I expect they were rather annoyed that you were the best they could do."

The centaur glowered at her.

"Thank you anyway," she said.

He grunted. Dust spurted and his hooves drummed as he made off back along the causeway.

"Well, that's that," Gladys said. "I hope your other way to get to the king really works, because the gods are going to throw fits if it doesn't."

The High Head strode among the trees. "It's quite simple," he explained. "The Goddess permits travel between any of her groves, and the king maintains a Royal Grove outside Ludlin. It does, however, take the power of at least two adepts to move from grove to grove."

"Ah," Gladys said to Jimbo as she gathered him into her arms, "I knew he needed us for something."

Within the trees, a spring dripped into a mossy stone bowl.

"That's pretty," Gladys murmured. "Peaceful. Nothing fancy."

Primitive place, the High Head thought. Bowl cracked and full of moss. "I'm going to put into your head my memory of the Royal Grove," he said, "and you must will us there. Is that something you can do?"

"I should *hope!*" said Gladys.

The High Head smiled and envisaged in professional detail the Royal Grove, such a contrast to this one, with its beautifully tended turf, marble bowl and statue, and its noble trees. Gladys took it at once and held it steady. In some ways, he thought, the creature would be a pleasure to work with. He smiled again and willed her sharply to a frosty grove in the north.

To Gladys, it seemed that the quiet little grove tipped about in a fuzzy turmoil. No matter. Working with Len had sometimes been like this too. She clutched Jimbo and held her will steady. Jimbo chittered and, almost certainly, put his contribution in. After a moment, everything settled down as it should. Gladys gazed around with pleasure at the large and beautifully tended grove. The trees tall and healthy, she noted, and that statue of the Goddess as Mother was truly lovely. It gave Her quite a look of Amanda's sister Zillah. And where *was* that girl?

Gladys wondered worriedly. She just had to hope Tod had found her.

"I see all this has to be royal," she remarked to the High Head.

He whirled around irately. She saw, with sadness, that he had meant to get rid of her. "There's no need," she told him. "I really could get quite fond of you if you'd let me. After all, I married you once."

The dark blood of fury suffused the High Head's face. He glared. Perhaps it was lucky that the Grove Guard arrived then. They advanced precisely from all sides, twenty or so men and one or two tall women in red and gold livery. Strong-eyed they all were, Gladys saw. A lot of power among them. The man—captain?—who came up to the High Head looked at least as much of an adept as he did.

"Your names, and your business in the Royal Grove," this man said coldly.

"I am the High Head of Arth, and I need to see the king urgently," the High Head told him. "There is a crisis in Arth."

The captain did not seem precisely impressed. "And I'm Gladys, dear," Gladys said. "And this is Jimbo. I'm from otherworld, and he's from—well, let's just say down below—but he's been with me for years, almost ever since my poor husband died. We have to see the king too. Your gods want us to."

As she had expected, they were a good deal more interested in her, and very impressed indeed by Jimbo. But it took nearly twenty minutes of explaining and some arguing, during which time Gladys was fairly sure a number of hidden tests were performed, before the captain consented to let them set foot outside the grove.

"It's by no means certain the king will grant you an audience," he said. "I'll send you to the palace, but my responsibility stops there."

3

Outside the grove was a driveway through more well-tended turf, leading down to a tree-bordered road where a large car was waiting for them. It was, Gladys thought, settling gladly into it, newer and far more comfortable than her faithful taxi, though its appearance was that of a car fifty years older. She thought she would enjoy the drive.

The High Head was by now seething for various new reasons. "These gualdians!" he said, flinging himself in beside her. "Think they own the entire Pentarchy! They look down their noses at me—the whole squad did—because I'm only a half-breed gualdian!"

"No, that thought came from you," Gladys told him. "But from the way they went on, I got an idea that Arth may not be too popular here. Is that right?"

The High Head remembered that consignment of servicemen—all those delinquents, one peculiar gualdian, and that sickly centaur. "That could be so," he admitted gloomily. "I fear the king indicated as much a little while back. How did you guess?"

"I keep my eyes open," Gladys said.

The car sped upward into the town piled on a hill beside a river. The style of the houses was no style Gladys knew—narrow and fairy-tale or thick and low,

with great doors—but, she thought, you did not have
to know a style to like it. Steep-pitched roofs, blue or
red, a chunky bridge and a spidery one, towers like mad
Chinese Gothic shooting up among the houses, all of it
rising to the grayish towered building at the top. "What
a lovely city!"

"It's not changed much," said the High Head, "but
they've put up far too many centaur dwellings since I
was last here. It's quite spoilt the East Quarter."

"And that tower?"

"Some newfangled factory."

All his comments were similarly depressing. Gladys
knew he was upset, but he began to annoy her. It seemed
to her that she had done all she could to show him
that they had a common cause, and he first tried to
lose her and now snubbed her every time she opened
her mouth. The car hummed slowly through a crowded
square where stalls were set out. Most were piled with
fruit, but Gladys saw meat, cheese, and clothing, and one
stall full of animals.

"Oh, I love markets! What were those animals?"

"I didn't see," said the High Head repressively.

As the car started to wind its way up the hill beyond
the market, Gladys lost patience. "You've spent too many
years in that Arth place of yours," she told him. "It's
turned you into some kind of gloomy prig. Relax, can't
you! Len could laugh at least!"

"I am *not* Len!" the High Head snapped.

"Yes you are," said Gladys. "You're Len in this world,
and I'm glad it was the other one I knew. I'd never have
married him if he'd been like you."

Though the High Head did not deign to make the
obvious reply, anger suffused his face nearly purple.
Three worlds were conspiring against him to wound
him! Three worlds were trying to make him both insig-
nificant and ridiculous! When the car gently stopped,

hood pointing into a large archway leading to the white-gray palace that crowned Ludlin, and its way was barred by a line of young gentlemen centaurs refusing to let the car go further, he could have screamed. A glance at the driver—another gualdian—showed him that the man was simply going to sit looking smugly impassive and let this happen. The High Head tore open the car door and advanced on the centaurs.

"I'm the High Head of Arth. Let me in to see the king at once!"

They stood in a row, shoulder to shoulder, wearing the same livery as the Grove Guard, and looked at him down their straight, somewhat horselike noses. "Sorry, sir," said the one in the middle. "We've had no orders about anyone of your description."

Though these guardsmen resembled Hugon only as a knife resembles a lump of ore, the High Head felt that the whole centaur race was out to thwart him too. He raved at them. He threatened them. He swore. The driver of the car opened his window to hear. An interested crowd gathered. Gladys climbed out of the vehicle, with Jimbo scuttling after her, and went to speak to the driver.

"What do we do to make them let us in?"

He shrugged. "Not much. Not if they've had no orders."

Instead of shaking him, as she was very tempted to do, Gladys looked around her. The archway, and the line of centaurs too, were imbued with power. She was not sure of the source of it, but she could feel it was too strong for both her and the High Head to break, even if she could persuade the man to work with her, which she doubted she could. He was in too much of a state. Such power was very surprising, but there must be a way to get in. Someone must know how. She turned and advanced on the crowd of spectators.

They had obviously never seen anything like her before. They all—centaurs, humans, and one or two oddities she couldn't place—backed swiftly away from her, looking alarmed, except for one of their number. This one, a little clerklike man in spectacles, with a string bag full of oranges, had obviously stopped to stare on his way back to work from the market, and seemed too bemused to move. Since he looked harmless and bewildered and was nearest, Gladys took hold of his arm.

"Sorry to bother you, dear, but *do* you happen to know how a person gets in to see the king? I wouldn't ask, only it's really important, you see."

The little man's bewilderment increased. "I was," he said, "under the impression I was invisible."

A nutter, Gladys thought. Just my luck! "No dear, I'm afraid you're not. Auntie Gladys can see you quite clearly. Sorry to have bothered you." She let go his arm and was turning away when she realized that everything around her had become strangely quiet. The crowd and the line of centaurs were staring. The driver was leaning out of his window, frankly gaping. Beyond that, the High Head suddenly looked like a frantic statue. She turned slowly back to the insane little man and found him smiling apologetically.

"Truly," he said. "I like to slip away to the market from time to time. I have a habit—stupid, you may say— of liking to choose my own fruit. And usually nobody knows, because it is a fact that, when I will it, only those who also have royal blood can see me."

"Only those—then you're—but I'm not—" Gladys managed to say.

"No. This puzzles me," agreed the little man. "You saw me, and you are not, as far as I know, one of my relatives. I'm sure I would have known if you were. You are—if I may say so—rather memorable."

"I'm from otherworld," said Gladys. "Do I call you Your Majesty?"

"A problem," he said. "If you are from otherworld, there is no conceivable way I can be *your* king—but since I take it you need to see me and I am beginning to gather that the person with you who seems so angry must be High Head of Arth, I conclude there is something urgent afoot. I think we should all three go to my office."

Five minutes later, still decidedly stunned, Gladys found herself with the king and the High Head in a plain paneled room in the palace. There was a desk under the window as plain as the room. The only personal things in it were a multitude of potted plants—everything from a tropical fern to a small rosebush—but watching the king first empty his string bag of oranges into a bowl on the table and then put a finger to the earth of the nearest plants to see if they had enough water, Gladys had no doubt that this was the king's own private place. Having done this, His Majesty Rudolph IX, King of Trenjen, Frinjen, and Corriarden, Protector of Leathe and Overlord of the Fiveir of the Orthe, took off his clerkly spectacles and cleaned them with a handkerchief.

The handkerchief, Gladys recollected, had been invented by Richard II of England. She was not sure about spectacles. "Were those glasses one of the ideas that came down from Arth, Majesty?"

He put them on again and gazed through them at her with round, magnified eyes. "I believe so—several centuries back. Why? Is that a bad thing?" She nodded gloomily. "Then sit down," he said, waving to the group of plain, cloth-covered chairs by the fern in the hearth, "and tell me about it. Shall we start with you, Magus Lawrence?"

The High Head, now very pale and harrowed, held on to the back of a chair and stood there stiffly. "Your

Majesty, what I have to say is very serious and for your ears only."

"I'm sure," said the king. "But my sense is that what the two of you wish to say is closely connected. And though I feel hostility from you toward this lady, I get no sense of danger from the lady herself. So please sit and proceed, Brother Lawrence."

Irritably, the High Head obeyed. While he talked, Gladys sat with Jimbo crouched against her and could have cheered at what had happened in Arth. Bless those dear girls! She was delighted, even though she could guess, from the way her leg was quaking with Jimbo's laughter, that harnessing the vibrations in that way had not been entirely intentional. But that young Flan always had her instincts in the right place. Maureen's motives, she had always suspected, had not been quite pure in choosing Flan, but it had turned out to be ideal all the same. The king, she was interested to see, did not seem too worried by any of what the High Head was telling him. He looked grave, he nodded, but he was in no way alarmed or scandalized.

"Thank you, Magus," he said when the High Head was done. "I sympathize with your indignation and shock, naturally, but I must tell you that I have felt for some years now that Arth was in need of reform. You must have realized the way I felt from the servicemen I sent you last spring."

"The louts," the High Head said somberly. "Your Majesty—"

"The majority were indeed louts," the king agreed. "We had to make up the numbers in some way, and neither I nor my advisers wished to waste any more promising young magecrafters on Arth. But the centaur and the gualdian were hand-picked by me, personally. Both are throwbacks to earlier times and so possess a large degree of wild magic. My hope was that this type of power would act to disturb the vibrations of Arth—which I suspect that it did—but I took care to balance them, in case of disaster, with a Fiveir heir with a trained birthright. And had these three had no effect, my next step would have been to go to Arth myself and force reforms upon you. I wasn't, of course, reckoning on direct action from otherworld. By the way—" the king put his hands to the sides of his glasses and focused an apparently anxious stare upon the High Head's harrowed face "—didn't young Roderick Gordano play any part in all this? I don't recollect your mentioning him, Magus."

"Your Majesty," the High Head said, "I have done nothing to deserve this—this high-handed one-sided action. I had no idea!" His voice cracked.

The king took advantage of the cracking to persist, musingly, "Though you tell me that young Philo and the centaur unaccountably took to the deeps of the citadel with the otherworld young woman and her child, you have not clearly indicated any *reason* for this."

The High Head rallied. "I inherited a tradition," he said chokingly. "I have been doing my best to continue it, Your Majesty. I—I behaved throughout as kindly and humanely as that tradition laid down. Tradition told me it was my duty to take in a party of women in distress. I did nothing wrong. I welcomed them, I tried to find out how to get them home. Meanwhile I warned them of our Oath and its connection with the vibrations—and my reward is that Arth and its values are now in ruins. How was I to know they were from otherworld? Tradition told me that the inhabitants of otherworld were not human!"

His distress was real. Gladys pitied him, even though she knew he was using it to bluster over the facts. The king thought so too. His hands continued to focus his glasses on the High Head. "Magus, I do not doubt you are a good man, though I could wish you were not so much inclined to the traditional. A little more real research into otherworld, a little questioning of tradition, might have helped. Now, if you recall, I asked you about Roderick Gordano."

The High Head appeared to pull himself together. "So you did, Your Majesty. My apologies. I am in a state of shock. I suppose the young man was one of the dancers roaring for my blood in Arth just now."

Gladys did not need the nudge Jimbo gave her. "Lawrence!" she said. "That is a whopper! You know it is. You sent Tod off to be a spy in my world. I know, because I met him on his way back here. No real coincidence, Majesty," she told the king. "There's only one way through—looks as if someone keeps it open—and he missed it slightly. So he got stuck, and I happened on him and put him right. He told me all what had happened to him on the way."

The king looked at the High Head. "Magus?"

"He was caught," said the High Head, with dignity, since he was caught himself, "making love to the young woman, Zillah. He deserved punishment. My practice is to send all such offenders to otherworld."

"Condemned," said the king pleasantly, "out of your own mouth, Magus. Transposing a serviceman anywhere except back to the Pentarchy is illegal, as I am sure you know. I am afraid you have given me my official excuse to remove you from your office. But I'd have had to remove you anyway. You see, it was not only Arth's extreme traditionalism which was disturbing me. Leathe seemed to have got its claws into you—"

"I *swear* that is not the case!" the High Head protested. "Last time the Ladies of Leathe were with us, I took every precaution—"

"Possibly," the king cut in. "Possibly you were unknowing victims. But I cannot otherwise account for the fact that Leathe has, for the last decade, been receiving a constant stream of ideas and inventions which the rest of the Pentarchy has never been allowed to have. Nor could I rid myself of a suspicion that the activities of Arth were actually *causing* the rising of the sea here."

"Oh, they were, Majesty," Gladys said. "This is what I came about. Your Great Centaur—"

The king turned his focused spectacles on her. "Then I think you should tell me now, Mrs.—er—"

"Gladys. Well, Majesty—"

"But first tell me about the invasion of Arth," said the king. "I can't imagine a person of your powers having no hand in that."

A shrewd man, she thought. She told him the whole story, aware as she spoke of the unfortunate High Head becoming alternately enraged and desolated in the chair opposite. Len would have managed his feelings better, she thought, though Len was always a bit inclined to be hidebound too. It must go with the man. Having told the king about the capsule, she gave him the facts as she had had them from the Great Centaur. "He was sick," she concluded. "It was the ideas that did it. He told me that ideas transpose matter—energy—in the most concentrated form there is. Your universe is bloated by this time, Majesty, and ours is getting drained. As I told Lawrence here, it does no good for Arth to trigger this global warming thing with us, because your world is getting filled with what you get from *us*, and to pull in just another idea from us is going to do more harm than good. It might help more for you to tell *us* what to do about *our* trouble."

"It might," the king agreed intently.

"But there's more," Gladys said. "I'm glad we've had this talk, all the four of us together, and you happened to mention Tod, because things are really falling together in my head now. It's what *you* said, Majesty, about Leathe getting this whole stream of stuff. I saw that stream, back in the early days. It's like a great mains sewer, and I'm afraid I know what it is. You see, Tod told me he was set to spy on the man in our Inner Ring—he's called Mark Lister, and he came out of nowhere suddenly with powers you wouldn't believe, which always did puzzle me, but I was only just widowed then and I'd other things on my mind, like a row with my daughter, and who was to replace Len in the Ring, and so I kind of let him pass, if you know what I mean. Anyway, Tod said our Mark was the image of a man called Herrel in Leathe—"

"Stop there," said the king. "I see. Herrel Listanian's been puzzling us for some time. So not only has the woman Marceny committed an abomination, but she's poisoned our world doing it. Good. Then I can safely close down Marceny."

"It seems to me you'd do well to close down this Leathe as well," Gladys observed.

"Unfortunately I can't," said the king. "The ex–High Head here will tell you how Leathe was legally established as the demesne of female mages soon after Arth was established."

"I could go on for hours about it," the High Head said bitterly. "It may have started as a safeguard, believe it or not, to separate male and female mageworkers. Now, to cut a long story short, Leathe is established by every magical and legal method possible. It would take a major revolution to unseat those women."

"You never know," said the king. "My hope is that it's begun." He sat forward. "I'm glad you came to me. Our Powers know what they're about. As it happens, I am in a position to complete the picture. A regrettable part of our situation with Leathe is that I, too, have agents who spy for me. And reports came out of Leathe this morning that a centaur, a gualdian, a small child, and a young woman have suddenly arrived on the estate of Lady Marceny."

The High Head and Gladys both cried out together.

"One at a time," the king said mildly. "Brother Lawrence?"

"It's impossible!" said the High Head. "I was going to say they couldn't get out of Arth—but if there's wild magic in question, I suppose I— But, Your Majesty, you *know* what they do to gualdians in Leathe. I'm one of the products of it—I *know*."

"Yes, indeed," the king said. "I have Philo very much in mind. My agent has instructions to assist him in every way. And you, madam?" He turned to Gladys.

She had her hands to her face. Jimbo was chittering and nudging her beaded knee. "Poor Zillah," she said. "Majesty, she's in love with Mark Lister, and she has power. The moment she sees the other half of Mark, she'll know. And she's going to try to put him together again. Majesty, Mark knows all the secrets of the Ring, *and* he's a computer expert. That's too many ideas."

"It is," agreed the king. "She'll have to be stopped."

"She will be," said Gladys, and the grimness of her Goddess Aspect came over her. "I must get there at once and stop her."

4

Zillah wished Marcus would settle down. He had had two-thirds of an Arth day, followed by most of a Leathe day, which ought to have been enough to tire any toddler, and he was still fretfully on the go. The possibilities of all the toys in the bag had long ago been exhausted. The room they were in was little help. It was not exactly a cell, but it was made of stone and only sparsely furnished. Since the light came from a barred grille outside and above the window, Zillah concluded it was a basement room, though she had not noticed going down any stairs when they had been brought here. The door was solid, and locked. Marcus was pounding on it at the moment. She wished he would stop, fall asleep for a while, or at least give her time to think.

She needed to think of the things Lady Marceny had said. Somewhere among the woman's saccharine words there had surely been something that might help her turn this hopeless situation around. But she could not think of anything, not with Marcus banging away at the door. She also felt she should worry about Philo and Josh, and think of Tod—a sort of moral duty to blame herself for causing disaster to people wherever she went—but she could not concentrate on that either. In fact, the only feeling she had room for, among the distractions

Marcus made, struck her as entirely crazy: it was joy. A placid joy. Herrel was here. He would come. She only had to wait.

She told herself, without success, that this could be nonsense. The light from the grid was evening light now. No one had been near them, even with food, since they had been put in this room. Hope should be fading—except it was not hope: it was faith. All the same, since some of Marcus's restlessness must be due to hunger, it was time to think of something else to take his mind off it.

Zillah got up off the flimsy cot-bed. "Here, Marcus. Stop banging, love. Let's build a house in the middle of this room."

Marcus turned and beamed. "Ow," he agreed.

They assembled what little furniture there was and disassembled it. Marcus was good at taking things apart. He happily reduced the flimsy bed to a pile of rods and laths. For a while, he was diverted by being allowed to do something he had so often been prevented from doing, but he grew fretful again when Zillah tried to encourage him to build the pieces into a hut. Zillah persevered. They had quite a creditable Eeyore-hut made when the door opened and Herrel sauntered in.

Marcus greeted him with loud friendship. "Ow, ow, ow, ow!" he shouted, pointing at the edifice and beating with a spare bed rod.

Herrel grimaced. "Ow indeed. Were you thinking of keeping a pig?"

"OW," Marcus repeated, conceiving he might have been misunderstood.

"Yes, I know it's a house, fellow." Herrel scooped Marcus off the floor, bed rod and all, and went on a remarkable walk with him, straight up the wall beside the window, upside down across the ceiling, and down the opposite wall. Marcus thought it was marvelous and flailed his rod enthusiastically. Showing off, Zillah thought. Showing me party tricks. Maybe showing me that's what he's like. These dispassionate thoughts did nothing to counteract her sheer joy. Herrel had come. Her faith was justified.

"More!" Marcus commanded, as Herrel descended to the floor.

"If that's what you want," Herrel agreed, and went on a second gravity-defying circuit, this time around the length of the room, up the door and down the far wall, forcing Zillah to back toward the window. She watched his gawky jester's figure as it walked upside down, head almost brushing the top of the Eeyore-hut. A Joker, the Fool, the Hanged Man. Herrel was telling her all these things. Possibly he was also enclosing the room in some form of protection. She noticed he said nothing of importance until he arrived back, upright in the place where the bed had stood. "The centaur's still in the grove," he said. "They can't budge him. And the little gualdian's disappeared."

"Phil—I mean Amphetron?" Zillah said.

"*Bilo!*" boomed Marcus from Herrel's arms.

Herrel tapped him on the mouth. "Shut up, you. Neither you or your mother are good at secrets, are you? Fatal to come to Leathe if you can't keep a secret. Yes, the gualdian. My mother sent sweet Aliky up to him a while back. I suppose the idea was to start with a bit of tempting kindness, but if the girl couldn't fetch the centaur out of the grove, I can't see her seducing a gualdian myself. Anyway, she never got a chance. She shot back down, screeching that the room was empty. Now there's a major search going on. Have you any ideas on this? My mother sent me to ask you. I'm supposed to be interrogating you cruelly."

Herrel said all this in a light, laughing manner and seemed to be addressing most of it to Marcus. Zillah tried to meet his eyes, but it proved almost impossible. He looked mostly at the top of Marcus's head.

"He told me—Ph—Amphetron—that he had no kind of gifts at all," she said. "His family think he's a runt." It seemed hard on Philo to devalue him like this, but it was the only help she could give him. If Marceny thought he was worthless and the search relaxed, Philo might just get away. She wished she could think of a way to help Josh. "They wouldn't really want him for stud, would they?"

"He's gualdian, runt or not," Herrel said lightly. "We always want gualdians for stud, and they always try to run. They seem to think it's a dishonor. Funny state of mind. Those that get away afterward seem to consider themselves outcasts and never go near other gualdians, so I'm told. And the ones that don't get away always kill themselves."

"No!" said Zillah.

"Oh yes," said Herrel. "I was there when my father cut his throat." Here he did look at Zillah. His face creased into a carefree smile, but behind it she sensed another face—a face not Mark's but truly Herrel's, and quite unlike the bearded jester smiling at her—and this face was screaming. It only had access to Herrel's eyes. Those eyes implored her. "I was only about this fellow's age," Herrel added, giving Marcus a little shake. "Zillah, why did you *come*?"

She wanted to take him in her arms along with Marcus and tell him that it was all right, the agony was over now. But he was facing her across the silly hut, too far away to reach. "I told you," she said, and managed to enfold him anyhow, in some way not physical, but powerful and sure, in an enwrapping essence of herself from across the hut. "I had to come. I was on Arth and I saw you in a sort of mirror, talking to High Horns."

"Arth?" he said. "Why Arth? You were safe where you were! You'd left me—Mark—him. I was even glad in a way. I tried to be grateful."

"Grateful!" she said. "It was so horrible, I left Earth!"

"Yes, but you set me—him—free by leaving, you know. I don't know how it was—maybe it was the effort I had to put in before that to make sure my mother didn't know about you—but the moment you were gone, he was practically a free agent. And I thought he might at least repair a bit of the mess over there in your world, and turned him loose with instructions to let otherworld know the way it was being exploited. She's just found out what he's done. She's hard at work trying to punish him at the moment. That's why I'm here. Zillah, *why* did you leave me—him?"

His face still smiled at her, but she ignored it and spoke to the face behind. "He—Mark—was so *shallow* somehow—it was alarming. Then one night I had a kind of vision of him—you—down a deep well with a woman feeding off you. I thought it was Paulie, but it wasn't, of course. And I was pregnant and there seemed nothing else I could do. I knew it was hopeless. It—it was very horrible for me too. You—he—didn't even *try* to find me."

"We knew better than that," he said jokingly. "You were safer away from him. But if I'd known about— What's this fellow's name?"

"Marcus."

"Barker," Marcus agreed sleepily.

"Marcus, I'd have warned you never to go near us— him." The smile left Herrel's face at last. "Zillah, you realize that if *she* finds out who Marcus is, you and I are both dead, don't you? Now she knows what I— Mark's done, she's got very little time for me anyway. A small child of her own flesh and blood is *much* more malleable."

"Then she shan't find out." Zillah put forth more enfoldings, around Marcus and around Herrel too. "Herrel—"

His head was on one side and he gazed at her. "Goddess!" he said. "The weirdest thing about it is that I've barely *touched* you in my own flesh."

The stone room was dense with misery.

"Fetch Mark back," said Zillah. "You need him. Don't leave him there for her to punish."

"I told you—I don't know how. I was out cold all through the ritual."

She was exasperated. "But you must know! You—it's *instinctive*! He's *you*!" Herrel was smiling again, hiding his screaming face. Zillah said furiously, "And I bet she used your own strength to cut you in two! She feeds on you all the time. How did you ever *let* her get that kind of hold on you?"

"I didn't." Herrel was entirely back to his light, joking manner. "I was Marcus's age. There was a ritual—very pretty and impressive—in which I was circumcised and she ate the foreskin."

"Oh, good *God!*" Zillah's anger became blazing disgust. "Why is witchcraft so damn *squalid*! I think that's why I've never— Look, Herrel, this has to be nonsense. A third of a person's body cells change every seven years. After more than twenty-one years, she can't have the *remotest* hold on you!"

Herrel laughed and jogged Marcus. He seemed hardly to have heard.

"All right," said Zillah. "If the hold is still there, then you've got the same hold over *her*. Mustn't that be true?"

"Perhaps Marcus can sort that one out." Herrel turned merrily away from her. "That do for you, Mother? Full confession from both guilty parties."

"Yes, thank you, dear. Very nice." Lady Marceny, dressed now in crimson velvet, approached him along

what seemed to be a wide stone terrace. Her train softly
dragged over the flagstones behind her. "I heard your
part very clearly, Herrel, and I'm quite vexed. But I see
you've got the child. I may forgive you for that. Bring
him along here, dear. The ritual's all set up."

Why am I not surprised? Zillah wondered. I'm not
even angry. Just numb.

There were women around her, all finely dressed. Their
gowns glowed in the orange-ruby light of the sunset
filling the sky beyond the trees at the end of the lawn.
Was the room where they had been an illusion then?
Shame penetrated Zillah's numbness. She and Marcus
must have spent half the day roving about an oblong
space on the open terrace. How stupid! But there was
no point in thinking about that now. The lawn, about
a foot below the terrace, was lit by nine tripods, each
holding a blazing fire. There was a low table at their
center. On it, knives caught the color of both the sunset
and the flames.

5

"How far is it to Lady Marceny's estate?" Tod asked his cousin as they hurried back along the causeway.

"No distance, as the crow flies," Michael said. "It's just across the border, but the estuary's in the way. Since this flooding, you have to go miles round by the road."

"I'd no idea it was so near!" Tod said. "I've never thought of you living next door to a menace like that."

"Surely you knew?" Michael said, making great booted strides. "This barony was set up to guard the border. That's what most of the centaurs do here. Until Paul came, we had to employ a mage as well."

"Paul? Amanda's new man? Is he a mage then?"

"Not exactly. He's from Hallow Isle—off the Leathe coast. The people there all get born with some sort of natural antidote to Leathe. It's genetic."

Michael, Tod thought, sounded a bit curt about Paul. He was glad to see his cousin was not a complete saint. "Is that why your mother married him?"

"No," Michael almost snapped. "Love. I thought we could leave Paul here while we—"

"No," Tod said. "I take him. You stay."

"Now, *look*—!" said Michael.

"You look," said Tod. "The woman's grabbed one gualdian already. You're gualdian on one side, and on the other you've got Gordano birthright—"

"I've yet to notice either," Michael said.

"Marceny will. Gods in hellband, she'll want you even more than she'll want me! My old dad will *never* forgive me if I let us both go."

That seemed to shut Michael up. As they came to the centaurs milling at the end of the causeway, Tod looked up at the great yellowing bowl of the sky. Given luck, they could reach Josh by nightfall. The foremost centaur had a pale wedge of a face, like a slice of white cheese, and was clearly in some kind of authority. Tod snabbled him. "You in charge here? Good. The centaur in the grove isn't a ghost. He's Horgoc Anphalemos Galpetto a Cephelad—know the family? Great. And he's stranded in Lady Marceny's grove, in bad trouble. Can you choose me all your fastest folk? We'll need to go in and out quick, and I don't want anyone left on the way. Tell them to form up round my car in five minutes."

"Quite the little Pentarch, aren't we?" Michael murmured.

6

The king appeared entirely unhurried. He gave orders—or rather, issued mild requests to centaurs, humans, and some of the odder folk, some in uniforms and others in sober suiting—all of which, Gladys noticed, were obeyed as if they were commands with the death penalty attached. From this she conjectured that the power he could raise was formidable. It seemed hard on such a small, mild man. And she noticed he was seldom at a loss. In fact, the only time she saw him disconcerted was when he courteously asked his guests what they wished to eat before leaving for Leathe. The High Head asked for passet, Gladys for sausages.

The gnomish-looking lackey stared. The king blinked. It was clear both requests were extraordinary. "And the ether monkey?" the king asked, recovering. "Will he eat?"

"No," the High Head and Gladys said in chorus. The High Head shot her a venomous look and explained, "Your Majesty, they are not from our band of the Wheel. They are said to live on base energies. No doubt these are plentifully available from this one's mistress."

"Well, well," said the king. "Magus, I realize your position is deeply unpleasant for you, and your future uncertain, but I must insist on courtesy. Would it reassure you if I try to discover what is going on in Arth?"

The High Head's face showed a terrible eagerness. Poor man, Gladys thought. "If—if that is possible, Your Majesty."

The king got up and ambled to his desk, where he stood looking out of the window and apparently tapping his desktop aimlessly. "As you know," he observed, "I seldom do this in person, but I think it is time that I did. Ah. There are not much in the way of tides just now, but something—I should say Someone—has favored me with an excellent wave band. Here we are."

The window in front of him rippled, dimmed, and became shot with flecks of light. Like a bad television warming up, Gladys thought. As in a television, sound came first. Laughter. Peals of it. One of the laughers broke off to say, "Arth here. Who is it *now*?"

"If it's Leathe again, tell them what to do with it," someone else said.

"This is the king," stated His Majesty, "wishing to speak to whoever is in charge."

"Oh—*Goddess!*" said the first speaker. This was followed by a muttered discussion, giggles, and the sound of a chair falling over.

"Yes, all right—she's bringing him," said someone else. "Find some coffee. Quick."

The window cleared with a *flick* to bright blue light, and a face twice lifesize looked out of it. It was swaying slightly. For an instant, Gladys had the notion she was seeing the Great Centaur again. But this was a man, trying very hard to look serious and businesslike. He said, with great care, "I am Acting High Head until the coming elections, Your Majesty. How can I help you?"

"Edward!" said the ex–High Head. He looked betrayed.

"Yes, you can tell me what's going on there," said the king.

"Well, nothing much at the moment," Edward replied.

"You'll have to forgive me, Your Majesty. We're all very drunk. We've been celebrating for a long time—the repeal of Oath and Constitution, you know." The High Head put his face in his hands.

"Do you intend to draw up new ones?" the king asked.

"In a bit," said Edward. "I mean, yes, of course, Your Majesty. Someone said they were working on it, I think." He seemed to realize that this was a little inadequate. He frowned importantly. "We shall ask for two hundred women from the Pentarchy the next time the tides are right. Then we'll abolish the service-year—and celibacy, of course—and— What? Oh yes. A lot of the mages and most of the cadets want to go home."

"That seems to be on the right lines," said the king, "but a little sketchy, High Brother. Add two things to it now. Perhaps if you have a Brother handy to write this down, it would assist you to remember tomorrow, or whenever your party is over."

Edward turned and made fierce gestures to someone out of sight. A hand appeared, passing him a block of paper and a pen. After a slight tussle, in which Edward attempted to retain the wineglass he had in each hand as well as the paper and pen, and the hand—possibly a female hand—firmly removed both glasses, he turned and nodded owlishly at the king. "Ready."

"Splendid," said the king. "Write, One: No further research is to be done on otherworld without written royal permission. Two: The function of Arth is, in future, to supply the Pentarchy with the same sort of inventions that we have hitherto gained from otherworld, and these are to be discovered purely by the Brotherhood's own unaided efforts." While Edward laboriously wrote, the king said over his shoulder to Gladys, "I'm ashamed of the way we've been sponging on your world—and they *can* do it themselves, you know. Some of the best brains in the Pentarchy are over there. Is there anything else I should tell him?"

"Ask about our women," Gladys said.

"Oh yes. Have you got all that down?" the king asked Edward. He nodded, looking as sober as only someone extremely drunk can. "Then the last thing I have to say is about the five otherworld women in Arth. What arrangements have you made to send them home?"

There was an instant outcry. Shouts of *"No!"* and "Don't you take our women!" and "They're *staying!"* filled the paneled office deafeningly. Edward's face was jostled out of the screen, replaced by several angry ones, two of them female, and then jostled back. Gladys sighed with relief. Flan and Judy seemed fine.

This time, Edward was icy cold sober. "I'm very sorry, Your Majesty. We have no intention of sending any of the women anywhere. They have asked to stay. We made them all citizens of Arth this morning." His image vanished with a crash and a slight tinkle, as if someone had broken a large sheet of glass. Evening sun dazzled through the window again.

The king turned away from it. "Well, there you are. I shall go there and try to sort things out in due course, but the next tides are not for nearly two years, I'm afraid, and by that time it will be *very* hard to remove anyone who wants to stay."

Gladys shrugged. "That's five more full sets of ideas."

"I know," said the king.

The dejection of all three was interrupted by a footman entering with a trolley. Gladys eyed the carefully sliced black pudding that was the Pentarchy's notion of sausage and politely said nothing. The king, however, was unable to resist murmuring to her, "How *can* the man eat passet?"

"My Len had a weak stomach," Gladys murmured back, "and I daresay he's just the same. Analogues, you know. Len used to live mostly on potatoes."

The ex–High Head heard her and looked at her with hatred.

Shortly the king looked at his gold fob watch. "We leave for the Royal Grove in five minutes. Both of you must visit a bathroom before then."

"I, Your Majesty?" said the High Head. "There is surely no need for me to go to Leathe?"

Gladys did not hear the king's reply, for a polite young woman arrived just then and led her away to a washroom with decidedly peculiar plumbing. Gladys wrestled with it, thinking that His Majesty was being rather hard on poor old Lawrence. The man's only fault was to be the wrong man in the wrong place at the wrong time. This mess, after all, went back long before he was born.

She came back to find the High Head dismally resigned. He sat silent in the car that drove them to the Royal Grove. Even Gladys did not guess that the thought of setting foot in Leathe again made the passet churn in his stomach. All he said was, to the king, when they were joined in the dim light under the great trees by seven soberly dressed men who all had the look of mages, "Your Majesty, I hope one of us is familiar with Lady Marceny's grove. It is usually important to—"

"No, Magus, but we have other reliable facts," one of the soberly dressed men told him, and he spoke with as much respect as if the one he addressed were still, in fact, High Head of Arth. "We arrive exactly at sunset in that time zone. The grove is of orange trees, and there is a centaur in it."

His facts were a little out. There were upward of a hundred centaurs in it, all milling about, shouting in deep bass voices. Gladys hurriedly picked Jimbo up, wondering if they had come to the wrong grove. The king's party was jostled every which way. But hardly had they realized this when one of the centaurs shouted, "Oh, all *right* then! Let's all go!" And the whole crowd of huge bodies went thundering away out of the grove.

"Follow them," said the king. "Quickly."

7

The journey was exasperating for Tod. He insisted on driving his car, which meant he had to keep to the roads, while the centaurs spread out across country. He and Paul had both been offered a ride on a centaur, but Tod bore in mind that they might have to make a swift and scattered retreat and that Josh would be exhausted. He folded the roof of the car back, which just gave room to cram someone Josh's size into the rear seat, and drove with the warm wind in his hair and Paul sitting solidly beside him.

No one had a reliable map of the Listanian estate—no doubt Marceny took care there were none. The centaurs tended to get lost at first, until it dawned on their unorganized minds that Tod was able to home on Josh. His birthright led him to be conscious of Philo, Zillah and Marcus too, though Tod did not tell them that. Once he had explained he knew where to go, the centaurs spread out in the lands on either side of the road, and Tod tended to leave them behind on the straights. Where the road bent, the centaurs cut the corners, and he nearly ran one down. In addition, he had not the slightest idea what kind of conversation to make with Paul. They exchanged stilted monosyllables until—Tod supposed it should not have surprised him—Michael suddenly bobbed up in the back, saying, "Hellspoke, Tod! Paul's a perfectly reasonable human being!"

Paul gave a great shout of laughter, and Tod jumped half out of his skin.

"Oh, Great Centaur, you fool gubbins!" Tod said disgustedly. "And you timed that perfectly, didn't you? There's no way I can turn back now, or even kick you out!"

Taking everything together, he thought it quite surprising he only drove down one road that dead-ended.

Sunset came and grew and flared on the meticulous drainage ditches. The land here was as flat as Michael's barony, though ten times tidier, and well before they reached the place, Tod could see both the grove and Marceny's mansion as a small clump and a black blot against the sky. The nearer he came, the more certain he was that he was faced with a choice. Josh was still in the grove, all right, but there was worse trouble at the mansion.

In the end the choice was made for him. The road did not go to the grove, but swept around to the left to lead to the mansion. "Michael," Tod said, hurriedly drawing up, "go and make sure they get Josh out of that grove and back to Riverwell. Stay near a road, and I'll try to pick you up on my way back. I'll take Paul to the mansion, if that's all right with you, Paul?"

"Fine," said Paul. "Take care, Michael."

Michael leaped out and ran, splashing through a dyke in a storm of spray, to accost the nearest centaur. Tod swung the car around and roared off toward the mansion, which seemed to be dark, except for a curious flickering among the trees at the back.

Paul said, "There's something over there with more power than I think I can handle."

"Now, why do I get that feeling too?" Tod said. He stopped with a shriek at the unlighted front of the house and ran up the steps and in through its open door, brushing aside heavy wardings and strong blocks to right and left like so many cobwebs.

8

There was more power than Zillah knew how to handle. She felt heavy with it, dead. As Marceny set off down the steps to the lawn, with her train of red velvet softly brush-brushing the stone, and Herrel followed carrying Marcus, the women around Zillah moved too. She was forced—by nothing she could see—to walk in their midst. The power was so great that she had to wade rather than walk.

And I might as well be dead anyway with Herrel on two sides at once, she thought, glancing at the girls around her. Pretty, pretty little faces. Don't any of them *care*? *They* seemed to be able to walk perfectly well, although the one on her right in the peacock silk was mincing rather. Zillah glanced contemptuously at the little witch. Glanced again. And her heart knocked, heavily, against the stifling load of power. The girl was dark, with dark eyelashes demurely spread on the cheeks of her pretty little face. Her small hands delicately held up her silken dress as she approached the steps. But she was Philo. No one could have been less like Philo, particularly with those tiny hands and—yes—dainty little feet tripping down the dim stone steps, but Zillah knew it *was*. There was an essence of him that she could sense, scared, small, very angry, and most definitely Philo inside the disguise. She

hoped he would look at her—wink—show in some way
he was there and still her friend, but he gave no sign.
Perhaps his anger was at Zillah for getting him into this,
or maybe he needed all his attention on maintaining the
illusion. Zillah feared it was the former.

As they went out onto the lawn among the carefully
spaced stands of fire, there was singing. Zillah thought
at first that it came from the numbers of dimly seen people gathered at the edges of the turf—presumably people from the estate or workers from the house—but she
was soon sure that it did not. It was heavy singing, in
one rich but untrained voice. Its tune dragged from one
powerful, slumberous phrase to another, bringing sleep
with it, numbness, submission, and probably death. Yes,
a deathsong, Zillah thought. It came from the source of
the heavy power that made it so hard to move. The lawn
was a tank, full of it like a heavy liquid.

Marceny took up her position beside the stone table,
right in the center, and Zillah instantly knew that the song
and the power came from Marceny, even though she had
not uttered a sound. Knowing that killed a slight hope.
Herrel had said Marceny was currently busy punishing
Mark; but any hope that this might drain her strength
or concentration went at the sight of Marceny's closed
lips and still face. Zillah could even feel, as a sort of
dim strand, the power being diverted toward Mark,
and it made no difference to speak of to the strength
singing here.

With silent gestures, Marceny sent people to their
places. One gesture, and a group of girls was sent to
the far end of the table; another, and Zillah was halted
among other women at the near end. Zillah was forced to
stand and watch Philo go with the first group, separated
from her by the length of the table with its gleaming
knives. The light from the sky had almost gone by
now. Marceny's red velvet gown glowed bloodily in

the flames as she beckoned Herrel, carrying Marcus, up beside her.

A practical color, Zillah thought bitterly. Very practical. But then black witches are, I've heard. We all know the Goddess has her dark side. That singing—

—is not the Goddess

It was as if someone spoke. Even more clearly than she had known the nature of Arth, she knew this. Whatever the power Marceny was using, whatever it was that sang, it was something other than any aspect of the Lady. It was very foul. It fed on Herrel, through Marceny, and on other things too. It was very strong. Well, at least I know what we're up against, Zillah thought. That sounded better than it was. The truth was, she did *not* know what this thing was. The hopelessness she had thought she felt without Mark was nothing to what she felt now. She was down at the raw end of a chasm where hope simply was not.

The singing stopped. An abiding silence settled.

"Give me the child now," Marceny said to Herrel. Her voice seemed a small, shrill thing in contrast to the singing.

As Herrel's arms moved, Zillah said, "Do that, Herrel, and you're dead meat!"

"He is anyway, dear. Both of you are," Lady Marceny pointed out. She put out her hands and took Marcus under the armpits. Marcus himself, frightened by the strangeness and remembering he disliked Marceny, clung to Herrel with arms and legs. Herrel simply stood there. Two young women went to help Marceny. Zillah had a glimpse of Philo, staring helplessly.

"Herrel, for God's sake, stand *up* to her!" Zillah screamed. She threw every protective strength she had around Marcus.

"Come along to your granny, dear," Lady Marceny told Marcus. "Let's have no more nonsense."

Marcus was removed from Herrel and dumped screaming on the table. He was truly terrified now. Zillah's
protections were broken. It was as if half her being was
wrenched from her. She had at that moment some notion
how Herrel must have felt when Mark was taken from
him. The two girls were undressing Marcus. Marceny,
with a firelit knife raised in both hands, was reciting
an invocation to the Goddess. The Goddess! That's rich!
Zillah thought. She could not move. The heavy power
pinned her at one end of the table. But Herrel was a free
agent. Zillah knew he was, even before he turned and
looked at her with his eyes screaming and his mouth
smiling. Asking *me* to help! Zillah more or less screamed
to herself. You're asking *me* to stop Marcus being made
like you! *You* could stop it, Herrel, in an instant, if you
wanted to. You're so strong that that *being* infesting your
mother feeds and feeds and you still carry on!

Herrel, of course, could not want to. He could not want
anything that had been taken from him to make Mark.

Zillah was in the act of kicking Herrel aside mentally
as useless, when she saw that this wronged him. Herrel
had done one small thing. He had done it for Marcus.
On the table, Marcus was screaming and threshing and
surrounded by a small, triangular space of his own. It
seemed to be the ghost of the Eeyore-hut. Marcus was
mentally crouching in it, disseminating the one protection small children have—fear. Fear beat in waves over
the two women trying to undress him and slowed their
movements. Even the knife in Marceny's hands showed
a slight tremor. And his screams were horrible.

What's *this* supposed to do? Zillah thought angrily.
Yet she knew. Herrel had made the circuit of that illusory
room, and made it just real enough for Marcus to use. It
was all he thought himself able to do. The slight breathing
space this gave, Zillah was supposed to use to confront
Marceny.

And I can't! she thought. Doesn't he know I couldn't even face my own mother? I just had to leave. I couldn't even look Marceny in the eyes, and he expects me to—

Ah then, she thought. I must fetch Mark here. There was no time to consider it impossible. They had Marcus undressed now. "Philo, help me!" she called out above the drone of Marceny's invocation, and threw her mind toward Earth and Mark.

Tod came out on the terrace to see Marcus naked and Marceny in the act of blessing the knife. His birthright, at the sight, ramped within him like an enraged beast. Maybe it was anger, maybe it was the strange negative presence of the man Paul behind him, but he felt it, for the first time for years, spring out of his control. It seemed to be going wild. He was terrified. And he could be no *use* like this. Then he heard the voice of his old tutor, saying, "Even now it will sometimes take over, and you'll find it knows what it's doing." Well, I just hope he was right, Tod thought, and let it go.

He found himself calling out in a great voice, far deeper than his own. "Stop this! This dirties the name of the Goddess. I forbid it!"

At the other end of the lawn, a flying pale shape crashed through the trees and burst among the watching people. Tod, to his astonishment, saw Josh, whom he had confidently thought to be safely on his way to Frinjen, gallop among the pans of fire and slow gradually as the heavy ponding of power caught him. Josh came to a halt between two fires, facing Tod, pawing the turf angrily. "Leave that child alone, woman!" he panted. "I tell you—"

A timeless stillness was suddenly present.

Oh, thank Heaven! Zillah thought. Space. The space Herrel had tried to give her through Marcus. Marceny and the women around her were still moving, but in the slowest of slow motion, and if Marceny was still chanting, her voice was too slowed and lengthened to hear. Zillah knew what had happened. Tod and Josh had accidentally—if such a thing could ever be accidental—taken up the positions of a ritual of their own. They stood to east and west. Philo was to the south, and Zillah herself to the north. There was someone strange with Tod, who had the effect of dimming the other women with Marceny, so that the heavy power was forced to draw in around the table to protect itself. What Zillah had here now was the space peculiar to magic—which might last a second or many hours—and in which she could work.

And how do I? she wondered. Power. They all had power. Tod's was trained, but it seemed to be running wild in anger at the moment. Josh and Philo had certainly been taught, but the tuition in Arth, it had always seemed to her, had been beside the point for both of them. Whatever they had was almost untrained. As for herself, anything she had was as feral as a wild animal.

Well, then we call it wild, she said, and called.

Wild it was. It lifted her in an exultant sheeting gust so long and so far that she lost all sense of time, or of her own body. She was all mind for a nano-second that seemed to last a thousand years. Understanding filled her. *This* was why she had always ducked out, refused training in witchcraft, run from Amanda's kind of education. The restraints of knowledge harmed this wild power. In order to use it, Zillah could not know what it was. It would only answer a being as untrammeled as itself. It was wildness. Zillah hung in its exultant aurora borealis, exulting herself, because she had always known this about wild magic really. The instant, and the knowledge, extended infinitely. Her forgotten body sheeted across time with her, or shrank to the smallest instant, most strangely. Sometimes she had been a giant for hours, and then a small blob for a century. The knack, she discovered, was not to let it distract you. After a millennia-long instant, she was in a house she only remembered seeing once before, where a wild sending stalked around the borders of its safety, rattling windows, howling in the chimney, and snapping trees. There was a jungle of huge potted palms. She thought she had found the wrong place, until she heard her sister's voice.

"I know, Paulie. But whoever sent it has harnessed wild magic. Part of the strength is the wild magic objecting. I can't stop it, and I don't think any of us dare go out, even if it is only after Mark."

Gladys's house, but most oddly empty of its owner. Amanda was there, standing by the hearth, and Mark was a little aside, staring at the potted trees. He looked pale even for him. Zillah took the wild magic prowling around the house, united it to her own fourfold power, and promised it freedom shortly.

"Mark," she said. "Come with me quickly. I need you back with Herrel."

Amanda straightened. "The sending's gone! I—*Zillah!* Zillah, what do you want?"

"I've come for Mark," she said. "He has to go back. It's necessary."

The frown Zillah knew so well collected above Amanda's nose. "Why is that?"

She might have known, Zillah thought, that things would not be easy with Amanda in it. Mark was now somehow on the other side of Amanda, looking puzzled. "Mark," Zillah explained, "is half of another man from another universe."

"We know," Amanda said, and turned to speak to another presence whom Zillah could only dimly discern. "Yes, but be quiet, Paulie. It's Zillah. She wants Mark." At this, the other presence seemed to raise an outcry, but Amanda turned impatiently back to Zillah. "Zillah, are you in this other world?"

"Yes, and in terrible trouble. That's why we need Mark."

Amanda raised her head and became more than herself. "Zillah, this man is badly flawed. For one thing, he's been spying on us."

"Not intentionally, or voluntarily," Zillah said.

"There are other flaws," Amanda answered. "Do you really want him?"

"The other half is even worse," Zillah protested. "I love him both. Amanda, he *must* come, or I'll die, Marcus will be enslaved, and Mark will probably die, too, when Herrel's killed. Please."

Amanda's head was still raised. She said, with unearthly sadness, "Zillah, I'm sorry, but taking Mark makes a terrible imbalance. You could destroy two worlds."

"Then I'll balance!" Zillah cried out. "You help. Wait a second."

The next second, or maybe at the same time, she had taken wing on the fourfold wild magic—some of which protested and was soothed—and was in the presence of Amanda again, only with a difference. This Amanda walked through a strange room with painted panels, and her hands were nervously clasped to her mouth.

"I tell you I can't *see* at this juncture," she said to someone out of sight. "It could go any way. How I *wish* I hadn't let them *all* go off! Or I should have gone too. What a hellbound coward I am!"

Amanda should always grow her hair that long, Zillah thought admiringly. It looked beautiful. "Amanda!"

The woman jumped and turned. "You need help?"

"Badly. Take on your Aspect and balance. Balance for your life! Here." Zillah tossed the woman she hardly knew what—a thread, or a spark, or a skein—and to her relief and gratitude, the woman made dismissing motions to the person she had been talking to and seized what Zillah threw in competent hands.

"A moment," Zillah heard her say. "I'm summoned as Priestess."

She was back with her sister, flinging her another version of the thread or spark. "Balance." This Amanda, not so used to balancing, needed Zillah's attention more. Zillah hung between the two, holding, helping, while energy poured and thundered. It dinned around her, fell in avalanches and slid like lava, smoking and roaring. The wild magic of the sending fled shrieking upon it and was gone. Clouds scudded like boulders. When it stopped, it seemed too soon, but Zillah was spent. She hung in front of her sister, knowing she was only there on energies Josh and Philo and Tod were lending her to use.

"Amanda, let me have Mark now. Please. I've done all I could."

"I know." Amanda was holding on to the mantelpiece with one hand. She looked exhausted. She waved the other hand wearily at Mark. "You have to ask him, Zillah. He's not a pawn."

"Mark," she said faintly. "Come home with me? Please?"

Mark seemed to see her for the first time. "Zillah? You *want* me?"

The look on his face set the other presence squalling again. " . . . about the insurance?" Zillah heard. "All those bills and our mortgage . . ."

"Always," she said, holding out her arms through the noise.

He walked into her arms gladly.

9

"I don't get on with all this transposing, or whatever they call it," Gladys grumbled to Jimbo. They had no sooner arrived in the grove and seen all the great rumps of those centaurs rushing away than they were somehow ahead of them, on a lawn lit by a set of barbecues and standing beside another centaur. This one was smaller and whiter, as far as she could see. She could hear the High Head muttering something about how little light there was.

The king's seven mages appeared to agree. They all raised light—something she would have given her *toes* to be able to do—great pearly blue globes of it between each man's hands. Then she realized they had arrived in one of those utter stillnesses which meant the working of magic was in progress. What she saw, the female in bloodred, the child on the table, and the knife, nearly caused her to rush forward and interrupt. But the king raised a warning hand, and she saw it was a different stillness.

It was over in that instant. A girl—Zillah—sagged onto the end of the table. The small white centaur started forward, and so did two other people from the terrace-thing at the back. The red woman seemed about to bring the knife down, but the man dressed like a jester calmly leaned over and took the child off the table.

"Not this time," he said. "Not him too."

The red woman stared and then screeched, *"Herrel!"*

The jester-man turned away. "Give me his clothes, Aliky. He's freezing."

At this moment Jimbo vanished from Gladys's arms. She cried out, "Jimbo!" and cried out again when she saw him briefly on the table where the child had been. He loomed like a mad spider in the queer light, and the shadows gave him far too many arms. In another jolt of movement, he was on the red woman. His voice beat and howled through her head, "WRONG GREED! FOUL EATER! *GREED!*" with such force that Gladys nearly fell over, although she knew Jimbo was not shouting at her. She saved herself on the flank of the white centaur and stared at him attacking the woman. She had never known Jimbo do such a thing before.

The woman screamed. It looked as if she hid her face in her arms. Then she grew other arms and flailed at the ether monkey. An instant later it was clear that there was another thing, many-armed like Jimbo, emerging from the woman's substance to fight back. There was, for another instant, a scrawl of flailing limbs and a hideous low howling, before the fabric of that world seemed to become too flimsy for the creatures, and for the woman too. Everything elongated around them, blurred and stretched, so that the tearing and howling was going on in a deepening pit composed of lawn, table, house, terrace—until it tore under the strain and snapped back, leaving a vibrating bare space.

10

W rapped together in the nightmare bodiless intima-
cy of the sepia space, Joe-Maureen looked up and
screamed. A fighting tangle of glossy black limbs, with
something fraying and shredding among them, plunged
toward them, filling the whorls with senseless howlings.
He-she struggled aside, threw herself askew, and then
threw himself backward. The tangle plunged wailing
past, barely missing them, and vanished on downward,
spraying them as it went with hot acid redness, that
lashed them agonizingly with salt.

"Blood!" screamed Maureen. "That was real matter!"

Joe's reply was "I want out. Up this way?"

"I don't care anymore," she said. "I'd do anything."

He said, "You might have to. You realize we're stuck
with one another after this, do you?"

She knew he was right. The nightmare enwrapment
meant that she knew he knew a myriad small, disgraceful
things about her, for instance, the way she had pushed
poor old Flan Burke into going in the capsule just in order
that Flan might not rival her in the troupe. And she knew
the same things about him. What he had done to that man
Wilfrid in Arth, for example. Wilfrid may have deserved
it, but Joe had been vile, just vile. These and thousands
of other pieces of knowledge bound them so tight that

407

nothing short of murder could release them—and even murder was out of the question, for what one thought, the other would know. "I'll settle for that," she said.

"Me too," he said. "Up now. I think this is how. It'll take a while."

Eventually there was a sense of rising. Altogether elsewhere, in the sealed flat, their two flaccid bodies stirred on the sofa.

11

G ladys was crying. "I'm all right," she told everyone mendaciously. "I knew Jimbo had an enemy.
I thought he was running away from it, but I see now
he was just waiting his chance to come here. But he was
a good friend of mine— Oh, good God, my girl! Haven't
you ever dressed a child before? Let Auntie Gladys. Put
him down on the table. Give me his clothes. Is this all
he's got? Lord, it's filthy!"

She was briskly heaving Marcus back into his pyjama
suit when the other centaurs charged in among the trees
and galloped shouting across the lawn, overturning the
fire tripods as they came. She turned around. Her face
was fit to look at by then. "If someone doesn't do something, I'll—!"

The king, in some tranquil, unguessed manner, contrived to surround the table in a bubble of peace. His
mages gathered into it. Against a dark background of
running centaurs all intent on smashing things, pursued
hither and thither by a redheaded young man in wellies,
who seemed to want to stop them, the king looked at
the weary company gathered around the table. Tod was
sitting on it with his arms around Josh.

"I don't think we *have* broken the law," Josh said
aggressively.

"Not at all," said the king. "It is a year since your service began. Besides, things have changed, over in Arth." He nodded pleasantly to the girl who had tried to dress Marcus. "Thank you, Miss Aliky. I think you'd better return to Ludlin with us. Your cover is probably blown." His round glasses went on to focus on Philo, leaning on the end of the table in the rags of a green cotton dress. "I take it you were able to help this young gualdian?"

Aliky giggled. "Not that much. He's better at illusion than anyone I've ever met. All I did was put the idea in his head, Your Majesty."

Philo grinned, soft but tired. "I almost had fun hunting the mansion for myself—but I was scared silly really, sir. I think only Zillah gues—oh!"

Everyone glanced at Zillah and Herrel perched face-to-face on the corner of the table, and saw that they were lost to everyone but each other.

"That makes two good women gone," Tod murmured regretfully to Josh.

The king had looked on to Paul. "Hallow Isle?" Paul nodded in a way that was near a bow.

Gladys by now had done up every snap on the pyjama suit. "There. Dirty but warm. Majesty, there is the matter of stopping this one's mother from—"

"Too late," said the king.

Gladys glanced keenly at Herrel. The jester's clothes now enclosed a normal man, with an air of Mark to him. "I see what you mean. *Now* what?"

"Things are actually much improved," the king said. "Zillah, I think, must have had the sense to call on someone to balance. And that abomination which inhabited Lady Marceny had sucked up a surprising amount. I felt a great wad of something tear loose when it went. This has made things a great deal better, although a little still remains. Zillah and her son, for instance. Excuse me, sir."

He tapped Herrel's shoulder, firmly. "Yes, you. Would you mind telling me your plans for the future?"

Herrel turned reluctantly, saw who it was, and stood up. "My idea was—well, Zillah wants to live here, and I suppose the estate is mine now. I'd like to secede from Leathe and make Listanian part of the Orthe. Is that possible, Your Majesty? It's been a dream of mine ever since I was a boy."

"It seems a good idea," said the king. "But—" He sighed and shook his head at Gladys, because Herrel had already turned back to Zillah. "So we are still less than balanced. I take it you are returning, madam?"

"Of course," said Gladys. "I've more than twenty cats—unless that daughter of mine has put them in the pot. There's no knowing with that girl. Yes, I am going back—just as soon as someone's told me what I do about global warming when I get there. That's what started all this—the mess Arth made of my world— and I tell you straight, I don't go without an answer, Majesty."

"Here is your answer," said the king. "You must take the ex–High Head of Arth back with you."

At this Gladys said, "Oh, look *here*! The poor man!" and the High Head said, "Your Majesty, I refuse."

"You may not refuse, either of you," the king said. "Magus Lawrence has in his head all the lore of Arth, which is a very great weight of ideas. He also started your global warming. It is therefore just that he try to put it right."

"Your Majesty, I don't know how—" the High Head was forced to confess.

"Then you must go there and try," the king said. "It is my will. Go now."

Tod had never felt the king raise his will before. The force of it astounded him. Everyone stirred under it, like trees in a breeze. The High Head bowed. Gladys stood

up in a clack of beads and held out her hand to him.
"Come along, dear."

He took her hand and they walked away toward a
wood in the distance, not quite in the space where the
centaurs still rushed about. "I have foresworn wom-
en," everyone heard the High Head warn Gladys as
they left.

"That's all right, Lawrence," her voice answered. "I've
been a widow for years. But you'll have your stomach
cared for. I hope you like cats."

The going of Gladys deprived Marcus of someone to
talk to. He was warm now, and no longer frightened,
and beginning to feel lively. He looked hopefully at Tod,
but Tod, for some reason, was doubled over in fits of
laughter. He looked at Philo and Josh and saw they
were in the not-just-now-I'm-tired mood. Aliky didn't
know enough; nor did the serious men holding lights.
He looked at Zillah. No, she and the man who walked
on ceilings were not-now-I'm-busy. That left only one.
Marcus pulled the king's sleeve and pointed a starfish
hand at the busily galloping centaurs.

"Ort bake ow," he remarked. "Bad doubt."

The king stared at him. "I do beg your pardon. I didn't
quite catch that."